# LITURGY OF THE HOURS:

- *Matins* at midnight
- *Lauds* at 3 a.m.
- *Prime* at 6 a.m
- *Terce* at 9 a.m
- *Sext* at noon
- *None* at 3 p.m.
- *Vespers* at 6 p.m.
- *Compline* at 9 p.m.

# PART ONE
## INCURABLES

# WITH
# TWO
# EYES INTO
# GEHENNA

# WITH
# TWO
# EYES INTO
# GEHENNA

JANE LEBAK

Philangelus Press
Boston, MA USA

With Two Eyes Into Gehenna Copyright © 2018, Jane Lebak.

ASIN: B07H9BWHZG
Library of Congress Control Number: 2018966215
Print ISBN:  978-1-942133-29-2

Dedicated to David

Cover art by Fiona Jayde

Also by Jane Lebak:
Relic of His Heart
Pickup Notes
Half Missing
Honest and for True
Forever and for Keeps
An Arrow in Flight
Sacred Cups
Shattered Walls
The Wrong Enemy
Seven Archangels: Annihilation
Bulletproof Vestments
The Boys Upstairs
A Different Heroism

# ONE

Sister Magdalena hadn't been allowed to leave her convent cell for three days, and she was only being summoned into the parlor now because of the man she'd killed.

The abbess didn't speak to her all the way down the stone staircase, and Magdalena didn't attempt to start a conversation. Every nun in the convent knew what she'd done, and because of that, no one was in evidence in the hallways. The abbess had even rung the bell, alerting all the sisters to retreat to their cells, usually a signal that a layman had been admitted into their enclosure.

Magdalena kept her eyes lowered, trying not to think of neither how hungry she felt nor about the terror that finally her punishment would come. Although sixteen was old enough to be executed by the Roman magistrates, even then, it wouldn't be over. No, next she would face her eternal Judge and His eternal consequences.

As she stepped into the convent parlor, her eyes jumped to the fireplace and the flames that were her future. Her breath caught, and she blinked hard.

In front of that fireplace stood a cardinal and a nun in an unfamiliar habit. Magdalena had never seen either before, but then again she'd also never been guilty of a capital crime before.

The abbess bowed to the cardinal, then gestured to Magdalena.

The cardinal said, "You may go."

The abbess stiffened. "Sir, as she is a member of my community, I am responsible and must stay."

"You are in no way responsible for her actions," said the cardinal, no expression on his face. "Please leave. You may take the ascoltrice with you."

Magdalena fought the shock that threatened to overtake her and instead stared at the swirls of the thick carpet. When outsiders visited, the 78-year-old ascoltrice nun's job was to listen. It was part of the regulations to make sure the nuns didn't break the rules of the community (although to be honest, half of them did it anyhow). But this cardinal had brought his own listening woman, so maybe that sufficed.

The abbess snapped at the ascoltrice to pick up her crocheting and go. Then, hands clenched, the abbess stalked out of the room herself, leaving the parlor door open. The strange nun followed her and shut it.

Now Magdalena stood alone at the center of the large room, the only place she had seen her family for even brief visits in the weeks since her simple vows. This was the place for parties, for visits, for quick views of the choir nuns' younger sisters on their wedding days. Not for a trial.

Perhaps that was why the cardinal wanted the abbess out: so he didn't contaminate the room in her memories. But the church attached to this convent had been built in the year 600. Surely after nearly a thousand years, someone else had committed a crime in it. Could Magdalena truly have been the first?

The cardinal was a thin man, black eyes piercing against his white beard. "Sister Magdalena DeCasalvis, how long have you been a Poor Clare?"

"Sir." She'd rehearsed this moment so often in her mind, but she'd never imagined talking about it with a man. She'd always imagined pleading her case before the abbess and the other high-ranking nuns, but not to a pair of strangers. Certainly not to a man.

If it had to have been a man, a priest, why couldn't it have been the convent's other confessor? Father Jacobi was younger but subtler, thoughtful, soft-spoken, smart. He'd have heard her explanation and ratified her guilt, but he at least would have acknowledged her cause.

This man, though—this cardinal—was old, unsubtle, and sharp-tongued. Cardinals were sometimes called "princes of blood." She'd thought it was their red hats and red cloaks, not because they condemned people to death. This one looked ready to order hers.

Magdalena steeled herself. "Who are you?"

His mouth tightened. "My name and rank are unimportant to you. Answering my questions will be your only concern."

Magdalena bristled. "I took my simple vows this past Michaelmas."

The cardinal stared through her. "And do you regret your pledge to become a bride of Christ?"

She tilted her head. "In no way, sir."

The cardinal nodded. "Then I would like you to tell me about the incident."

*The incident,* of course, could mean anything from dropping a tea cup in the dining room to...well, to homicide. This man didn't appear to be the type to employ euphemisms, so he was probably testing her to see how much of her own guilt she would omit.

That meant she had to get it right the first time. She had to impress him both with her honesty and her desperation.

"I was in the library reading the biography of Saint Clare." Trying to read, that is. With only the most rudimentary skill, she had to sound out each word and then work back over each sentence to attach meaning to what she'd just deciphered. "I fell asleep. I'm not used to waking up during the night to pray the Office, not like the older nuns. Not yet." Now she never would be. "When I woke up, there was—"

Her stomach clenched, and she bit her lip, blinking hard. The strange nun said, "There was a man in the room."

She was short and wore a black habit and wimple over a white tunic, and she wasn't much older than Magdalena's own mother. Her voice bore no accusation. Just as the cardinal had, she spoke with the same declarative tone as, *A visitor dropped a tea cup.*

Magdalena's voice wobbled. "It was one of our confessors." The younger nuns hated the man, and the boarding girls did everything possible to avoid him. To Magdalena he seemed unnaturally slick, like the frilly men her mother worked for, not a man she would have guessed to have a calling to the priesthood. But he was well-educated and well-bred, and apparently well-used to taking whatever he wanted.

Oh, if only she'd been found by the other confessor. He'd have awakened her and asked questions about the book, not...not...

The nun said in her soft voice, "We've heard the abbess's account of your actions, but we are primarily interested in what you have to say."

Magdalena clenched her hands against her chest. "Do I have to?"

"It's very important." The nun's voice lowered in tone. "I suspect we haven't heard the whole story."

Magdalena's hands tangled themselves in the long cuffs of her habit. Now not only would she have to confess to murder, but also to unchastity. "I woke up with him touching me." Touching her breasts. Squeezing them like a ball of dough being kneaded for bread, his breath on her cheek as he leaned over her and pressed her between his body and the life of the virginal Saint Clare.

The nun said, "Go on."

Magdalena shook her head. "Who are you?"

"It doesn't matter. Keep talking."

With gooseflesh as though she could be cold beneath a woolen habit in a fire-heated parlor, Magdalena said, "I cried out, but he put a hand over my mouth. So I fought him."

"Fought?" prompted the cardinal, intent.

The nun urged, "How?"

Magdalena shook her head. "Why? I fought him, and I didn't mean to kill him, but he died. I did the thing my cousins told me to do to any man who wanted to touch me, but I didn't expect him to collapse and—"

To die. To die because she'd hated the man and hated his touch and hated the taunt in his eyes when he told her to give him what he wanted.

The other nuns had known she was in the library. They'd been laughing in the parlor, sharing tea and gossip about the new nun who wasn't able to arise for prayers at three o'clock in the morning. When the chattering nuns had gone back upstairs, they'd found the priest dead in the library with froth and blood on his face. They'd found Magdalena's discarded book on the desk, and moments later they'd found Magdalena in her room struggling to scrub the blood out of her habit.

The nun stepped closer. "If you can't tell me, then show me what you did."

Magdalena backed up further. "So you can convict me? I've already admitted my guilt."

"Come here." The nun had her sit at a desk, and then stood behind Magdalena. The cardinal remained at the door, arms folded. The nun said, "Is this how he stood?"

"He was much closer. He'd crushed me against the table. I was like this." Magdalena laid her head on the lacquered wood. "He was overtop of me with his hands here." Magdalena touched her breast and reached up to cover her mouth with her other hand. "Stand back so I can show you what I did."

"Just do it," said the strange nun.

She was already in trouble. Magdalena kicked back her chair so it flew into the nun's leg.

The nun caught it. "Excellent! Then what?"

Magdalena spun and grabbed the nun's shoulder with her left hand, then folded her right hand the way her brother had shown her and drove it straight at her throat.

The nun caught Magdalena's wrist in her calloused palm. "Really?" She examined how Magdalena had made her hand flat as a paddle, the first two joints of her right hand tucked under so her knuckles would impact as hard as an axe head. "You crushed his vocal chords?"

"That would kill him," murmured the cardinal, barely audible from across the room. "Done at speed."

"I didn't mean to!"

"You meant to drive him off," exclaimed the nun, eyes bright. "As you should have. But if you break the little bones in a man's throat, right near his Adam's apple, he can't breathe."

Exactly as it had happened. The man hadn't drawn breath ever again. At first Magdalena had jumped back, wielding a bronze statue of the Blessed Virgin Mary to smack him across the head if he'd come at her again. Instead he'd dropped to his knees, hands at his throat, gagging. He'd gone red, then white, ribs heaving, and to her horror, Magdalena had realized she was watching a man drown right here in the air, on the second floor of an enclosed convent on the edge of Rome. She had murdered a priest. A priest. She'd murdered a priest, and he wasn't dead yet, but there was nothing she could do because in moments a priest would be dead because she'd murdered a priest.

She'd dropped the statue with a clang and slammed the door as she fled the library, as though that could prevent God from seeing what she'd done. Then up the stairs she'd torn all the way to her cell where she'd barred that door as well, then dropped to her knees and prayed for God's mercy on her blood-stained soul. She'd filled the basin from her pitcher, trying to give a similar mercy to her blood-stained habit. The water had turned red, but it was futile. She'd committed murder.

The strange nun flexed her hand into the position Magdalena's had been in. "That kind of punch? That was taught to you by your brother?"

"My cousins."

From the door, the cardinal said, "Cousins on your father's side?"

"The side with the money?" Magdalena's eyes narrowed as she regarded him over the nun's shoulder. "No, sir. You learn such things when your family doesn't have any money."

The nun said, "What if I did this?"

She wrenched Magdalena's arm around. Magdalena yelped with surprise, then ducked and twisted, casting her weight to the side and throwing the nun off-balance. Yanking free, Magdalena backed away, but the nun rushed her.

"Defend yourself," called the cardinal.

Magdalena fell into a defensive stance, and the nun aimed at her with a high kick. Again Magdalena retreated, but when the nun moved closer, Magdalena lunged for her midriff to tackle her off her feet.

The nun slipped behind to pin her around the chest, her forearm against Magdalena's throat.

"Impressive." The cardinal folded his arms. "Sister, that will suffice."

The nun released Magdalena, who staggered forward and pivoted, arms raised.

"No one's going to hurt you." The cardinal picked up the chair. "Please join me at the sofa. I will summon your abbess. Perhaps we should have some tea as well."

Magdalena perched on the very edge of the couch, but the other nun sat across from her.

"I could hand you over to the magistrates," said the cardinal. "The magistrates know of the priest you killed, and his family is powerful. You will be tried and quite probably put in prison, if not executed."

This much she'd expected.

"Although you have relations with some connections," he mused. "One of them might intervene rather than endure a scandal." The cardinal's eyes bore into her. "I could tell the abbess that the best place for you is to remain here to do penance for the rest of your days, and that they should always be observant about which men are allowed in your presence."

Magdalena said, "As perhaps they ought to have from the start."

The nun chuckled. "You do have some spirit, don't you?"

That wasn't as disapproving as Magdalena had expected, so she looked up, puzzled.

The cardinal continued, "I assume you know your penance would be for the most part involuntary, as the dead man had until three days ago been the lover of at least one of the more influential nuns. At your age you can look forward to sixty years, perhaps, of infamy and ashes in your dinner. That would more than amply expiate the man's death."

Of course. Of course the man had been intimate with more than just one nun. And of course it would be her fault that she had so seductively fallen asleep over a biography of Saint Clare.

The cardinal rubbed his beard. "As for the man himself, I have no doubt he's in Hell. He was a stain on the priesthood and would, if allowed to live a long life, have brought scandal on the Church and on His Holiness Pope Pius. The Lutherans require no more ammunition in the form of criminal priests, so as far as I'm concerned, you've performed a useful service to the Church, and as such you're unworthy of such a sentence."

"She's hardly trapped." The nun turned to Magdalena. "These walls won't hold you once you get a mind to leave. Did you spend your childhood scaling walls? Distracting fruit sellers so your brother could get a meal for you and your younger sister?"

Magdalena's eyes widened. "Leave my sister alone. She had nothing to do with anything."

The other nun shook her head. "Such a one as you needs a purpose other than high walls and safety. An eternal purpose." She folded her hands in her lap. "I will provide a third option. I invite you to join my order."

Magdalena's head raised. "What?"

The sister seemed serious. "We're the Catherinites, a small mendicant order who received authorization only in 1556, during the reign of Pope Paul IV."

Magdalena's eyebrows shot up. The people of Rome had celebrated Pope Paul's death with weeks of rioting. Pope Paul had thrown cardinals into prison for heresy and promulgated an index of banned books so long that the booksellers had to construct special hidden rooms just to sell them. His approval wasn't entirely sufficient for Magdalena.

The nun noted her look. "By special order of the pope, we are Theatines who designed our rule according to the life of Saint Catherine of Alexandria. We maintain a hospital and a boarding house. Our convents are here and in Trent."

Although Magdalena couldn't at the moment come up with the life story of Saint Catherine of Alexandria, neither a hospital nor a boarding house sounded like a cause for rioting. In fact, either option sounded better than a life behind enclosure. She couldn't leave Rome, though. Her sister needed her here.

The nun must have seen the way she'd brightened, because she leaned forward. "You would work hard. You would be expected to take vows again, including a vow of obedience to the pope. You would follow our rule, which is more stringent than fried sweet buns and cushioned parlors."

Magdalena sighed. "I can't afford to join a different order. My family isn't rich."

The cardinal chuckled derisively. "You're from Farnese stock. I was surprised you didn't send word to Cardinal Alessandro Farnese as soon as your abbess locked you up."

She was from Pope Paul III's stock, specifically, and tangentially related to Cardinal Farnese as well as many others. "I'm the illegitimate child of an illegitimate child." Magdalena folded her arms. "My mother scraped together as much as she could to pay a dowry to the convent, and that's the last of our fortune."

She wouldn't mention where the rest of it had come from.

The nun waved a hand. "I am unconcerned with your heritage or your money. As I said, we are a mendicant order. We own no property, and therefore you require none. But as such," and she took in the parlor with a gesture of her hand, "we have none of these luxuries."

Her hand was rough and worn. But strong. Magdalena couldn't forget the strength of that nun's grip on her wrist.

"Will you let me stay in Rome?" Magdalena said.

The nun replied, "The Roman convent maintains the hospital for incurables."

That sounded like work Magdalena could do, and until a few months ago had already been doing.

The cardinal said, "I still am not convinced you would be a worthwhile contribution." He looked Magdalena in the eye. "Tell me: that man you killed. Would you do it again?"

Magdalena raised her voice. "I didn't go out of my way to tempt him. I never in my life would have laid hands on a priest!"

"An admirable answer, but my question stands." The cardinal's eyes drilled into her. "Would you do it again?"

Would she? Would she kick back the chair and scream, then hit him hard enough to stun him, only to discover her cousin's trick resulted in an eternal stun? Would she knowingly send a man to Hell before letting him violate her body?

She glared into the cardinal's eyes. "With all due respect, sir," and here she took a deep breath, "I would."

If anything, she'd hit him harder.

"Why?" The cardinal's nose wrinkled. "For your purity? For your family's name?"

"Because he had no right to touch what was consecrated to God!" Magdalena exclaimed. "Didn't God kill the man who touched the Ark of the Covenant? And that was just to keep it from falling. This man wanted to put his hands on the Ark and push."

The nun with the rough hands laughed out loud at the cardinal's startled expression. "Are you convinced now?"

The cardinal frowned. "She certainly has plenty of opinions. But given her fire, I'm not going to lay hands on her either. She comes by her own free choice, or else she stays."

The abbess swept back into the room along with one of the servant nuns, who as directed carried a tray with tea and fried sweet buns. The abbess glared at Magdalena with a hatred suddenly made plain in light of the cardinal's words. Had that foul man been the abbess's own lover?

"We have concluded her interview," the cardinal said. "There has not yet been any decision as to her disposition."

The abbess sent Magdalena a smile warm as mud. "We want only what is for the best."

"There are so many considerations," said the cardinal in a languid voice. "Her eternal soul requires extra care and subtle direction, and of course, Cardinal Farnese doesn't want scandal to touch the Curia."

Magdalena struggled not to choke. Hadn't she just said Cardinal Farnese might recognize her name, but only to spit over his shoulder?

The abbess straightened. "She cannot remain here!"

"Of course she must," said the cardinal. "She's taken vows to be the bride of Christ. What God put apart, no man should rend asunder."

The abbess's eyes blazed. "Sir!"

The cardinal shook his head. "Her family paid a dowry."

"A poor one," snapped the abbess. "Scarcely enough to cover her food, and with no annuity."

The cardinal opened his hands. Magdalena realized right then that he was playing all of them, and with a mastery born of decades. "Regardless, you accepted the money. In good conscience, how could I dispense her from her vows?"

"We would pay that money back to her whore of a mother," said the abbess, and Magdalena's fists clenched. "We'd pay it back double. I want her gone."

The cardinal smiled, a calculated expression that left Magdalena wondering whose teeth were sharper.

The cardinal did have a point. Remaining here meant the rest of a long life enduring scorn and hatred and the thousand daily injuries dealt by women to women behind walls where the world never could penetrate, but that also meant the women couldn't escape when inevitably the world did.

Except for now. She could take the route of the magistrate: escape to a trial and then a different prison. Or, finally, an unknown prison with an unknown order, doing what looked like hard labor under the tutelage of a nun who apparently beat up her novices for fun. Moreover, she'd be under the supervision of a manipulative cardinal who wanted prime seating when nuns defended themselves to the death.

She could remain here and figure out how to break out of the convent. Her cousins could be counted on to hide her for a few days. They might even smuggle her out of the city.

The abbess said, "Everything she has belongs to us, including herself. We can eject her from the convent and right onto the streets, and who's going to believe the daughter of a whore versus one of the established convents of the city?"

"She's not a whore!" Magdalena exclaimed.

The abbess ignored her. "Bear in mind that one day this one will be found by the family of the man she murdered. After that day, there will be no further word from her, and the city streets will be cleansed of an unimportant piece of garbage."

The nun from outside folded her rough hands and looked to Magdalena. "What would you care to do?"

Much as it would thrill her to annoy the abbess by saying she'd stay and then breaking out once it got dark, Magdalena preferred not having ashes in her food even one more night. "I would care to leave, thank you, and remove a piece of trash from the convent. Let me go collect my belongings."

The abbess waved a hand. "Everything you have is forfeit. You gave up all your property when you entered here."

Which was, doubtless, why the abbess had a palatial bedroom filled with cedar furniture, paintings, and jewelry. Magdalena stood. "You are correct, abbess, and I apologize." She reached for her wimple. "Here, allow me to return your property."

She removed her head piece, then loosened the buttons at the top of habit.

The visitor nun's mouth tightened as she fought a laugh, and the cardinal turned to the window. Magdalena pulled her habit over her head and stood in her undergarments, barefooted and bareheaded.

She tossed the habit at her former abbess. "Just before I step out the door, I'll be sure to breathe out the last of your air."

# TWO

Her new abbess was Sister Bellosa, and she hustled Magdalena into an enclosed carriage waiting on Via dei Fori Imperiali while the cardinal collected her dowry money from the convent.

Sister Bellosa pulled a blanket from beneath the seat to wrap up in. "If you had personal belongings, they've remained behind."

Magdalena shook her head. "I had nothing of value."

Not entirely true. Her family had given her a few tokens after her simple vows, and she had a few letters from her mother, painstakingly printed by her brother Domenico. Magdalena had been able to hear echoes of her mother's voice in those pages. There also had been handkerchiefs embroidered with finely crafted rosebuds, made by both her mother and her great-aunt. Those she'd never get back.

Bellosa instructed the driver to get started. It was night already, but Magdalena didn't feel hungry. The only thing she'd eaten since a sparse lunch (probably dusted with ashes) was that fried sweet bun in the parlor, and in her nervous stomach it sat like stone.

"We're going to the convent of Saint Sebastian," said Bellosa. "Our convent is small, deliberately so. It attaches to a church and a hospital for incurables. Because of our mission, we are not enclosed."

Magdalena said, "Our mission being the hospital for incurables?"

Bellosa shook her head. "Our mission being protection of the papacy."

"How do you protect the papacy from a hospital?" she said. "Or are you saying the pope has an incurable disease?"

"Neither," said Bellosa. "For now, be patient. You'll understand soon."

Patience was not an easy virtue tonight. Magdalena didn't sit back at all during the ride through streets she'd assumed she never again would see. But here she was, leaving walls she'd vowed to stay behind, and under circumstances similar to what had driven her there.

I left the world because I didn't want anyone to die, she thought repeatedly, and now I'm leaving the convent because somebody did.

She'd enter a different convent instead, one which apparently dealt every day with death. Maybe that irony alone was expiation enough.

Magdalena's back and head hurt from the jolting carriage.

"I'll need to send word to my mother." Wrapping her hands in the blanket, she swallowed. "Quickly. I don't want her to go back there, or my brother and sister." After a hesitation, she added, "She's not a whore. We all have the same father. He never married her because he already has a family."

"The condition of your mother isn't my concern." Bellosa waved a hand as though to scatter that line of thought. "You'll have to change the way you understand the world. Once you take our vows, we are your family, and we are your connections." She looked up. "Since we aren't enclosed, you can still visit your mother. Your brother and sister can visit you too, although your brother shouldn't enter the main parts of the convent."

Magdalena straightened. "Really?"

Bellosa took note of her voice, then flagged the driver to stop the carriage.

The motion slowed, then ceased, and when they were at a standstill, Magdalena looked outside to see if they'd arrived. They were in fact very close to her own part of Rome, the streets she'd run through with her cousins and the vendors where she'd pocketed the occasional fruit if their meals came too far apart. Some of the doorways looked familiar, and even though no one walked the streets to see her, she clutched the blanket closer around her shoulders.

"Consider how much freedom you want," Bellosa said.

Magdalena studied her. "What do you mean?"

"I mean, Cardinal Simonetta secured your release from your vows. There were no conditions on that release." Bellosa gazed outside the carriage as though admiring the impoverished street where they'd stopped. "What you did, no one has to know. No one knows right now. I can return your dowry to you, and you can leave Rome. Perhaps you won't have a glamorous life, but with that money, you could go abroad and become whoever you want, tell whatever story. You could call yourself a young widow and take up residence as a governess."

Magdalena recoiled into her seat.

"I could drive this carriage to the doorway of your mother, and you could gather your family to leave this city. Perhaps not as far as you alone, but you could take them north, away from your shame and hers."

Magdalena closed her eyes. "I can't do that."

"What about your sister?" said the other nun.

Fiora. Fiora could come with me.

25

"The life I'm leading you to is not an easy one," said Bellosa. "No religious sister's life is, but ours will be harder still. It requires your entire devotion."

Magdalena forced a smile. "No fried sweet buns in the parlor?"

"No parlor at all." Bellosa spoke flatly. "Never a full night's sleep. You will be called to serve Christ in ways you haven't imagined."

Magdalena's voice softened. "Do you think I'm not strong enough?"

"No one is strong enough." Bellosa pressed her lips together. "But you're clever, and you've a clear sight to what's important. You refused to let anyone destroy you. That's why I wanted you, but the work is endless."

Magdalena bowed her head. "I am the bride of Christ. Let Him dispose of me as He wishes."

Bellosa signaled to the carriage driver, and travel resumed with a jolt.

By the time they reached their destination, the street was full dark. A relatively small church stood surrounded by buildings of equal height, and Magdalena's new abbess stepped out of the carriage. "Remain here. While I appreciate your respect of the other convent's property, you need more than a blanket."

Magdalena waited for so long that she was cold before Bellosa returned with an ankle-length cream-colored robe. Magdalena struggled into the linen garment within the carriage, and when she had it tied, Bellosa escorted her inside.

A nun just beyond the gate greeted them, wearing a black habit identical to Bellosa's. The abbess said, "Ring the bell and assemble the sisters in the church."

Candles lit the sanctuary of the church only poorly, and the air bore the faint tinge of incense. Shortly the first three benches filled up with nuns in black habits. Magdalena couldn't make out the details in the dark, but she assumed they were shapeless like Bellosa's and very much unlike the fashionable and stylized habit worn by the richer sisters at her former convent.

A mendicant, or begging, order. That fit better with Magdalena's life until now, to be honest. They'd been always borrowing or begging from anyone they could find, especially the upper crust paternal side who would have much rather preferred to have nothing to do with them.

Bellosa removed the garment from her habit so even the abbess stood in just her white under-sheath. "Sister Chiara," she called, "come forward as well."

A girl approached, maybe four years younger than Magdalena. She too was wearing only a linen sheath.

Bellosa said, "Both of you, proceed to the front."

As Magdalena realized what was happening, she stumbled. The girl at her side grabbed her arm, eyes glimmering. Up at the communion rail dividing the church, the abbess summoned two other sisters. Magdalena and Chiara were made to kneel on the stone. Beside Magdalena, Chiara had her hands clasped at her chest, her eyes fixed on the crucifix behind the altar. Even kneeling, she seemed to lean forward, eager.

This ceremony in Latin, which Magdalena assumed constituted her simple vows, was very different from the vows she'd taken at Santi Cosma e Damiano. The nuns chanted the *compline* prayer around Magdalena and Chiara, but from there they moved into a number of other prayers followed by a long litany. Then Bellosa sprinkled both of them with holy water. First Chiara and second Magdalena were told to lie prostrate, and Sister Bellosa spread a black cloth over each. *For my daughter was dead, and now has come back to life,* she sang in plainchant, her voice clear as it echoed off the stone.

The black cloth buried her. She was dead. Death surrounded her. Death filled her sin-stained soul. Death was what she deserved.

More prayers passed over her while she lay against the cold stone: the *De profundis*, several of the psalms, and then the *Te Deum*.

Sister Bellosa called, "Do you vow poverty, to relinquish all material goods in this world for the sake of the Kingdom?"

I do.

"Do you vow chastity, promising the powers of your body to God alone for the sake of the Kingdom?"

I do.

"Do you vow to resist heresy in all its forms, to resolve to uphold the law of God as defined by the Church in all her doctrines and all her dogma?"

I do.

"Do you vow obedience to the pope, on whose orders we serve for the sake of the Kingdom?"

I do.

The black cloth came away from her, and Magdalena found the church brilliant with lights, every nun in the pews holding a candle. A nun resettled the black cloth over her shoulders as her new habit, and then Magdalena and Chiara were handed candles of their own. Chiara turned to Magdalena with tears streaming over her smiling cheeks.

Bellosa engulfed Magdalena's soft hands with her rough ones while another sister clipped Magdalena's hair close to her scalp. Then it was Chiara's turn. The girl's brown locks tumbled in a heap around her feet, and she beamed with splendor as Bellosa hugged her.

"Welcome," she said to both. "You are now Theatine mendicant nuns, and you are the bride of Christ."

# THREE

As a bride of Christ, Magdalena awoke to the three o'clock bells to say *lauds,* the early morning prayer. She pried herself out of the straw mattress and back into her habit, then plodded to a candle lit chapel crammed with Christ's other brides.

After that, she returned to her bare cell to sleep, only to awaken in three hours to find a nun laying out new clothing on the wooden chair in the corner.

"*Prime* is in a few minutes," the woman murmured. "I'm sorry to rouse you. I'm the clothier, and I'm told you came with nothing."

The complete outfit consisted of a white tunic under a black garment. It had wide sleeves, and on her head Magdalena would wear a black wimple. On her waist she wore a rosary made of a knotted cord, each knot big enough to make the rosary unwieldy to pray on—and uncomfortable to sit back in. She had no shoes, but the other nun was also barefoot. "I heard what you did to your former abbess." The other nun gave a demure smile. "Thank you for saving me the trouble of returning their habit."

At the door, the nun turned. "By the way, what's your name?"

That was the extent of Magdalena's introduction to their routine. As at the other convent, *Prime* led to a recitation of the rosary, and following that came breakfast. While St. Sebastian's food was lower quality than Santi Cosma e Damiano's, it was filling. Chiara sat at the table beaming as though this were her wedding feast. Which, in a way, it was.

Bellosa dismissed the other nuns to their duties and had Magdalena accompany her to her own cell, which Magdalena assumed as the abbess's cell would be outfitted like a palace. Instead it was just as bare as her own. The only concession to Bellosa's status was an extra chair.

"In addition to being the abbess, I am the mistress of novices." Bellosa reviewed the order's daily schedule, starting with all the hours of the Little Office of the Blessed Virgin, plus the rosary, the *De profundis,* and the *Veni Creator.* They had adoration on Fridays, plus fasting on specific holy days and feasting on others. "We always take meals in common," said Bellosa, "and every sister works for an hour at daily exercises. In addition, we tend the hospital for incurables next door. We wash their laundry and cook meals for the inmates and the doctors, plus we prepare the dead for burial." She signed herself with the cross. "Finally, we care for the church building."

"I can cook," Magdalena offered. "That was one of the things I did before entering Santi Cosma e Damiano, and they were training me up to work in their kitchen." Magdalena paused. "What are daily exercises? Are they like the Jesuits' meditations?"

"You'll attend exercises next, but first we'll measure you for new garments. I'm not sure how the clothier worked at Santi Cosma e Damiano," added Bellosa, "but while all our sisters' overgarments come from the common closet, your exercise garments must be fitted."

Magdalena cocked her head. "Don't the nuns from noble families have their own personal habits? And what are exercise garments?"

"This will be an adjustment for you." Bellosa squeezed her hand. "Try not to think of the families we came from. Here, we all wear the same clothes because we're all alike. There is no difference in the cut, style, or the quality of the cloth. Our exercise garments are personal only because they have to fit well."

Bellosa summoned the clothier, whose name turned out to be Gilia. She was a few years older than Magdalena, light on her feet and wiry with strength. Gilia measured her all over, including her feet.

"While I appreciate your thoroughness," Magdalena said, "I thought we don't wear shoes."

"It depends on the work. Our sisters in Trent find it very cold, so they also wear wool socks." Gilia looked at the measurements she'd written and then rechecked Magdalena's shoulders. "Do you have any skill at sewing? Embroidering?"

"Passable." Magdalena's nose wrinkled. "I can mend."

That done, Gilia escorted Magdalena to the "exercises."

A cousin who had gone to the Jesuits had written home that *exercises* were guided prayers accompanied by readings about spiritual growth, with the aim of making the young Jesuit priest more Christ-like in every fashion. These exercises took months to do. Instead of the chapel, though, Magdalena arrived in a wide room with a wooden floor. Chiara was already there.

"Agnella isn't here yet, so we'll wait." In the daylight Chiara had dark eyes, and the wild angles of her shorn hair foretold that it would curl when it grew again. Right now she was wearing clothing like a man's, with loose leggings and tight sleeves. Her feet remained bare. "I didn't want to ask last night, but what's your name? And thank you! Because you came, they pushed up my simple vows by several weeks. I was supposed to wait until the Ember Days, but instead, here we are!"

The girl couldn't be any older than thirteenAt that age, Magdalena hadn't yet witnessed the events that sent her into the convent, but Chiara seemed so sure of herself.

"You didn't even need formation, so you were already a nun?" Chiara said. "Where did you come from?"

It was hard to keep up with Chiara's conversation. "Santi Cosma e Damiano."

Chiara brightened. "Oh, they're an old convent! I was a student at San Marco, but it wasn't working out right, and the prioress started writing letters trying to get rid of me. Sister Bellosa came for me about three weeks ago. It's so much better here. You really feel you're doing Christ's work."

At that moment another nun entered the room, and both novices fell silent. Magdalena soon learned this was Sister Agnella, the exercise mistress. Agnella said, "Let's begin with prayer," and led them in a Hail Mary followed by a prayer Magdalena repeated phrase by phrase: *O Lord, we have consecrated our bodies to you. Please protect our bodies and give them health and strength. Amen.*

Although none of this made sense, Magdalena kept her mouth shut and followed directions. Agnella would demonstrate a stretch, and then Chiara would do it and Magdalena would attempt to imitate it.

Each stretch had a name. "Matthew" had her up on her toes, fingertips reaching toward the ceiling. "Mark" had them crouching on the floor, head down and hands spread. "Luke" was again tall but with the arms spread at the shoulders and fingertips splayed. "John" had them in a half-squat, arms extended behind and head tucked.

After several repetitions, the exercises grew more complicated. Agnella would demonstrate, then have each do it separately and very slowly, correcting them, then have them work together and work faster.

When the bell rang for *sext,* Chiara slithered back into her full habit, and they rushed to the chapel to say the noontime prayers. Next came lunch.

As soon as they said grace, one of the nuns turned to Magdalena "Which convent rejected you?"

Magdalena dropped her spoon.

"Culled out," Bellosa corrected mildly.

Chiara said, "Santi Cosma e Damiano!"

"They're a respectable convent," said Agnella. "What did you do to get kicked out?"

"Culled out," Bellosa repeated serenely, ladling food onto her plate.

Magdalena looked to Bellosa for guidance, but Chiara giggled. "Don't worry. We've all been *culled out* from other convents."

"Except for those of us who escaped," muttered Agnella.

Chiara's head pumped in a nod. "That's what makes this such a special order. It's a second chance for misfit brides of Christ."

Bellosa said, "The cardinal of the Datary pays attention to reports of nuns who might interest our order. I'm very selective." She smiled at Magdalena. "You I sought out specifically after Cardinal Simonetta received their letter."

Chiara beamed. "Please tell us!"

"Please do not pry," said Bellosa. "None of you were compelled to tell your own stories."

Magdalena eyed Agnella, who claimed to have *escaped* rather than been selected, and she found herself being studied in turn. In a year, would she too think of herself as having escaped Santi Cosma e Damiano?

After lunch, the pair of novices tended patients in the hospital.

"The senior nuns do exercises in the afternoon," Chiara said as they carried the hospital laundry back to the convent. "But we're allowed in there at any other time to practice."

Magdalena shifted the laundry to her hip to open the door. "I never heard of anything like the exercises."

Chiara nodded. "No other convent does them. Oh, have you found the library yet? I'll show you after dinner."

At every turn, Saint Sebastian's became more and more different from Santi Cosma e Damiano. Every nun's cell was the same as every other nun's, unheard of at the wealthier convent. When the nuns all ate at the refectory together, there was laughter and not simmering tension between cliques.

And as for not being enclosed, while it meant any man could enter the convent through the hospital doors, Magdalena had already spent the first sixteen years of her life unenclosed. Being unenclosed meant she could see her family again.

It was smaller too. The nuns here numbered fifteen, and perhaps the size was key to the lack of tension. Fifteen couldn't form factions the same as eighty. And with only fifteen, surely there were positions and jobs enough that all the nuns held some particular status.

She met the priest charged with the church above, where she'd professed her vows. He kept a respectful distance, repeated her name to himself so he wouldn't forget, and said he would pray for her during this time of adjustment. "I serve as your order's confessor, but of course you're allowed to confess to any priest you wish. I'm just the most convenient." Then he offered her access to any of his books if she ever needed them.

Yes, so very different from Santi Cosma e Damiano. She'd never have to kill a man like this.

Bellosa sought out Magdalena again in the afternoon, saying they'd sent a messenger to her mother with the

WITH TWO EYES INTO GEHENNA

pertinent details. Her mother hadn't written a letter (her mother could barely read) but she'd returned a verbal message: *Stay safe.*

Her mother was worried. Of course her mother was, but the one to be worried for was herself and the other two children.

The nuns prayed *none* at three o'clock, *vespers* at six, and *compline* at nine. After *compline,* Magdalena collapsed onto her straw mattress.

This was the rest of her life, then. This was the beginning of how it would end, and she faced (as Cardinal Simonetta had said) seventy years of the same.

She could do this.

That was her last thought before exhaustion overtook her. She could do this, and it was good.

———————

Sunday was a day of rest, except that it wasn't. The incurables didn't rest from their illnesses on the Sabbath, and therefore neither did the nuns. They served as the choir for the Sunday Masses, but then immediately resumed cooking for the hospital's inmates and caring for the dying.

"We put off the laundry as much as possible on Sunday," said Chiara, hauling a basket of soiled clothes down to the courtyard, "but I suspect it's because we're so long at choir rather than just because we're supposed to rest." Even so, they needed to do some washing, and there was one yellow, hollowed-out man they expected to die today and whom they then would need to tend for burial.

"God rested on that first Sunday," Magdalena said, almost as a comfort to herself, "but He's worked every Sunday since."

Chiara laughed. "That's a good point. I'll meditate on that when we're at adoration."

Ah, so their order had Eucharistic adoration on Sundays as well. A life of contemplation, Magdalena decided, but done actively.

Agnella appeared in the courtyard. "Magdalena, you have visitors."

Magdalena exclaimed, "Me?" followed by, "Oh! Is it my mother?"

"Go!" Chiara pushed her toward Agnella. "Give your mother a huge kiss and then give her a second one just from me."

Magdalena tried not to hurry Agnella through the hallway, but even so, she accidentally stepped on her heels. "During the next exercises," Agnella muttered, "I'll teach you to walk."

She opened the door into a guest parlor Magdalena hadn't realized they had, and there was her mother. Magdalena flew across the room to embrace her, and her mother burst into a sob. Face pressed into her mother's shoulder, Magdalena inhaled the scent she had lived with every day of her life until the day they locked the grille behind her at Cosma e Damiano.

"Oh, sweetheart," her mother whispered, hand in her hair. "What happened to you? What did they do?"

Then came a sudden slam into her side. Her sister Fiora, younger than Chiara, had a grin lighting up her crooked face. Magdalena looked up, and standing at the far wall, fiddling with the buttons on his sleeve, was her brother Domenico.

The door behind her closed. Agnella had left.

"I can't believe you're here," whispered her mother.

Magdalena led her mother to the couch, and her mother sat beside her, stroking her hand. Her voice soft, Magdalena said, "Did they tell you what happened?"

"Some." Her mother looked pale. "Are you in danger here?"

She shook her head. "I'm more worried about you."

Mother gave a brave smile. "I'm not worried about that louse's family. The Marcolis could start a feud with us, but why would they publicize their shame? As long as we say nothing, they'll do nothing."

Magdalena frowned. "Marcoli? I didn't even know his name."

Mother huffed. "Giovanni Marcoli, and may the devils say it every day. I've asked around, and those people would never set foot in our part of the city. They're far too fine for us." Mother's eyes darkened. "They may go after your father, and I hope with all my heart that they do. But if they hassle him and he hassles them back, this would be no more than either of them deserves. They'll get nothing from us."

Magdalena glanced at Domenico. It was to some extent true that any family would hesitate to carry off a vendetta against the unmarried mother of a nun who'd defended her own honor. They might take up matters with her father, but her father could to some extent deny (with full truth) that he'd had anything to do with raising her. In the stories told by the avenging family, of course, Magdalena would become the harlot of Santi Cosma e Damiano, seductively leading her confessor into sin and then, after his virtuous refusal, murdering him to keep her secret. That too wouldn't stand up to sustained scrutiny.

It didn't matter. The Farnese family name had endured quite a bit of scandal so far, emerging none the worse for wear. Not too long ago the Farnese pope had elevated his sons...or rather, his "nephews," to cardinal status, with all the income and stature that bestowed. One of them, Cardinal Alessandro Farnese, had become quite powerful.

Since the family itself was founded on a chain of illegitimate children, another few illegitimate children stashed in convents couldn't do much damage. Some snickering in the market square never killed anyone. Unlike, say, herself.

Magdalena glanced at her brother. "I'm worried about Domenico, though." Domenico wasn't a brute. While not sickly like Fiora, who never would overcome her limp or the fact that half her teeth had never come in, Domenico wasn't strong like her cousins. He was smart as a fox, and half the mischief they'd played had been brewed in his own hearth of a brain. But if the Marcoli family had their own branch of street urchins, then her brother and cousins would become their targets.

These vendettas ended only in blood. One such vendetta had been what sent her into Santi Cosma e Damiano in the first place.

Domenico tossed his head. "I'll be careful. I don't know any Marcolis, but we know to listen for anything." His eyes lit up. "Erico said good job, though. He brags to everyone that he's the one who taught you how to do it."

Mother's eyes were puzzled. "What did you do?"

"Hit his Adam's apple with my hand flattened out, hard." Magdalena's shoulders drooped. "I just wanted to stun him."

Domenico laughed. "Erico's going to be insufferable forever, isn't he? But if the Marcoli family comes for us, he'll go strutting in front of them so they try to take him first."

Fiora lurched over to the couch and settled on Magdalena's other side, head against her shoulder. "I thought Erico was just telling stories. He's never killed anyone."

"You'd think he took out a fleet of Turkish pirates, the way he keeps his nose in the air." Domenico smirked. "Ask him to teach you too. Maybe it'll save your life."

Leaving Fiora had been worse than leaving Mother. With a right leg shorter than the left, Fiora wasn't able to keep up with the other children. Magdalena had minded her for years, hauling a two-year-old around the city on her hip when she herself was six. She'd braided flowers into Fiora's tangled hair and taken in seams on her own outgrown clothes so

Fiora had nice dresses. Mother and Aunt Lucia had apartments in the same building, with the cousins forever running from one place to another, but Fiora couldn't manage the stairs very well. Everyone had taken turns hefting the child up and making sure she had a place with them. But it had been Fiora who drove away their erstwhile father.

A Farnese, even an illegitimate Farnese, couldn't tolerate a crippled daughter. When he'd seen his imperfect spawn, he'd blamed the mother and never come back. Magdalena had been four at the time, so at least she'd known the man.

Magdalena hugged Fiora to her side. She was back outside the grates now and able to hug without having to reach through bars. She could smell that familiar combination of Fiora's sweet skin and Mother's rosewater. Maybe, as Fiora grew up, Magdalena could find a way to keep protecting her too.

# FOUR

Even after three weeks, *lauds* was still the toughest part of Magdalena's life. Three o'clock in the morning saw her slouching out of bed to stagger into the chapel where the nuns prayed for a quarter hour, and then she'd shuffle back to bed.

No doubt it was holy. The Church had maintained for generations that prayers throughout the watches of the night were holy. But it was holy because it was hard.

After *lauds* on this night, however, Agnella kept Magdalena and Chiara behind, along with the clothier Gilia. "Exercise clothes," Agnella whispered, "and then return to me. Wear your rosaries."

It made no sense, but in quiet obedience Magdalena pulled on her loose black clothing. In the hallway, Agnella gave each nun a black scarf to cover her head.

With a full moon and no clouds, Rome slept around them all, the women camouflaged in black in bare feet and with covered heads. Agnella whispered the prayer before exercise, then had them do their basic stretches in silence. *Matthew. Mark. Luke. John.* After several repetitions, she started at a jog through the street.

Without hesitation, Gilia took off after her. Magdalena and Chiara followed.

"What is this?" Chiara hissed.

"No idea."

Rome slept in silence, but Magdalena could feel the presence of the unaware citizens. The refuse of horses littered the streets, complement to the human refuse in the drainage ditches. Garlic's sharp smell competed with the sewage, and even with everyone indoors, the city reeked of unwashed people. Still, with no human activity, the air felt cleaner, and Magdalena awoke as they sprinted.

Agnella stopped beside a wall taller than her head. Alongside it was a tree. She jumped at the wall, springboarded off it toward the tree, and made her way onto a high branch. From the branch, she scaled the tree further and made it onto the top of the wall.

Magdalena blinked. "How'd she do that?"

"Watch." Gilia took off. It was a study in motion, the way she seemed to run up the side of the wall, pivoting in midair, getting her foot onto the stone and pushing upward as if the wall were a step. From a good way up the wall, the tree branch was an attainable goal. Magdalena hadn't thought of doing it that way before.

If you could run up the side of a wall, you could go anywhere. You could get into any house. Or out of one.

The Catherinites had run and jumped up the walls in the exercise room too, but only to get some height and then land with their legs and arms poised like a frog's, touching down in silence. This though? How useful. How fun.

Magdalena ran, sprang, propelled herself upward, and missed the branch.

Chiara giggled. "I won't make it either." When she tried, her hands hit the branch, but she couldn't pull onto it.

Agnella sprang down, her limbs absorbing the impact, and she rejoined them. She pointed to a particular stone, then moved Magdalena back a few steps. Magdalena started to speak, but Agnella pressed a finger to her lips: silence.

Okay, that made sense. Having the city awaken to a gaggle of leaping nuns would overly complicate their lives. But the jump-pivot-fly connection? That still made no sense.

Agnella demonstrated again, and this time Magdalena noted where she placed her foot and how she swiveled her hips to change direction in midair. Just as Agnella hit the tree branch and pulled up, Magdalena took off for the wall, jumped, contacted with one foot, and propelled herself into the branches.

The tree shook. She struggled to work her body onto the branch, but then she had to drop.

Chiara did make it, and that left only Magdalena on the pavement, an untenable situation. Plus, she wasn't sure how much tree-rustling it took before someone looked out into the roadway.

She ran, jumped, dug into the wall with her foot, and gasped as the branch hit her solar plexus. She was folded over the branch! With a scramble, she made her way gracelessly into an upright position.

Sure, she was fearfully and wonderfully made. God must be laughing at her as she made a thousand clumsy mistakes getting this done, but it wouldn't be the first time she'd amused Him. She climbed the rest of the way to join the other nuns.

Agnella led them along the wall until it reached a building, and then she scaled the side.

Magdalena had plenty of experience doing this, so she made it without difficulty. By contrast, a winded Chiara looked terrified. Without waiting, Agnella led them along the roof until it connected with an adjoining building, and this they ascended as well.

At the far end of this rooftop was a gap before the next. Agnella ran, sprang off the very edge, and landed with a roll on the other building. Her shoulder took the brunt of her touchdown. Seconds later, Gilia did the same.

Chiara hung back.

Magdalena squeezed her hand. "You?"

Chiara closed her eyes and shook her head. Magdalena swallowed hard and recited the prayer before exercise, then ran as hard as she could and jumped, flying into space. She landed in a hard thud—but on the roof, not in a splatted mess on the pavement.

"Quieter next time," Agnella breathed into her ear, a thousand times subtler than the crash of her landing. "Practice silence."

Chiara didn't want to come, so Agnella jumped back across, again landing in a silent shoulder roll before springing to her feet. Magdalena and Gilia waited under the moon while the two nuns spoke, heads together. Agnella had her hands on Chiara's shoulders. Finally they moved together to the edge of the building, Chiara petrified in the moon's bluish cast. She backed up again with Agnella. Chiara did the sign of the cross, then ran, hurled herself and cleared the jump by quite a distance. Agnella followed, again landing in a shoulder-roll that made no sound.

"One more," she whispered, and they followed.

At the corner of this building stood a tower. They scaled the outside, then slipped onto the stones at the top. From here Magdalena could pick out church spires in the full moon. She could see the darkness of the poorest neighborhoods. She could even recognize the outline of the Apostolic Palace where the pope himself was in residence.

On the peak they sat while Agnella recited in Latin, "I will extol you, O Lord, for you have drawn me up and have not let my foes rejoice over me. O Lord my God, I cried to you for help, and you have healed me. O Lord, you have brought up my soul from Sheol; you restored me to life from among those who go down to the pit."

Magdalena closed her eyes the better to hear her own breathing. She could even hear Chiara's beside her. Her mind followed through the delicious Latin of the psalm, the words of King David who had never experienced a city as grand as Rome and yet whose joy somehow captured the thrill of sitting at its peak in the full moon.

"Weeping may last for a night," Agnella recited, "but joy comes in the morning."

Agnella stood, now the tallest thing in this part of Rome, wisps of her hair broken free from the kerchief binding her head. Her smile was broad and bold in the moonlight. "Let's go home, sisters. Joy comes in the morning, but *prime* starts at six o'clock."

# FIVE

After seven weeks, Magdalena still went to bed certain she could do this for the rest of her life.

The convent's endless work invigorated her so much more than life behind an enclosure. Instead of attempting to embroider amidst the gossip of richer nuns, she carried food to the mortally ill and hauled back their laundry. She stayed awake past *compline* to pray the rosary with those actively dying, holding their hands as they received their final anointing from the kind priest at Saint Sebastian's. She'd wipe spittle and vomit from their chins and murmur psalms over them as they faded into their final sleep.

She'd fled to religious life as an escape from death, but here she found death not so scary an opponent after all. In the right way, at the right time, death operated for the glory of God. She talked to elderly men and women about running the race and fighting the good fight. She reassured them of the glorious crown that awaited. She tended their open sores and thin skin with a gentle hand, while as the weeks passed, her own skin became as rough as Bellosa's.

More than her hands had toughened. Daily work in the exercise room supplemented the hours of lifting and hauling she did at the hospital, and soon her muscles stopped aching every time she got out of bed. She and Chiara were transferred into an afternoon session where the exercises became more complicated.

Though plain, the food satisfied her. All that hard work left them hungry, and the kitchen nuns made sure there was plenty of meat.

During dinners in the refectory, Gilia would read aloud to the other sisters. Her books of doctrine proved far more interesting than the *Lives of Saints,* what the nuns of Cosma e Damiano had been limited to. Night by night, the nuns of Saint Sebastian's spent their time pondering the documents released by the first two periods of the forever-on-hold Council of Trent, intended to counter the Lutheran heretics. Bellosa said, "You need to know sound doctrine in order to recognize heresy. Without enclosure, heretics are something we all may encounter."

Once a week Magdalena had a visit from her mother and Fiora. Bellosa didn't insist on an ascoltrice to listen to their conversation. "We are all ascoltrices here," Bellosa said. "Remember that God Himself is always listening."

Domenico didn't come, perhaps intimidated by a community of toughened consecrated virgins, but Fiora became the convent's darling. The other nuns complimented Fiora's handmade clothes and the embroidery she brought, and this was even before Mother unpacked a basket with bread and cheese, plus a large jug of homemade rosewater.

Magdalena carried her mother's donation to the kitchen, where an older nun named Nezetta was arranging a tea tray. "Please bring this to your mother," Nezetta said. "I've added an extra biscuit for Fiora."

Magdalena returned with the tray, and her mother thanked Bellosa for the convent's generosity. "And thank you so much for accepting my daughter under the circumstances."

Magdalena's ears picked up the tension in her mother's voice, but Bellosa responded first. "Is something the matter?"

Mother sighed. Fiora had with unerring instinct detected that the extra biscuit was for her and was carrying it to the sofa. "We encountered some Marcolis." She wrapped her hands around one another. "Erico got into a fight."

Magdalena rushed forward. "Was Domenico hurt?"

"He's fine." Mother shook her head. "The boys who attacked Erico in the market were the sons of a man who works as a caretaker for the Marcoli family. I've no idea what's going to happen, but I'm worried about Domenico."

Agnella said from across the room, "Fiora, do you know what to do if a man tries to strike you?"

Fiora pursed her lips. "Should I do what Magdalena did?"

"Come with me." Though smiling, Agnella's face was tight. "We have an exercise room, and I'll show you how to use it too. To get stronger."

Magdalena said, "She can't run."

Agnella's eyes glinted. "Then she really needs to know how to defend herself."

After Agnella left with Fiora, Magdalena sat closer to her mother. "What can I do to help?"

Bellosa said, "I have no compunction about involving the church hierarchy. There's more than one priest in the Marcoli family, and they might back down if their hirelings' involvement in a vendetta prevents certain family members from advancing in the Church."

"They're not doing anything worse than scuffling in the streets right now." Mother's cheeks were pale. She must not have slept well for days. "I've been keeping Fiora with me, bringing her to the kitchens when I go to work, or leaving her with Lucia while she does the mending. I'm afraid to send her out to the market, but I'm also afraid for Domenico when he goes out to work. Erico was attacked on the docks."

Domenico pulled in decent money unloading ships. While it wasn't a lot, it made the difference between eating or not.

Bellosa bowed her head. "I will see what I can do. Pray and trust in God."

Mother said, "That's all I can do." Then Bellosa left the room, and Mother changed the subject to gossip about one of their extended relations.

After a time, Agnella returned, Fiora at her side glistening with sweat but bright-eyed. "You can come back whenever you want," Agnella said. "Or do those exercises on your own at home."

Fiora looked delighted. "Can I teach Domenico?"

"Domenico's a boy." Agnella shook her head. "He'll manage fine on his own. What I taught you doesn't come naturally to girls, so you'll need to work harder."

The bell rang for *none,* so Magdalena and Agnella escorted Mother and Fiora to the convent door, where Mother hugged Magdalena with a desperate tightness. "Pray for us," she murmured. "God listens to your prayers."

Magdalena hoped so, especially since this situation was her fault.

As they locked the gate, Agnella said on the way to *none,* "I watched how Fiora's leg moves, and I may be able to brace it."

"Really?"

"She needs to build up strength, and then the bone will straighten a little. Next time she's here, I'll take care of her."

Bellosa kept Magdalena and Chiara behind in the chapel after *none.* She looked them over, had them straighten their habits and get their rosaries tied on correctly, then asked them accompany her up the stairs to the main church.

Before the Communion rail at the front, Cardinal Simonetta awaited them. Had Bellosa summoned him because of the threats against her family? But no, they'd only just found out about it, and in any event, Chiara had been summoned too.

"Sister Bellosa, how are the novices?" Simonetta advanced through the slanting beams of colored light emanating from the stained-glass. His expression took on a more critical humor as he examined the pair. "Are they satisfactory?"

"Quite," said Bellosa.

"Both appear to be in excellent health." He looked at Chiara. "How old are you?"

"Thirteen."

He looked at Magdalena. "And you're...sixteen?"

She nodded.

"They're terribly young," he grumbled.

"I know you would prefer nuns over age forty," Bellosa said, "but the older sisters don't have the same conditioning and flexibility. All of us can haul the laundry or unload a cartload of flour, but in terms of reach, stretch, and speed, the youngest have the advantage."

Simonetta fingered his beard, then shook his head at Chiara. "This one, at any rate, is far too young."

Magdalena locked her teeth together. Chiara didn't mind being talked about like a horse at auction, but how dare he? Cardinal or not, he owed them respect as brides of Christ. Imagine the fun if she were to ask how many boys at her age, or even Chiara's, had been advanced to being cardinals solely for being the pope's *nephews*. For that matter, how had Simonetta himself obtained his position? With enough money, you could bid on any position in the Curia. Some positions, she was sure, had been formed solely to generate that kind of income.

She held her tongue. Bellosa instructed Chiara to return to the convent.

Magdalena stood alone. She could ask what to do about the Marcoli vendetta. She could, and then doubtless he could reply that he'd done his duty by removing her from immediate danger, and that Farneses could look after themselves.

"We have a concern," Simonetta said, "and I need your help to resolve it."

Oh, did he? "Sir?"

"Are you familiar with the Index of Banned Books?" When she nodded (because who wasn't familiar with that particular brainchild of Pope Paul IV?) he said, "We've heard that a certain cardinal has come into possession of one of those books. He's influential in the Curia, so of course we cannot turn him over to the Roman Inquisition, but certain of us are very concerned that he might be corrupted by heresy."

Beside Magdalena, Bellosa shook her head.

"We've no idea how he obtained the book," Simonetta continued, "but we need to part him from it before the damage is irreparable. Asking him directly would cause him to hide it, and we don't want to accuse him in public lest we cause scandal." Simonetta stepped closer, and breathed his words as he towered over Magdalena. "We need you to retrieve it."

*Retrieve it.* Magdalena's eyes widened. "How?"

"We believe he keeps it in his personal chambers," Simonetta said. "We require you to penetrate the building and deliver us the book."

He made it sound so intriguing, but in reality he was asking for petty theft. Nothing Magdalena hadn't done in her previous life.

Bellosa sounded concerned. "Sister Agnella can accompany you, at least in part. But she doesn't have your youth and flexibility."

How flexible did you have to be? Agnella had climbed a church tower last month. "I could get into the building by delivering laundry or food. If someone in his residence gets ill, you could dispatch me to tend the person."

Simonetta smiled, and it was a cold wind. "You're clever, but I want you to do it tonight."

Tonight. Magdalena thought about her brother, about her cousins, who had climbed walls in order to slip into windows and creep outside again with coin purses and jewelry. How much of her dowry had come from those after-dark activities?

Still, his request sounded as though he enjoyed making it more difficult than it had to be. "How will I know which book?"

"I've written down the title. It's in Latin. Can you read Latin?"

She'd rather have died than admit to this man how little she could read. "Yes, sir. I can read Latin."

Simonetta again wore that half-amused smirk. "Don't bristle at me. We have one chance to save this man's soul from Lutheranism."

"Forgive my impertinence." Magdalena braced herself. Simonetta had said, after all, that he *needed* her. "I'm very concerned about my family. You remember the circumstances under which I came to Saint Sebastian's. The other family has tracked down my relations, and I'm distracted by worry." She paused, and then added, "If you were somehow to help them, the relief would make it easier for me to carry out this assignment."

"Would it indeed?" Simonetta's voice was bland as he handed her a paper with a string of indecipherable words.

Bellosa spoke before Magdalena had the chance. "One letter from you might put paid to the incident, and Magdalena could free her mind to focus solely on the work you're asking."

"I'm asking you to protect the papacy." Simonetta scowled. "You took a vow to do so, did you not?"

Magdalena raised her chin. "I know my vows."

"Then you know your duty. Bring the book back to the convent. In the morning, I will fetch it for transport to the Roman Inquisition."

# SIX

After *lauds,* Agnella and Magdalena stripped off their outer habits, revealing their black exercise clothes. They tied on black scarves. Effortlessly they jogged through the avenues, their bare feet making less sound than their hard breath.

At a palace a mile from the convent, Agnella stopped. She pointed to a series of windows on the darkened third floor. Their layout exactly matched the drawing Agnella had sketched earlier this afternoon.

They waited at the feet of the building for several minutes, but nothing moved. The darkness of every window, unbroken, told of a household asleep.

*Matthew,* Magdalena thought as she worked through the early exercises to steady her muscles. *Mark. Luke. John. Matthew again. Mark. Luke. John.*

Her heart trilled as she flexed her fingers within her leather gloves. O Lord, we have consecrated our bodies to you. Please protect our bodies and give them health and strength. Amen.

Silent as a black cat, Magdalena raced across the street to the wall surrounding the building. Without slowing she jumped, planting a foot right on the stones and vaulting upward. Her stomach hit the top of the wall, but she pushed with her arms to complete the leap.

Seven weeks ago, she couldn't have done this. Seven weeks ago, she'd been hungry in a cell and awaiting execution.

Behind her, Agnella landed. Without waiting, Magdalena raced along the wall toward the house. The moonlight gave all the guidance necessary, and momentarily they'd reached the building.

She looked up the side of the palace, then found the drain spout from the roof. Rain could go down, and Magdalena could go up. She pulled off her gloves and shinnied up the pipe to the second floor, where she rested on a window ledge. Her brother and cousins had done this often enough, and she'd never been too proud to help. She climbed the rest of the way to the top all in one trip, then grabbed the tiles and slithered onto the roof.

With the terra-cotta cold under her chest, Magdalena waited for her breathing to ease. Silence was of greater import now than speed. But as she paused, she scanned the city spread before her.

Rome. Rome wreathed in black. Rome, the city of saints, bejeweled overhead with God's diamonds and the one luminous sphere of the moon. Distantly she could pick out the glory of the Apostolic Palace. And in all this, only she remained awake. She and Agnella, with a book awaiting her in a cardinal's bedroom.

Magdalena crept across the roof to twin spires jutting up at the front. The window she needed was directly between and beneath.

Tall like a church spire, she gathered herself. *Matthew. Mark. Luke. John. And go.*

Magdalena unhooked the cord rosary from her belt, looped it over the head of a gargoyle, tugged, and then scaled the wall until she reached a window. Her hands had a grip on the rosary knots, and when she reached the end of the loop, she swung to the side and through the open window, landing like a frog on her hands and toes.

The landing wasn't soundless, but she stayed still. *No one rouses after only one noise.* Anyone who hears the first waits for a second. In the absence of a second sound, they assume the first was innocent. *I am of no importance. Go back to sleep. I'm nothing.*

During those minutes, her eyes adjusted to a room without moonlight, and shortly she identified a four-poster bed. In the bed, someone slept, his breathing steady and slow. She couldn't pick out the images on the tapestries, but she noted the chests, the armoires, and a sideboard. Across the room, a shadow looked like a desk with a chair: her target

Toward this she crept, tracking always the faint breathing of the sleeper. In. Out. The carpet absorbed her footfalls, and at the other side of the room, she reached the book.

She couldn't read its title in the dark, but she ran her fingers over the leather binding. As Simonetta had told her, it was long as her forearm and thick as her fist, clasped shut with a leather strap.

After a slow trip back across the room, she examined the book in the moonlight. The gold-embossed Latin letters matched the ones she'd memorized from Simonetta's paper. It was lighter than she'd predicted. Shouldn't a condemned book be full of weighty thoughts?

She ran her fingers along the leather strap. The words written in here must in a way be magical, to beguile even a cardinal to heresy. What would someone pay for a book like that? What kind of person wrote those words in the first place? Maybe such creation happened under the tutelage of Satan, demonic script rising and swirling together to form a sweet poison that looked like medicine for an ailing church. Only instead of sweetness, it became venom that the reader didn't realize until a moment too late. Once bitten with that venom, was there any way to put the snake back into the book?

She fingered the clasp, suddenly hungry to find out.

But no, it was forbidden. Simonetta had said as much.

Careful now. She had to get it out of the room. Not read it. Just remove it and put it in a place it couldn't hurt anyone.

Crouching beneath the window, Magdalena untucked her shirt and pressed the book against her abdomen, then secured it with her belt. Bulkier than before, she raised herself onto the window ledge and looked out again on Rome. Rome, with so many church spires and beautiful buildings, the jewels above and the filth below.

*Lord, protect me,* she prayed, and she leaped for the rosary hanging between the windows.

It went taut, and Magdalena feared for a moment that it would snap, or the gargoyle would let go of the roof and tumble to the courtyard, taking her with it. But it held, and she crept up the dizzying side of the building, then reversed her way back down. Descending the pipe took less time than ascending, but eventually she rejoined Agnella at the wall.

She pointed to her chest, and Agnella nodded. They fled along the wall back to the street, then alighted like butterflies. Agnella ran down the street, but Magdalena stopped.

Agnella sprinted back to her.

"We need to bring this to Cardinal Simonetta," whispered Magdalena.

Agnella replied in a similar tone, "We're to bring the book back to the convent."

"Too dangerous. The book is in the Index, and we don't want the Roman Inquisition breathing down our necks." Maybe not even the Roman Inquisition. Given how tempting it was to open the book in that dark bedroom, how could she sleep the rest of the night knowing it was in the same building? In the silent convent, she could linger over the pages and not be discovered until *prime.* Anyone could. Magdalena shouldn't take that chance. "Let's do this the right way. Where's Simonetta?"

A wicked grin overtook Agnella's face. "Well, then. You keep surprising me with your spirit."

Agnella ran, and Magdalena struggled to keep pace as they worked their way deeper into the city. This was the ecclesiastical part, the places the cardinals lived. Many of them had palaces in other locations, of course, but here were their in-city homes. The nuns met no one at this hour, but they ran in silence anyhow. Eventually they stopped before a building that seemed just like all the others.

Agnella whispered, "Second floor window. That would be his office."

Magdalena whispered, "I want to put it in his bed."

Agnella shook her head. "Too dangerous. His rooms would be in the interior or toward the back."

Magdalena took a deep breath to steady herself, then scaled the wall, always careful of how the book's weight unbalanced her. Although it was light for a book, it still threw off her sense of balance. But her fingers found holds in the stone and so did her toes, and at the window ledge she entered.

The desk stood beneath the window. Magdalena sprang to the carpet, then listened. When the house failed to respond to her presence, she laid the forbidden book on the cushioned chair. Simonetta would find it, but it would remain hidden from view by his servants.

From there she moved back to the window ledge, then eyeballed the distance to the ground.

Descending was always worse than ascending because you had no way to see where your feet needed to go. So instead of climbing, Magdalena leaped from the window, landing like a spring.

The impact jolted up through one leg, but the rest of her landed like a frog. Agnella waved to her, and they moved.

As soon as she tried to run, her ankle screamed in protest. Limping, she stuck to the shadows, and shortly Agnella reappeared.

"Ankle," Magdalena whispered.

"That was dumb. It was too long a jump."

Magdalena smirked. "I've jumped further."

"Onto grass. Can you walk?"

With no choice, Magdalena hobbled to keep her weight off the bad side.

When they reached one of the main streets, Agnella said, "Where did you come from? I mean, before Cosma e Damiano."

"I'm the bastard daughter of a bastard son." Magdalena huffed. "And if you go back further, I'm a Farnese."

"Good blood." Agnella sounded grudging. "Nasty men, but good blood. With connections like that, how did Simonetta bring you to us?"

"Scandal."

Agnella sounded disgusted. "They caught you sneaking a man into your convent?"

"Hardly!" Magdalena's shock squeaked out in her voice, and she lowered it. "I killed a priest."

Agnella stopped. "Really?"

Magdalena paused to rub her ankle. It wasn't bleeding, but it felt thick. Tight. Agnella took the wrap from around Magdalena's waist and tied it over her ankle, down around the arch of her foot, and back up again. "That should get you home, at least. What did you do to the priest? Who was he?"

Magdalena tested her weight on that foot. The wrap seemed to help, so she took a step. "I think I can make it this way. Thanks."

"The priest," Agnella repeated. "What happened?"

It was the note in her voice, the urgency. Magdalena said, "He was one of the convent's confessors—"

Agnella spun out a curse long and violent enough that Magdalena wondered if she'd memorized it from an ancient tome pried from the hands of a dead man—or maybe even the book they'd just left in Simonetta's house. Agnella finished with a hissed, "Confessors! Let them all be dragged screaming into Hell with demons clawing at their ankles and shoved under the waves of the lake of fire by nuns wielding hot pokers."

Agnella stepped closer to her. "Have you heard of *Le Convertite*? In Venice? Two hundred nuns lived there, in a convent for *fallen women*." She sounded disgusted. "Most of us were converted prostitutes, but some were young widows and others...you didn't always know why they were there. But we fled into that enclosure for safety. We couldn't stay pure in the outside world. We took vows there because the walls would free us from temptation. And once we were all barred up in God's bridal chamber, the snake slithered inside the walls speaking Latin and Greek."

The hair stood on Magdalena's arms. "What did he do?"

"What do you think he did? Women who had sold their bodies came to him as their lifeline to God, some barely more than girls themselves. He'd dangle hope, but he'd also ask questions, and if you said no to his touching and propositioning, he'd let you go with a laugh. How funny! He was just testing you." Her voice grew sinister. "But then a few days later the abbess would accuse you of some petty infraction. You'd be locked up in the convent prison, and he'd come in to bribe you or beat you until you agreed to let him have you. Or else he'd just force you."

The hair was standing on Magdalena's arms. She couldn't feel the pain in her ankle over the whine in her ears.

"We waited for another priest to come in so we could all confess to him, just so someone would know, but the snake never let another priest in. Nuns died without being confessed because the snake didn't feel like getting out of his bed, or because he wasn't in the city. Still no one from the magistrates investigated. Our bishop didn't visit. No one from the Curia provided any help whatsoever."

Magdalena blinked back tears.

"We reported him, but always someone would stand up for his good name. Father Giovanni Pietro Leon was a saint, *bella figura,* and we were only women. Defiled women, at that. Prostitutes turned nuns, or married women with no husbands, blemished and obviously of bad character." Her voice went hard like a knife blade. "But then they caught him, for real."

Remembering Agnella's comment when she'd first arrived, Magdalena ventured, "And you escaped?"

"I escaped because at the end, they threw a hundred of us out of the convent. I fled to Rome and thought maybe I could at least earn some money the old way, but then I found out about our order. I went to Bellosa, and she decided I'd fit in."

They were quiet a moment.

Magdalena said, "What about the snake? Was he imprisoned?"

"Executed." Agnella spat the word. "It took five tries to cut off his head. The scene was so horrible that his friends wrested the blade from the executioner and tried to finish him off, but even they couldn't do it." She spoke quicker now. "I hope he felt every minute of that death's agony, and that when it finally ended, I wish Satan made it his business to be right there to yank out that brute's filthy soul with his fangs. It is my most ardent desire that now Giovanni Pietro Leon can relish every minute of eternity enjoying whatever the old dragon chooses to do with him. And if the devil runs out of ideas, I have several suggestions."

In silence they moved through the shadows of buildings, now closer together than in the rich parts. Magdalena wasn't sure how much further it was to home. She'd get barely an hour of sleep, but at least she would have an hour.

Agnella didn't look back. "Your confessor? How did he die?"

"He snuck up on me in the library." Magdalena swallowed. "He had his hands all over me. I hit him to force him away. Instead he died."

"He didn't assault you during confession? He was an amateur. Too confident." Agnella sounded bitter. "I wish I'd killed the *saintly* Giovanni Pietro Leon."

Magdalena ventured, "At least the man's dead."

"I blunted the swords they used on him." Agnella turned around, and even in the low light there was no mistaking her smug eyes. "I'm the reason they had to hack him to death. But it's not enough. I wish I had his blood on my hands the way you do on yours."

# SEVEN

Bellosa had to shake Magdalena to wakefulness for *prime,* and with a worried expression, she pulled Magdalena and Agnella aside while the other nuns began the rosary. "Where's the book?"

"We delivered it directly to Cardinal Simonetta." Every step hurt, but Magdalena didn't dare limp. "A forbidden book would have tainted the convent."

Bellosa's eyebrows raised.

Agnella folded her arms and leaned against the wall. "I escorted her to our favorite cardinal's residence, and she deposited it at his desk."

Bellosa stared, horrified. "The book, was it unopened?"

Magdalena's eyes widened. "Of course I didn't open it! If I don't want their heresy polluting the convent, why would I tolerate it polluting my soul?"

Other than sheer curiosity, of course. But it was better this way. Let Simonetta deal with the curiosity. Then again, maybe he'd already read it. Surely someone needed to read the books to determine they deserved to be banned.

Bellosa turned to Agnella. "You let her bring it directly to him."

Agnella wore an inexplicable smirk. "I thought it fitting."

Bellosa glared at Agnella, then looked back at Magdalena with more weariness than sternness. "In the future, obey your orders exactly as given."

"I don't want to tangle with the Roman Inquisition."

"I can handle the Roman Inquisition." Bellosa sighed. "But now, I'll have to handle Simonetta. Agnella," she added, her voice sharpening, "I will speak to you later."

"Speak to me now if you like. The book is delivered, and the work is done. This afternoon," Agnella added, "I'll start Magdalena on some more advanced exercises."

After their rosary, the nuns had breakfast. "Are you hurt?" Chiara exclaimed. "Sister Bellosa, Magdalena is hurt!"

Bellosa murmured, "I'm sure she's quite fine," and then looked right at Chiara and interrupted before she could say anything else. "Please, go ahead and finish your breakfast."

Magdalena nodded at Chiara, who returned her attention to her porridge.

Bellosa's revenge on Agnella consisted of dispatching her to Simonetta's residence with a letter. Magdalena got to work carrying laundry and provisions to the hospital for incurables. Walking hurt, but the more she walked the less it ached.

They met for *terce* at nine o'clock. Immediately afterward, Magdalena was summoned to the church where Cardinal Simonetta glowered, arms folded and eyes dark.

Bellosa strode forward, so she missed hearing Agnella's barely audible snicker. Magdalena braced herself for the walk across the stone floor, then bowed in front of him.

"You were to bring it here," he snapped.

The lack of a preamble meant her delivery of the book had crossed so far into his definition of "unacceptable behavior" that he didn't think she required an explanation. It also meant she should refrain from asking him to intervene with the Marcolis.

"I didn't want to expose the Catherinite convent to scandal," Magdalena replied. "I saw no benefit to bringing it to Saint Sebastian's where another nun might find and open the book or where a hospital visitor might recognize a forbidden text and report us to the Inquisition."

Agnella sounded uncharacteristically mild. "When handling poison, sir, it's best to minimize the intermediaries."

Simonetta focused a glare on her so penetrating that it was a wonder Agnella didn't crumple to a heap on the polished stone. Instead she met his furious eyes, defiant.

His anger made no sense. Neither did Agnella's attitude. Some larger conversation must be taking place, unspoken but decodable by every participant other than herself.

Simonetta turned to Bellosa. "Her actions were highly irregular."

"I acted to prevent scandal." Magdalena raised her voice, "If anything, my actions were more efficient than yours. I relieved you of the need to come here at all. You have the evidence you require."

Simonetta barked, "Do you know what was in the book?"

Magdalena shot back, "Heresy."

He drew back.

"She didn't open the book," Agnella said, "so how could she know what it contained?"

"Other than the judgment of His Holiness Pope Paul IV," Magdalena said, "I have no reason to believe the book contained anything at all. But the Church says it's dangerous, so I believe it's dangerous too. Too dangerous to bring behind our walls," she added. "I brought it to you as our order's protector."

Simonetta said to Agnella, "This wasn't your idea?"

"It was her prudential judgment." Agnella's eyes narrowed. "Sir."

The cardinal paced, then returned. "Very well, then. I will consider the matter, and Sister Bellosa, I will be in contact as necessary."

———————◇———————

Agnella transferred Magdalena into the main exercise group. "Today, though, don't do any jumping. We need to protect your ankle, so whenever the others work with their legs, you will remain to the side and pray. Pray for healing, and also pray for Cardinal Simonetta to discover his sense of humor."

The new exercise session opened as did the previous one, with a prayer for protection of their consecrated bodies, and then the standard stretches. After this, Agnella unlocked an armoire in the corner and handed out long staffs. For the next hour, the nuns did their exercises holding the staffs, swinging them or thrusting them. Agnella had them pair off and pretend to strike one another with an exaggerated slowness, scripting their attacks and blocks.

"Are we putting on a play?" Magdalena said.

"Exactly." Agnella nodded. "Keeping practicing this, and when it's time to perform, you'll act your part without thinking about it."

She struck Magdalena in the shoulder. Magdalena pivoted, bringing up her arm, but Agnella knocked away her staff. It rolled to the wall with a clatter.

"Almost." Agnella's eyes narrowed. "How often do the street urchins refer to convents as 'brothels' and 'whorehouses'? So be it. But if any man tries to take these *whores*, he'd best be prepared to lose the use of his arm or one of his eyes."

Magdalena folded her arms. "I was given to understand we should die to protect our virtue, not kill."

"Better to go lame or blind into paradise than whole and with two eyes into Gehenna." Sister Agnella tossed Magdalena's staff back to her. "Try again."

Fiora arrived shortly before *none,* and Agnella exclaimed, "Oh, our newest exerciser! Come in!"

Fiora handed Agnella a basket of bread. "Beautiful," Agnella said. "Magdalena, bring this to the kitchen."

Mother's bread. Magdalena breathed in the scent of it and hoped some of it made its way to their dinner table and not all of it into the hospital.

She returned to the exercise room to find Agnella fitting a crutch under Fiora's arm. "If we get this the right height," Agnella was saying, "not only are we going to make you more mobile, but you, my sweetie, will have at your disposal your very own weapon."

Magdalena couldn't remain. She had bandages to fold, plus one elderly woman who needed bathing. By the time the bell rang for *none,* Fiora had left.

After *none,* Bellosa announced that she would be keeping certain of the nuns with her, including Magdalena and Agnella. In their full formal habits, six nuns assembled in the main church, and shortly they squeezed into a carriage to ride to the residence of Cardinal Simonetta.

"Now you'll get to see it in daylight," Agnella murmured as she slipped in behind Magdalena. "It's really quite splendid."

Because of the traffic on the Roman streets, it took longer to ride there than it had taken to sprint. Magdalena's stomach churned from the motion and the smells, not to mention the noise.

Inside the convent, there was always a measure of quiet. Even in the hospital for incurables, the few people who cried out in their illness were notable because of their cries, not because they melded into the general tumult. The Roman streets, however, churned with chaos the way an ant colony churned with shiny bodies. Fruit sellers and bread sellers littered the air with their voices, plus people calling greetings and others shouting threats, as well as the occasional church bell, and always the sound of clopping hooves and creaking wagons.

Less than a year ago, Magdalena would have considered this the backdrop of existence itself. She'd given up the noise along with the rest of her life. It was still a jolt to realize she'd been given it back again.

As a servant escorted the nuns into Simonetta's parlor, Magdalena craned her neck to gaze up the wide staircase of marble and dark wood. A trip to the office she'd entered was not, apparently, on the docket for today. The first-floor parlor made her only more curious about the upstairs, bedecked as it was with a woven rug and cushioned furniture. The servants brought trays of fruit as well as tea and biscuits.

"Fancy stuff," Agnella said. "The priests always seem to have that."

"He must get a rich benefice from his position," said Gilia. "How many scudi a year do you think a cardinal earns?"

"How much do you have to pay up front to be elevated to cardinal?" Agnella shot back. "There had to have been money aplenty before he ever took the red cap."

"Look at the art," Bellosa told Magdalena. "Many of those were his own commission, but he's inherited quite a bit."

Magdalena settled herself on a couch to take her weight off her ankle, but she obeyed her abbess and admired the paintings and the statues. This was a luxurious existence, no doubt, but how did the life of someone like Saint Francis fit into this kind of situation? All Magdalena's life she'd been surrounded by people doing the work of God, who then retired to homes like this every evening. Even her former convent had been of a piece with this, and they followed the order of Saint Clare.

You had to eat to survive, and you needed shelter. So the Church paid for these things, and it made sense that the higher positions received greater payments. But on the other hand, wasn't Saint Clare great too? Wasn't Saint Francis?

Agnella said, "Don't look surprised. This isn't his only house, you realize."

Magdalena straightened. "Where is the other?"

"Pesaro. He was made bishop there," Bellosa said, "following in the footsteps of his uncle, the previous bishop."

"His uncle, or his *uncle* uncle?" Magdalena leaned forward. "You know, the way Pope Paul III was the *uncle* of Alessandro Farnese?"

The other women in the room snickered. "It's not entirely clear to me what you mean," said Bellosa primly. "He's currently the cardinal in charge of the Datary, so he hasn't been back to Pesaro in some time, and therefore he's resigned that position."

Half the bishops in the Church hardly ever set foot in their diocese, if at all. The only unusual thing was in Simonetta's actually resigning the post rather than just collecting the payment of its benefice and hiring someone else to do the job.

"The *Datary*," Gilia said with emphasis. "That makes him the Eye of the Pope."

*Oculus Papae.* Not only a cardinal, but the cardinal of the Datary? Magdalena had heard that term, and only now did she realize how outrageous it had been to crawl into this man's second-story window to leave a stolen book. When was the last time someone had outright defied him?

Magdalena hid a smile. Too long, clearly.

The door opened, and in strode Cardinal Simonetta, Eye of the Pope. The nuns all stood, and he instructed them to sit, then drew over a chair. "I trust you are comfortable. I've brought you here because the Church needs your help."

The other nuns sat at attention, so Magdalena ordered her thoughts. *Help* yesterday had meant stealing a book. What was meant by today's *help*?

"I've had Sister Bellosa choose the sisters she feels are best suited to this particular service," Simonetta continued. "Sister Magdalena," he said with an icier tone, "necessity compels us to count your assignment as completed, although irregularly. The Church has a matter of greater delicacy and urgency that needs our attention, and your work last night has ensured you a place in its completion."

"Thank you, sir." The words slipped out before Magdalena had time to think twice.

He turned back to the group of nuns, a group that Magdalena now realized consisted of the convent's younger women. To be more specific, the younger women in the advanced exercise class. Bellosa was over forty, and Nezetta was even older. But Agnella was in her mid-twenties, Gilia nearly the same, and then herself at seventeen. The only young nun missing was Chiara, whom he'd said yesterday was too young.

Flexible. Strong. Skillful. And trained to defend themselves with weapons.

Simonetta said, "The pope has decreed that the Council of Trent will resume this year, after several years in abeyance. And yes," he said, cutting off Agnella's stifled sigh, "we have every reason to believe it actually will resume this time, and that in this third period it should complete its work."

The never-ending Council, the very late response to the Lutheran schismatics. And it would never end, therefore never bring back the heretics.

"We have much to do in order to restore orthodoxy and re-unite the heretics and schismatics from the northern countries back under the umbrella of Rome." Simonetta sighed. "The politics makes the council's continuation extremely tenuous, but the pope wants it to take place, and the Holy Roman Emperor very much wants us to succeed. The French are in the teeth of heretical revolt right now, and the Spaniards are insane with ideas of reforming the *head* of the Church. England may not dare send any bishops due to the Acts of Supremacy and Uniformity, and it's an open question how many we can get from the East. But the pope has ordered us to proceed."

Simonetta paced to the window. "Five of you must go."

Magdalena's ears rang, and her vision went dark. *Go? Go to Trent? Leave Rome? How far away was Trent? How far would she be from Fiora?*

"Pope Paul IV made certain your order had a convent in Trent just for this eventuality," Simonetta continued. "The work we perform at Trent is more important than any work I have ever asked. Corruption is rampant, and Emperor Ferdinand as well as King Philip and King Charles are exerting tremendous pressure on His Holiness to *reform the papacy* in such a way as to diminish us all."

He strode back to them. "Your vows against heresy compel you to act. There is no other way."

Bellosa said, "I assure you, sir, that we want nothing more than to protect the Church."

"You will travel up to your northern convent," he said. "It's in *German lands,* one of the stipulations from the start. They believe it will soothe the Lutherans to think they stand on their own ground. But there you must go."

German lands. That had to be hundreds of miles away. Magdalena ventured, "You said five of us...?"

"I will not be going," said Bellosa. "I'm required here, as this convent's abbess."

Magdalena blurted out, "But—doesn't the convent there already have nuns?"

Trent wasn't even on the Italian peninsula, was it? In German lands—how could she see her mother again? What would she do if the Marcolis caused problems?

"What you want isn't as important as what the Church needs." Simonetta raised an eyebrow at her. "Need I remind you of your vows?"

Bellosa rested her hand on Magdalena's.

Simonetta delved more into detail, and Magdalena struggled to retain information that was meaningless to her. The politics alone was insanely complicated. The Spanish bishops would be very reform-minded. The French bishops wanted to do anything they could to limit the power of the pope. The Holy Roman Emperor wanted to keep his German lands under tight control, but he doubtless intended to use the council to strengthen his own power instead of bolstering the Church's. No one knew what England was going to do, assuming England participated at all. And so far, no envoys to the Eastern parts of Europe, northern Africa, or the Near East had returned with assent that they would attend. "The Polish bishops have a very delicate situation," said Simonetta. "And the sad truth is, most bishops don't want to attend, on the grounds that they don't think the council is going to take place."

If the council failed to happen, that would at least get Magdalena back to Rome. But how long would it take to declare this third attempt a failure?

"Our sisters in Trent run a boarding house," Bellosa said to the nuns. "We planned this to ensure we had full access to the bishops and the envoys of the kings. Several of our order also service the palace of Trent's bishop, Cardinal Madruzzo."

Magdalena said, "Surely they won't bring forbidden books to the council, so what are we to do?"

"You are to listen," Simonetta said, emphasizing the last word overmuch. "You are to report any heresy you hear so I may make the proper response. I've attended the previous two periods of the council, and it would horrify you to hear the heretical notions they float during the general congregations, let alone amongst themselves. Cardinal

Morone and Cardinal Pole, from the first period, were both later accused of heresy. This time, I myself will be in attendance as one of the five papal legates. I will be setting the agenda, and I will be reporting back to His Holiness Pius IV. You will be my ears and my hands among the swarming throngs."

Magdalena said, "If they show up."

Simonetta glared at her. "You certainly do talk a lot."

Since he'd noticed, Magdalena had nothing to lose. "You're using nuns as spies?"

Agnella said flatly, "As enforcers."

Magdalena started.

Agnella kept her voice flat. "The penalty for heresy is death."

Simonetta's voice had gone stern. "At such a location, at such a precarious time, we can't summon the Holy Roman Emperor or conduct a heresy trial. How can we hold public executions when highly placed men are voicing opinions so desperately clung to by the general population?" He shook his head. "Moreover, we've made a guarantee of *safe conduct* to any Lutheran theologians who care to present their errors in public. We can't promise *them* safety and then publicly turn on our own. Therefore, on occasion, on very rare occasion," he specified, "the Catherinites may be tasked with completing a sentence after a verdict of heresy."

The longer he spoke, the closer Magdalena came to vomiting up the flaky biscuits and hot tea.

No wonder they'd sought her out. She'd killed a man.

She'd done it once. Only once, and that by accident. He'd been trying to pleasure himself on her, and she'd killed a priest.

No. No, get calm. The Church was the bride of Christ even more than she herself was, and if she was allowed to defend her purity, so was the Church. A heretic was in his own way pleasuring himself at the expense of a Church he thought would be too ashamed or too scared to defend herself.

That was why kings executed heretics. In a Church council bent on stamping out heresy, surely heretics would surface in order to pervert the faith even further. Imagine what they could do with their heresies once they had even a shred of approval from a Church council?

The Church was at her most vulnerable. Now. In the moment of decision, the Bride must be protected.

Magdalena thought again about the staff Agnella had handed her today. It had been heavy in her hands but swift in its motion and brilliant in how it extended her reach. Wielding a weapon like that to defend Christ Himself would make it all the lighter. This wasn't just about removing books from the hands of impressionable clergymen. It was about removing the already-swayed clergymen from the flocks of sheep who would follow them with full trust right into Hell. The Church had souls to save and only one way to save them.

"I don't anticipate it coming to that," said Simonetta. "But the convents of Saint Sebastian and Saint Martin of Tours will need to stand at the ready to defend the faith."

# EIGHT

Fiora made her way into the chapel just before *terce,* surprising Magdalena with how quickly she moved with the crutch. Agnella watched the girl's motions, then frowned as she studied her feet. There was no way to speak, not in the chapel, so Magdalena shifted over enough for Fiora to kneel at her side.

After prayers, Agnella took Fiora into the exercise room, but she also asked for Gilia. Curious, Magdalena followed them and found Agnella examining Fiora's twisted foot.

"It's not just a matter of length," she said. "Your leg is shorter on this side, but your foot doesn't flex properly. Let's see what we can do to brace it."

Gilia set a paper on the floor and traced Fiora's foot. Agnella looked up. "We have only a few days left," she said to Magdalena. "I need to get this done quickly. You don't have to stay," she added, which was as good as a dismissal.

So Magdalena went to the hospital of incurables, cleaning an elderly man who sweat a foul-smelling liquid from every pore in his body and whose sheets needed to be boiled daily. She struggled to see Christ in this man's terrible body, and when she bathed him, she tried to imagine his stench as the stink of sin that clung to every human soul. The man didn't seem ashamed. Maybe he couldn't smell himself any longer. Or maybe he did know and pretended it wasn't there as the only way to maintain his dignity.

From there she moved to the bedside of a woman in pain, and she tried to soothe her. There was also a child Magdalena had to spoon-feed a thin broth, and every one of these people needed their laundry washed and their souls prayed for.

When the time came for *sext,* Agnella didn't come to the chapel. A nun's absence wasn't entirely unusual: if you were holding a basin for a vomiting man, you didn't just put it down because the bells rang. But Agnella's absence was curious because to the best of Magdalena's knowledge, she wasn't at the hospital.

She was, however, present for lunch, and Fiora sat at her side. The girl was in a bright mood, and she chattered at the nuns throughout the meal. Magdalena was about to shush her when Agnella signaled her not to. In her eyes glinted a defiant light.

After lunch, Magdalena found Fiora and Agnella sitting on the exercise room floor, holding a plaster form. "Behold," Agnella said. "One of the doctors showed me how to make a cast of the body, and here I've made your sister's foot."

Magdalena knelt beside her. "Why?"

Fiora beamed. "She says I'll be able to walk without limping!"

"I want more than that." Agnella frowned as she studied the form. "I want her to be able to run fast enough to save her life."

Magdalena swallowed hard. "Surely she's not in that much danger."

"Domenico and Erico say they'll protect me."

"They can't be with her all the time." Agnella ran her hands over the deformed arch, the crumpled toes. "It's good to hit an attacker with your crutch when he thinks he's got an easy victim." Her voice dropped into a bitter tone. "But the reason to hit him is to put him on the ground so you can run to safety. Fiora can't run. We need to fix that."

She pivoted the plaster foot in her hand. "Gilia is making a pair of sandals like the ones she made you. The top will be flexible, but not the bottom. Here." She held up a piece of wood. "I've measured your sister in every direction I can. One leg is three inches shorter than the other, but I can't just elevate her three inches. Her foot is crooked, so I need to marry the arch of the lift to the bend in her bones."

Fiora took the plaster foot and held it out to Magdalena. "It's me. See?"

Magdalena said, "And then...she'll be able to walk?"

"For a time. It's a shame about Trent because over time she's going to outgrow the sandals we make. Her muscles will strengthen, and—who knows—maybe the curve will change as her foot gets stronger." Agnella turned to Fiora. "I hope that's exactly how it does work, but when that happens, the shoe won't fit any longer."

Fiora said, "You can make me a new one then. Right?"

Agnella glanced from Magdalena to Fiora. "Don't borrow trouble from tomorrow. I'll stay up all night if I have to in order to get the shoe ready by tomorrow morning. Gilia will get the form fitted to the shoe, and then you'll be able to run home." She stood. "For now, though, you should get back to your mother."

Magdalena said, "Tomorrow, if you can, come here with Mother."

A dreadful conversation that would be, having to say that after losing her daughter and getting her back again, Mother would lose her once more.

Fiora beamed. "So she can see me run?"

Magdalena steadied herself. "Yes. I want her to see you run."

"Magdalena," said Agnella from the library door, "get into exercise clothes and come with me."

They were an hour before compline. Once dressed, Magdalena followed Agnella up into the main body of the church. Gilia was already waiting in her loose black clothes, and shortly Chiara sprinted across the marble floor. "I've barred the doors. We're alone."

"Wonderful." Agnella made the sign of the cross and said the prayer before exercise.

First they did their basic stretches. Then Agnella said, "You three needed a more challenging workout, but it's raining." Grinning, she exclaimed, "Follow me!"

She took a running jump and, using a side altar as a springboard, leaped onto one of the ornate balconies. Gilia made the jump, pivoting her hips mid-spring so she could change directions without losing momentum. Chiara gulped, then followed, slamming into the rail and scrambling until she could lever her whole body on to the railing.

Magdalena went last. Agnella didn't wait. She shot right off the balcony into another springing jump toward one of the stained-glass windows, then from the window ledge to another balcony.

Magdalena slammed into Chiara on top of the first balcony. Chiara wouldn't move, but Magdalena put a hand on her shoulder. "It's like in the exercise room. This is just real life."

Chiara craned her neck. "It's so high."

"It's fine." Gilia looked perfectly calm. "Agnella wouldn't have you do this if you weren't ready."

Agnella called, "Follow, sisters!"

Magdalena slipped around Chiara and mimicked Agnella's jump, reaching the window ledge and then springing sideways toward the balcony. Agnella was already moving again, and Magdalena watched her motion just enough to figure out where she needed to go and how she needed to aim in order to reach the next landing point.

Agnella sped up their tempo, and the four sisters climbed all over the church. The two nuns and two novices scaled the columns, made their way onto the top of the pipe organ, and ran along the narrow backs of the pews. They never ventured into the main sanctuary, but they climbed the candelabras and bounced off the statue niches.

Breath heaving, Chiara whispered, "Isn't this sacrilegious?"

"We're consecrated," Agnella replied. "That makes us the body of Christ, and each church is our home." She stretched. "Once more before *compline*."

They climbed the side of the choir loft, then clung to the grate to make their way across hand-over-hand. Magdalena's abdomen and upper arms howled from the effort.

Halfway across, Gilia fell.

Chiara screamed, clinging to the metal with strained fingers.

Agnella swept across the choir loft with a swiftness that put her previous motions to shame. "Magdalena, Chiara, don't look down! I'll get her."

Magdalena fought terror, but no, no, breathe. Fifteen feet in the air was not the place to panic. She passed the point where Gilia had fallen, then forced herself to keep moving. At the edge of the loft she looked back, but Chiara still clung in place, eyes tight and lips trembling.

"Chiara! Stay calm!" Magdalena inched back. Chiara's whole body was shaking now, and doubtless her hands were wet with sweat. "Do you need me to come for you?"

"I can do it. I'll do it." Chiara moved one arm at a time, then one leg, then the other, all with a deliberation born of fear.

The moment her feet were safely on the floor, Magdalena swept over to Agnella's side. Grey as ash, Gilia was bleeding from her head and shoulder, her left hand pressing her right arm against her stomach. Agnella kept her voice calm. "Let's get her downstairs."

Gilia couldn't even get to her feet, so Agnella and Chiara half-carried her down the stairs. Magdalena remained in the church to extinguish the candles. Using her black sleeve she soaked up the blood from the wooden benches, then carried the final candle with her into the convent.

Bellosa met her in the hallway, taking the candle from her hand. "Go directly to *compline.*"

"How is Gilia?"

"Go to *compline.*"

Chiara huddled in the chapel with the rest of the sisters. Magdalena took her place at Chiara's side, but through the whole prayer, she thought only of Gilia. She prayed for mercy on her fellow nun and for what was broken to be mended. Distraction wasn't a problem: she wanted only to know that Gilia would be all right, so every word of the prayer ordered itself toward begging God to restore Gilia to safety and health.

When prayer ended, Chiara tore down the hallway to the infirmary. Magdalena followed.

As they came in, Agnella looked up from Gilia. "Peace. It's not as bad as it could be."

Chiara knelt at Gilia's bedside, clutching her hand. "I'm so sorry. Is the pain awful?"

Gilia smiled bravely and squeezed, but sweat beaded on her face. "It's suffering for Christ. Should the servant expect to escape what her own master had to endure?"

Her voice wavered, and Chiara didn't let go.

Bellosa looked over from the fireplace. "She's going to heal, but it will take a while. Are both of you unhurt?"

"It was just her," Magdalena said.

Bellosa nodded. "You should sleep. Agnella and I will keep watch."

Chiara clasped her hands at her chest. "I can stay."

Bellosa shook her head. "Please obey. We accept the risks associated with total discipline over our bodies. Gilia is not the first to be injured, nor will she be the last."

"I can pray for her now," Chiara insisted.

Magdalena put a hand on Chiara's shoulder. "Obedience. At *lauds,* if she needs us then, we'll take over."

Back in her cell, Magdalena didn't immediately extinguish her stub of a candle. Over and over, her mind returned to Gilia plummeting from the grate, but also to the feeling of climbing all over the interior of the church like a consecrated spider. Ascending to the high spots on the walls and looking down over the benches: was that what an angel would see? Perched on tiny ledges beside statues of the holiest people history had to offer, was there a greater perspective from there on all that humanity could achieve? Or had you only gotten yourself high enough to hurt yourself if you fell?

A light knock preceded her door creaking open, and Chiara slipped inside. The youngest of their order pressed her face into Magdalena's black exercise shirt, and she let Magdalena's shoulder muffle the sound of her sobbing. Arms wrapped around her, Magdalena held Chiara while she shuddered. Finally the girl whispered, "I was so scared."

"I know." She didn't know, actually. Did Chiara mean she was so scared up on the grate, or that she was scared for Gilia? But rather than ask, Magdalena held her and waited.

As Chiara kept crying though, Magdalena guided her to sit on the bed. She held the girl while the candle burnt lower.

"She's not going to die," Magdalena whispered. "You did nothing wrong. No one blames you."

"I'm so scared," Chiara repeated.

The night lay heavy and thick, like air with too much candle wax burnt into it. Chiara huddled next to Magdalena, whose eyes closed longer and longer, and at some point she started awake to find the candle guttering out and Chiara out cold at the foot of the bed. She laid down, unwilling to disturb the girl but at the same time worried the other nuns would be scandalized to find them together. At Santi Cosma e Damiano, the abbess had been very insistent that nuns not sleep in the same cell. Magdalena didn't understand why. She'd found that the worst adjustment in the early nights when her cell seemed so isolating. She'd always slept in the same room as her mother and Fiora.

Tonight she slept fitfully, tentative in case she might stretch and kick Chiara off the bed, never fully asleep because she feared this would be the first night someone peeked into her cell and found her unalone. There wasn't enough room for two, and the lone blanket was pinched in an awkward place so she couldn't get either of them properly covered. But at last came the bell for *lauds,* and Chiara gasped aloud because she had no idea where she was.

"Come," Magdalena whispered. "It's time for chapel."

They were neither of them properly dressed, but none of their sisters voiced an objection. Magdalena half-slept through the prayers, hoping God would forgive her exhaustion while at the same time fearing what she'd find in the infirmary.

Bellosa came to *lauds* a couple of minutes after they started. Agnella came not at all, and Magdalena neither anticipated nor saw Gilia.

They'd barely done the sign of the cross to finish before Chiara fled her seat. Magdalena waited until the other nuns had left, then said to Bellosa, "How is she?"

"Often awake." Bellosa seemed drawn. "She's in pain, but I believe she will heal in time."

"Go to sleep," Magdalena said. "I'll take over."

Bellosa didn't object.

At Gilia's bedside, Agnella sat beside a candle while she prayed her rosary. Finishing a decade, she looked up. "She drifts in and out. That's harder than if she were awake the whole time, because then you sleep too. Then she awakens just as you start to drift away."

That had been Magdalena's whole night so far. "We'll sit with her now," Magdalena repeated, and Agnella left the room to rest a couple of hours before *prime*.

Unsure what to do, Chiara touched Gilia's forehead.

"Leave her to sleep," Magdalena whispered.

The girl looked up, eyes huge.

"She needs to heal."

Chiara positioned herself alongside the bed, resting her head on the straw mattress. Soon she'd fallen back to sleep, and Magdalena fought the urge to doze as well. Her fingers traveled the beads of her rosary as she prayed her way through the first half-hour, but shortly her eye caught something out of place on the infirmary floor: wood shavings.

She finished the closing prayers, then crouched on the floor to touch the slender curls. There were only a few, and those near the walls. Lifting the candle, she hunted around the room until she found their source on one of the tables: a humped piece of wood the size of her hand. Or rather, the size of Fiora's foot.

The plaster cast of her foot lay on its side, but the twisted wood stood like the beginnings of a carved statue. There was no knife in evidence, and the block had been sanded smooth on top, although on the edges some nicks remained where the knife had gone deep.

Magdalena fitted the two together: the plaster foot and the wooden riser. They matched up, and she imagined Fiora standing straight.

She could re-create her sister's foot in her mind. She'd never really thought about it before, but here in the silent hours of a sleeping convent, she realized she also could perfectly remember her mother's feet. Her brother's, too.

People never admired feet, their shape or the way the toes spread or the curve of the arch. Yet somehow she'd absorbed all this information, and when she set the plaster form back on its side, she still could picture how Fiora's foot would marry up to the wood. All that remained was sealing the wood to the bottom of a shoe, and then Fiora would run.

Run, and run, and run, either away from or toward. Wherever she wanted.

Gilia stirred, so Magdalena moved quickly to the bed. "I'm here."

Agnella had splinted Gilia's arm with a long black wrap, much as she'd done to Magdalena's ankle. Gilia's was also braced it with a thin piece of wood. Magdalena tucked the blanket around her, then added a log to the fire even though it was already stifling. At least building the fire made her feel as if she'd accomplished something.

Gilia murmured, "I won't be able to go to Trent."

Chiara wasn't awake to hear, so Magdalena said, "Don't think about it now. You might be whole by the time we need to leave."

Gilia shook her head, then flinched. "No, listen." She squeezed Magdalena's fingers with her left hand. "What we do, we need to be strong. I won't be strong enough. They won't take the chance." Her brow furrowed. "Can you read and write?"

Magdalena shrugged. "Only a little."

"They'll need an annalist. Someone who can write Latin." In addition to being their clothier, Gilia was the convent's record-keeper. "I could teach you the codes, but the writing. You could pick it up." Her voice got softer. "You're smart enough to learn quickly. You can bring the annals to Trent."

Magdalena tightened her grip on Gilia's hand. "It's late at night. You aren't thinking clearly, and you need your rest."

Chiara raised her head, blinking.

"The records are important." Gilia closed her eyes. Her voice came thin. "We have to keep them."

"What about the records?" Chiara moved closer. "The records are safe. You got hurt, but the records are safe."

Gilia breathed hard, struggling to keep awake. "Someone needs to keep the records."

Magdalena stroked her hair. "You need to rest."

"I can keep records," Chiara said. "I can read and write. You can trust me to do it for you."

Gilia's cheeks burned with a high pink flush around the white of her skin. "Did you get the book?"

"No one touched your books." Chiara kissed her forehead. "You need to sleep. Your books are safe. We'll keep the records. It's you we're worried about."

Gilia closed her eyes. "You can't keep records until you've gotten the book."

"Of course," Magdalena said. "You'll be up in the morning, and you can have your books and keep your records then."

Chiara said, "But for now, we'll pray." She unhooked her rosary from her waist. "Our Blessed Mother will help you get better."

By the time they'd finished the first mystery, Gilia was back asleep. Magdalena whispered, "Let's stop. I don't want to wake her."

Chiara slipped away from the bedside. "I forgot to apologize."

"You didn't do anything wrong. You weren't even near her."

"No, but she kept looking at me. She was distracted by me, and that's why she slipped. She's so good," Chiara whispered. "She's so confident. She was already here a year, so she professed her final vows the week after I arrived."

Magdalena said nothing, but Chiara added, "It's her right arm that broke. I bet that's why she thinks she can't do it anymore."

Magdalena paused. "Why can't she write with her left hand?"

Chiara shook her head. "You're supposed to write with your right hand, the same way you're supposed to hold your fork or your spoon. That way you don't smudge your ink." She glanced at her hand as though she could imagine ink all over herself even now. "She's been the annalist for a while, but they really wanted to know if I could write when I first arrived. I suspect that's why I'm here."

Magdalena said, "Did you have any schooling?"

Chiara nodded, but before she spoke, Gilia sighed and shifted. She didn't awaken, but after that their conversation ended.

# NINE

Gilia's prediction was, in some respects, accurate. She would not be going to Trent.

Magdalena and Chiara slept straight through *prime,* but afterward Bellosa awakened them to get an update on Gilia and send them to breakfast.

"She's very concerned about the records," Magdalena said.

Bellosa's eyes widened. "What did she say?"

"She wasn't making any sense," Chiara said, "but she was worried about the book of records. I told her we'd get the book and keep her records, and after I promised it would be taken care of, she went back to sleep."

Bellosa relaxed. "Well, I'll talk to her when she awakens. She has no need to worry about anything."

Agnella didn't appear at breakfast. Magdalena drank her tea and hoped it would awaken her enough to do all her own work over at the hospital, plus cover for Gilia's and Agnella's.

After *terce* at nine o'clock, there was a meeting in the visitor's parlor. Bellosa called together the nuns who had been selected to go to Trent.

"Gilia can't go," she said simply. "Her arm won't have healed before we leave. It will be drafty and rough on the road, and that's not even considering if she develops a fever

WITH TWO EYES INTO GEHENNA

during travel. We also don't know how much strength she'll have once her arm heals. She has to stay behind."

Agnella looked dreadful, both sullen and worried. It was her exercise that had resulted in the injury, and her desire for one last game.

"I'm going to send word to Cardinal Simonetta and ask his direction." Bellosa sounded far more grave than she had early this morning. "Gilia is not easily substituted because of her particular skills, but we should be able to cover for her. She was already concerned last night about the record-keeping."

Record-keeping. What did it entail? When Magdalena had arrived at Santi Cosma e Damiano, a nun had entered her into the convent annals, then recorded all the property she brought in and payment of her dowry (indicating that there would be no annuity for her upkeep). A convent probably kept records of how they spent their money: payments for food and cloth, payment of taxes, and payment for any repairs or services. That would require knowledge of writing, plus the ability to do sums, but not necessarily Latin. Gilia must have been senseless from pain when she said that. Records probably also meant planning how to parcel out the money the convent already had versus the money the convent would need to spend later.

Bellosa sat back. "Of our options, the best replacement is Chiara."

"She's too young," said Nezetta. "She's never been sent out."

Agnella huffed, folding her arms. "The *cardinal* says she's too young. I disagree. Physically she's ready to go out on her own, and I'm confident that with a little polish she'll do just as well as the rest of us."

Magdalena added, "Chiara thinks Gilia fell because of her."

"Complete nonsense. You were in between them." Agnella's eyes darkened even more against the shadows on her skin. "If I had to blame Chiara's youth for anything, it would be for her assuming guilt where none is to be assumed. The monsters in the world always take advantage of that, so the sooner we break her of those thoughts, the better."

"Cardinal Simonetta will object," Bellosa interrupted, "but I'll lay out our case as best as I can. He wants the younger nuns traveling to Trent, and the older ones remaining here to take care of the hospital and train up new younger nuns. I was never in favor of separating our two novices anyhow," she added. "Novices should learn together."

"And the records?" Nezetta said.

"Chiara can read and write," Magdalena said. "She told me last night."

Bellosa's hands wrapped around one another in her lap. "For now, I would rather not lay that responsibility on her, especially if we're focusing on her training. Agnella, I'll talk to her about the guilt, regardless of whether she goes. But do I have your assurance that otherwise, she can keep up with everyone else?"

"Absolutely." Agnella glanced at the ceiling. "I'd pit her against our red-hatted patron any day of the week, and I know who'd win."

The other nuns chuckled, but Bellosa shook her head. "I'll avoid mentioning that part of your assurance." She stood. "Return to your duties. Don't mention this to Chiara until Cardinal Simonetta responds."

"You're the abbess," Magdalena said. "Why can't you just tell him this is your order, and you're going to do what's best for the order?"

"Because he knows more what's best for the Church," said Bellosa, "and the Church is more important than any order."

Magdalena stopped off in the infirmary. Chiara was mixing white gunk in a bowl while Gilia sat on the mattress, pale but looking alert.

"Are you feeling better?"

Gilia nodded.

"Agnella is making her a more durable splint, so she showed me how to mix the plaster." Chiara looked into the bowl. "It's mostly flour and egg, but there's some water too. When this dries, it's going to either be hard as marble or a little tasty."

Magdalena said, "Or both. Good thing you aren't fasting."

Gilia forced a smile.

Chiara said, "Oh, when you were talking about books, I started looking around in case you meant a specific book. On one of the infirmary shelves, I found one! It's fascinating, too. *De humani corporis fabrica librorum epitome*, written by Andreas Vesalius. There's so much interesting information about our bodies! God made us marvelously," Chiara gushed. "There are drawings of how the muscles work together and where all your bones are located. So when the Bible says we're fearfully and wonderfully made, that's true. But apparently he looked at dead bodies in order to draw all the secrets our bodies are keeping."

Magdalena shuddered. "I'd rather they kept those secrets."

Agnella appeared in the doorway. "Out, you two. And leave my book alone."

Chiara recoiled. "It's not forbidden, is it?"

"Ask yourself if a convent would keep a forbidden book." Agnella checked the plaster mixture and nodded. "You, head over to the hospital," she said, pointing to Chiara. "After lunch, we'll still have exercises, but I may transfer you into Magdalena's group."

Chiara's brows furrowed. "Why?"

"To keep our two novices together."

Magdalena straightened, and Agnella gave a sardonic smile. "Apparently that's important."

Magdalena beamed.

"And you," Agnella said, turning and waving her hand, "your mother's in the visitor's parlor. Send Fiora to the exercise room. Keep your mother entertained until I bring her back."

Magdalena gave a tentative, "You were working all night?"

Agnella nodded. "Plenty of time in the small hours. It took two tries. The first one went into the fire." She pointed to the hallway. "Your mother is waiting."

Why did Agnella always make it sound snide when she talked about Magdalena's mother? Other nuns had visitors too, although not Agnella. Maybe she'd left all her family in Venice. Maybe after whatever event had landed her in *Le Convertite*, her family had left her behind instead.

In the parlor, Magdalena caught Fiora in a lopsided hug as the girl launched herself at her by using the crutch. "Go to the exercise room and talk to Sister Agnella."

Fiora gave a cheer, then lurched off down the hallway.

Mother handed Magdalena a basket of bread. "What's wrong?"

Magdalena stared at the wicker handle in her hand, and her shoulders slumped. In Trent, no one would be able to take one look at her and identify her mood. Nuns got to know one another, but it couldn't be the same as one's own mother, a woman who'd seen you every day of your life up until the moment she handed you over to a community that would never give you back.

Magdalena swallowed hard. "It's been a difficult night. One of the nuns got hurt. She broke her arm, and we've been tending her. But..."

She struggled to find the words, standing there with only a basket of home-baked love between them, to tell her mother one halting sentence at a time that she was leaving. Leaving for German lands.

"Trent?" her mother whispered. "All the way to Trent? For a council that will never take place?"

To be fair, it had already "taken place" twice. A bigger issue than its never starting was that it might never finish. Simonetta had said the pope was committed to making it happen, but popes had been committed to making it happen (or making it finish happening) several times in the past. An entire generation of German heretics had grown up Lutheran in the time it took to complete the council set on reconciling with them.

Her mother's head bowed. "How long will you be away?"

"For as long as it takes," Magdalena said. "Our order is devoted to ending heresy, so we need to be present there."

Her mother's head raised. "Your order is devoted to a hospital for the dying."

"That's what we do in the meantime." Magdalena forced a smile. "We pray every day for orthodoxy and theological purity. We learn everything we can about the dogma of the Church, and that's why the cardinal of the Datary is sending a contingent of us."

"But you? You're so young. You haven't been here long." Mother shook her head. "Surely an older nun would have even a better grasp of dogma and doctrine. You aren't a trained speaker. You can't persuade cardinals and theologians."

With no answer she would be allowed to give, Magdalena squeezed her mother's hand.

From the hallway came laughter. Fiora flung open the door. "Mother! Mother, look!"

She clomped across the room, her arms outstretched to keep her balance. It wasn't quite a run. Not yet. Her muscles weren't strong enough, and unused to using her leg, she was very off-balance. But still—she could do it.

Their mother gasped, hands flying to her mouth. "Oh, sweetheart!" She embraced Fiora, and when she looked up, tears streamed over her cheeks. "Thank you," she said past Magdalena's shoulder.

At the door, Agnella stood with her head bowed and her hands clasped. When Mother hugged Fiora again, Agnella left the room.

# PART TWO
## HAERESIS

# TEN

Having lived her entire life in Rome, Magdalena had imagined Trent on the same template. Trent was smaller—that much she knew for certain. It was "in German lands," but since she couldn't quantify what rendered a thing German, that hadn't impressed itself on her either. So in her daydreams, she'd fabricated a truncated version of Rome where people spoke another language. The only thing she knew for certain was that all would be strangers, none of them relatives.

The first day's travel held all sorts of delights for Magdalena. The five nuns (including Chiara) rode in one coach, as well as their baggage. They drove first through the city, then into the foothills. And from there, into the sparse areas. It was wild and brilliant: farmland and pastureland and houses with space all around them.

The nuns prayed the rosary or read the psalms as they rocked over the uneven road at a steady pace, wheels creaking and the air cluttered with dust. Magdalena watched the world in its untamed freedom, startled by the green and the sheer distance they could visualize all around whenever they crested a hilltop. Sometimes they'd pass vineyards. Vineyards! She'd never seen one before, so she tried to fit what she saw into the parables Jesus had told. So many rows where plants would stretch toward the sky. Maybe grapes were just pre-wine, the same way the nuns were pre-saints.

By day's end, the carriage's motion bothered her, and she longed to move about, but at least they had some opportunities to get out in order to give a break to the horses. Then they'd climb back inside, and Magdalena would wait for new visions of the feral earth.

The second day was less new, and conversation lagged. They'd sung hymns on the first day. Today they didn't. They estimated when to do the liturgy of the hours, but sometimes it felt far too long between prayers, and others far too short.

Occasionally they'd pass through a city, the stop-and-go of their progress frustrating in a way Magdalena had never experienced even though Rome's streets were entirely stop-and-go.

Florence. Bologna. Venice. Agnella's face was set like stone when they passed nearby, although fortunately they did not have to travel through it.

Then came the third day, when no one spoke and no one sang. Magdalena prayed for strength because if she saw even one more vineyard or one more green vista from the top of a hill, she might just let go of whatever sanity still remained.

Chiara chose that time to say, "Who founded our order?"

Nezetta, the oldest of their group, said, "I was in the initial community of nuns."

"Really?" Magdalena pivoted to look at her. "You met Pope Paul IV?"

She nodded. "A priest named Cajetan had started a food bank, a hospital, and an actual money bank. Then he founded the Theatines to combat heresy." She was crocheting lace as they rode; she turned her work, then resumed on the back side. "Cajetan had a companion named Gian Pietro Carafa, the bishop of Chieti. He became the first superior of the Theatines."

Agnella said, "And later on became Pope Paul IV."

Ah, that was one connection made a little clearer. "Our order was initially intended to pray for the souls of the dying," continued Nezetta, "but the pope cultivated a special relationship with the nuns of our order."

"Not special like that," Agnella said quickly to Magdalena. "Not the way some priests cultivate a special relationship with specific nuns."

Nezetta said, "He canonically recognized us in a secret bull and then established specific ecclesiastical ties, and the Catherinites took on the additional role of praying against heresy."

No one could discuss Pope Paul IV for more than two minutes without uttering the word "heresy." *Haeresis.* Heretics and heresy had consumed the dreams of Pope Paul IV. In every corner lurked heresy. In the much-hated Spanish empire they bred heresy. He'd even called cardinals on the carpet in his pursuit of heretics. He'd ordered Cardinal Giovanni Morone imprisoned, tried for heresy, and then returned to prison even after a Curial tribunal insisted he'd done nothing wrong. Morone, at least, was back in everyone's good graces.

Pope Paul IV had also condemned another cardinal who'd participated in an early session of the Council of Trent. Reginald Pole, archbishop of Canterbury, knew he wouldn't get a fair trial and simply did not return to Rome. Months later, he died of influenza.

"How does this connect us with the Council of Trent?" asked Chiara.

"Were you at the previous periods?" Magdalena asked Nezetta.

"And why are there all these periods?" Chiara continued. "Shouldn't the council just meet and get it done?" She shook her head. "And I still don't understand why we're going."

"We'll be on site to pray and guard against heresy," Agnella said. "I told you that."

Chiara huffed. "We could have prayed from Rome."

Nezetta said, "Do you think all Rome wasn't praying for the previous two periods? This Council started in 1545. Pope Paul III should have held it in Bologna, where there's a library and enough space to house all these bishops, but Trent is what they decided, the pope and Emperor Charles V." She waved a hand like a woman dismissing the antics of strutting boys. "They held eight sessions before they closed it down in 1547 because they were afraid of plague."

Chiara said, "There was a plague?"

Nezetta shook her head. "No plague, other than a plague of endless talking. Pope Julius III restarted the council's second period in 1551, and they had another five sessions. That took only a year. And since then, everyone has thought the council deader than Abraham because it's been so long asleep."

Magdalena said, "So it still may not happen, and we can go home?"

Agnella sighed. "It's been dragging on since 1545. We'll probably linger another three years before they decide it's not going to happen. And of course if the current pope dies, it ends immediately."

You couldn't wish for the death of a pope. Even Chiara didn't have any more questions after that.

On the fifth day, they started as early as possible. They arrived after dark, and the driver asked directions to the convent of Saint Martin. He found it just as the church bells tolled eight o'clock.

Even before the five Roman nuns had finished unloading, out bustled the abbess. She was short, shorter than even Chiara, and had a pinched face as though every day she spent at least an hour sucking a lemon. Nezetta said, "Sister Lena? Our new Abbess?"

Sister Lena folded her arms and nodded.

Nezetta said, "Thank you for your hospitality."

"Hospitality?" Sister Lena barked a laugh. "We're already at capacity, so don't expect any. Come inside. I hope you didn't bring much."

Sister Lena had them bring their luggage into the parlor. "Are you very stiff from the journey? Have you eaten?"

They hadn't eaten yet, and Magdalena wondered how anyone wouldn't be stiff after five days in a carriage. All business, Lena showed them to the refectory, where she herself served out a large bowl of chicken stew and rolls. "Try to finish before *compline*."

With her stomach tense under Lena's assessing eyes, Magdalena could manage only a small portion.

"No trouble on the road?" the abbess continued. "Good. Some of the bishops had problems, but mostly the ones coming east to Trent. There's nothing good over that way." She shook her head. "I've had a letter from Sister Bellosa introducing you all. Which of you are the novices?" When Magdalena and Chiara identified themselves, she said, "Come with me."

Magdalena finished her roll in one bite, then wiped her hands on her habit as she followed. Chiara got ahead of her, gaping at the hallway, the carpet, and the candle sconces.

"Yes, it's a finer building than the Roman convent." Lena sounded annoyed by the frippery. "Hospitals have to be practical. But since we're a boarding house, a place where people ostensibly choose to go, we need to make it look nice. No one cares if the nuns live in a hole in the ground if the nuns are merely caring for the dying," she added. "And to tell you the truth, I preferred it that way. Everyone demands a boarding house be brighter, finer, and better in every way than they'd keep their own houses. But despite the ornamentation, we're doing a good work, as you'll see tomorrow." She led them to a large room that resembled the exercise room at home. "Well, then." She dusted her hands against each other. "Has Agnella been testing you?"

Lena swiped out one leg and hooked Magdalena by the ankle, spun her, and flipped her onto the floor so she landed hard on her back. Chiara cried out, but Lena turned on her as well, striking at her head. Chiara threw up a forearm to block the incoming blow, but Lena jabbed her other hand at Chiara's waist. Chiara went to her knees, clutching her side.

Magdalena rolled to her feet and took a ready stance. Lena pivoted back to her with a high kick, which Magdalena blocked with her forearm. After Chiara's fall, she knew to expect a second blow and so blocked a second kick when Lena struck with her other foot.

"Nice!" Lena went for Chiara again. The girl ducked, but Lena crashed one arm over Chiara's chest with her forearm locked around her opposite wrist.

"Well then," Lena said, "it seems you've more to learn. For one thing, if someone rushes you, don't get out of the way. Give them something to run into, ideally your fist." She released Chiara as the bells rang for *compline*. "Agnella loves climbing the walls like a monkey, but this isn't Rome. In Trent, you need to get in close."

---

After ensuring she hadn't actually broken either novice's ribs, Lena escorted them to *compline* with the Tridentine nuns, and then showed all five Roman nuns to cells. The convent was out of space: they were sharing not only cells but also their actual beds. "You're small," Lena said by way of dismissal. "I'm sure you'll fit."

The travel, not to mention the beating they'd gotten, left both novices exhausted. They slept through to *lauds* like a pair of corpses. After *lauds,* Magdalena lay awake and eventually moved to the floor for relief from Chiara's elbows.

After *prime* and breakfast (a high-quality breakfast because they ate the same food they served the guests), they returned to their cell to unpack their belongings. Chiara repeated all the information she'd gathered from the Tridentine nuns. "They say the city will be crowded to the point of violence. Whenever the council reconvenes, bishops arrive by the dozens, and every one of them brings a retinue. Then you have the envoys of all the world's princes, plus the papal legates, the heads of a dozen religious orders, and an army of theologians." Chiara giggled, and Magdalena imagined ranks of wizened men wielding pens and dusty books. "The result is, there's nowhere to sleep, nowhere to go that there aren't already a dozen people, and the market sellers raise their prices so high you'd go bankrupt. The travelers here get upset at the costs, and the residents get moody because they want their city back."

Magdalena fastened her rosary at her waist. "I can't blame them."

"The out-of-towners are sport for the locals," Chiara said. "It gets very hot in the summer and very cold in the winter, and travelers get sick from it because they're not used to it. Remember how Nezetta says the first session of the council ended because the papal legates though there might be plague?"

They met in the chapel for the rosary, although throughout the chain of *Aves* and *Paters,* Magdalena found herself remembering the rhythm of walking horses and the smell of the free air.

Afterward Lena called the Roman nuns and some of the younger Tridentine nuns to join her in the exercise room. She led them through preliminary exercises and stretches identical to Agnella's. Lena remarked on that with an overstated relief.

Agnella had her arms folded. Darkly, she said, "I hear you beat up my novices."

"They're alive. I was glad to see you did at least some work with them." Lena shook her head. "Come here."

Agnella and Lena stepped to the center of the room, and the other nuns backed to the walls. Lena crouched with her arms raised, and Agnella mimicked the stance. Lena counted to three, and then they sprang at each other.

Chiara gasped, palms at her mouth, but Magdalena leaned forward. The women moved quickly but with precision, striking and avoiding in a way that seemed prescient.

They backed off from each other, Agnella grinning.

"My." Lena looked pleased. "You aren't terrible after all."

Agnella didn't laugh, and they returned to sparring, almost beautiful in their speed. Magdalena judged every motion for its deadliness, for its potential impact on an opponent. Agnella: was she fighting that terrible Venice priest? When she struck, was she striking at a father who'd abandoned her? A vanished lover?

Again they backed off. Lena shook her head. "You rely too much on distance."

"God gave us a whole world." Agnella's breath heaved. "He wants us to use it."

Chiara clutched Magdalena's arm.

Lena turned to her own nuns. "The Romans learned to survive in the city, so in instances where the buildings themselves play a role, trust their expertise. Let them have their way when it makes sense. Up close, however, we have primacy."

She turned to the Roman cohort. "You're going to have to improve your close-quarters work. Unless you altered it to make your lives easier, our rule is the same as yours in terms of the schedule. Where you would work in the hospital for incurables, you will instead be working for the boarding house and our other contracts. But where you climbed walls at home, you'll need to learn hand-to-hand combat here." She rubbed her hands on the legs of her exercise clothes. "I'll pair each of you with one of mine so you can learn our basic techniques."

Lena pointed from Chiara to one of the Trent sisters. Naked on Chiara's face lay nothing short of fear. Then Lena sent Magdalena to another spot, and Chiara was at her back.

Lena walked between the paired-off nuns. "We're smaller than men. We're lighter, but that makes us faster. But most importantly, they don't expect us to do anything. We're weak and fair, and all of that is to our advantage. Nuns are omnipresent. Men don't notice us. Their ignorance is our weapon." She gestured to the tallest of the nuns, who came to stand opposite her. "You need to bring down someone taller and stronger. Like this."

Lena and the tall nun walked toward one another, and as they passed, Lena pulled the rosary cord off her waist, whipped it up and around the other nun's shoulders, and then threw her body to the side so the taller nun went off balance. Lena caught her, set her upright, and then pulled back her rosary.

"Get them off balance quickly. Use anything you have, and always keep your eyes on your surroundings. The world is your weapon." She turned to Chiara, who looked about to faint. "Is something the matter?"

Agnella sounded grim. "Nothing is the matter. My novices can handle themselves."

Lena said, "Last night, I learned Romans punch with their arms. That's not good. You punch with your whole body, and you do that by using your hips." She punched slowly at nothing, pivoting her hips and core as she moved. Her whole body would be behind that motion. Magdalena's eyes widened as suddenly it made sense. The whole body, moving as one. Not arms and legs striking an opponent, no. But rather, just as Paul had written: many parts, but all one body.

Then Magdalena had to call her attention back to her sparring partner Tadea, a nun who was taller and stronger and far more experienced.

⸻

In the dark, Chiara whispered, "Do you understand any of what's going on?"

Crammed together on the straw mattress, they lay cuddled up in the only position they'd been able to find that worked for both of them.

The blanket tightened as Chiara clutched it in her hands. "Close combat? Weapons? Does Lena think we're soldiers?"

"This convent is different." Magdalena was facing into Chiara's back, so she could breathe her words without having even to whisper. "The Trent nuns have been working as personal guards."

"But why?"

"We're *in German lands*. There must be Lutherans everywhere." Magdalena's hand tightened against her stomach. "Huguenots too. They've been killing priests up in the northern territories. The German princes started a war with the Holy Roman Emperor over the questions the council is supposed to answer. Do you think they want the Church to succeed?"

Chiara whispered, "What are a single order of nuns supposed to do? Why hold the council here if it's so dangerous?"

"It's all about politics. The Germans wouldn't come if we had it in Italy. Neither would the French."

Chiara shuddered.

"Heretics," Magdalena breathed. "They'll do anything."

"We're the brides of Christ." Chiara shook her head, and Magdalena could feel it against the pillow. "Husbands are supposed to defend their wives, not the other way around. Men lay down their lives for their women."

"That's why no one suspects we can help."

"Maybe they suspect that because we can't."

Magdalena smirked. "Lena looked like she could take down a fully armed Swiss Guardsman."

Chiara chuckled. "Agnella is going to be aching tomorrow morning."

"Me too." Magdalena had been swept off her feet several times. "But they're training us to disable taller and heavier opponents."

Come to think of it, those were the things Agnella had been teaching Fiora. How to use her crutch to knock out someone's legs, and then how to use the special shoes to run for her life. Lena might have added to that teaching: give Fiora a knife and teach her to go in close so she'd never have to deal with her attacker again.

"I still don't like it." Chiara shivered. "I want to stay in the hostel and bake bread in between the liturgical hours."

Magdalena said, "Why did you join this order? Didn't you know they did this?"

"Did you? Every one of us got kicked out of some other place." Chiara deflated into the bed. "I entered my first convent as a boarding student, but I was always in trouble. I asked too many questions and kept trying to change the way they did things. I was eight years old, and they got angry when I spoke out of turn. And the library! They had a hundred books, but they only ever wanted me to read two. Two? Why bother reading at all? I was hungry for books. I'd sneak them back to my room and read for as long as I had moonlight." She sighed. "When I was twelve they wrote to my mother and said I wouldn't be allowed to profess there. She complained to her uncle, who's a cardinal. Great-Uncle figured he could force them to accept me if he talked to the right people. He went to Cardinal Simonetta at the Datary, who then asked Sister Bellosa to take me on even though I'm young."

Ah. Connections. "So your family is noble?"

Chiara said, "I'm the youngest of six, and I have four sisters. How much money can a family have? There wasn't going to be a proper dowry for me, so I had to become a nun."

Several of the nuns at Santi Cosma e Damiano had been in the same position, effectively surrendered to the convent for long-term storage in order to benefit their families. That was their job: to pray for everyone in the family to be blessed and simultaneously to free up money for other girls in the family to get married. In return, their families made the convent generous donations.

Chiara said, "What about your family?"

"Cardinal Farnese is my great-uncle."

Chiara straightened, pushing Magdalena back against the wall. "Your great-grandfather was a *pope*?"

If only blessings were heritable. "Everyone was born on the wrong side of the bed all the way down to me. My brother isn't going to be named a cardinal when he turns seventeen, and Farnese himself wouldn't recognize me if I carried a decanter of wine into his office."

Chiara chuckled. "Still, that's got to annoy Cardinal Simonetta. Your family ranks his."

That was an interesting thought. Anything that irritated Simonetta was something to be treasured, even her lousy Farnese relations. "That's the only reason I'm not in prison right now."

Chiara lifted her head. "Why would you be in prison?"

"Bellosa fetched me from Cosma e Damiano because I killed a man."

Chiara gasped. "Why?"

"He was touching me and kissing me while I was asleep."

Chiara stayed really, really still. "And you killed him? Without any training at all?" She sounded awed. Then, "But how did a man get behind the wall? Santi Cosma e Damiano is enclosed."

"Priests can get in."

Chiara's voice was horrified. "You killed a priest."

"Simonetta absolved me." Magdalena's voice picked up an edge. "He wanted to make sure I didn't confess that to any other priest but himself. It might cause scandal."

Chiara whispered, "A priest trying to rape a nun *should* cause scandal."

For a moment Magdalena wondered if that too hadn't been part of the plan. In Rome the Marcoli family was influential, so if she'd been arrested and sent to the magistrates, the name of their family would have been tarnished along with her own. She'd have been sent to prison or executed, but could it be that Simonetta was solving several problems all at once? He'd added a known killer to his order of militarized nun operatives, and at the same time curried favor with a powerful Roman family. Clever.

Chiara said, "The priest you killed...did he hurt you?"

Other than the memory of his hands kneading at her breasts, and the garlic of his breath tracing over her neck and ear? "I awoke in time. I was in the library, not in my cell. He hadn't forced me down."

Chiara grabbed her knees to her chest, pressing her back into Magdalena's stomach. "I'm so sorry. I didn't know." She shuddered. "There was a priest I never trusted at my convent. When he was around I made sure to seem especially dull. I'd slouch so my habit hung like a curtain because I wanted him to think I was disfigured and ugly. When we had to confess to him, I'd rough up my hair and look as awkward as a street urchin." She shuddered. "He said I was unfit to be a bride of Christ."

"Well, now you can be a defender of Christ." Magdalena put a hand on Chiara's shoulder. "He can't hurt you here.

After Lena's done with us," she added, "no one will be able to. At least not without crawling away, dragging a broken leg."

In the dark, Chiara snickered. "Maybe that's for the best. Even if we never have to protect a cardinal, at least we can protect ourselves."

# ELEVEN

The Council of Trent had established a rhythm for itself (an infamously slow rhythm) in its first two periods. It also had established several precedents, like in no way starting on time (as in, delaying for months) and having a threadbare attendance of bishops at the opening sessions (quite possibly owing to the months-long delays).

A whole new vocabulary engulfed Magdalena.

"Reform" and "doctrine" were the two big watchwords. The Holy Roman Emperor wanted reform tackled first; the pope wanted doctrine. The legates from the first council period had compromised: the agenda for each session would feature one reform item for every doctrine item. They'd pair the two, and both would be voted on simultaneously.

As for a "session," that was a meeting when all bishops in attendance would vote on something the council had decided. The first session of this period, on January 19, 1562, would be a declaration that they were reopening the council. Most sessions would begin with a Mass and then hold pronouncements and a vote. It could be an all-day affair or a half-day, but it would take place at the Tridentine bishop's residence and the attached Cathedral of Saint Vigilius.

At the sessions, no one held discussions. Debates (and actual arguments) took place at "general congregations," with bishops making speeches on whatever item was on the docket, one after the next.

Theologians had their own special congregations where they could present their analyses to the bishops, which would later be reported at the general congregations.

After all the bishops had a chance to speak about a question at a general congregation, the papal legates would draw up a final document they knew could be approved. Then the session. After that vote, the papal legates would announce the agenda for the next session.

Simonetta was one of five papal legates. Magdalena had never heard of the others.

"Some agenda items take months," Lena muttered as she and Magdalena carried bread baskets to Cardinal Madruzzo's palace. "The way they talk, you'd think there was a special music that emerged whenever a bishop heard his own voice. They agree, and they agree again, and they agree a third time. Or they disagree and repeat themselves for an hour. Enough." She huffed. "We're hardly a university, but even the uneducated can understand the first time. Or the tenth."

Magdalena said, "Maybe it's only the bishops who need it repeated over and over," and Lena laughed out loud.

"You need to watch your tongue." She sounded amused. "Especially when you say things that might be true."

They delivered the bread to the servants at Madruzzo's palace, then made their way to the cathedral. Magdalena kept staring at a sky unimpeded by buildings. After a week, this morning was the first she hadn't had a headache. "Trent air is different," Agnella had warned her. "The air hits you hard until you get used to how bland it is. Then you'll go home," she added, "and you'll have another headache for a week because it's so rich."

Magdalena scanned the crowded streets. "It's so quiet."
What would Mother think of all the missing sounds? "It
smells different. People don't push you when they walk by."

"Wait a few months." Lena huffed. "The second period
wasn't well attended, but even then we had bishops and all
their servants scurrying around demanding our little city
have the same amenities as Paris and Rome. How can you not
have copies of every papal decree in your library? What, you
have no library? No port? Where are the couriers?" She shook
her head. "Trent is a stopover town for travelers. They're
supposed to keep going the next day, not linger for two years
debating the finer details of justification."

They rounded a corner, and Magdalena thrilled at the
sight even though she'd seen it a dozen times.

Rome had cathedrals by the dozen. Every time you
changed sides of the street, another church spire appeared,
and when you drew close, you'd find the cathedral of Saint
Whoever, but already you could see behind it the grand
church of Our Lady of Another Important Title.

Here, though, they faced head-on into a square church
front topped with a spire, and a rose window with each petal
taller than Magdalena herself. Among the shorter buildings
of Trent, it stood out in a way no church building
distinguished itself in Rome. At the end of a street lined with
flat buildings, each boasting a balcony, the church stood as a
focal point and a statement: it was the center of their lives.
The center of the universe. Magdalena's eyes watered.

Coaches and carriages delivered people to the low front
steps, and they proceeded with pomp beneath the columns
and then through the doorway arches. It was a parade of the
holy.

Lena said, "We'll enter through the side. The heads of
the major orders are invited to the council, but we're not the
Jesuits or the Franciscans. Officially we exist to bring the
bishops their tea."

She led Magdalena through a servant entrance and then up into the body of the church.

While from the outside the building had seemed the center of the universe, from the inside it became the universe itself. Cavernous, the cathedral expanded toward the top of the world, its massive cupola painted as if to look like heaven. Dark wood. Square columns. An image of the Blessed Virgin seated on clouds and attended by saints and angels. A marble altar. An organ large enough that Fiora might raise her head and detect its notes back at home if only the wind blew in the right direction. And everywhere, everywhere, were ornate carvings, alcoves, and side altars.

"Keep control." Lena bowed before she entered the church. "I know you Romans. You enter a church like this and long to climb all over it like monkeys. Well, the last pope to own a monkey was Julius III, and our feet are not going to leave the floor."

Magdalena checked out the tiny ledges. Climbing like monkeys? Why yes, she could find footholds in that column, or over that altar. There were handholds on that wall and niches where you could brace yourself beneath the pipe organ. And if you climbed high enough, surely there was space atop that column to perch and watch everyone underneath.

No one would look up to find you. They'd admire the mosaics and the paintings and completely miss the black-clad nun.

What about the outside? Surely the sisters could climb the outside as well, although if you fell from here, you wouldn't break just your arm. Most likely you'd die.

But you'd die having ascended to heaven and brushed the stars.

Lena led Magdalena to the main gathering space where the bishops and cardinals were assembling for the first session. She left Magdalena at the door and deferentially approached Cardinal Simonetta, who wore the reddest of his red hats and capes. The color set off the dark of his eyes and the point of his chin, and Magdalena scanned the throng for other cardinals to see if they looked just as proper.

Servants rushed in and out, so Magdalena cleared the doorway and kept her posture demure. As Lena had predicted, no one noticed her. A nun in a church, barefoot, wearing a habit, gaze cast down: what was there to see? That was a rosary at her waist, not a weapon. Her hands were rough from scrubbing floors, not from combat maneuvers. The lightness of her step was from humility, not half a year's training never to make a noise.

Lena summoned her. Magdalena crossed the room to Cardinal Simonetta's side, keeping her eyes lowered.

"Sister Magdalena," said Lena, "the cardinal wishes you to deliver this note to Cardinal Gonzaga, the head of the papal delegates. He's still at his rooms in Cardinal Madruzzo's palace, but you'll need to hurry to reach him."

Magdalena slipped her way back through the crowd. Only with her first breath outside did she realize how much the air inside the church had begun to smell more like Rome. Maybe it had been the scent of clothes that had last been hung to air under a Roman sun. Maybe the many Italian bishops had carried the air of Rome in their lungs and in their luggage.

She sprinted through the streets for the bishop's palace, ignoring the looks from the town-dwellers. She wasn't winded by the time she reached the palace, and she slowed to a rapid walk in the hallways. One of the servants directed her to Gonzaga's suite, and she rushed down the correct corridor.

As she rounded a bend, she crashed into a red-cloaked man.

"I'm so sorry, sir!" She bowed her head. "I was sent by Cardinal Simonetta."

The old man sighed. "Simonetta. *Miserere mei.*"

*God have mercy?* Magdalena backed up. "Did I hurt you?"

She looked up to find a bony face with old eyes. He was wearing a red hat. Ah, a cardinal! "Are you Cardinal Gonzaga?"

The man said, "My dear sister, I wish I were so great a man. I am merely Girolamo Seripando."

Another of the papal legates. If that "God have mercy" meant anything, Cardinal Seripando was hardly one of Simonetta's admirers. "I'm so sorry, sir."

"Please, don't think of it again," the cardinal said. "Come, I'll show you to Gonzaga's suite."

Seripando walked slowly, and his height reminded her of a rickety building. He said, "What is your order? I don't recognize your habit."

"The convent of Saint Martin of Tours," she said. "We're Catherinites, Theatine nuns."

"You are not many in number, then. I knew Cajetan, your founder. Such a smart, intelligent man. So genuine. I presume you are not enclosed."

That wasn't a question. Standing in the hallway of Madruzzo's palace, obviously she wasn't enclosed. "We're a mendicant order, sir. We run a hostel in Trent, as well as a hospital for incurables in Rome."

"Amazing work." Seripando's voice had a comfortable inflection, as though you could stretch it out and wrap yourself in warmth just by listening. "You are the gentle hands of Christ, welcoming the stranger. Visiting the imprisoned, in effect. Feeding and clothing the naked and the hungry. And, one supposes, burying the dead. All these are worthy deeds for the brides of Christ."

He didn't mention smiting the wicked and executing the heretic, but Magdalena didn't correct him. He guided her down a different corridor, and there he flagged one of the servants. "Please let Cardinal Gonzaga know he has a message."

He turned away. "Thank you for your efforts, Sister."

How odd, to be thanked by a cardinal for changing sheets. She inclined her head. "It is your service I thank you for, sir."

"We are all in service to God." Seripando laid a hand on her arm. It was surprisingly firm. "One work is no better than the next, so long as all are done with love."

When Cardinal Gonzaga appeared, Magdalena handed him Simonetta's note. As she turned to leave, Gonzaga said to Seripando, "Are you heading to the cathedral? I'll come with you," and then both cardinals invited Magdalena to accompany them.

Hilariously, they jolted across the short distance in a carriage, and then when they arrived, were ceremoniously unloaded. Stifling giggles, Magdalena bowed her head and trailed the cardinals, thinking about how she'd explain this in a letter to her mother. *As it turns out, the very great men of our Church hire two horses and a cushioned carriage to travel the same road I passed in less time by running on the feet God gave me.*

But Seripando and Gonzaga were both old, and if anyone deserved being treated like royalty, surely either of them qualified. As the head papal delegate, Gonzaga was authorized to speak as though he himself were the pope. Seripando, based on the little she'd heard, had been influential in the previous two Council periods. In the prime of his life he had become the head of the Augustinians and reformed the entire order. If after all that he felt like riding two blocks in a carriage, she'd grant it to him.

Once in the cathedral, Seripando separated from them to talk to an unfamiliar bishop while Gonzaga sought out Simonetta. Magdalena followed Gonzaga. When the two cardinals met, however, Simonetta paid no attention to

Magdalena, so she retreated to the side wall and admired the double rows of windows and how the interior was divided into three naves.

Shortly the session began with a prayer. There were more in attendance than Simonetta had predicted: there were four papal legates (all in red with red hats) and one still to come, plus a hundred bishops and archbishops, a dozen abbots and seniors of other religious orders, and a throng of theologians. The crowd already strained the available space, with more slated to arrive.

The four cardinals in red really did look striking amongst the sea of finery. Maybe "princes of blood" was the right thing to call them. They were the lifeblood of the Church."

On the outskirts, the Catherinites moved about. Domestics. Brides of Christ, tenders of the home fire and at the same time fierce protectors of the family.

# TWELVE

Lena tugged Magdalena's sleeve after the session. "Simonetta is concerned. We'll meet in his quarters." Then she disappeared into the milling bishops to call the others.

They waited for Simonetta in his suite's sitting room, praying the rosary because the session had interrupted their daily rule. With Magdalena were Lena, Agnella, Nezetta, and two more Tridentine nuns.

When Cardinal Simonetta arrived, they were in the middle of the fifth mystery, so he finished their rosary with them, and then Lena stood to address the nuns.

There was no preamble. "The cardinal is concerned that some of the attending bishops may be heretics already."

Magdalena's brows contracted. "Bishops?"

"Are you already talking, Sister?" snapped Simonetta. "Yes, bishops. And if not themselves, quite probably members of their retinue."

Lena looked grave. "Some bishops brought twenty attendants, if not thirty. I know because we're housing many of them, but how can any bishop properly vet thirty people?"

"I want you closer at hand," Simonetta said. "Madruzzo agrees with me. One of you must be assigned to each of the papal legates, and others of you to certain key envoys."

If they wanted to root out heretics, of course, the first place they should turn were the secular authorities sent by the Holy Roman Emperor and the king of Spain. There were so many of them, none theologically trained, and any one of them could have smuggled in ideas fit to poison the Church. That's what Pope Paul IV believed had happened with Giovanni Morone at the first segment of the council, and that was why he'd imprisoned the man.

Secular envoys had no reason to adhere to orthodox teaching and every reason to want to diminish papal authority. Politically, it would be better for the Holy Roman Emperor to change the Church so as to end the wars with his northern princes. Princes who, she well knew, had only sided with the Lutherans in the first place so they could diminish the emperor's power.

"We will always report to Simonetta," said Lena, "but Cardinal Madruzzo knows our mission to protect the Church. He will inform the legates and our other assigned clients that we will be assisting them."

Agnella folded her arms. "How exactly do they require assistance?"

Simonetta said, "You will listen. You will observe. You will report back to me."

Agnella's eyes narrowed, and Magdalena could read her thoughts: observation didn't materially assist the other legates and the bishops, did it? It only assisted Simonetta.

Simonetta continued, "You will note if they discuss forbidden ideas or if they want to undermine the pope's authority. I want to know whatever they say about *reform of the head,* and when you give me this information, I will send it back to the pope." He paced to the windows. "These councils are dangerous. Councils have tried in the past to limit the pope's authority and deadlock the Church. The Holy Spirit must guide us, not the envoys of foreign governments or dissatisfied Spanish priests." Shaking his head, Simonetta returned to the center of the room. "Secondarily, you will provide physical protection. The more doctrinally sound a man is, the more the man becomes a target for Lutherans. Heretics have shown willingness to destroy and even to kill in an effort to corrupt whatever they want. They've rejected one set of laws, and there is nothing to prevent them from rejecting every human norm."

Lena said, "We've practiced close-quarters exercises for just this sort of situation. You can act in an emergency to protect your assigned legate or envoy or bishop. That's my concern more than protection against heresy." Here she glanced at Simonetta with a hardness to her eyes. They must have reviewed this point of contention repeatedly. "Our order can't safeguard a man's mind. We can safeguard his body."

Agnella still looked annoyed. "Shouldn't that be the purview of the Swiss Guard?"

"Not even the dumbest brute would strike when the guardsmen are in appearance," said Lena. "But guards can't be everywhere."

Simonetta stepped forward. "Moreover, you can let me know if their minds have been breached. At that point, I will act to safeguard the Church."

With Lena standing a little behind Simonetta, he couldn't see the bald fury in her eyes. She said, "My chief concern, as was Madruzzo's, is that in preparation for the council, Madruzzo hired numerous servants. These men and women have access to all parts of his palace, and while he took recommendations, of course he can't know who has ties to the Lutherans or the Huguenots. They may be walking the halls. They may be listening at our doors. Within limits, you'll have to stay close."

Agnella glared at her. "And at night? In their beds? Surely we can't protect them there."

Lena sighed. "Not there. In the night hours, they're on their own."

Agnella said, "Then we're not going to be very effective."

Lena looked at Agnella with a frustration Magdalena recognized at once: physical protection wasn't the primary reason, was it? Yes, they were trained as guards. But Simonetta wanted them first and foremost as spies. Lena said with a forced banality, "Whatever these consecrated celibates take into their beds is their own problem."

Simonetta said, "Now, if you will, your assignments."

Simonetta kept Lena for himself, although presumably she wouldn't have to report him to himself for heresy. Agnella had the Spanish envoy, Count Claudio Fernandez de Quinones Luna. Simonetta's nose wrinkled when he said the man's name. He was one of those dreaded reformers, and Simonetta added that this man had already tipped his hand.

When Lena turned to Magdalena, she said, "Did you like Cardinal Seripando? Since you've already met him, you can take care of him."

He of the soft voice and the rickety walk, and who could have ignored her when she walked back to the cathedral but instead insisted she ride.

Simonetta lowered his voice. "Don't allow Seripando's status as a legate to deceive you. He's already deceived the pope, but I know him from long ago. At heart, he's a reformer. He would give the council far too strong a hand in Church affairs, and he's shown his ear to the princes of the world." Simonetta's gaze bored into Magdalena's, and fear curled through her. "He himself may be a heretic, and sister, he's got the ear of the man in charge of the council."

<hr />

Years ago, it hadn't been Mother who taught Magdalena to read and write, but rather one of the caretakers at the home where Mother worked as a cook.

In the mornings, Mother had brought Magdalena and Domenico with her and left them in the courtyard of the manor house. They'd spent their time in the garden, and one day they'd met an old priest who enjoyed the sunlight and carried a worn breviary. He worked as a gardener when his bones and joints allowed him to. The rest of the time, he prayed in front of a statue of the Blessed Virgin holding the Christ child.

Magdalena had been six when the priest asked if Domenico could read. When Domenico said no, the man made a point of bringing a slate and a pencil and showing him how to make letters. Magdalena had watched, so they'd learned together.

It was the same with Latin: you could pick up a lot of Latin once you mastered the basics. Once you could recite the *Pater noster,* you could start recognizing a number of other words in the liturgy. You might not be able to piece together everything the priest was saying, but you could hear the flat note when he got the words wrong or skipped an entire section. The reading Magdalena learned was Italian, but the letters were the same in Latin, so when she found an inscription, she spent time sounding it out.

One day, one day stood out in glorious victory when she'd stood in front of the courtyard's statue of the Blessed Virgin and sounded out, piece by piece, "Ave Maria, gratia plena. Dominus tecum." She'd shrieked and shown Domenico, and they'd laughed out loud and run around the statue, calling to each other, "Ave Maria!" Then the old priest had risen from his rose bushes and told them to hush.

Magdalena couldn't remember now, but she wondered: had that palace been her father's house? Had her mother slaved there as a cook all those years, and when her father had wanted a midday snack, it had been her he sent for?

That had ended after Fiora's birth. After Fiora came, Mother had been sent to another kitchen, and Magdalena had cared for Fiora with the help of an older cousin.

Domenico had continued learning. He'd brought home pamphlets, sounding them out loud while she read over his shoulder. They'd found a prayer book once, abandoned in a dark church, and brought it home to work through the text. On some pages were drawings of Christ and the apostles, or pictures of saints with their own reading-like system of codes as to who they were and what they had done.

With no money for paper or ink or pencils, Magdalena hadn't learned to write. What they had should go to Domenico, so he'd practiced tracing the letters on any pamphlet they found. When he was done, he'd write up the sides and around the edges. Magdalena kept thinking someone who could write might be able to get a better job. Maybe he wouldn't spend his days bent double on the docks, unloading ships.

The letters from home, therefore, came from Mother but were scribed by Domenico. It was so expensive, so expensive. The paper. The pencil. The payment to a courier to tuck her letters in with the cartons of paperwork flying between the legates and the pope, or between the envoys and their authorities. The letters wouldn't come frequently, and for that reason alone, Magdalena expected Mother would make sure they sounded happy.

Dear Magdalena,

We miss you so much now that we can't come to see you every week, but we hope to hear from you soon. We told everyone in the family that you've gone off to Trent for the council, and no one understands why you had to go, especially if the council goes the way it has before. It's been thirty years in progress, no?

"Seventeen years, Mother," murmured Magdalena. "There's no need to exaggerate when the actual truth is just as ridiculous."

Mother's letter continued,

You saw Fiora walking with the shoes and the stick, and how well she was doing. She's so pleased. I think she's getting stronger every day, and she's excited to help us now. She's begun taking in laundry along with my sister, and the money helps. She wants to buy lots of paper to send you lots of letters.

Fiora. Taking in washing. Able to carry heavy burdens and walk through the streets with them. It was like a miracle.

Domenico has returned to his job at the docks—

Returned? Magdalena frowned. When had he left it?

—and his new employer pays almost as much as the previous one, so we're doing well.

The letter went on to talk about all her cousins, except (notably) Erico. Mother gave a description of a procession through the streets, and then at the end, one worrisome sentence.

Was that cardinal able to write a letter to the Marcoli family?

# THIRTEEN

Before a general congregation, Cardinal Seripando sat in his suite reviewing his notes while Sister Magdalena wandered about, distracted. She went first to bring his tea, then came back get a cup, then found herself standing in the bedroom rather than in front of the fire with the kettle, and then back in front of the kettle holding the tea canister but no cup.

Chiara entered the suite to remove his breakfast tray. "My dear," Seripando said as Chiara walked through, "are you limping?"

"I fell yesterday." Chiara sounded cheerful. Unspoken was that she'd fallen because Lena, teaching them to block a low kick, had taken Chiara's legs out from beneath her. The graceless landing left a palm-sized bruise on her hip. "It doesn't hurt as long as I keep moving."

Seripando sounded concerned. "Perhaps if you rested, it wouldn't hurt then either."

"Working is good for me. It was worst when I woke up stiff for *lauds*," Chiara said, "and then had to sit in the chapel for a quarter hour at prayer." She smiled. "I'd rather be moving around."

"Perhaps you can pray *terce* while making beds at the hostel rather than sitting again in your chapel." Seripando turned back to his notes. "Sister Magdalena, will you please add this to the books we're bringing to the general congregation?"

As with most of his books, the title was in Latin. She took the heavy tome. "How many languages can you read, sir?"

"Four." His voice had grown on her over the weeks, and while before she'd compared him to a rickety building, now she understood him more as awkward than weak. His mind was nimble, and when she heard him in private conference with one bishop or another, he showed a facility with ideas that left her astonished at how he could raise or lower his diction to convey any concept. If he had a flaw, as far as she could tell, it was that he assumed everyone was as smart as himself and grasped ideas as quickly as he did.

She found herself in the next room, holding a book and wondering what to do with it before remembering she was supposed to set it with the other two books, and she carried it back out to the main sitting room.

Seripando had a second flaw: he was, as Cardinal Simonetta warned, a reformer. Magdalena had begun to suspect their patron assigned her to Seripando because of her basic writing skills. Those skills had rapidly improved because Simonetta demanded reports on anything Seripando said that that might mean reform. With all the practice Seripando's reforming ideas provided, Magdalena would have to write Simonetta a long letter tonight.

And her mother. She needed to write Mother a long letter as well.

"My dear," Seripando said, "you're so unsettled, and you keep carrying things into the wrong room. What's weighing on your mind?"

Magdalena looked up. "I'm sorry, sir. I'll be more attentive."

He shook his head. "Tell me how I can help. How can I pray for you?"

"I got a letter from home." Magdalena said, as Chiara left with the tray. "Let me carry those for you, sir."

He shook his head as he held his books. "I feel best with these close to my heart. Besides, I want to make sure they actually come with me." His wrinkled face broke into a smile. "This is a copy of a document we generated in the first iteration of the council, on justification. It's quite lengthy, but so fine and so precise. It's quite a treasure, and we should almost thank the Lutherans for forcing us to develop it."

That was something to include in her report, since Simonetta preferred her letters to be long even if she had to bundle up the tiniest crumbs of information. Short reports always garnered a nasty remark about how she'd chosen that day not to pay attention.

"Now tell me," Seripando said, "about this disturbing letter from home."

Magdalena sighed. "My mother hinted that there was trouble with another family. A vendetta. I'm afraid for my brother and my cousin, but I don't have any real information." Magdalena spotted one last book, a leather-bound tome that reminded her of the one she'd retrieved the night before being assigned to Trent. "You wanted this one too, right?"

Seripando laughed. "Ah, my good girl. You aren't the only one misplacing books this morning! Yes, if you please. We must both pray: you for your family and me for your peace of mind. The Holy Spirit doesn't want you to worry. Pray with strength, because you are a bride of Christ."

A bride of Christ who had been dispatched three hundred and fifty miles from her family.

As they stepped into the hallway, Magdalena said, "How do you make time to read all these?"

"Reading is a joy, my dear." He called the nuns *my dear* so often that it felt natural. "How are we to know our Lord unless we do our very best to experience Him? By prayer, surely, and by our merciful works where we find Christ in others, but also by studying the Bible and reading many edifying books. In all these, God is apparent."

Magdalena said, "Isn't today's general congregation about the other sort of books?"

Seripando sighed. "The Index of Banned Books is a well-intentioned idea, although poorly implemented, but reforming that shouldn't be the work of the council. Who would have time to read every book ever written and then determine its fitness for Christian eyes?"

"Cardinal Hosius would," Magdalena quipped too quickly to stop herself. But that was part of the joke: of the five papal legates, Hosius was always reading and Simonetta was always writing.

Servants bustled in the halls, carrying trays or wheeling carts or hauling baskets of laundry. They tended to cling to the walls, making way so the guests of Cardinal Madruzzo to walk down the center.

"The difficulty we encounter with Hosius and the other *zelanti*," said Seripando, nodding at a maid, "is that they balk at reforming anything the popes have done. So my esteemed peer's reading and judging would be of no use."

The zealots had identified themselves quickly in the course of the council, far more quickly than Magdalena would have expected any group to fall into factions. Of course she should have predicted it, but she hadn't wanted to believe bishops would take sides against one another. Everyone against the Holy Roman Emperor's envoys? Certainly. Everyone against the Spanish Crown's interests? Naturally. But bishop against bishop, and legate against legate...?

Of the anti-reformer *zelanti*, Simonetta was their head, always stepping into the breech to protect the pope and his authority. He had to. The pope had no voice in the council other than the men he had sent to represent him.

The principal legate was Cardinal Ercole Gonzaga, a wonderful man, nearly deaf, who envisioned a Church where pastors took care of their parishes and bishops tended their dioceses. Simonetta had warned the nuns, however, that Gonzaga had fallen under Seripando's influence and should be considered in the reformer camp.

"How are you going to review the Index without being able to read the books?" Magdalena asked, stepping aside for a servant to wheel a cart past her. "They're already banned. Reading them to un-ban them is sinful."

"As you've seen, though, there are exceptions, and exceptions to exceptions." Seripando shook his head. "Half the reason we need this Council is because too many times, we enact a commonsense regulation only to find the exceptions have ruled the day, and it is no longer commonsense."

As they turned a corner, a servant leaped toward Seripando with a knife.

Without thinking, Magdalena threw herself between the knife and the cardinal, raising her book as a shield. "Sir! Back!"

She dropped the book to block with her left arm. Her forearm connected with the attacker's wrist hard enough to send his knife crashing into the wall. Before he could regain his wits, she struck his head with her right hand and then kicked his abdomen twice in rapid succession.

Seripando stood, shocked. The attacker tried to dart around her, but Magdalena yanked the rosary off her waist and caught it around his neck, throwing her weight to the side. Off balance, he hit the floor, and she tightened the rosary around his neck, yanking backward. As he rolled onto his stomach, she dropped onto his back, knees into his spine and a strangling pressure on his windpipe. "Sir! Summon the guards!"

Seripando hurried down the corridor, calling for the Swiss Guard. Magdalena kept the attacker pinned even when he stopped struggling. He was a lot larger than she and might be carrying more than just the one knife. It took so long for the guard to come, too long. Magdalena wished she could pray, but in the moment she couldn't remember even the *Ave Maria*.

Simonetta had been right. The Lutherans had tried to kill one of the legates. They'd tried to kill *Seripando*. The nicest, most cautious of the legates—and the one most likely to have recommended the reforms the heretics wanted in the first place.

Two Swiss Guardsmen raced up the hall, and finally Magdalena released the attacker. The man gave a gurgling gasp and raised his head, but the guards shouted at him to stay down, drawing their swords.

"Easy, there." One of the guards hauled the man to his feet. The attacker was pale, blood streaming from his nose where Magdalena slammed his face into the floor. "Your pride's probably wounded worst of all, beaten up by a nun."

The second guard laughed with a roar. "That little thing took you down?"

Seripando urged, "Be careful. He had a knife."

Magdalena lifted the heavy book she'd dropped. Only then did she realize her hands were shaking.

Lena rounded the corner. "Sister! Are you all right?" She took in the attacker, then picked up Magdalena's rosary. She eyed the guardsman holding onto him. "You're going to take him away? We can't have someone accosting nuns in Cardinal Madruzzo's own palace."

"Of course we're going to lock him up." The Swiss Guardsmen started laughing. "For his own protection! Maybe you'll punch him again, and he'll need to go home to sit on his mother's knee." They led the man away, taunting him all the way down the hallway.

Magdalena staggered to the wall. Her brain felt distant from her body, and she couldn't tell if she were about to hit the ground herself. The man's knife lay at the junction of wall and floor. The blade gleamed with sharpness, the hilt dark with its own density. If that brute had connected with Seripando, so old and so slow-moving...

The book weighed heavy in her arms. The leather binding was slashed. She hadn't even realized the assassin scored a hit.

Lena put a hand on her shoulder. "Come with me."

Magdalena said, "I have to help the cardinal carry his books to the general congregation."

Seripando drew up close. His voice wavered. "My dear, you are not all right. You're pale like a ghost. You need to sit."

Shaking, Magdalena studied the carpet around her leather-clad feet. Here in Trent the nuns wore flexible leather slippers because of the cold. She couldn't feel the carpet under her toes, but right now she couldn't feel anything. She should have felt gravity. She should have felt anger. Terror.

Her abbess had a demanding note in her voice that should have cut through everything. "Where is Chiara?" Instead, Lena's voice came from far, far away. Faint, as if carried on the wind.

Magdalena's response sounded the same. "In the kitchens."

"I want more guards here with Cardinal Seripando, and then I'll walk you back to the suite. You are under orders to stay there until you are able to return to the convent." She put a hand on Magdalena's arm. "Chiara will carry the cardinal's books, and I'll consult with Cardinal Simonetta. When I want you, I'll send for you."

Chiara shrieked when she saw Magdalena. "You're so pale! Did he hurt you? Did he hurt the cardinal? What a monster!" But Lena urged her to keep moving, so Chiara kissed Magdalena on the cheek. "Here's a leftover biscuit from breakfast. Eat something and then go home. I'll be praying for you."

Magdalena slipped the biscuit into her pocket. She took the attacker's heavy dagger and wrapped it in a cloth, then slipped into the pocket of her habit. The weight made her feel more secure, although she'd done well enough without a weapon. Then, although she didn't feel steady, she left Madruzzo's palace.

As Magdalena walked, she kept reliving the attack. A servant. She hadn't thought about servants being a threat. She'd been lax. She'd been distracted by phantom problems from home and hadn't watched for the real problems nearby. When no physical attacks had occurred immediately, Magdalena had concentrated on the theological ones and let herself enjoy the cardinal's company.

And that man—that man, yes, she'd sent him to the floor with a bleeding face and quite possibly a few broken ribs, but he'd come at them with a knife. At Seripando, rather. He'd expected her to flatten herself against the wall like a good little girl and let the menfolk do what they did best, the breaking and taking and wrecking.

She reviewed every movement, and after the fifth time she realized she'd done exactly as Agnella and Lena had taught. The hours of exercise had carved deep grooves in her reflexes so that when the hand had come at her, she'd blocked with intent to disarm. She'd kicked with intent to subdue. She'd used the book as a weapon because it was the only weapon she had, and then she'd used the rosary exactly as it was designed: to bring down a taller and stronger attacker. God used the weak to confound the strong, and the rosary was the tool of the Blessed Virgin who loved the weak.

By the time Magdalena reached the hostel, her fists and jaw alike were clenched, and her brow furrowed. She didn't look up, only went to the chapel and knelt in prayer, the dagger warm with her body heat. *Thank you, Father. Thank you for putting me in a place where I could protect the cardinal. Thank you for protecting my consecrated body and using it for your kingdom. Help me keep doing your will so your Council can complete the work you intend it for.*

She reached for that huge rosary on her waist. Rather than using one of the smaller rosaries, she prayed on the unwieldy beads, the long rope. This had saved her and saved the cardinal.

Before she finished, Sister Lena joined her in the chapel and prayed in silence, waiting. She'd brought Agnella as well. When Magdalena returned her rosary to her waist, Lena said, "Cardinal Simonetta will send for us when he's ready, but I need to know if you're hurt."

Agnella said, "Did he touch you? Because if he did, I'll let the prison guards know he violated a nun." Her voice dropped. "Sometimes accidents happen in a prison. Someone can break a wrist or an ankle. Sometimes spit gets into the prisoner's food, and the milk is curdled before it even pours into the cup."

"He didn't harm me. Let the magistrates deal with him." Magdalena shook her head. "Is Cardinal Seripando all right?"

Agnella said, "He's shaken up, the poor thing. Men like that, so insulated. I'm sure he's dwelt on martyrs and the heretics who are willing to kill, but all from behind the pages of a book. He lives in his head." She made the sign of the cross, looking heavenward. "Lord preserve us from theologians. They can preach on the spiritual significance of any single word in the Bible but have no idea how to boil an egg."

Lena said, "He noticed the book was damaged and asked me to repair the binding. And then he remembered himself and asked me to check on you, in case you were damaged too."

"I've no binding to repair." Magdalena smiled. "I should go back to the general congregation. I really am fine."

Agnella examined Magdalena and revealed a bruise spreading up her arm. She hadn't even noticed it, although now she made a belated connection with a stiff feeling on that side. "You blocked him hard. Good. I wish you'd blocked him hard enough to break his wrist." She looked over the rest of her and declared her whole. "The only places he hurt you were where you struck him, and he got the worst of every contact."

"Regardless," said Lena, "you're not returning immediately. I'll tell Seripando you're resting. As, in fact, he should be too. He had quite a scare, but he's out there doing his work."

"I should be doing mine," said Magdalena.

"There's work for you here," said Lena. "You're under orders to do it."

So for the rest of the day, Magdalena worked in the hostel, scrubbing floors stained by mud and boot prints. She said the liturgical hours with her fellow sisters. In her little free time, she stitched together a leather sheath for the dagger so it would fit snug against her forearm, invisible beneath her swishing habit sleeves. The dagger felt balanced in her hand, and it was well made, forged all in one piece and with, she noticed belatedly, a lion's head decorating the pommel at the edge of the grip. It kept her company for the rest of the day.

*Sext* and *none* passed without incident, but before *vespers*, Cardinal Simonetta summoned them to Madruzzo's palace.

Lena, Agnella, Magdalena, and three of the Tridentine nuns gathered in their cardinal-sponsor's outer parlor. Simonetta had supper brought in for all six. One of the Swiss Guard stood outside the door, but the nuns kept watchful eyes on the servants as they delivered the food.

Simonetta dismissed the servants, then took a seat. "Sister Magdalena, that was fine work today protecting

Cardinal Seripando. I'm very thankful you were there to save his life and possibly his soul." Of course, he still considered Seripando a heretic and therefore in eternal jeopardy. "The Swiss Guard questioned the man who attacked today. Like all paid thugs, he's a brute who was more than happy to say who put the gold in his pocket rather than spend the rest of his life in a stone cell. He's a mercenary, and he's being extradited to Innsbruck where the Holy Roman Emperor will consider his case. The emperor loves Cardinal Seripando, so may God have mercy on the poor man." Simonetta's mouth tightened. "It's now the mercenary's employer who concerns us."

At the unspoken threat, Magdalena's skin tingled beneath the dagger.

"By now he must know his previous plan failed. He won't know why." Simonetta paced the room. "I have a secret authorization from the pope to order any heretic's execution when speed is of the essence. We cannot send a courier to Rome and wait ten days for the pope to return his decision. In that time, the man can and will strike again, and again thereafter. We have to act decisively."

He turned to Lena. "These are your chosen sisters?"

She nodded. "Since we're unsure of the exact situation, I covered for every eventuality. We can move in close and direct, or we can work from a distance."

Magdalena's head spun. An execution. An actual execution.

Simonetta cast his eye over the six. "In exchange for clemency, the Swiss Guard are having the man write a confession as to who hired him."

Tadea's head picked up. "Really? Can I have a copy of that?"

Simonetta looked irritated. "Your records can wait. The assassin claims to have been hired by Bishop Cavanei from Pinerolo in northern Italy, but I've no idea where he maintains his residence."

Lena said, "Might he have replaced the real bishop?"

"Quite possibly. We need to remove him from operation tonight."

Such a man might have plans against all five legates. It made sense that Simonetta wouldn't sleep until they dealt with him

Cavanei had obtained an apartment in the center of town, near the river, where he lived with a retinue of ten, including a cook and a butler and a woman who may or may not have been his concubine. Simonetta added that last with a disgusted wrinkle of his nose, as though priests didn't take concubines on a regular basis.

Agnella said, "When should we act?"

"Tonight," Lena said before Simonetta could respond. "Once he's aware that his plan failed, he's going to flee. I can't see a criminal staying under the circumstances, so we'll need to intercept him quickly." She rubbed her chin. "Is there any reason you can think of, Cardinal Simonetta, to send him a message?"

"Why would we alert him?" Agnella exclaimed. "Asking him to report to the palace is equivalent to letting him know he should run right away."

"He doesn't know about the Catherinites," Lena said. "I'm not suggesting we surround his home with Swiss Guards. I'm more interested in sending him a letter and having one of us deliver it so we can learn more about his apartments. Is he on the committee to study the Index of Banned Books?"

Simonetta shrugged. "He's not on any committee, nor has he done more in three weeks than mark himself as attended for the general congregations."

Tadea said, "We could deliver a letter asking if he would meet early with you to present his opinion on the preliminary document."

Lena shook her head. "Devious minds look for devious plans. He'll ask himself, why are the legates making sure he'll be present the day after his man was sent to kill one of them? No, he'll suspect our intent before reading three sentences."

Agnella said, "And what if he does? A man like that deserves to worry, and moreover, what will he do? He might try to hide or fight, but most likely he'll run. If we keep his quarters surrounded, he can't escape."

Magdalena said, "If he does escape, we've still ensured the safety of the legates."

Lena looked grim. "Our orders aren't to drive him away. They're to execute. He's in the city, and we need to keep him here. Moreover, the follow-up is easiest if he remains local."

Simonetta fingered the edges of his beard. "He has a retinue of ten. I'm unsure you'll be able to carry it through without drawing him out of his residence."

Lena said, "Sir, with all due respect, you give the verdict. It's up to us to carry it out. Trust us to determine the best way of doing it."

# FOURTEEN

Magdalena returned to the convent in time to prepare supper. Lena and Agnella had disappeared into Lena's cell to devise a plan, but whatever they came up with wouldn't require action until after dark.

On returning from the storage room with a new flour sack, she found Chiara seated beside the fireplace. In her hands she had an amorphous white cloth, along with a spool of thread and a crochet hook.

"Everyone's tense." Chiara pronounced this with finality, but also a little frustration. "Lena, Agnella, Tadea, Nezetta, you're all brusque and very nearly rude. When I try to point out that it's a good thing you were there to help Cardinal Seripando, they only bark out their agreement like little lap dogs and go back to being grumpy."

"Now who's being rude?" Magdalena smiled at her, but Chiara was focused only on her lacework. "What are you making?"

"An altar linen. Cardinal Madruzzo had a priest in his office talking about reform of the Curia, which," and she sighed, "I've discovered is another subject that will make everyone tense."

Tense, or overly cautious. It was hard to decide which. Simonetta had standing orders with all the nuns that whenever anyone spoke about *reform of the head,* or reform of the Curia, he was to be notified in great detail. Every attendee of the council understood this was not a subject to be broached at all in public because as soon as they did, arguments would bring the council to a halt. Already the legates had put off discussing serious pastoral reform twice because the attendees couldn't agree whether a bishop's authority came from God or from the pope, and every careful attempt at wording around the issue had caused even more argumentation.

They might continue the council a thousand years and never reach a satisfactory conclusion on that score, and all the while diocese after diocese would have to function without its bishop, and Magdalena's family might well be involved in a war.

Chiara continued, "This priest complained that his parish had such a small benefice that it looked shameful and shabby compared to the ones in the city. Christ loved the poor and was born in a barn, he said, but does that mean a country church should look little better than a stable? His church doesn't even have altar linens, and his vestments are threadbare."

"Ah. So you took his arm on the way out and asked his name and his town and told him you'd look for him in a week."

"Don't flatter me. A month." Chiara sighed. "If he sends me his vestments, I can repair them, too. Lace-making gives me something to work at during the general congregations and the meetings of the theologians."

Magdalena started kneading the dough. "You could be listening."

"I'm always listening," Chiara snapped before realizing Magdalena was joking. She smiled. "After you've learned a lace pattern, your hands move on their own. In my old convent, some of the nuns would sell their lace to have a little pocket money, and then they'd send the money right back out into the street to buy things for themselves."

The sisters had done the same in Santi Cosma e Damiano, only with embroidery. "The work keeps them busy."

"Sister Lena keeps us busy. Scrubbing floors keeps us busy. So does baking bread." Chiara sighed. "I want to create art. The Eucharist is beautiful, and I think Jesus should be surrounded by beautiful things when we celebrate it."

Agnella stopped at the kitchen door holding a letter. "I'm looking for Tadea."

"Sorry." Chiara shrugged. "Not here." After Agnella left, she said, "Do you know how to crochet?"

Magdalena shook her head. "I can do some simple stitches, but nothing intricate like you're making. My mother didn't have time."

Chiara said, "Oh, I'd have figured as a Farnese, you'd be embroidering and crocheting and tatting."

Magdalena said, "I'm not really a Farnese. Bastard daughter of a bastard son. My mother was a cook."

Chiara's eyes widened. "Farneses can cook!"

"She's not the Farnese. My father was, and he'd send someone by every so often to make sure we were alive and give us money to keep being alive. He lived across town in his obnoxiously large house with his respectable family." Magdalena chuckled. "We did all right. My mother kept jars of rosewater steeping all over our apartment. The three of us slept in one room, and the rosewater took over everything else."

Chiara's eyes widened. "That's amazing! Why so much?"

"She sold it all. My brother and I, and sometimes my cousins, we'd head out to the fields in the summer and pick all the roses at dawn. We'd hear the bells ring for *lauds* and race to the field with baskets as big as ourselves, and we'd pick the fields clean before the bells for *prime*. We got the

best blossoms that way. Mother would set them up, and
they'd rest. All summer we'd do that, and she'd sell her
rosewater to the chef of every one of the grand houses and
palaces in Rome. Doing that would make enough money to
keep us in bread and clothes until the next summer."

Who did that for Mother now? With Domenico having
to work on the docks, was Fiora able to head to the field with
baskets? Could Mother work all morning and then fetch
enough flowers to make rosewater?

Chiara seemed wistful. "You lived with the essence of
flowers all around you. Their visual beauty faded, and then
you created scented beauty, and you sold it and made tasteful
beauty."

Magdalena smiled as she finished putting up the bread
dough. "My mother would like to hear you say that. She
worked as a cook and spent her whole days baking and frying
and boiling, and she taught me everything as she went along."

"Then Lena should put you in charge of feeding the
guests." Chiara pulled her thread to create more slack and set
to work crocheting her next row. "They're so demanding. I
would serve Cardinal Seripando in your place, although I
wouldn't have been able to save his life this afternoon."

Lena stepped into the kitchen. "Magdalena, are you
finished? I need you to run a letter over to Cardinal
Simonetta."

Magdalena dusted her hands on her apron and hung it
by the door.

Lena handed her the wax-sealed note paper. "Make sure
he reads it, and tell him I want an immediate answer. And
don't open it."

Magdalena put on her shoes and went back into the
street, walking the half-mile to Madruzzo's palace, and then
taking as long again to navigate the halls inside to make her
way into Cardinal Simonetta's suite. "Don't open it." The
letter was sealed: did Lena expect her to unseal it, read it,

memorize the contents, and then re-seal it? If she expected someone to open a message, why entrust that person to deliver it? Chiara was right that everyone was tense. It made them thoughtless.

A servant asked Magdalena to wait while he retrieved Cardinal Simonetta from a conference with Cardinal Hosius. In Simonetta's parlor, she took the time to say a decade of the rosary in relative silence. Although at first Trent seemed quiet, life here had its own distinct noise. At St. Sebastian's, she'd been able to find hush while tending the dying, or in her cell beneath the old stone church. Here, because the boarding house had access to the nuns' residence, quiet became scarcer. Overhead footsteps and boisterous guests all interrupted her thoughts on a minute-by-minute basis, and the longer the council continued, the more attendees crowded Trent.

So in these few minutes, she took the opportunity to settle her thoughts. They had an assignment to complete tonight. She prayed to be ready for whatever God required.

Simonetta entered the suite, and as Hosius left, Magdalena first bowed and second handed him Sister Lena's letter. He took it with a curt, "Thank you," then turned as if to leave.

"She asks that you reply to it now, please."

If anything, he looked even more irritated. He broke the seal and read with a frown. "Very well. Come along."

She accompanied him to his desk in the next room. Before he'd put ink to paper, however, Cardinal Hosius returned. Simonetta muttered, "A moment, please." He took Hosius back into the parlor, and Magdalena returned to silence. Trying to remember how far she'd gotten in her rosary, she took a seat near Simonetta's desk.

A page of his writings caught her eye, and she leaned forward. *Seripando.*

The letter was written in Italian, not in Latin, so Magdalena edged closer to decipher it. After all those reports, her skill had improved. With concentration, she could even read upside-down.

This appeared to be the second page of a letter, and Magdalena decided after a moment's reading that it was written to the pope as a report of the council's goings-on. Not unusual. The pope wanted to be kept in the know as to the council's discussions, and all of the legates had written numerous letters, dispatching them by courier to Rome and then awaiting a response in at least a week's time, but usually quite longer. The pope would have to decide what he wanted, and usually that decision was made only after a meeting with the Curia. Then someone (the name that cropped up most often was Cardinal Borromeo) would write a return letter, get the pope's approval, and send it by courier up to Trent.

For that reason alone, the Church should have staged this ridiculous Council in Rome. The Catherinites could have moved Lena down there and watched her cope with a hundred thousand people rather than lording over a town of five thousand.

Magdalena kept reading. Most of the contents were taken from her reports, but terribly distorted. Everything Simonetta had written about his fellow legate Seripando made it sound as though Satan had entered into the old man and was pulling marionette strings in an attempt to gut the papacy. Simonetta's letter mentioned Gonzaga in the next paragraph, painting a picture of two old men conspiring after hours in a locked parlor to ensure the downfall of the papacy, sharpening their swords to disembowel the church.

Did Simonetta have a second source on Seripando? Magdalena hadn't seen anything like this behavior. And Gonzaga, the cheerful half-deaf Gonzaga who knew everything there was to know about anything worth knowing—how could he be this scheming prince? How could the pope have made the man a legate at all, let alone the principal legate, if he were a snake and an underminer?

She reached the end of the page but didn't dare rifle through the private papers of the Eye of the Pope to find the rest. Simonetta and Hosius parleyed in the next room, but the men could enter at any moment.

The joke among the bishops was that Hosius was always reading and Simonetta always writing; that Gonzaga never heard anything and Seripando never dared anything; and that the last legate, Markus Sittich von Hohenems, never read nor wrote anything, never heard nor dared anything. His Latin was so bad he probably didn't even know the *Pater noster*, but he'd been made a cardinal because he was the pope's nephew. (Quite probably an actual nephew, not a "nephew.") Why wasn't Simonetta writing nasty things about Sittich? Get that embarrassing man deposed and the council could only improve.

Lots of popes promoted their nephews (both kinds of nephews). Magdalena's own grandfather had received a position in the Curia at age eighteen because his "uncle" (grandfather) had become pope. Pope Pius IV had promoted his nephew, Carlo Borromeo, to be the bishop of Milan and then elevated him again into the Curia. But to be fair, Seripando did think highly of Borromeo. "A genuine, worthy man," Seripando had murmured. Sittich was the first papal relative Magdalena had encountered who was blindingly incompetent.

But what she could see of the letter hadn't complained to the pope that Sittich was the laughingstock of the council, only that the gentle-voiced Seripando wanted to stop the Curia from selling red hats as a fund-raising tactic.

Seripando held many such opinions, and the cardinal of the Datary hardly needed Magdalena to collect them: Seripando said them in public to anyone who would listen.

Seripando believed bishops should reside in their own diocese, rather than collecting the benefice and living somewhere else. Seripando believed one man could only be the bishop to one diocese, and not the bishop of several dioceses. He thought the same of priests, that they should be responsible for preaching in their own parishes and not living elsewhere while paying a vicar to do their preaching. He wanted pastors to be *pastoral*.

It was part of Seripando's gentle touch, the way he called her (and all the rest of the nuns) *my dear*. He envisioned the Church as a shepherd right there among the flock, picking straw out of wool and getting mud on its boots and occasionally being stepped on by a distracted hoof.

Yes, it might diminish the papacy to make all these changes. Who would pay for them all? That always seemed the primary concern.

But did it really matter if Seripando thought the bishops derived their power from God or from the pope? Why would it, as long as he got the bishops to talk about it productively?

Simonetta entered the room to find Magdalena leaning back in her chair, fingers steepled and eyes closed. "Don't get up," he said as she started to rise to her feet. "I'll just be a minute and send you on your way with a reply."

He jotted a few words, then sealed the paper and handed it to her. "Don't open this," he said. "Those are orders from the Church."

Again, "Don't open this." They should just fill their letters with enraged hornets and identify the spies that way. Of course he could trust her with a paper, forbidden or otherwise. Unless, that was, he never trusted anyone.

---

After all the planning, Magdalena got left out in the cold. Literally.

Sister Lena had sent Tadea into his apartment in plain clothes to deliver a letter. "It looks just like the assassin's handwriting, and it asks for Cavanei to meet him because today's attempt failed and he wants to know what to do next."

"It's not quite that obvious." Tadea waved a hand. "It's using mostly our prisoner's words, and he was good enough to tell the guards where Cavanei had met him before."

The letter instructed Cavanei to meet tonight, or else the assassin would leave town. Then Lena sent herself, Tadea, and two other Tridentine nuns over to the meeting point. Agnella, who hated the plan, was dispatched to the apartment building in case Cavanei returned. As an afterthought, Lena gave her Magdalena. "You're bruised. I don't want you fighting, but you can watch."

In her exercise garb, Magdalena perched in the tree with her eyes adjusted to the night and her ears attuned to the sleeping city's every sound. She wore gloves and leather shoes, a black hair binding and black exercise gear. One person had ridden by on a horse but never picked out the black-clad human on the branch stretched over the street, although the horse had gotten nervous because he could smell a person where no person ought to be.

The convicted bishop's quarters had lights flickering in two windows. On the bottom floor a light moved from room to room. That would be the maid, tidying up for the next day, or possibly the cook prepping the kitchen for the next morning's work. On the second floor the light stayed in one place, and Magdalena figured that was a bedroom.

Tadea's delivery of the letter had gone as planned. Half an hour later, on schedule, Cavanei had left the building in the direction of the meeting place. That left them watching an uninteresting, unimportant building just in case Cavanei returned.

In the chill, Magdalena recited *Pater nosters* in her head as she tried to keep herself from getting nervous. There was no need for nerves: eventually Lena or Tadea would walk by and retrieve them, the job having been completed at the meeting site.

Someone left the bishop's apartment. Magdalena leaned forward to watch as he walked up the street, opposite the direction of the meeting area. Heading toward what? Based on his clothes, it might be the butler. Interesting that he'd have an errand tonight.

Five minutes later, more hooves. The same man walked back beneath her, leading a saddled horse.

Riding in the dark? Why?

Across the street, Agnella signaled by waving a white handkerchief. Magdalena moved out further on the branch to get a better look.

The butler stood at the door with the horse. It opened. Closed. Opened again, and this time a man exited. He carried a satchel, and he looked from one side to the next, then again.

Magdalena didn't need a signal now. This was wrong. The man who had left: was that not Cavanei? Suspecting a trap, had he sent some dupe to the meeting place in his stead while all along he planned to make a solo escape from the city? Was he just going to leave his entourage to the whim of the Swiss Guard and the city's magistrates?

The butler fixed the bags to the saddle, then helped the man to mount. No, he couldn't get away. But to chase him down? To break cover when she didn't know for certain—

Above, Agnella called, "Cavanei!"

The man turned.

Their target!

He urged his horse into motion, and Magdalena gripped the branch with both hands. As he passed beneath, she swung from the branch with both feet forward, crashed into his chest, and knocked him from the horse.

He swore as he hit the cobbles. She got to her feet and slapped the horse on the rear. It took off.

Scrambling upright, he swore, but she already had the knife from its sheath. When he sprang at her, she slashed, ripping his sleeve but not connecting.

"Leave me alone!" The man rushed her, but she ducked and spun, hitting him in the back with her elbow.

He didn't stop. Magdalena tore after him, knife in her hand. In these darkened streets, even without a horse, he could disappear in a heartbeat.

He turned into a side street. When she followed, something heavy crashed into her head.

She went down onto her knees. He brought his knee at her jaw, but she dodged so his knee only grazed her temple. She lunged forward, slamming him in the groin with the top of her skull.

When he went down, she unsheathed her dagger from its holster and plunged it right into his stomach, up under his rib cage.

He looked up at her, rage and pain on his face, as he lurched forward. She clutched the dagger, slippery with his blood, but he collapsed, and he didn't get up.

She waited, ribs heaving, head ringing.

His blood coated her gloves. Should she go back and find Lena? Stand vigil over his body? What if he wasn't dead and managed to crawl away?

So in an alley smelling of urine and garbage, she prayed the requiem over him, followed by the *De profundis*. She prayed for herself, thanking God for His protection. She prayed for the papal legates to be safe, especially Cardinal Seripando. Rats came to investigate the dead man, but she chased them away.

When she heard footsteps, Magdalena edged further into the shadows, but then she heard, "Magdalena?"

Agnella. Magdalena whispered, "I have him. I completed it."

"I couldn't get to you fast enough." Agnella sounded disappointed, but then her tone picked up. "I'll go tell Lena. She'll be delighted."

Delighted. Agnella would be smug and a hair's breadth away from insubordination, and Lena would be equal parts amusement and annoyance. Magdalena had the better part standing vigil over a body.

Finally Lena arrived, Agnella at her back. She checked him for breath, then checked for a pulse. And then, with everything a certitude, she stood and rested a hand on Magdalena's shoulder. "Congratulations. Your name will now be recorded in our annals."

# FIFTEEN

A winter's Sunday. As with the hospital in Rome, the boarding house didn't have a day of rest even when everyone else did. The Tridentine nuns' day of rest included making meals for the hostel, cleaning the rooms and hallways, and taking care of every fussy detail their guests might desire.

After having fed guests their lunches, Chiara tugged Magdalena's sleeve. "Come with me."

She led Magdalena away from the convent and toward the Augustinian church. Seripando was an Augustinian. It was late in the day, so with no one was in the nave, she hitched up the skirt of her habit and scaled the walls to the rafters crisscrossing the ceiling. Magdalena girded up her own skirt and discarded her shoes, then followed Chiara to the first of the beams. "Keep going," Chiara whispered, and they climbed higher, further into the ceiling until they reached an alcove housing a stained-glass window.

They both fit into the shelf area. Awaiting them was a leather-bound book, a hand-span wide and a finger's width thick.

"I found Tadea writing in this the day after that horrible man attacked Cardinal Seripando," Chiara whispered. She needn't have worried, as high as they were. "When I came into the room, she locked it up, but I've been keeping watch ever since. Last night, the chest was unlocked, so I pulled out the book."

Magdalena studied her with a furrowed brow. Chiara continued, "Remember Gilia and her records, how important they were? And how Bellosa wanted so badly not to talk about them? It made me crazy inside. I think these are them."

She opened the book and traced a finger along the columns. "These aren't just finances or a record of matriculation and attrition. For one thing, they're written in Latin, and why would anyone keep records in Latin? For another thing, the Catherinites hold all our funds in common. If you ask, Lena will show you the convent finance book. I've seen it. She records all the income from the hostel, all the gifts from the people who make donations, and all the expenses. You can review how much flour we buy and how much cloth, and when I take some of the crochet thread to make someone a veil for her wedding, how much we paid for the thread and how much the bride's family pays us for the veil." She shook her head. "So when I found this, I had to have it."

She paged through, each sheet of thick paper whispering as it passed from one side to the next. "I'm not very good at reading Latin, but a lot of these are names. On this whole column," she said, tracing it with a roughened fingertip, "every entry is 'Heresy.'"

Haeresis.

"I think this word at the top is 'Verdict.'" *Sententia.* "Then another date, followed by the name of a sister and a code. I haven't deciphered the code." She looked at Magdalena. "What is this?"

Magdalena swallowed hard.

"Don't lie," Chiara whispered. "You know what it is."

Below them, a door opened, and both nuns fell silent. A woman walked through the nave toward the sanctuary at the front. She knelt at the altar rail, silent, motionless as a hunted rabbit. Above her, Magdalena remained equally motionless.

Chiara let a few pages slip through her thumb, and then stopped them from fanning forward, traced her finger down the page, and came to rest on a name. Magdalena's.

Magdalena's eyes fixed on the name occupying the same line as hers. She'd never seen Cavanei's name written out, but here it was, in an elegant serifed script jotted into a ledger unlike any Chiara or she had ever seen before.

Of course the Catherinites would have to keep such a record. If this book had been known to the compilers of the Index, it would have been banned and then burned.

Magdalena took the book from Chiara's hand. Above her name were listed the names of the other sisters of her order. Tadea. Agnella twice, Bellosa four times. While the woman at the altar rail prayed in silence, Magdalena paged back through the book until the names became less familiar. Nezetta, though, showed up in the early entries. Her name appeared on the same line as Cardinal Reginald Pole.

While the woman prayed below, Magdalena prayed above, counting out a rosary on her fingers as they waited. Magdalena prayed for the wisdom to answer Chiara the way God would want her to. She prayed for the woman below and whatever she was praying for, this unknown woman who had a much simpler life. The purpose of the convent was to keep a woman's focus off worldly matters and squarely on God. In the convent, a woman wouldn't have to be busy with the things of the world. Everyone had said so. But here Magdalena was busier about the world than ever, and the world kept intruding, with no walls able to keep it out.

The woman below lit a candle, made the sign of the cross, then left the church.

Chiara said, "Come with me."

She climbed out on the rafter, further up, further out. Soon they were right at the peak of the ceiling, directly over the center aisle. The height was dizzying, and only a year ago Chiara had blanched at being up twenty feet.

She stretched out along the beam. "Why did you become a nun?"

Magdalena propped herself where two beams joined, dangling a bare foot. "Death," she said. "I was running from death."

Chiara said, "How so?"

"I told you we're Farnese stock." Magdalena let the wood take her weight, felt the rosary hanging from her waist over the empty space. "We weren't noble, though. We were hardworking, and the men were hard-drinking, plus I had cousins all over the place. My mother's brother had a daughter. She fell in love and got engaged. Then she found out he had a woman on the side, maybe more than one woman."

Chiara waited, but Magdalena had to gather herself. "My older cousins didn't take it well. They—" Magdalena steeled herself. "They got drunk. They hunted the guy down, and..."

It had been a day unlike any other. Or rather, exactly like any other, and for that very reasoning the most frightening day of her life. Such a day should be marked by storms, by an eclipse, by an earthquake. Not by clear skies and sellers hawking loaves of bread.

"Her fiancé... in the street, they beat him to death."

Chiara whispered, "But—"

"Because he made a fool of my cousin. She loved him. He broke her heart. I think she'd have taken him back. She didn't get the chance." Magdalena met the eyes of Chiara, who had stretched out on a beam over her head. "But what he did... Did he deserve to die? Beaten like an animal and left in the gutter?"

Chiara said, "Why would that make you a nun? That might make her a nun, but not you."

"Because that's how men are. I can't tell you how often I heard men bragging about this woman or that whore, how often I saw women fighting in the market because some man was her husband but this other one's lover." Magdalena tilted back her head the better to look at Chiara. As she did so, her hair bristled against the back of her neck. It needed to be trimmed again, and now she knew why. It had nothing to do with beauty or renunciation. An attacker could grab you by your long hair.

Chiara said, "So if you fell in love...someday your cousins would kill him?"

"Any man I'd love enough to marry is someone I'd also love enough to save his life. So I saved it. I made myself off limits. Whoever he is, he can't break my heart when he finds another woman, and my cousins can't go out in the market and break his head." Magdalena forced a smile. "I hope he appreciates it."

Chiara sounded stunned. "That's not what I thought at all. You're so spiritual. I figured you were like me, always planning to take the habit."

"I came here to avoid death." Magdalena looked ruefully at her hands. "And then I ended up working at a hospice."

"Those are holy deaths. Good deaths. Not men taken in adultery and murdered by drunks." Chiara shook her head. "I was in the convent school from when I was little. I never heard the things you're talking about. I didn't realize men had so little self-control."

"Why do you think priestly celibacy is such a problem? The Lutherans made a huge stink of it because nearly all the German priests had concubines or whores living with them, or secret marriages, or five children being raised on the Church's donations. Men aren't like women. They see something they want, and they take it."

Chiara protested, "But surely some of them are continent."

"Are they? I have letters from home. My brother gets into fights in the streets because of the man who tried to use my body. They had a truce and then my older cousins got involved, and now my cousin Erico has a broken shoulder. They're not continent with their fists. How can they be continent with body parts that are even more impulsive?"

Chiara urged, "And the book? What's that all about?"

Magdalena said, "More death."

"But how? These are people who died, and the nuns are people who lived. What is the connection? Why a verdict?"

"Chiara." Magdalena looked up at her, braced in the rafters by a body honed to perfection by hours of exercise fitted in among the liturgy of the hours. "The Church sentences heretics. The authorities sentence them to be killed. We're trained to kill."

Chiara didn't react with surprise, only thoughtfulness. It was the look of a woman scaling an intricate facade and wondering where was the next place to put her hand. She was fourteen now, but with an expression of always judging the world and predicting her next steps.

"Does no one suspect?" Chiara said. "A human body doesn't just perish because it's sentenced to do so. Don't the authorities wonder why these men die?"

"If the authorities don't already know, then they never see," Magdalena said. "When a man dies, who do they call to prepare the body for burial? Nuns. In these cases, we make sure the nuns are ours. We do it, and he's buried."

After Magdalena had completed her assignment, Lena had acted with swiftness and a tactical mind that would have impressed a Roman emperor. The bishop's body had been cleaned, his wound wrapped and sutured, and he'd been carried to the nearest church. When a pious soul found his body the next morning, looking as though he'd died in prayer, the magistrates had come. Bishop Madruzzo immediately requested Sister Lena and the Catherinites of St. Martin to tend to the poor man's body, and Madruzzo conducted a funeral that afternoon.

"Is that why St. Sebastian's runs a hospice?" Chiara said. "To ease us into the handling of death?"

"We keep a hospital for incurables because caring for the dying is a work of mercy. So is instructing the ignorant," Magdalena said. "If you carry the ideas forward, preventing the ignorant from being persuaded to heresy is another work of mercy. The Church has a responsibility to teach truth and to suppress lies."

Chiara said, "Your name was last in the ledger." No accusation in her eyes, only a statement. "You came to this convent upset because you killed a man. But that wasn't the man you killed, was it? So you did it again."

Magdalena nodded. "I may have to do it more before this council is over. Heresy is a disease—contagious like the plague. Officials will shut off entire cities due to the plague and leave everyone to die rather than risk a spread through the whole world. When people try to escape and carry the contagion out, the soldiers send them back. They'll even kill them."

Chiara sighed. "I didn't want to believe people could be that stubborn. If you explain to them how they're wrong, won't they reflect and amend their thinking?"

"Have the Lutherans?" Magdalena paused. "Have the Huguenots?"

"No." Chiara looked sad. "God have mercy on them. We can't execute all of Germany."

"We can't let the Church become Germany either."

Chiara said, "The council promised safe conduct to any heretic who came to us from the Germans or the French."

"Those are never the ones we target." Magdalena met Chiara's eyes. "It's only our own. We have to clean our own house."

"Cardinal Reginald Pole was in there. Nezetta was on his line. His arrest was called for at the same time as Cardinal Morone, but Pole didn't come. So she must have been assigned to go to him." Chiara's eyes darkened. "Do you remember that story? I do. It was Pope Paul IV, and everyone hated him for it because they had a trial for Cardinal Morone and the tribunal said there was nothing wrong. But Pope Paul kept him locked up like a prisoner for the rest of his papacy. He's still a cardinal, so they must have let him out afterward because he wasn't a heretic." Her eyebrows raised. "What if Pole wasn't a heretic either?"

Magdalena shook her head. "When these men became priests, they promised to trust the judgment of the Church. If the Church convicted them of heresy and they weren't heretics, then I guess they were martyrs."

Chiara stretched. "This is more than I thought it would be. We need to go back."

"Will you put back the book? What if the chest is locked where you took it from?"

"I thought of that. It's in Sister Lena's office, so I'll slide in the book with other things. It will look as though someone forgot to put it away properly, and at any rate," Chiara added, "that's true. I only got to the book because the chest was unlocked."

They climbed back to the ledge, Magdalena first. Chiara tucked the book into her habit. Much tinier than the book Magdalena had liberated for Cardinal Simonetta, this ledger had no risk of unbalancing the younger nun. They descended the wall, springing down the last fifteen feet. Magdalena retrieved her shoes, and they walked back through the chill to the convent.

Chiara said, "Not every nun's name is listed. I hope they never send me."

"You're here because you've never found a book you didn't love." Magdalena smiled. "Maybe your job will be to tend to the books."

# SIXTEEN

"The French," Simonetta muttered while writing.

Seripando looked up from yet another draft of the reform statement on the episcopal duties of bishops with the faintest smile on his lips. It relieved Magdalena to see he was more amused than concerned by Simonetta's irritation. "Pope Pius very much wants them to attend."

"And yet he's afraid of what will happen when they do," Simonetta retorted, not looking up from his paper. "Now we get to find out the demands of the mighty Cardinal of Lorraine, Charles de Guise."

"We're already relatively certain what de Guise has on his mind." Seripando looked at Magdalena. "Will Saint Martin's supply him a nun as well? He's an important man, and anyone with terrible intentions would be certain to consider him a target."

"You would have to ask Sister Lena," Magdalena said. "When does he arrive?"

"This afternoon." Simonetta huffed. "All of France intends to parade into Trent with their coterie and a retinue large enough to entire fill Madruzzo's palace on their own. Here." He held out his cup to Magdalena. "I need more tea."

As she prepared tea for Simonetta, Seripando said, "You will see them, my dear. Gonzaga and I are going to greet them at the gates and escort them into the city, so you will be at my side. Bring the other novice too. Chiara? It's certain to be a spectacle, and surely she'll enjoy the sight."

Magdalena brought the tea to Simonetta, who said only, "The French. Finally putting in an appearance to prove to us the Spaniards weren't as bad as we thought."

After an early lunch, Magdalena brought Chiara to the grand hall of the palace, where they waited with Cardinal Seripando for the appearance of Bishop Ercole Gonzaga. Nezetta followed him, several steps behind but keeping her eyes alert for any dangers. Magdalena's cheeks heated up: she'd let her mind wander, but she should be doing the same.

"Come," Gonzaga said. "Cardinal de Guise would be irritated in the extreme if we cause his retinue to delay their entrance."

As they went to the waiting carriage, Chiara whispered, "Is Cardinal de Guise that awful?"

"He's a lovely man," Seripando said. Magdalena often credited him with supernatural hearing because she herself had barely heard Chiara. "But he's rather conscious of status. That's a French idiosyncrasy, but he's a brilliant man, very earnest, very willing to do whatever is necessary to help the Church."

The date was January 2nd, and a brittle cold crept in around the edges of the carriage. Magdalena and Chiara pressed against each other to keep warm, clutching their shawls tight around their habits. Lately they'd both taken to wearing their exercise clothes beneath their traditional habits, but against this weather, none of their garments were much help.

At their intended destination, they breathed into their hands while the noise levels rose outside. Finally a servant fetched them out. It was time.

Chiara and Magdalena stuck close to the legates, wide-eyed as they moved through a crowd forming up into a procession the likes of which Magdalena never would have dreamed of participating in.

Rome had processions all the time, of course. But in relation to the sprawl of the city you hardly noticed the crowds. In Trent, it felt as though the whole city had gathered. Perhaps they all had.

The legates climbed a low series of steps so they had a higher-than-head view of the plaza, and the nuns accompanied them.

Over a hundred bishops had gathered in the Porta Santa Croce, along with all the legates and all the government envoys. So many colors and so much noise. A band played. Cheers erupted. Then, to cheers, the French arrived.

A dozen French bishops processed into the square, accompanied by theologians and abbots. And all their servants. And among them, a tall man in red.

"Behold." Seripando leaned in between Chiara and Magdalena. "The Cardinal of Lorraine."

Magdalena stood on her toes. Beside her, Chiara gasped. "He's so young!"

He was young in comparison to all the other bishops and theologians around him. He must have had top-notch patronage to rise through the ranks so quickly, but here he was, poised to be one of the most influential of the council attendees, and he was only just old enough to have been Magdalena's father.

Chiara breathed into Magdalena's ear, "He's handsome."

Magdalena whispered back, "He's probably got a concubine. Or two."

Chiara shook his head. "Absolutely not. If he did, *that* one would have complained about it."

Magdalena followed Chiara's gaze to Simonetta, who looked as though he'd been handed a well-thumbed copy of the collected sermons of Martin Luther. She giggled, and Chiara snickered too.

Seripando said, "Easy, daughters."

"I'm sorry." Magdalena clasped her hands around each other. "So many Frenchmen."

In addition to all the officials came hundreds of liveried individuals, and even more in uniforms Magdalena couldn't identify.

Simonetta strode over. "Where are we going to put all these people? Trent isn't big enough. Prices will rise even more."

"Madruzzo freed up a suite for de Guise," said Seripando. "Of the rest, I'm not sure."

Simonetta sighed. "The pope doesn't have money in infinite supply."

A horn sounded, and the legates remained in place at the top of the steps while the procession approached. When they reached the front, the procession stopped, and they bowed to the legates.

Gonzaga bowed in return, then descended the steps with Seripando. Simonetta remained at the top with Hosius, but Magdalena slipped through the crowd to make sure she was close to Seripando.

Thank goodness that embarrassment of a cardinal, the fifth legate Sittich, had already been sent home. Magdalena couldn't imagine how badly he'd have mucked up the proceedings.

As de Guise shook Gonzaga's hand, he looked at the nuns who had come up close, and he caught Chiara's eye. Chiara's fingers dug into Magdalena's arm.

The pair of legates walked with de Guise at the head of the procession, taking a route via the widest of the city streets all the way to Santa Maria Maggiore.

De Guise positioned himself between Seripando and Gonzaga, and Gonzaga said, "I presume you have a memorandum to present."

"Thirty-four articles," de Guise said, his mouth a clever smile. "We worked hard to get it to a mere thirty-four."

Gonzaga chuckled. "The *zelanti* are going to wring out their handkerchiefs."

Seripando said, "The pope heard that you had a meeting with the Lutherans."

"I had hoped they would negotiate," de Guise said. "I tried to conciliate them by any means possible, but of course there are so many issues we can't compromise. The Huguenots were the same way."

Seripando put a hand on de Guise's arm. "Of the thirty-four, which are your most important? Because right now, we're at a crossroads about episcopal reform, and we could use your skill as a mediator."

Gonzaga added, "Not that you've succeeded so admirably with the Lutherans."

Magdalena tensed, but de Guise laughed heartily. "True enough! But I would hope my fellow bishops aren't as hostile as the heretics."

"They're perhaps more so," Seripando said. "As unable as we are to compromise with one another, it's no surprise we can't compromise with the schismatics in the north and in the west."

"Communion under both kinds," de Guise said. "There's no reason to keep the sacred cup from the people. We also want the Mass said in French, and for priests to marry."

Magdalena shot Chiara a look, eyebrows arched, but Chiara shook her head.

Gonzaga nodded. "That's perfectly reasonable for discussion. I'll want to see the articles before you present them. Would the next session be acceptable to you? Mid-January."

De Guise nodded. Gonzaga added, "Do beware the *zelanti*. They'll fight you tooth and claw for every concession."

"It makes no sense." De Guise looked at Gonzaga, and Chiara's eyes widened as she got a better look at his face. "We're on the same side. We serve the Church."

"They don't think so. Or rather, in their zeal to protect the papacy, they think reform of any kind serves only the devil."

"If the devil wants French peasants to understand the beautiful words of the Mass," de Guise said, "then the devil isn't very good at his job."

"Similarly," said Seripando, "if the devil prompts souls to thirst for the Eucharistic cup, then we have a much less effective enemy than we thought. Just bear in mind that the pope gave so many of these bishops their livelihood. They feel a distinct loyalty, albeit misplaced, and whenever you suggest the pope has perhaps assumed too much power, they bristle like porcupines."

"If union with the Germans is an idea of the devil," de Guise added, "then the devil is of the same mind as Christ who wanted all Christians to be one." He sighed. "Now, tell me about these nuns who follow us so closely while watching only the crowd."

Chiara went white, and Magdalena shot a helpless look at Seripando.

Gonzaga said, "They're bodyguards."

De Guise laughed in shock, in rapid succession taking in Nezetta and Chiara and Magdalena. "What?"

Magdalena lowered her eyes. Under the scrutiny of de Guise, Chiara would be beet-red and skittish as a centipede.

Seripando said, voice low, "The one on the end saved my life. Most likely you will be assigned your own escort."

It wasn't difficult to imagine which nun would get the assignment. Unassigned and highly-skilled, Chiara was the obvious choice. Plus, she'd occasionally covered for Magdalena with Cardinal Seripando.

On the other hand, propriety dictated that a beautiful young nun not be assigned to such close quarters with a man in his prime as handsome as de Guise. Perhaps Nezetta, older than de Guise, or Sister Lena herself—although Simonetta was unlikely to surrender the honor of having the abbess as his personal attendant.

For that matter, Lena might assign Chiara to Seripando and transfer Magdalena to de Guise, but the thought made Magdalena's stomach tighten. It shouldn't. She forced herself to breathe deeply as she walked, telling herself that she needed to go where the Church needed her. And also that she shouldn't get attached to any one man. He was just a cardinal, just a representative of the Church to whom she'd sworn allegiance. The fact that he was nice made no difference. If assigned to someone else, she should leave without a backward glance.

Should. She squared her shoulders and continued the walk to the cathedral, but she watched only the crowd.

# SEVENTEEN

In addition to three hundred people, de Guise had brought Trent a library.

Tadea gave daily reports about the dozens of bishops and theologians who visited de Guise in order to read his books. To Chiara's relief and frustration, Tadea had been reassigned to shadow de Guise. Chiara filled in as before, working wherever they needed her.

It turned out her vow of chastity (and his) wasn't the cause of her distress.

"It's not fair," Chiara whispered one night in bed. "All those books, and I could read them."

"Simonetta thinks you're too young," Magdalena said.

"I'm not too young to read," Chiara muttered. "I'm not too young to do all the other nonsense he wants me doing. I'm not too young to empty chamber pots or sit up all night with the dying or scrub floors. But dust the shelves of a cardinal with a thousand books? Only an old nun could do that."

Magdalena giggled. "Simonetta hates de Guise and wants to deprive him of your company."

Chiara snorted. But there was no way to change the situation.

Chiara sometimes worked assisting Madruzzo himself. Because Madruzzo didn't express any theological opinions, Simonetta had in some respects crossed him off the list of people who concerned him, so he did nothing about Chiara's occasional service. Chiara spent some mornings in the palace, some at the hostel, but oftentimes drifted about assisting the other nuns. When Simonetta was furiously writing a proposal or a position paper, he might have Chiara functioning as his runner.

One day in February, when Seripando was about to take a trip to de Guise's library, the old man addressed Simonetta with a disarming calm. "I'll need the little novice today."

Simonetta looked up from his desk, puzzled.

"I am making a trip to de Guise's library for books." Seripando was absolutely deadpan, but he had to be up to something. If you rang for the servants, they'd bring a cart and enough manpower to carry fifty thousand books. Seripando continued, "I'll need help sorting and fetching, and because she can read, she would be most useful."

Simonetta glanced at Chiara. Magdalena could see into Simonetta's mind just as if it were a crystal wine glass: it would be convenient to know which books Seripando selected, and he'd expect a list on his desk before *none* tomorrow, alphabetized by title and author's name.

"Of course." Simonetta waved Chiara over to them. "Don't work her too hard. She's a child."

In the hallway, a giggling Chiara took Seripando's hand as if he were her delighted grandfather—which he almost looked like, with his eyes sparkling against his wrinkled face. "Thank you! I was beginning to think I'd never see the books!"

"I hope they live up to your standards." Seripando sounded amused. "Do you think Heaven has a library?"

"Wouldn't it have to?"

Magdalena said, "Why would it? God already knows everything."

"But He wants to teach it to us," Chiara shot back. "That means He must have a university. If there's a university, surely it has a library. At the very least, there has to be a copy of the Bible, and once you have one book in Heaven, it's not a far leap to having lots of books."

Magdalena shook her head. Seripando said, "My dear, don't discount what she says. I too hope God has a library filled with majestic and edifying books."

Magdalena didn't interject that maybe for some, that would be Hell. Reading was still a chore for her, and it seemed that the bookmakers took a special pleasure in putting out their work in a Latin so convoluted that Julius Caesar himself would have struggled.

Chiara said, "Doesn't the Bible say there's a Book of Life in Heaven?"

Seripando beamed. "Indeed there is. Now Heaven has two books to start its collection. We must assume God will gather several thousand more to keep them company."

Chiara looked at Magdalena. "By the way, I found us in the Bible too."

Magdalena stared at her, puzzled. "You found us?"

She nodded. "In one of the psalms, it says, 'With God I can fight an army; with God, I can scale a wall.' Who else could David have been writing about?"

That was getting uncomfortably close to things they shouldn't talk about, so Magdalena didn't reply.

At de Guise's suite, Tadea showed them in, but the cardinal himself swept out of the next room to greet them. "Girolamo Seripando! Come in, be comfortable. You brought two nuns with you," he added. "Am I so dangerous?"

"The only true dangers lie between the covers of a book," Seripando retorted. "I wanted to do some research, and our youngest novice has been thirsting for your library since the

167

moment of its arrival. I smuggled her in so she can rest happy at night."

Chiara blushed redder than a cardinal's hat. "You're very welcome then," de Guise said. "I would mourn to see one of our industrious Catherinites perish because of a book."

Chiara stepped into the library room with a gasp. "It even smells like books!"

Magdalena wouldn't have identified it so quickly, but the air hung thick with the smell of leather and animal glue, dust and paper. Madruzzo had provided tall shelves, and books stood at attention along all the walls. Additionally he'd provided several desks, and two large lecterns stood at the end.

De Guise said, "My friend, which books are you seeking today?"

Seripando settled himself in the chair nearest the fire, and Magdalena brought one of the small tables closer. "Thank you, my dear." He turned to de Guise. "How are we to proceed, Charles? Have you received news about our Church's two newest cardinals?"

De Guise looked abruptly serious. "No news has reached me."

"Allow me then to introduce the new members of the Curia." Seripando rubbed his temples. "Federigo Gonzaga, our dear chief legate Ercole Gonzaga's *nephew,*" (Magdalena wasn't sure which kind) "who is an honorable eighteen year old—"

De Guise huffed.

"—and Ferdinando de' Medici, who may in fact share a birthday with our sweet Sister Chiara."

Chiara turned her head. De Guise muttered in French as he paced to the window.

"Tell me again," de Guise said in a flat, angry tone, "how we are to trust the pope to reform the papal court."

"I wish I could tell you. I don't know whether this is a move by Pope Pius to remind Gonzaga of some presupposed allegiance to the papacy," Seripando said, "or whether it's such an ingrained tradition that even desiring reform, the pope cannot stop."

De Guise said, "I cannot expect the pope to solve a problem he doesn't understand."

Both Tadea and Magdalena paid attention for tonight's reports.

"Then it's the job of the council to make him see it." Seripando raised a hand as de Guise started to object. "But carefully. Carefully, otherwise we will find ourselves holding a council that no longer exists."

De Guise frowned. "He wants the council to go forward. Pope Pius backed down last year when Gonzaga threatened to resign."

"Understood, but he also doesn't want the council to go *too far* forward. He wants it very carefully in place, somehow reforming the Church and at the same time changing nothing. Gonzaga thinks he may be able to accomplish this, and he's already done so much." Seripando chuckled. "Some of the more obstinate bishops have no idea how well he had them in hand several times when it appeared we'd achieved a permanent stalemate. But even Gonzaga can't reform the Church without reforming it."

De Guise kept glaring out the window.

"The pope is wise in many of the wrong ways." Seripando glanced at Chiara as she settled on the floor with one of the smaller books. "He harassed and stonewalled Gonzaga until Gonzaga sent his resignation. It was our dear Carlo Borromeo who intervened and negotiated peace between them."

De Guise's nose wrinkled. "Yet Borromeo is another of the pope's relations."

"Oh, but give him credit," Seripando murmured. "Borromeo is at heart a reformer, even right at the side of the pope. He's sensible and spiritual. Borromeo recognized that if his uncle accepted Gonzaga's resignation, all the reform-minded bishops would leave, and after them the envoys and theologians. I read the letter Pius sent to Gonzaga, and it is filled with Borromeo's phrasing."

"I'll trust your judgment." De Guise shook his head. "If you're right, I wish Borromeo were pope."

"Not now, please. If the pope dies, the council ends immediately. Then we'll have to hold a fourth period, and heaven only knows when that will happen." Seripando signed himself with the cross. "May Pope Pius IV live another twenty years if that's what it takes."

De Guise laughed out loud. "He may need to live as long as Methuselah."

"Perhaps after two centuries, perhaps His Holiness will mellow about a bishop's residence requirement."

De Guise moved quickly to a chair alongside Seripando. "Talk to me about residence. It seems the bishops have already fought, resolved it, fought again, and now are deadlocked, and I cannot for the life of me fathom why."

Seripando waved Magdalena over. "My dear, if you wouldn't mind freshening up our tea?"

Magdalena had to leave the room for a few minutes while the two cardinals had yet another discussion of the impediments to bishops being bishops in their own diocese as opposed to collecting the money for a diocese (or two or three) and living elsewhere. And the wording. The endless fine points of the wording, *jus divinum* versus whatever other turn of phrase the reformers favored. She could recreate the argument on her own without either man present. She'd let Tadea write this report.

By the time Magdalena returned with the tea pot, de Guise and Seripando had changed topics.

"By moving to Innsbruck, the emperor is close enough to Trent that he can more effectively influence the process," Seripando was saying. "For him to move his court here, the emperor must be incensed at the progress reports he's getting from his envoys."

De Guise said, "Not that I blame him."

"I fear his pressure is not going to have the effect he desires."

De Guise rubbed his chin. "It's only a hundred miles to Innsbruck, correct? I will go speak to him in person. At the very least I can assure the emperor that not every attendee wants a permanent stalemate, and maybe I can enlist his help in some practical matters."

Seripando smiled wanly. "This Council is the very opposite of practical."

"He wants it to succeed, and he has his own influence with the pope. Imagine," de Guise said, "if we could get the emperor to grant us full freedom in formulating our decrees so all our documents don't have to go through Simonetta and then back to Rome, where they get debated and then rewritten and then sent back to us as boneless statements. Imagine if we had a greater contingent of bishops from outside Italy, or maybe even from Germany, to outnumber the *zelanti*. And with all due respect, sir, imagine if the legates were not the only ones who could propose our agenda. The French and Spanish reform items could be discussed and worked in full. Once it's known to the larger Church that we're tackling those items, surely we'd draw more bishops from France and Spain."

Magdalena glanced at Tadea, wondering if she'd be sent along with de Guise on such a long trip. And then, with a skip of her heart, she had a second thought. A second self-serving thought unworthy of a bride of Christ.

"I would advocate for this all," de Guise said. "I would have the emperor visit the council himself."

"Sir," Magdalena said, "are you sure you can travel so far? The council looks up to you."

"The council needs no single man when the Holy Spirit is in charge." De Guise sounded amused. "A hundred miles isn't such a long trip. A few days at most, and we need this support for the council's success."

Magdalena turned to Seripando. "And you—would you also travel to Rome to speak to the pope?"

Rome. She'd have to accompany him. She wouldn't be there more than a few days, of course, and there would be five days each way in a carriage...but she'd see her mother. She'd be able to hold Fiora and watch her walking with her stick and her shoes. She could teach Fiora other ways to defend herself from the increasingly nasty Marcoli family.

Seripando shook his head. "I don't expect a summons to Rome until the council concludes, no more than I expect His Holiness to come here."

De Guise muttered, "I wish Pope Pius would come here."

"I have no such wish. The *zelanti* would become more than insufferable, and half the reformers would leave." Seripando looked directly at de Guise. "Pius's strategy seems no less multifaceted than Gonzaga's, in that he carefully commits but does not commit, and the rest of us dance on the ends of our tethers as we seek a means to complete our work." Seripando looked back at Magdalena. "So you need not worry, my dear. I will not stuff you into a carriage and force you to travel."

She inclined her head. "I would gladly accompany you every step of the way."

"You never complain about anything." Seripando's face broke into a grin, and he turned his eyes on Chiara. "The closest that any one of you has ever come to complaining is our dear Chiara, who very much desired to read the books, which you, Charles, have so inconsiderately locked away in your library."

"What have you found?" de Guise asked her.

Chiara held up a book. "It's a little life of the Blessed Virgin."

"As told to a mystic," de Guise said. "I wasn't certain about bringing that one. It's not forbidden, but it's an example of how a book can be at the same time not forbidden but not necessarily edifying."

Chiara frowned, then kept reading. Magdalena hid a smile.

De Guise stood. "I have other business to attend to, but please feel free to use the library as long as you like. I'll make travel arrangements for Innsbruck, and with God's grace, we can prod the council into moving forward."

# EIGHTEEN

Cardinal Seripando started up from a paper he was reading in his office. "My dear, I apologize," he said to Magdalena. "I forgot to mention this earlier, but Cardinal Simonetta desired to see you."

Magdalena paused with an empty breakfast tray in her hands. "Right away?"

"I can spare you now," said Seripando.

Lena met her at Simonetta's door, looking grave. "Come in."

Agnella and two other sisters were already there.

"I have orders." Simonetta looked uneasy. "Orders from the pope, and they're explicit. I cannot find a way around them."

He extended a letter, but none of the nuns took it. Magdalena finally accepted the paper, which Simonetta seemed to expect her to read aloud. Of course it was in Latin, and she didn't have a hope of sounding it all out. She wished Chiara were here.

Then in the middle of a paragraph, that word: "*Haeresis.*" She kept scanning. There was its mate: "*Sententia.*"

"An execution," she said. "And it's..."

Her eyes flew over the paper scanning for a name.

"Cardinal Ercole Gonzaga?" she exclaimed. "But—he's a legate! The chief legate?"

Simonetta made his way back to his seat. His uneasiness made all the more sense now.

Magdalena shook her head. "Sir, no. Write the pope again. Assure him Gonzaga isn't a heretic. Gonzaga wants reform, but he's not against the Church. He loves the Church. You can hear it in how he talks about the Eucharist, and—"

"Sister Magdalena, hush." Simonetta wrung his hands. "I'm not the decision-maker."

"You're the news-bringer," she shot back.

Simonetta's eyes stared into her like live coals. "Mind your manners."

Lena stood. "She's in shock, sir. Please forgive her breach of protocol. If the pope has ordered this, of course we'll carry it out."

Gonzaga was an old man. An old man in a position of power, certainly, but not that dangerous. Why not just remove him from the Council? Why not promote him to a position where he'd talk to no one and influence no one (which was, coincidentally, the fate Sittich von Hohenems had earned for himself by being an embarrassment to the papacy)? If the pope were to summon him back to Rome for consultation, it would look natural to keep him there, then just send word that Gonzaga's health wasn't up to a return.

The council had been in its third session for a year. If the principal legate were going to do harm, wouldn't he have done it by now?

But no. Magdalena had to steady herself. There had already been two occasions where Gonzaga had threatened to resign, and both times it had turned into a terrible uproar. How shameful it looked for the papacy that the pope's own legate couldn't run the show. Private executions were necessary when and only when having the individual censured in public would cause great harm, great scandal, or great disruption.

If Gonzaga left or was sent home, the reforming bishops and the reforming envoys would leave. They'd said as much last time. That's why the pope had refused his resignation, and that's why Carlo Borromeo had interceded so he would stay.

But now the pope had said... The pope had decided. If after an examination of the evidence and a trial the verdict had been conviction of heresy...and heresy dangerous enough to warrant death...how could she object?

She stared again at the letter, wrestling with the unfamiliar words. Simonetta had access to the legates that even their order didn't have. The legates spoke amongst themselves while setting the agendas. Gonzaga might have been heretical out of her presence.

Other sources. Surely the pope wouldn't make such an important decision based only on one man's letters. Someone else must have been gathering information and exercising prudential judgment.

Lena said, "Is there a date on the order?"

Simonetta shook his head. "I assume sooner rather than later. I will write to Rome when it's completed, of course."

Magdalena handed Lena the paper, and the abbess folded it and slipped it into her sleeve. Simonetta looked surprised, but Lena said, "I'll have our annals-keeper read and record. Afterward, I'll burn it."

Simonetta said, "How will you take action?"

Lena met Simonetta's gaze, steady like a stone staircase. "That's for us to decide."

He said, "It has to be done circumspectly."

"Sir, we carry out the pope's orders, and the pope has put his trust in us." There was undue emphasis on the word *pope*. "We will let you know whatever is in your best interest to know."

Simonetta's face hardened, and Magdalena stared at the carpet to keep composed. He wanted command over them, but he couldn't entirely object.

Outside, Magdalena said, "What are we going to do?"

"We're going to let that man stew for a while about the fact that he's not actually the one who gives us orders. We're in the service of the pope, not in the service of the pope's lap dog." Lena huffed. "Did you ever hear of Cardinal Innocenzo Ciocchi del Monte?"

Agnella made a disgusted sound. "That brute? Isn't he still in prison?"

"He's out again. He always gets out. In my most sinful moments I hope he'll stop at Saint Martin's for an overnight, but his presence would be the proximate occasion of mortal sin." She shook her head. "He got promoted to cardinal because he took care of the pope's monkey. By contrast, no one is promoting me to cardinal, therefore I will not spend my time mollifying any of the pope's pets. If Cardinal Simonetta is unhappy, let him write poison pen letters about me too."

Agnella gave a sardonic laugh. "He's got his pen in his hand right now. Those subversive nuns are an enemy of the papacy and have taken it upon themselves to determine how best to carry out the pope's orders to perfection, not consulting me even though I have nothing useful to add."

Magdalena's eyes widened. "You know he does that?"

"Of course he does that," said Lena. "It's a game to curry favor for himself and slowly sideline everyone he doesn't like." She shrugged. "If the pope chooses to authorize another community of nuns to take over our work, I'm more than happy to cede our commission. But he won't."

Agnella said, "We're too good at what we do."

Good enough that they were talking freely in the street and drawing no attention. For all any passersby knew, the nuns might be talking about ministering to the needs of fussy legates and annoyed envoys and exhausted bishops. Criticism of a former pope about whom rumors swirled like flies around a rotten orange? Not at all unusual. Any random conversation in Rome's streets would have heaped far worse insults on clerics who still held their positions. And bravado, of course. Always the bravado.

It was bravado that was bruising her brother and wrapping her sister in fear. Bravado that kept her mother on a bed of pins every day, wondering if tonight was the night she would stitch a burial shroud for her son.

At the convent, some of the nuns went into the exercise room. Magdalena followed Lena and Agnella into the abbess's office. Lena asked Tadea and Nezetta to crowd into the room with them.

With the door finally shut, Magdalena said, "We can't do this. He's a legate. He's a high-standing member of the Church."

Agnella shook her head. "It's unsettling at first, but other than when there's an immediate danger, we're only ever sent after clergy and high-ranking church officials. We're never dispatched for commoners or theologians writing in German lands to their fellow Lutherans. That's not our job."

Lena said, "Agnella's absolutely correct. I'd have to check our records, but while we might have handled a theologian or two, I'm pretty sure there are no sentences we've carried out against a member of the laity unless, like the brute who tried to kill Seripando, they're pretending to be clergy. If they can pretend to be priests, they can die like they're priests."

Agnella said to Magdalena, "Taking out that assassin was the aberration."

Lena waved a hand. "You can't hang priests in the public square or set fire to them on hilltops. It's bad for the faithful and causes the laity to live in fear. Plus, their execution would galvanize our opposition, especially when what they're opposed to is the power of the pope. Have the pope kill someone who questions papal authority and you might as well sign papers authorizing another schism."

Lena unlocked her chest, and Magdalena had a fleeting fear when Lena didn't immediately come up with the record book, that maybe Chiara had taken it out again, and then relief when Lena withdrew the ledger. She handed it to Tadea, who recorded all the details from the letter into their proper places. After the list at the back, there were lengthy sections in the beginning that required paragraphs of writing, all in Latin.

"Suggestions?" said Lena.

Nezetta said a word Magdalena didn't at first recognize, but there was quick agreement from Tadea. Lena nodded. "I thought that might work, but I wasn't sure."

Agnella said, "I don't trust it. I'd rather climb through the window and ensure it happens quickly, all at once. In the morning, the servants make the discovery and then we swoop in before the doctors arrive. Madruzzo will have us prepare his body for burial. The doctor won't disturb him, and we'll get him encrypted by dinner time."

Lena shook her head. "With this many guards and soldiers, that's madness. The Swiss Guard are likely to want Gonzaga examined when he doesn't awaken, and their presence would keep us from gaining access. Also, there's always the possibility of a struggle, meaning blood. We can't risk observation in this kind of overcrowding and with someone as high-profile as the principal legate. A direct strike has worked when our target wasn't prominent enough to require an inquest, or when there wasn't a security force available on a moment's notice."

Agnella said, "The dosing is going to be tricky though. If it takes several days, what if the doctors recognize the symptoms?"

"I can dose him properly." Nezetta's voice was calm, factual. "I brought the ingredients with me from Rome. We resorted to this method with Reginald Pole, and no one suspected then either."

The hair stood on Magdalena's arms.

Agnella said, "Most doctors can recognize poison."

Poison?

Nezetta fingered the sleeve of her habit. "This formula doesn't behave like a poison. Dose it low enough and death comes on like a head cold, then pneumonia, and finally fatality. He'll die of illness." Nezetta opened her hands. "Trent has harsh weather. He's been doing hard work and keeping long hours and visiting with people from all countries. He doesn't sleep enough. He's old. Given all that, they'll assume the obvious. The doctor will order him to bed, and we'll tend him."

"That leads to a different consideration." Tadea looked up from her book. "The first Council period ended early because of rumors of plague. Are we likely to set off another flight?"

Nezetta shook her head. "Plague has distinct characteristics. Gonzaga's death will look exactly like a body wearing out in response to the constant fighting."

Magdalena said, "Which will be true, won't it?"

Agnella caught her eye. "Exactly true. If he weren't fighting the pope's authority, he wouldn't be about to die."

# NINETEEN

With a bow in her back, Nezetta was the oldest of the Catherinites. She had tended the sick in Rome with a gentle hand. She spoon-fed the incurable dying who were too weak to do more than swallow thin gruel, gently dabbing the corners of their mouths after every mouthful.

That night, she spent all her hours mixing and cooking. The result was a stoppered bottle. She set the iron bowl directly into the fire and filled it with boiling water. "That isn't good for food anymore," she reminded Lena, and then with the morning light tucked herself in her thick shawl to head for Madruzzo's palace.

The weather turned brittle, so Magdalena stayed indoors. She prayed in the chapel. She attended every one of the liturgical hours with her sisters.

Nezetta didn't return that evening. Snow accumulated on the street, so the hostel guests demanded meals delivered to their rooms along with additional firewood. Magdalena mopped puddles of melted snow out of the entrance. She kneaded rosewater buns the way her mother had taught her to do on days when inclement weather kept them indoors back in Rome. While the snow fell, she made enough buns for everyone in the hostel. With those set to rise, she prepared additional batches of fried sweet buns. It wasn't a Friday, and it wasn't yet Lent, so the nuns had one apiece before dinner and then delivered the rest to their guests, still hot, as a surprise.

Fiora had never seen snow. Magdalena had seen it only once as a very small girl. It had come in the morning and been gone by noon. Instead she had known winters of thick fog and an otherworldly morning stillness that splintered into the cries of the city streets as the day came on. In Trent the snow came and stayed. It snuck through your clothing and clung to your feet, and you lost sensation in your toes as you walked to the cathedral.

She'd written home a long letter, trying to explain the constant smell of smoke and how the low skies kept it trapped, and when it back drafted into the houses, letting it out meant letting the chill inside. She'd tried to illustrate for Mother and Domenico and Fiora the snow starting out as an unbroken layer that got ruined when the first sturdy soul headed outside. Once that happened, it never returned to the same kind of smoothness, no matter how the wind blew. It was just like sin on a blameless soul, and only a miraculous wind of the Spirit could have blown it back into something like it once was. She wrote about endless puddles in the walkways and how the flakes clung to your hair outside, dry, only to soak you through when you came indoors and they melted away.

Fiora would laugh at that. She'd write back asking Magdalena to send her a parcel of snow so she could run it through her fingers and feel it dripping down her neck. But by the time Magdalena's letter got to Rome, and by the time a reply returned, perhaps it would be spring. Instead she'd press flowers and send those in her letter.

Outside, the wind howled. Inside, the warm convent smelled of rosewater. Beauty, Chiara had said. Rosewater took the visual beauty of a flower and turned it into the beauty of taste and smell. But did it also give a beautiful touch? Could the softness of a rose petal be considered beautiful, or the slippery quality of the rosewater when you added it to your baking? Did the petals make the faintest of sweet sounds as they absorbed the water in their jars and sank to the bottom to begin their long steep? When that happened, was it the sound of beauty?

For *lauds* in the dark hours, the convent was frigid. Magdalena wore her shoes to prayer and stayed bundled in her shawl. Afterward, she and Chiara huddled in bed, pooling their warmth and breathing under the covers to save the heat of their lungs. It wasn't better in the morning, but they built the fire and set kettles to boil before rushing to *prime.*

Lena said to Magdalena, "Today you'll come with me to the palace." Bundled in everything they owned, they walked through the snow with numb toes and clumsy fingers. It was the last day of February.

While walking, Lena said, "Witness the final reason Agnella's plan was delusion. Icy stones and ledges, wet handholds, and slick rooftops. Nezetta will have remained warm the whole night, tending the fireplace in the legate's suite."

"Agnella can't predict the weather," Magdalena said. "Neither can you."

"Agnella just likes to climb walls," Lena retorted. "The weather or the lack of moonlight only adds to her fun, but I'm less interested in her thrill-seeking than in completing our task."

When they finally reached Madruzzo's palace, the Swiss Guards ushered them immediately into a parlor to warm themselves. The hearth was large enough to stable a horse, and it must have taken a whole tree to fill it with fire. Sensation returned to Magdalena's hands and feet like needles pushing through her skin, and shortly the little perfect crystals in her hair yielded in the presence of such prodigal heat. Water dripped down her neck.

The nuns knew not to exhibit too much curiosity, so when Magdalena arrived at Cardinal Seripando's suite, she began by preparing his tea, clearing away his breakfast dishes, and straightening the room. Seripando had a meeting with two theologians to discuss reception of the Eucharist under both kinds, then wrote a note for Magdalena to deliver to a bishop staying elsewhere in the palace.

When she returned, the bells were tolling noon. A servant stood outside the suite with a wheeled cart containing Seripando's meal on a tray. "Here," Magdalena said, rushing to open the door for her. "Come in."

Seripando looked up with a smile. "Oh, dear, I've no space..." he said, looking over his desk.

"I'll set you up over here." Magdalena hurried to one of the chairs near the fireplace. "You should sit closer to the fire anyway. You don't want to catch a draft."

He walked slowly to the chair she positioned near the fire, and she laid out his meal for him. The servant departed.

"This is too much," Seripando murmured. "My dear, you hardly eat at all. Please, come have some as well."

Magdalena objected, but he was already portioning out part of his meal onto one of the smaller plates. She moved an upholstered chair near and sat opposite him.

"Is the weather truly brutal today, my dear? You shouldn't come from the convent on such days." The cardinal studied her. "The nuns of Saint Martin take such good care of us, but surely this is an imposition. There are plenty of servants in the palace."

Magdalena smiled. "The pope ordered us to be at your service."

"Posh. You mustn't obey if it puts your health in jeopardy. Yesterday you stayed home because of the storm," he added. "Today it isn't storming, but it's just as cold. You could have remained in the convent today as well."

Magdalena smiled as she sipped her tea. "Idle hands do the work of the devil."

"You would by no means be idle at the guest house." He laughed. "I've heard from Chiara about the labors there. You'd be at work before sunup and after sundown, plus you'd be in and out of the chapel praying the liturgy of the hours, not to mention your other prayers." He pointed a bony finger at her. "I know your kind. You are busy about the work of the Lord. But the Lord doesn't require you to freeze. If it sets your soul at ease, I hereby dispense you from coming to the palace during unseemly cold."

"Dispense me?" Magdalena laughed. "Are you the pope?"

"It's not only the pope who can offer a dispensation." A smile softened Seripando's face. "A bishop or a priest has certain authority to dispense."

Magdalena thought a moment. "If priests have the power to offer dispensations, then why is there such an argument about how bishops derive their power?"

"Ah, so you've been listening. Be careful about these questions, or Ludovico Simonetta will mistrust you as well." He took a bite of beef in a creamy sauce. "You're referring to the *jus divinum* argument. Some bishops believe that if it's a divine law that a bishop must behave as a bishop, or a priest as a priest, then that makes the pope somehow less the pope."

Magdalena frowned. "How can they argue against bishops doing the job of bishops?"

"You speak like a Roman. You've never lived in a diocese without the bishop in residence. There are many, many, many. This is a scandal, and the Lutherans rightly objected to it. Why should a bishop live somewhere other than his diocese? How can a bishop do his job while luxuriating in a palace hundreds of miles from his diocese? Moreover, how can that absent bishop soon be the bishop of seven dioceses?"

Magdalena's eyes flared. "But surely they can!"

His worn face grew very sad. "They *can*, because they do. I argue that they cannot do it *well*, let alone do it in a way befitting a servant of Christ. Instead, worldly priests or bishops collect their benefice, spending the money without performing the duties. The first segment of the council addressed exactly this problem, but my dear, the situation is not improved. We thought it prudent to mention that under certain extraordinary circumstances, it might be best for a bishop to live elsewhere. As with the sessions for this council, for example. Or in case of war, a bishop might have to flee for safety."

Seripando sipped his tea and looked out the window at the too-bright glare of daylight on snow-covered rooftops. "But in response to that concession, every bishop immediately applied to the pope for a dispensation, and of course he granted it. Thus the push for stronger wording: if a bishop's role comes from divine law, no pope can dispense from it."

Magdalena frowned. "Why not?"

"The pope can't dispense against a sin." Seripando didn't seem annoyed by having to teach. If anything, he seemed to enjoy it. "The pope can dispense obligations that are merely a matter of practice, such as abstaining from meat or attending Mass if you're far from home. But he can't dispense a mother from the obligation to ensure her child's welfare, or a husband from the obligation to remain faithful to his wife."

Magdalena huffed before she thought about it. "Is that why so many cardinals have children?"

"Ah, you did say you were a Farnese," Seripando murmured. "There is no dispensation involved in those cases. That's sinful human nature as old as Eden, and a culture in Rome that embraces these sins as funny rather than a grave scandal that reeks before Heaven."

Magdalena recoiled. "I'm offensive to God?"

"Never." He patted her hand. "You are made in God's own image. In response to the evil of fornication, God brought forth a truly blessed creation." Seripando sighed. "In response to several generations of the evil of fornication, in fact. You yourself may be the product of sin, but that doesn't make you any more sinful than a child conceived in a lawful marriage."

Magdalena rubbed her chin. "Would...would Cardinal Simonetta feel the same way?"

Maybe this was why Simonetta dithered about writing to Rome to stop the feud. Maybe he thought of her and her brother and sister as the refuse of the street, and that it would only be to Rome's improvement if they were gone.

"Ludovico would think nothing of the sort. He's a stern man," Seripando clarified, "but he's stern about things of the Church."

"My great-uncle was a thing of the Church. My great-grandfather was a thing of the Church."

Seripando chuckled. "In which case, my fellow legate should think you very good and therefore beyond reproach."

Magdalena laughed out loud. "Never! He says I talk too much." She picked up her tea cup. "Do you have any children?"

"You've gotten very comfortable with me, my dear. Perhaps you do talk too much." Seripando grinned, his eyes wrinkling. "No, I have none."

She shrugged. "It doesn't seem like an impertinent question. Gonzaga has five."

Seripando shook his head. "He admits to having had a wayward youth. In his old age, he's repented. If you ask him, he will tell you outright that part of the reason he yielded to temptation, or in fact sought it out, was the callous way everyone viewed sexual sins in the clergy. But you see now why we would benefit from *reform of the head*," Seripando added. "Because when everyone knows the pope himself is keeping a bedtime companion, why would those working beneath him do better? Not our current Pope Pius IV, but certain others have done this. And yet *reform of the head* is exactly what Ludovico Simonetta and Stanislaus Hosius— and Pius himself—do not want to have."

Magdalena glanced out the window. "It doesn't benefit the pope to limit the pope's power."

"The pope's primary job should not be the benefit and comfort of the pope!" Seripando retorted. And then, when Magdalena let slip an incredulous expression, he continued. "Pastors should be pastoral. Shepherds cannot tend their sheep by messenger from inside the palace walls. The Holy Roman Emperor wants reform. The princes of Spain want reform. The French want reform."

"You can give them reform," Magdalena urged. "You can vote on it."

"And we could by doing so convince the pope to disband the council." Seripando leaned back in his chair, weary. "I hope it won't come to that. Many if not most of the Italian bishops are beholden to the pope. He's made their lives easier, done them favors, or elevated them himself. They're not going to jeopardize their own interests, and therefore," he added, his eyes growing dark, "they won't ever vote for anything that remotely resembles *reform of the head*."

"That's not fair." Magdalena's hands trembled. "How can the council get anything at all done under those circumstances?"

"As you can see, very little has been done. I've attended all three periods of the council so far." Seripando rubbed his beard. "I've spent more years in Trent than ever I wanted to. You see how slowly the wheel turns. A thousand years may pass, and Christ Himself may return, and we'll have to ask Him to wait while we pass a measure pushing our vote on the current docket to the next session."

WITH TWO EYES INTO GEHENNA

He chuckled, a soft, creaky laugh that left Magdalena unsure whether she should join him or just sit by in horror. "Surely it won't take that long."

"Exactly those words were uttered halfway through the first time we attempted to hold this council." Seripando shook his head. "I'm afraid the council has taken a toll on all of us. The weather here is terrible, and this city is not gentle on old men like me. Gonzaga took ill last night."

Folding her hands, Magdalena looked at her lap.

Faint church bells came to them through the windows. "Oh," Seripando said. "I don't often hear them in this part of the building. Is it time for *sext*?" He leaned over and put a hand on Magdalena's. "Say the Office with me today. I'm not one of the sisters of Saint Martin's, but I would enjoy the company."

Together they prayed, and Magdalena fought a tightness in her stomach that wasn't from a rich cream sauce. Gonzaga had taken ill. Nezetta had begun the process of completing his sentence. It was only the rhythm of the familiar prayers, the trust they engendered and the hope Magdalena craved, that kept her from running the halls to beg the operation to stop.

# TWENTY

On March 2nd, with the weather wet and the air heavy, everyone in Trent feared the worst for Gonzaga.

Lena and Agnella seemed tense. Simonetta fretted when they saw him, but no one spoke during the times they met in passing. If Lena and Simonetta conferenced while she worked for him, Magdalena didn't know it. For her part, she stayed with Seripando as much as possible.

Worry lined the old cardinal's face. She caught him from time to time praying in low Latin whispers, a tiny sound that tugged at her heart. Meanwhile, in the same building, Nezetta fed Gonzaga medicated death by spoonfuls in order to heal the Church.

Seripando prayed all the liturgical hours with her now. He scheduled his meetings around them, and Magdalena took comfort in their routine. His worry for Gonzaga was bringing him closer to the Church. This was good. He'd abandon his heresies, and all would be well.

After *none,* Magdalena answered the door to find a servant with a message. "Would Cardinal Seripando please come to visit Bishop Gonzaga? They have sent for him."

Seripando leaned on Magdalena's arm as they walked. He wanted to hurry. "Is there an emergency?" Magdalena asked.

The servant said, "I don't believe so. Bishop Gonzaga asked for him, that's all."

Still, Seripando didn't slow his pace.

When they arrived at Gonzaga's suite, the room smelled of illness. The scent drowned Magdalena in an instant, bringing her back in time to that moment she'd struck her confessor in the throat and shot shards of bone into his Adam's apple. It was the stench of blood in a urine-filled alleyway where she'd ended the life of a bishop-impersonator intent on murdering papal legates. But it wasn't the smell of blood, nor the smell of the hospice. This time it was just the smell of death. It weakened her knees.

Nezetta sat in a corner, crocheting. The white thread came up from a basket at her feet and ended in loops strangling other loops to create fabric that created art. By her elbow, on a small table, sat a tray filled with a variety of stoppered bottles. One of those contained poison.

Seripando walked forward holding Magdalena's arm, and she accompanied him as though he were carrying her rather than she supporting him. At the bedside sat the superior general of the Jesuits, Father Diego Laynez. "Cardinal Seripando." He stood. "He asked to see you."

Seripando took the younger priest's hand. "I'll sit with him a while. Why don't you get some rest? You look exhausted."

Laynez looked no less exhausted than Seripando, but he acknowledged and left the room.

Seripando lowered himself into the chair Laynez had vacated, and he reached for Gonzaga. "You've got everyone worried, but it's time to show everyone your toughness."

Gonzaga forced a smile, then coughed painfully. Magdalena rushed toward him, helped position him more upright on his pillows, and straightened his covers. When Gonzaga kept coughing, Nezetta brought him a cup with hot tea. Magdalena didn't know if it was dosed.

It didn't matter. Gonzaga pushed it away, and as he did, the loose sleeve fell away from his hand to reveal his arm. Grey spots pockmarked his arm, each the size of a button and looking lifeless while the skin surrounding it was yellow.

With him upright enough to breathe easier, she tucked his covers back around him. There was a little whistle every time he inhaled.

Seripando said, "You don't have to talk. You aren't alone. I'm with you, and the sisters are with you, and Christ is with you."

Magdalena tidied the room, but not much needed to be done. She longed to throw open the window to the afternoon air and release the smell, but the chill would be such a shock to Gonzaga's lungs that he'd die right there. Seripando himself might take cold. Seripando asked her to search on Gonzaga's desk for his breviary, and when she found it, he had her fetch a lamp. He read passages out loud.

Lord, let Gonzaga forget his heresy, Magdalena prayed. He's coming to You, so please, let him come with a clean soul. Let him repent the harm he wanted to do to Your Church before he arrives at Your doorstep.

A servant of Madruzzo asked if anything was needed, and Seripando requested holy oils and more candles. Shortly these things arrived by the hand of Madruzzo himself, so Magdalena avoided him, stoking up the fire and straightening out the papers on Gonzaga's desk. She didn't worry about Gonzaga's privacy. Too soon there would be no more secrets.

Madruzzo and Seripando performed the last rites. They gave Gonzaga final absolution. They administered Holy Communion. Then they anointed him, praying in Latin while Gonzaga slackened into the cushions.

After they finished, Magdalena nestled each little vial into the case in its velvet niche, the crucifix tucked into its own compartment, and shut the lid with a click. Madruzzo bid goodbye to Gonzaga, bending and kissing his forehead.

Seripando sat heavily, grief lining his face.

Magdalena accompanied Madruzzo to the door, but when he reached the hall, he turned to her. In a low voice, he urged, "Stay with Seripando. He's going to need someone nearby."

This wasn't just an execution, Magdalena thought as she returned to Seripando in the room of death. This was taking too long with too many bystanders, like Agnella's tormenter with the blunt axe and twenty death blows. Every inch that Gonzaga came closer to death was a part of Seripando being executed as well.

Gonzaga slept. Magdalena said, "Let's pray the rosary," so Seripando prayed with her and Nezetta. They had no sense of time in this room and couldn't hear any church bells echoing over the snow-covered rooftops. Maybe it was time for *vespers* but maybe not. And yet they traveled through the sorrowful mysteries: whipped alongside Christ, mocked at His side, burdened with the instrument of His own death, and then nailed to it to hang until all the life had been wrung from His body.

Father Laynez returned, still looking worn, but maybe having gotten rest and a meal. You couldn't eat here, with the miasma of death all around. "Thank you for keeping watch for me. I'll call you back if I need you again."

Seripando shook his head. "I will stay."

The soft words did what nothing before had done. Not the smell of the room or the depressed grey circles on Gonzaga's skin. Not the chrism with its sharp scent and not the Latin prayers. Seripando's soft refusal brought Magdalena to tears, and she pivoted to keep him from seeing. Until she could get them under control, she busied herself finding a second chair for Laynez. If he saw her tears, he kept silent about them.

The sun set. Dinners arrived and remained uneaten. Nezetta spooned heated sweet liquid into Gonzaga's mouth. *Stop.* Magdalena wanted to shake her. *Stop. It's nearly done.* But Nezetta would have him drink that cup right to the bottom, and Magdalena's assignment was Seripando.

The other nuns should have returned to Saint Martin's by now. They'd be saying *compline* and readying for sleep. Chiara would be warming up their bed on her own, breathing on hands tucked up under the blankets while Magdalena added more wood to the fire in an already-stifling room. Gonzaga needed to be upright to breathe, and Magdalena kept a full kettle boiling on the hearth to moisten the air. With the night impenetrable outside, she found an extra blanket and placed it around the shoulders of Seripando. He never noticed.

He was her concern. Her job was not to see to the death of Gonzaga, but to sustain Seripando.

She kept the lamps lit. She answered the door when the servants knocked, and she sent messages back via those same servants. The palace staff cleared away the uneaten food and brought a tray of lighter fare. Magdalena encouraged Seripando to take some broth, but after a few sips he set it aside.

Did angels gather around a dying man? They must. This room must be filled with angels coaxing the soul to repent, guarding its fragile edges as it pulled away from its human shell like withered autumn leaves one at a time letting go of their branches to flutter aground. In the midst of so many angels, of so many prayers in His name, surely Christ Himself was with them.

Maybe the room was filled with angels, but Magdalena couldn't know. She also didn't know at what time of the night Gonzaga died, only that she hadn't heard church bells in hours, and that it would be hours more until the sun rose. It happened with the same slippery smoothness that water took on when you infused it with roses, only the opposite. At first there was one thing with two natures, and then the soul had slipped away and it was two things with one nature each. Before the separation had been a great theologian and bishop. Afterward there lay in an elegant four-poster bed the material husk of a man while his spirit returned to the Almighty. Humans hadn't been designed to separate from their bodies. Death was the final insult, like trying to boil the roses back out of the water.

Seripando had dozed on and off through the night. He was the one who discovered Gonzaga unbreathing and his body cool. It was he who covered Gonzaga's face with the blanket and told Father Laynez to extinguish the lamps.

Nezetta stood. "Magdalena and I will prepare the body."

Seripando said, "She's worked all day. Let her rest."

Nezetta said, "She needs to do the work of the Lord."

"I will walk you back to your quarters." Magdalena's voice was raw. "Then I'll return here to help."

To her, Seripando had always been an old man, at first rickety and later just awkward, but now he felt fragile. Magdalena guided him through the corridor, light flickering from the candle in her left hand while she supported him with her right. Every so often he'd murmur to himself, but she couldn't make out the words. He sounded defeated.

"He worked so hard for this council," Seripando whispered. "He wanted to see it through."

"He can pray for us." At least Magdalena hoped that was the case.

"Of course. But it never seems just when God calls a soul home before it completes the work God Himself entrusted to it. Moses didn't enter the promised land. David didn't get to build the Temple. It happens to the best of men," Seripando mused. "I never understand why God leaves it to another man to finish the work of the first one."

JANE LEBAK

Magdalena said, "Maybe it's to keep us humble. Maybe that way, no one man can become a hero beyond criticism."

Seripando chuckled. "Be careful with that line of thought. They'll brand you a reformer."

Magdalena smiled. "Then we can take another approach. Maybe sometimes the work is so important that God wants to share the beauty of it with more than one person."

"Ah." Seripando relaxed. "That sounds sweeter to my old ears. *Precious are the feet of him who brings good news,* and therefore precious are the hands doing the work of the Lord. In this way, God makes more hands more precious, and His very generosity gives Him an excuse to love us more profligately."

They reached his suite, where Magdalena escorted him all the way in to his bedroom. She set the candle on his bedstand. "Would you like me to stay?"

"You can go back to your work." The defeat had returned to his voice. "There's no need to sit at my bedside in waiting. I am not a dying man."

# PART THREE
## PRINCES OF BLOOD

# TWENTY-ONE

March 3rd dawned painfully early, after Magdalena got a few stiff hours of sleep crammed on the couch in Gonzaga's suite. She and Nezetta had prepared the body, pockmarked with sunken grey circles from shoulders to toes. In the deep dark, as they dressed the body for viewing, Magdalena wondered if those circles penetrated all the way through the layers of skin and muscle. Did concave circles dot Gonzaga's heart and lungs and liver? One at a time had every one of his vital parts succumbed to the little dead areas?

Magdalena checked on Seripando immediately, only to find his suite soundless and him still asleep. In his outer parlor, she took refuge on his sofa and started praying the rosary, only to fall asleep and then startle awake to the pealing of church bells. Many, many church bells.

She ran to the window but from here could see no church towers. The angle of the light meant it was probably the hour for *terce*. She felt unsteady, maybe hungry and maybe nauseated.

It must be that at the general congregation, Madruzzo had announced Gonzaga's death. Now every church in Trent was tolling their grief. Over and over, as the word spread, each new church would ring its bells. There would be announcements nailed up on the doors for those who could read. There would be a funeral, most likely not today and maybe not tomorrow either, so every bishop and dignitary could pay Gonzaga their final respects.

Simonetta, in his suite...was he grim with the knowledge that the pope's orders had been carried out to the letter? Or was he at the general congregation, feigning surprise and agreeing that yes, this was an immeasurable loss?

Sometime today Simonetta would pen letters to Rome. The pope would likely not replace Gonzaga with another legate. Simonetta and Hosius together outnumbered Seripando alone as a reformer. Given his sole possession of the pope's ear, Simonetta would become principal delegate, and the pope would have then no question about them meddling in "reform of the head" because no one alive had the power to do so, even if they had the inclination.

*It is with great sadness that I inform you of the death of Ercole Gonzaga.* How do you say such a thing when the one to whom you were writing was the one who ordered the death? What are the correct words when that death wasn't a tragedy so much as a necessity for the Church's survival?

So many letters would fly off to Rome that surely Magdalena could include one for her mother. A courier didn't care for one extra sheet of paper, and Seripando often slipped her letters in with his own. If the couriers were charging him, he'd never asked for extra money from her.

Magdalena drew up a chair near the window to see that the snow hadn't melted since yesterday. In this suite, it was so much cooler than last night in Gonzaga's over-fired rooms.

When the church bells stopped tolling, she let herself into Seripando's bedroom. The fire had guttered down to a grey heat, so she stirred it and laid on another log. The fireplace tools clanked by accident as she set them back.

He roused. "Sister Magdalena?"

"It's me, sir. I didn't mean to disturb you. I'm sorry."

"Did I sleep so late?" He sat up, groggy. "Open the windows. We've let the darkness remain in here too long."

She drew the curtains so vertical light streamed into the room. "I'll bring in your breakfast. The servants delivered it earlier, but I didn't want to disturb you."

She wheeled in the tray with its covered plate of biscuits and dark bread, then set the tea kettle on the fire.

"Send word downstairs," Seripando said, hoarse. He pushed himself out of bed, looking unsteady. "Find out what arrangements Madruzzo has made. There will be a funeral, but when?"

Magdalena pulled the rope, but when no servant appeared, she went downstairs herself. Bishop Madruzzo was absent, attending the general congregation, and servants rushed everywhere to make arrangements. The master of the house said Cardinal Simonetta was in charge of the funerary arrangements.

Magdalena returned to Simonetta's suite, where a servant at first said she couldn't enter and then realized she was one of the Saint Martin's nuns and escorted her into the parlor.

Simonetta looked startled by her appearance. He was already meeting with Lena, Nezetta, and Agnella.

Lena swept over to her. "How are you? Did you get some rest last night?"

Magdalena nodded. "What's this?"

"We needed to report back, in the aftermath. Why aren't you with Cardinal Seripando?"

Magdalena shook her head. "He wanted information about the funeral."

"We will hold it tomorrow at noon," Simonetta said. "Bishop Madruzzo wants it at Santa Maria Maggiore, and Bishop Gonzaga will be laid to rest temporarily in the tombs beneath the church."

There was a momentary silence, and Magdalena shifted uncomfortably. "Do you need a report from me?"

"That can wait," Lena said. "I'm sure Cardinal Seripando is very shaken by Gonzaga's death, so you need to stay with him."

"I'll come speak with him soon," Simonetta added. "But he shouldn't be left alone now, not even for five minutes."

Magdalena hesitated, but no one offered any more comments, so she slipped out of the room.

Half an hour later, Lena and Simonetta arrived at Seripando's suite, and Lena sat with her in the parlor while Simonetta went into his office. "It's difficult to watch them die by stages." Lena shook her head. "Nezetta knows just how to administer that concoction so it mimics a natural sickness, but it's so effective that it's difficult to watch. Even the doctors don't realize it's not pneumonia. Only a few Spaniards know this potion exists at all."

Magdalena shivered. "Now I understand Agnella's insistence on just climbing through the window."

"Different circumstances require different techniques. Imagine if Gonzaga had been found slain in his bed." Lena spoke low, very nearly into Magdalena's ear. "We're careful, but if someone had gotten to his body before we did, or worse, if someone found out after we'd arranged his body? Where would sympathy go?" Lena shook her head. "We'd have created a martyr. The moderate members of the council would feel a push to finish Gonzaga's work for him, and that's the opposite of what the Church needs. Even worse, bishops might fear for their own lives and call off the council entirely, something his holiness doesn't want under any circumstances. This way, it's just tragic, but the council will go on." She patted Magdalena on the knee. "Ours is a difficult path, and it requires fortitude in ways you never thought of before."

Magdalena couldn't look up. "Have you ever climbed to the ceiling of a cathedral?"

Lena chuckled. "Do I look like a Roman?"

"I have." She squared her shoulders. "That takes fortitude too. You can't decide halfway up that it's too difficult to go on."

"This is the same. You can't decide halfway through that it's enough just to scare the person. Nezetta is a stable woman for this work. You shouldn't have been in there last night."

"Cardinal Seripando wanted me there," Magdalena said. "You just said I can't leave his side."

Lena chuckled wryly. "He shouldn't have been in there either. A man of his age and constitution should have been frightened of catching the same illness. Madruzzo certainly was. Seripando should have stayed away until he was told the end had come. You didn't try to warn him about contagion."

No, that hadn't occurred to her. She'd known it wasn't contagious and hadn't thought about how someone would have reacted in ignorance. Of course she should have told him she feared contagion.

Simonetta returned to the parlor. "Did you do as we discussed?"

"Not yet." Lena took Magdalena's hand. "You need to take your final vows, and—" she kept talking even though Magdalena gasped, "—it's time to initiate Chiara."

Magdalena glanced at Simonetta. "You said she was too young."

Lena said, "She's proven herself trustworthy."

Simonetta said, "Because you began your work together, it's fitting that you conduct her initiation. It's an important work, and the person in charge should be someone the initiate looks up to but also is familiar enough with to behave normally."

Magdalena studied Lena. "What are you talking about? Is this initiation something we didn't do in Rome?"

Simonetta pulled up a chair. "I sent you to retrieve the forbidden book, remember? Every sister of the Catherinites has to pass the book retrieval as a test of your skills and your nerve. Sister Agnella accompanied you to gauge your performance, but not to help."

Magdalena frowned. "She showed me where your residence was."

"Yes, and you nearly failed the initiation for that reason," Simonetta said, "but Sister Bellosa convinced me that was initiative instead of arrogance." He looked annoyed. "We will set up a similar test for the other novice. We'll lay out the forbidden book, and you will take her out at night to retrieve it. In the morning, that book is to be at your convent, not in my parlor."

"Yes, sir." Magdalena didn't dare glance at Lena, in case Lena hadn't heard this story from Simonetta before. Although given his penchant for telling tales, Lena had probably heard it five times.

"We should do it in about a week. You'll also spend time until then in prayer and adoration. Before Chiara's test, you'll take final vows." Lena didn't make that sound as momentous as she should have. In most convents, final vows were a large celebration, followed by a party in the parlor with your family on one side of the grate and you on the other. But in most convents, you didn't climb walls or wear daggers. "We conduct our book tests during the full moon because it's easiest to see then. The weather will have time to clear, and you'll have opportunities to assess any weaknesses in Chiara's training."

Magdalena shrugged. "She's an excellent climber. I've seen her climb carrying all sorts of things." For example, a forbidden book to the crown of a raftered church ceiling. "Why would she need to be tested at all?"

"It's part of our rule." Lena shrugged. "Once she completes that, she'll learn the rest of our order's mission, and she'll be better able to assist us with the council."

*She already knows.* That was the danger of picking out the smartest and most restless nuns from convents where they felt stifled. When you put a bunch of headstrong women under the same roof and gave them the skills to carry weapons and climb masonry, you might suddenly find nuns sitting on statuary holding books you thought you'd locked up. Suddenly your secrets were a whole lot less easy to keep. This meant, undeniably, that Chiara had gotten that book back into its slot undetected, and it also made Magdalena's job a bit easier. She wouldn't have to hide anything from her. She could just take Chiara, retrieve the book, and come home. After that, there would be no more concealment.

---

The full moon came on March 10th.

At *compline,* Lena called Magdalena to kneel at the front of the chapel. Lena began the litany of the saints. At its close, she went to stand before Magdalena.

"Sister Magdalena of the Theatine order of the Catherinites, having lived and abided by our rule in the period since your first vows, what is your desire?"

Head bowed, Magdalena responded, "With the help of God, I ask to profess my eternal vows to the order for the glory of God and for the service of the Church."

Lena said, "May God, who created you and saved you and abides in you, now sustain you in your profession of final vows."

Magdalena prostrated herself, and Lena sprinkled holy water over her. "Your religious consecration represents the eternal union between Christ and His Bride, the Church. Your vows commit you to imitate Christ's totality of love and self-emptying, placing the Kingdom of God above all earthly considerations and offering the service of all your heart, all your soul, all your strength, and all your mind."

Magdalena said, "Amen."

"Do you vow poverty, to relinquish all material goods in this world for the sake of the Kingdom?"

"I do."

"Do you vow chastity, promising the powers of your body to God alone for the sake of the Kingdom?"

"I do."

"Do you vow to resist heresy in all its forms, to resolve to uphold the law of God as defined by the Church and all her doctrines and all her dogma?"

"I do."

"Do you vow obedience to the pope, on whose orders we serve for the sake of the Kingdom?"

"I do."

Sister Lena had her rise, then placed her hands on Magdalena's head. "Heavenly Father, we ask you to bestow on your daughter Magdalena the crown of virginal excellence, that as she sacrifices her body and her will here on earth, that even more may be added unto her in the Kingdom of Heaven. We ask this through the merits of Jesus Christ Your Son, who lives and reigns with You and the Holy Spirit, one God, forever and ever."

"Amen."

Lena stepped back. Her eyes were glistening, a realization that shook Magdalena's heart.

Lena smiled. "Congratulations, Sister Magdalena."

The other nuns applauded, and when Magdalena turned, Chiara glowed with joy.

# TWENTY-TWO

After her first *lauds* as a fully professed nun, Magdalena and Chiara returned to their cell to don exercise clothes, shoes, and leather gloves.

In perfect silence they scaled the wall to the convent roof and made their way from building to building. When a jump could take them across a gap, they jumped, but other times they climbed half a story up a ledge or sprang down to land in silence on the roof of a lower building. All the while the moon watched overhead, high and clear. Only a week ago, they'd both stood at Seripando's side during Gonzaga's funeral.

The targeted building towered over the one they stood on now. Magdalena pointed to a pair of windows, and Chiara nodded. While Magdalena remained in place, Chiara found handholds and made her way up the side like a spider. Even in the full moon it was hard to pick her out of the darkness, but Magdalena knew where to watch.

Magdalena huddled around herself, wishing she'd been able to bring a shawl. The snow had evaporated, but the air remained frosty. The longer she waited, the more her body heat began to dissipate.

Meanwhile, the black shape of Chiara's body appeared at the rim of the roof, then vanished.

Watching the front of the building, Magdalena observed Chiara cross over, then lower herself down. Unlike in summertime Rome, Chiara had to work open a glass window before she could enter, but shortly she must have gotten it open because she swung her legs over the ledge and disappeared.

Hugging her knees in a squat, Magdalena waited. The winter night made no sounds. In Rome she'd have been able to hear insects, but Trent was the echo chamber of death itself. Nothing moved and nothing called to its fellows.

Then, solitary in the hills, came a howl. A wolf. She smiled. Maybe it was the great-great-great grandson of the wolf Saint Francis had negotiated with. Maybe it was just a wolf who wanted everyone to know that although the humans had packed together into cities, the cities themselves were in fact alone in the wild, dots of human defensiveness in the midst of God's creation full of feral things, life that grew and did as it would without any discipline and without any concern for what it consumed.

Chiara emerged from the window and made her way back up the side of the building. Something was wrong. No, no, Magdalena tried to reassure herself that Chiara didn't look unsteady or uncertain at all, that it was a trick of the eye combined with the lack of light. Chiara seemed off-balance, but she was moving more quickly now than when she'd gone in. Had she been discovered? Discovery wasn't part of the plan. Simonetta had promised that this suite would be unoccupied when Chiara entered.

A minute later, Chiara appeared at the edge of the roof and began her descent. She really wasn't moving well—now it was certain, even in the pale light. What had happened to scare her? Had the book not been there? Was she rushing back to find Magdalena so they could make another attempt before daybreak?

Chiara didn't know it was a test. She shouldn't be nervous about it.

When Chiara got back to the level of this roof, Magdalena rushed to her. She wasn't supposed to help, but at the edge of the roof she offered her arm and assisted Chiara away from the ledge.

Chiara dropped to her knees. She covered her face with her hands, shaking with a terrifying violence.

"What happened?"

"That wasn't a book. That wasn't real." Chiara sobbed as she shuddered. "What did you do to me? What did you do? Why did..."

Magdalena tried to hold her, but Chiara pulled away.

"What's going on?" Magdalena whispered. "Did you get the book?"

"That wasn't a book." Chiara pitched forward onto her hands and knees. "It wasn't a book."

She vomited, and Magdalena sprang back instinctively. Chiara heaved again, and then she wiped her face with her sleeve, crushing tears and mucus into the fabric.

"You tricked me." Chiara slumped to the side of the foul puddle she'd just disgorged. "It's a book. It's not a book. I hate you. You knew."

Magdalena tried to get her upright, but Chiara struck her away. "We have to get back. I want to go home. Now. Right now."

Magdalena hissed, "You need the book!"

"You're not listening! I know it's not a book!" Chiara staggered to her feet and lurched to the roof's edge. "You don't have to pretend."

She wobbled, then said, "I can't do this. We have to get to the ground. I can't."

Refusing Magdalena's help, she started down. It wasn't far. It was only a story and a half, nothing she hadn't done a hundred times already and sometimes with an object in each hand. But before Magdalena's horrified eyes, Chiara slipped and plummeted to the dark ground.

Magdalena hurried to her. Chiara was shaking all over. She wasn't just cold: there was more vomit on her clothing. The younger nun didn't struggle anymore when Magdalena got her onto her feet and started walking her, one arm over her shoulder. Chiara staggered like someone drunk.

What on earth had happened? Magdalena wanted her indoors, in front of the fire and with the other nuns to look her over, but she couldn't hurry her and wasn't sure Chiara would be able to keep on her feet. Every so often Chiara would stop, and Magdalena would coax her into another walk. The cold was numbing her fingers and feet. They should have been sprinting over rooftops with a book in custody, triumphant. Instead they were faltering home with nothing but questions, and with Chiara damaged.

At the hostel, Magdalena brought Chiara in the front door and right downstairs to the convent. Chiara whimpered, "Our cell. Take me to our cell," but Magdalena pushed her the other way, toward the infirmary. Once there, she lit candles and stirred up the fire, but Chiara got out of the bed and tried to make it down the hall. She collapsed. Magdalena attempted to lift her into the infirmary bed, then thought better of it and ran down the hall for Lena.

Magdalena didn't knock, just flung open the abbess's door. "Sister Lena. We need you. Now. Chiara."

Lena sat up, squinting in the light of Magdalena's candle. "Did you bring the book?"

"She's saying it wasn't a book. I don't understand, but Chiara's hurt."

Lena's eyes widened, and she made the sign of the cross. "Where is she?"

Magdalena raced back to the infirmary, but Lena stopped to bang on a cell door. Magdalena didn't pause to see whose. When she reached the other hallway, Chiara had made it back into the corridor and was crawling toward her cell.

"Back," Lena ordered behind her. "You need medicine."

When Chiara raised her face, tears streaked her cheeks. "You knew. You tricked me."

Magdalena said, "She keeps saying that."

Ignoring Magdalena, Lena wedged herself under Chiara's arms and half-dragged her to the infirmary. "Lie down. Let's see."

She stripped off Chiara's gloves, and although her hands looked okay, Chiara yanked back. Lena took her wrist, and Chiara screamed.

"Did you open the book?" Lena demanded, stern. "This is important! Chiara, did you open the book?" To Magdalena, "Get me scissors."

Nezetta appeared in the doorway. "Magdalena," Lena insisted, "the scissors."

Flustered as she was, Magdalena couldn't find them right away. When she finally handed them over, Lena took Chiara by the wrist. Chiara howled, and Nezetta moved in to secure her.

"Don't cut off my arm!" Chiara shrieked. "You're cutting off my arm!"

Lena sheared along the seam of Chiara's exercise shirt, opening it from bottom to top, and as she did, Magdalena retched. Chiara's arm was bright red and swollen to twice its size.

Nezetta stoked the fire higher and set a pot to boil.

Lena whispered, "You opened the book."

"It wasn't a book." Sweat beaded all over Chiara's terrified face. She was shivering, and Magdalena brought her a blanket. She only thrust it away. "Let me out of here! I have to get away!"

Lena said, "Magdalena, we need to secure her. Now."

As Chiara tried to stand, Magdalena squeezed behind her and held her around the chest. Chiara thrashed, but Lena was able to cut off the rest of the shirt to expose her arm. Nezetta brought a basin with tepid water mixed with a handful of salt, and they made Chiara immerse her arm in it while Magdalena pinned her. Nezetta then set some of the coals from the fire into a small kettle and dusted an unfamiliar incense over them. The scent of sandalwood filled the room.

"Theriac," Lena said, but Nezetta already had removed from their cabinet a jar the size of an orange and set it on the table. She took a tiny spoonful of the salve and told Chiara to keep it under her tongue, then lifted the swollen arm out of the water and rubbed more salve into the skin. Chiara gasped when Nezetta touched her arm, but the older nun crooned at her, soothing. When Chiara settled and her skin was more slippery, Nezetta rubbed it in so she smelled of cedar, musk, and lavender. Then they returned her arm to the salt water.

Chiara's face was flushed, but her skin was pale everywhere else: at the edges of her eyes and all around her lips. She shook with a fever.

"Chiara," Lena whispered, "can you answer me? Where is the book?"

"I dropped it. When I realized...I left it there. I wanted to get out. Get home."

Lena kept her voice low. "So you opened the book?"

Chiara swallowed hard. "It wasn't a book."

"I know it wasn't. Did you open it?"

Chiara shot a nasty look at Magdalena. "You tricked me. I'm going to tell Jesus what you did."

Lena said, "Can you move your hand?"

Chiara shook her head.

Nezetta said, "I found the bite marks. They're near the bone on her wrist."

Magdalena said, "Bite?"

Lena glared at her. "Yes, bite! It's an Italian asp. Its bite shouldn't be reacting this quickly." She shook her head. "It shouldn't be reacting at all. This isn't right."

Magdalena didn't move from between Chiara and the wall, not even when Chiara tried to push her away. Magdalena was more awake than she'd been in all her life, even under the moon on the rooftops in Rome. Even those mornings gathering flowers. Every instant kept pressing itself into her awareness, like roses pressed all around by tonic water. She watched as Nezetta made a medicinal preparation and Lena murmured to the young nun. She listened to Chiara's breathing and the rasp of Chiara's voice. She watched the swelling travel up Chiara's arm, and she noted every crackle and pop of the fire as it devoured the logs and aroused the room to a livid heat.

Chiara sweated and shook, and eventually she slackened back against Magdalena with her eyes closed. Chiara was exhausted. Even if it hadn't been the middle of the night, that much shivering and agitation would have exhausted anyone, but she was dying. Lena brought the blanket to spread over her, and this time she didn't resist.

Nezetta's hands, hands that had so carefully measured out the ingredients to take the life of Ercole Gonzaga, now measured out ingredients to preserve the life of Sister Chiara Pasqualigo of the Catherinite convent of Saint Martin. Lena, who had swept their legs out from under them without a second thought in the exercise room, crooned encouragement and worked to keep Chiara calm. Magdalena cuddled her. Chiara, who had shared her cell and her bed for the last year, seemed finally to take comfort in that. It was a familiar presence, something most likely to lull her to sleep.

"Stay with us," Magdalena whispered.

Chiara whispered, "It was a test, wasn't it?"

Lena bit her lip. "Yes. We needed to know you wouldn't look."

Chiara's voice faltered. "I failed."

Lena stroked her hair. "You did."

Lena fetched a priest who lodged in the boarding house. He was bleary-eyed and with his coat thrown over his pajamas, but after one look at Chiara, he immediately set up for last rites. Chiara made no response, so he prayed over her in Latin, then broke off a tiny piece of the Eucharist and set it on her tongue. He anointed her eyes with oil, then her nose and ears and on and on and on, and he prayed again, resting his hands on her. The whole time, Magdalena joined the prayer silently in her own head, afraid Chiara would die before he finished.

But she didn't. With her anointed, the priest left, and Nezetta started the rosary.

Lena said in a flat voice, "Should we amputate her arm?"

Magdalena gasped. "No! You can't!"

Nezetta looked grim as she stopped her recitation. "It won't do any good. The poison's in her whole body."

Lena said, "If your arm causes you to sin..."

Nezetta shook her head. "Her arm isn't causing her to die. Her blood is, and we can't remove her blood."

Magdalena squeezed Chiara's good hand, but Chiara didn't squeeze back. Nezetta resumed her prayers.

When Chiara started wheezing with every breath, Nezetta slathered alcohol on her chest, then made a poultice of garlic and several other herbs. She heated up heaven-only-knew what and added it to the salve on Chiara's arm. The tight skin was red all the way to her shoulder, but her fingers were pale and cold. Her hair was sweaty. And sometime before the nuns awoke for *prime,* she stopped breathing altogether.

Magdalena kept holding her. Lena said she was gone, but Magdalena thought no, no, they just had to get her warmer and Chiara would recover from this. Asps don't kill with their bites, and why would she have been bitten by an asp anyhow? She'd only climbed a building to get a book, nothing more. Could the fall have hurt her? But no, her skin was cold and her eyes were unresponsive and she wasn't breathing...and Lena pried Magdalena away. The abbess laid Chiara flat on the cot to cover her with a sheet.

Magdalena stood, head bowed and fists clenched at her chest, struggling to breathe and wondering if, after all these exercises and commissions and spiritual promises, she'd forgotten how.

# Twenty-Three

Magdalena attended a funeral that evening. Chiara lay in state all day, and people came from the hostel to pay final respects and pray for her. Several looked in vain for someone to talk to about things Chiara had done for them to make their stay in Trent more comfortable, and finding no one, they talked to the abbess. Sister Lena agreed with everyone that it was tragic. Magdalena sat in one of the seats and remained by the body.

Chiara, gone. Just a body.

In the evening, one of the bishops said a funeral Mass in the church, and they laid Chiara to rest in the tombs belowground. There were no architectural fixtures here, nothing for her spirit to climb on and cling to if human souls really could ghost the places they had died. It would have been different in the main church, where Magdalena would have imagined Chiara sitting on the ledges alongside the stained-glass windows, or maybe now that she was free of all human concerns, dancing on the spires adorning the altarpiece. Chiara could climb the clock tower and watch, sparkle-eyed, whenever the church bells tolled.

After the funeral, Magdalena found the basket with Chiara's crocheting in the corner of their cell. She knew nothing about lace-making, so she left it alone.

"May I come in?" Lena said behind her.

Magdalena's mouth tightened. "You're the abbess. You set the rules."

"I set the rules, but that also makes you my responsibility."

Magdalena folded her arms. "You haven't been doing a very good job."

"Apparently not." Lena stepped into the room. "Every one of us has undergone the book test, and there have only been a few failures through the years."

"That can't be true. There's only recently been an index of banned books," Magdalena said. "Before then—"

"Before then, we had other means of testing loyalty and secrecy. The development of the Index dovetailed nicely with the testing we were doing already, so we utilized it."

"And the snake? Why not just fill the inside of the book with sawdust or horseflies so once they escape, they're impossible to put back? Why not have someone observe the pickup?" Magdalena turned to her, lowering her voice. "But now I understand why Cardinal Simonetta got enraged when I put the book in his office. He thought I'd brought him a venomous snake as a gesture of defiance. I kept remembering that all day. When I said we should deliver the book directly to him because I didn't want it in Saint Sebastian's, Sister Agnella called him a snake. I didn't realize it was a private joke."

Lena shrugged. "She does overstep her boundaries."

"Because someone else greatly overstepped theirs."

Lena didn't turn away. "I know her history. I know yours as well."

"I didn't do anything to deserve this." Magdalena folded her arms. "I'd rather be tried for murder in front of the magistrate in Rome than dealing with this."

"You've done nothing wrong, and you're not being punished."

"Chiara's dead!" Magdalena exclaimed. "She didn't do anything to deserve this either!"

"She opened the book."

"She was insatiably curious and loved books! If I'd known what was in there, I could have told you she wouldn't pass that test!" Magdalena's voice grew shrill. She couldn't stop it. No matter how she tried, it just kept pitching up. "In a hundred years she wouldn't have been able to pass that test! She pried into everything! She was kicked out of her first convent for smuggling books, and she was starving for more knowledge. Then you put her in front of a forbidden book when she knew she could handle dangerous ideas just the way she handled dangerous weapons. I never would have let her go out there! I'd have told her just to stay on the sidewalk and claim she couldn't break into the room."

Lena said, "Then she couldn't have stayed with us."

"She could have gone somewhere else," Magdalena said. "You could have sent her to another convent—alive. She'd be alive right now. She'd be crocheting lace for unappreciative priests and baking bread for self-centered magistrates, but she'd be alive to be unappreciated rather than filled with snake venom in a crypt."

This brought a shadow to Lena's eyes. "The snake bite wasn't meant to kill. I don't know why it did."

"That doesn't help Chiara."

"I didn't say it would help Chiara. But it was never the intention that anyone who failed the test would die to preserve the order's secrets." Lena opened her hands. "I'm not any happier about this than you are."

Magdalena said, "You're not even sad."

"I have to keep this convent running." Lena's voice lowered. "They need me functional, not weeping in my cell over things we can't change. While we're down here, there are sisters upstairs changing bed linens and scrubbing floors and stoking fires, and there are other sisters at the palace seeing to the legates."

"So go." Magdalena gestured toward the hall. "Go take care of your convent, and I hope you'll forgive me if I decide to mourn the death of one of our sisters as if she mattered to anyone else in the world."

Lena squared her shoulders. But then instead of returning the volley, she walked from the cell, shutting the door at her back.

Magdalena dropped onto the bed. In the next moment she thought about Chiara and how this had been their room for so long, their bed, their cell. She slipped off the bed and onto the floor. Lying on her side on the stones, she tucked her knees to her chest and closed her eyes. Struggling to stay as quiet as possible, she cried.

---

Magdalena skipped *lauds* and *prime* and morning Mass. It was the second day after her final vows, but right now she didn't care if skipping them was a sin. Someone knocked, but she didn't answer. She slept on the floor of the cell and ate nothing and spoke to no one.

When the convent quieted, she slipped out to the kitchen in case there was some leftover bread. Across the door of her cell lay a tray with a covered plate and a small pitcher. She carried it to the kitchen, but finding no one there, ate beside the hearth and its low red glow. Whoever had left her the tray must have wanted her to feel better. There was a fried sweet bun in addition to her biscuit, and the tea had been sweetened before it had grown cold. She drank it as it was, tepid. Tepid seemed about right for this morning.

Voices rose and then faded in the hallway. One of the nuns came in, nodded to her, and then left again.

It was ridiculous to stay in the convent right now. The longer she lingered, the greater the chance someone would want to talk to her, and she wanted to hear from no one. They'd all known what was going on, or if they hadn't, they'd been kept just as ignorant as she. The truth was, frustratingly, that she couldn't bear to talk to any of the sisters, and yet they constituted her whole world.

Breaking her biscuit into little pieces, Magdalena thought, no. They weren't all her world. Cardinal Seripando had lost a friend too. If she served him today, he'd notice her sorrow. His gentle words would soothe the roughened places in her heart. She wouldn't have to tell him how Chiara died. In fact, she probably shouldn't. Part of their rule was secrecy. She hadn't been permitted to tell him about her exercises, let alone why she'd been able to save his life from that assassin.

But Chiara's death—that was an actual fact, not something hidden.

Now that she thought of it, wasn't it odd that he hadn't attended the funeral yesterday? But most of the bishops and cardinals hadn't. Simonetta hadn't. Having been gone to train Chiara and prepare for her vows, Magdalena hadn't kept up to date on the schedule, but maybe there'd been a general congregation. Those took all day, but even so, there should have been time to pay respects. At least Madruzzo had visited.

Magdalena put on her shoes, then took her heavy shawl. Lena hadn't told her not to go to work today, so she'd track down Seripando wherever he was. After a year, she knew all his ordinary places, and if he were in a meeting, surely Madruzzo's servants would know where to find him.

On the streets, she detected a moisture on the wind that heralded spring. Last year there had been mud, so much mud between the end of winter and the beginning of the warmer weather, rain every day for a week and then at the end of it all, the first of the leaves prying themselves open as the days grew longer.

She stopped first at Santa Maria Maggiore, but although Simonetta and Hosius were in attendance, she didn't find Seripando in his customary spot. Outnumbered by them, he must be having a terrible time with those two, but maybe he'd relented in his heretical urges.

Magdalena asked one of the Swiss Guard if they knew where Seripando was, and they directed her to the palace. The guards there passed her through without any recognition that she'd been gone for a week, and no one questioned her as she went upstairs to Seripando's quarters.

The servant admitted her. She left her shawl and shoes in his parlor, then went in to his office to let him know she'd arrived. He wasn't at his desk, but hearing voices from the bedroom, she knocked.

A servant opened the door, and Magdalena stepped inside to the smell of death. The same smell as before.

Seripando lay in bed. In the corner, crocheting, sat Nezetta.

# TWENTY-FOUR

Magdalena flew to Seripando's bedside. Nezetta acknowledged her, but Magdalena didn't look at her as she took the cardinal's hand. "Oh, sir," she said. "I had no idea you were sick. I'm so sorry."

He squeezed her fingers, and she eased back his sleeve to reveal recessed grey circles on his weathered skin. "I heard the young novice died suddenly." Seripando's voice was steady, so unlike how he had sounded at the end of Gonzaga's life. "I'm sorry. I would have come to pay my respects, but I took ill in the morning."

Magdalena pulled up her chair, tears filling her eyes.

"I'm sorry," Seripando said. "I shouldn't have reminded you of your friend. Sister Chiara was very sweet, and so very good to me."

The tears overflowed while Magdalena sat at his side, voiceless, unable to move. He said, "My dear, my dear," and she laid her head on his chest.

The door squeaked, then shut, and Magdalena couldn't find the resolution to move, just let her tears soak into the blanket while the world went liquid around her and she melted down. Seripando patted her shoulder and said reassuring things she knew were lies, lies, lies because he couldn't possibly know the reality of his situation, that a nun sat in the room with him dosing out poison in fateful drops based on a verdict rendered by Seripando's sponsor in a city five days' journey from his deathbed.

The door opened again, and Seripando said, "Ah, Sister Lena."

Then Magdalena raised her head. Lena looked grim. "I'm so sorry, sir. Sister Magdalena shouldn't be here now, behaving like a child."

"She's had a terrible loss." Seripando patted Magdalena's hand. "She can stay."

"She needs to leave." Lena sounded firm. "Sister Magdalena, come with me."

Magdalena's legs were jelly. She forced them to work, one step after the next after the next like little drops of poison spreading their grey flaccid circles along a healthy man's lungs and liver and heart.

Lena brought Magdalena from Seripando's suite down the hall to Simonetta's. In his parlor, Simonetta loomed by the window.

"You didn't waste time," Magdalena said.

"You're still too opinionated," Simonetta said, "Did you say anything to him?"

"Agnella called you a snake." Magdalena trembled. "At the time, I thought it was a metaphor."

"Be that as it may, we aren't here to discuss Sister Agnella's working relationship with me." Simonetta folded his arms. "Sister Chiara's failure to observe secrecy was a lapse of her training and not my fault."

"Nothing dirties your hands. You pass along messages from the pope or else you're bowing to the observance of our rule. We went ahead and book-tested Chiara on *your* orders," Magdalena said, raising her voice, "and that's not your fault either, even though you did it in order to distract me from what you were about to do to Cardinal Seripando."

Simonetta's face had gone white. "Remember your place, Sister."

"I am well aware of my place, but I'm becoming aware you don't know yours." Magdalena folded her arms. The expected reproach wasn't coming from Lena. "Chiara was too young and too curious. You recognized it, but to you her life was an acceptable loss because you thought I'd object."

"Was I wrong?" Simonetta retorted. "I heard how you behaved after Cardinal Gonzaga died. You took vows, Sister. You vowed to defend the Holy Roman Catholic Church, and you vowed to obey the pope and to fight heresy. Am I incorrect in these assumptions?"

Magdalena said, "Was Chiara a heretic? Did I miss the written order for her execution?"

"Chiara's failure is separate from yours."

"My failure?" Magdalena's eyes widened.

"You're far too emotional."

"What have I failed to carry out so far due to my emotions?" Magdalena took a step toward him, and Simonetta recoiled. "I took down an attacker in the palace hallway, and I used the man's own knife to disembowel his employer in an alleyway. You seemed to think me perfectly in control of my emotions then."

"Then I suggest you regain control of them now," Simonetta said. "You are to return to your convent and bake bread or do whatever it is you do there, and leave the work of the council to us."

Magdalena said, "You mean the council that's in its third period and shows no signs of ending before the pope orders the execution of another hundred bishops who disagree with him?"

Simonetta said, "Do you dare defy your superiors?"

With her abbess standing right behind her, Magdalena could count on this standoff to be decided without further argument on her part. She might be sent back to Rome along with the next batch of letters. She might be sent there in a box. She didn't care.

Sister Lena sounded puzzled. "If I may, sir, is your intention to end the Council?"

Simonetta snapped, "You know perfectly well it is not."

"Because, sir, if the nun known to be Seripando's personal assistant is kept in seclusion while he's dying, especially because she also was present at the death of Cardinal Gonzaga, you're facing rumors of plague." Lena continued with a sweet tone Magdalena heard almost never. "How long will the French delegates remain if they think they stand a chance of getting sequestered in German lands? Or if they think a quarantine might prevent further food from coming in?"

Simonetta exclaimed, "No one's talking about plague."

"You don't have as many ears to the ground as I have." As Lena stepped forward, Magdalena could see her again in her peripheral vision. "I assure you, questions began the instant Cardinal Seripando retired to his bed yesterday. Magdalena's absence has been noted. Moreover, Cardinal Seripando is known to have impeccable etiquette, so his absence from Sister Chiara's funeral is on everyone's lips."

Simonetta frowned at Lena, unsure whether he should accuse her of lying.

"A rash decision on your part will end the conference by Sunday. If you don't think you and Hosius can handle the reformers, send Magdalena home." Lena folded her arms. She hadn't specified whether *home* was the convent of Saint Martin's or all the way back to Rome itself. "I can handle *her* behavior. I'm her abbess. You have no such authority over the reform-minded bishops, but because you'll be named chief legate within the month, you have one chance to make sure the reformers don't get the best of the council."

Simonetta walked to the window, rubbing his chin.

Lena didn't look at Magdalena at all, and Magdalena's heart raced.

A flying kick would send that man crashing through the window. It was two stories to the ground. Magdalena could avenge Chiara right here, right now, and let Simonetta finish thinking on the way down about the best way to handle her *emotions.*

Simonetta turned. "You're sure you can manage her?"

Lena folded her arms. "I'm an abbess, not a scullery maid."

"Because I need to be sure—"

"This is an unwise time not to be sure of our services." Lena stepped back. "If you order me to remove Magdalena, she doesn't go alone. I will take your orders as an admission that you lack faith in all the Catherinites. You can then write to Rome to find out if the Curia has any other way of carrying out the pope's orders."

The room spun on its axis.

Simonetta huffed. "If you can't control her, there will be penalties."

Lena chuckled. "Who are you going to contract to carry out these supposed penalties? The Swiss Guard? By all, means, sir, send those men to besiege the convent. They can prepare tea for our houseguests." She took Magdalena by the arm. "If you choose to override my authority, I will abide by your objection. But if you want this assignment completed, I will see it completed on my terms."

With that, Lena escorted Magdalena from the suite and out into the hallway.

As soon as the door was shut, Magdalena grabbed Lena by the sleeve and leaned close to her. "The orders? You saw them? They were written?"

Lena fiddled in her tremendous sleeves and produced a letter. "Our rule requires it for proper recording."

Magdalena found the papal seal, the word *haeresis*, the name Girolamo Seripando, and everything else she expected. The date on the top was February 28th, the morning Nezetta had begun dosing Gonzaga and three days before Simonetta had ordered her to prep Chiara for her book test.

Lena huffed. "I'm not ignorant. Your behavior is abominable, but his isn't much better. If you go back into Seripando's suite, you will behave like the professed nun you are. I've put myself on the line for you, and I expect you to justify my actions. Make him as comfortable as you can, just as you did with Gonzaga, because charity and care for the dying is a part of our rule. You're compassionate, and unlike Simonetta, I see that as a good quality. But no matter what, you are not to interfere with completing his sentence."

Magdalena bit her lip. "Rome didn't even give him a chance to repent of his heresy before issuing the condemnation."

"He's had enough chances. The legates have him outnumbered, but he retains plenty of influence. They can't have him raising up scions to carry on his cause." Lena put a hand on Magdalena's shoulder. "You like him best, and I don't want you distraught. You've been through enough. But I'm not Simonetta with his smug assumption that you're a fragile girl who needs someone to decide what her glass heart can handle. If you want to be with him, then you know yourself best and what you can do." Lena sighed. "Pray with him. If you can get him to repent his heresy before death, all the better for his soul when he faces God on the seat of judgment."

# TWENTY-FIVE

Nezetta was just as glad to have company while she tended the dying man, but often it was Magdalena alone. Magdalena, who'd been by Seripando's side all along—Magdalena because it was odd to have Nezetta tend first one dying legate, then another.

Magdalena learned from Nezetta how the poison worked, how often it had to be dosed, and the effects she should expect. The older nun taught her the mechanism, although not the recipe, which she'd obtained from a hundred-year-old Spanish woman's forbidden books in exchange for looking after her disabled daughter. Nezetta said, "I'm getting old. Lena agrees it's important for someone else to know the procedure."

Doubtless the recipe was inscribed in that ledger stashed in the locked box. No further brewing was required, though: Nezetta had enough remaining from Gonzaga to properly dose Seripando. "Gonzaga was already in fragile health," she said one morning in the outer parlor. "I thought at first I'd made it too strong, or started him off too fast, but as you can see, it's just his health. Seripando's progress is typically what should happen."

"If the doctors recognized it," Magdalena said, "or if we got orders to reverse the sentence, would you be able to?"

Nezetta nodded. "There is."

"I'm not going to try, so don't tell me." Magdalena sighed. "I just wish there's some hope."

Seripando was weak and dizzy, but he could get out of bed long enough to sit up in his office working on the documents on the sacrament of holy orders for the next session. He sent instructions to the Congregation of Theologians, and he still said Mass on occasion, although Father Laynez to support him. All the while, the grey circles spread on his skin, slowly puckering downward and killing him by inches.

"You can read?" Seripando said to Magdalena on the morning of the 16th. "Read to me. I will tell you which book and which chapter, but my eyes aren't very good right now."

She spent the next hour reading to him, sounding out some of the words she couldn't understand. The book was Saint Augustine's *Confessions*. Although the book appeared to have been read a thousand times, and he may have had it memorized, Seripando had her read it again anyhow.

Sometimes he would ask if she understood the sentence she'd just read. Oftentimes no, she didn't, so he would explain to her. Then she would read again, and he'd stop her and go back to teach her more. A few times she said she didn't understand just because when he explained, he explained in nuances so deep and multilayered that she realized all over again that no, she hadn't understood it at all.

In halting Latin, Magdalena read,

Where then did I find Thee, that I might learn Thee? For in my memory Thou wert not, before I learned Thee. Where then did I find Thee, that I might learn Thee, but in Thee above me?

"Do you understand?" Seripando didn't wait for her answer. "He's saying that even our desire to know God is a gift from God Himself. Without that first gift, we wouldn't know to reach toward God. At every point in the process, we rely on God to give us yet another gift to get us closer to Him."

Magdalena sat, puzzled. "Then where is the merit?"

"The merit is in the asking," Seripando said. "It's in conformity to God's will as much as we can. Before we can even do so, however, He has to stir up in us the desire for more. Many times, that desire takes the form of unhappiness or suffering, and only later do we look back on it and give thanks."

He had her continue reading.

All consult Thee on what they will, though they hear not always what they will. He is Thy best servant who looks not so much to hear that from Thee which himself willeth, as rather to will that, which from Thee he heareth.

"Dwell on that thought." Seripando sighed. "So many times we have God's answer right in front of us, waiting to be grasped, but we avoid believing in it because that answer is not what we want to hear. But the way God works isn't going to be the same as the way people work. It's always better to give in to God's will than to force our own will upon a situation."

Nezetta glanced up at Magdalena from across the room, and Magdalena registered her warning.

"Why are you teaching me?" Magdalena patted his hand. "You should save your strength. I'm already the bride of Christ."

"Then you must learn more about your husband." He sounded peaceful. "I want you to read to me now because even after fifty-five years, I still crave to know more about my God and my Savior. Always."

Magdalena leaned forward. "You, sir? You're one of the most respected theologians in the Church."

He focused on her. "Then one of the most respected theologians in the Church has asked you to read to him from a spiritual book. Go on. This passage is so special to so many."

Magdalena wondered for the first time if this book were on the Index of Banned Books and if Nezetta were going to turn her over to Simonetta for heresy.

Too late loved I Thee, O Thou Beauty of ancient days, yet ever new! Too late I loved Thee! And behold, Thou wert within, and I abroad, and there I searched for Thee; deformed I, plunging amid those fair forms which Thou hadst made. Thou wert with me, but I was not with Thee.

Magdalena felt caught up in the yearning and the grief Augustine expressed over all that lost time, all the ways God had pursued him and all the ways he'd ignored or belittled God. Yet through all that, God had waited for him. No, not even waited. God had worked ceaselessly to bring Augustine back, and then once Augustine returned, God had embraced him and rewarded him and loved him as though he'd never left. The only thing lost was the time they could have spent together.

"You'll find yourself feeling this intensely when you get older," Seripando said.

"You're preaching to me," Magdalena teased.

"I'm a preacher. You have to sit with me, so you should expect a measure of preaching." But he was at ease. "Any way you can become closer to Christ will make you a better nun. Men who have been priests since they were twenty are still becoming better priests when they are sixty, and when they do, they look back and lament the time lost. Even if at the time they were doing the best they understood to do, someday they grow in holiness and look back to despise whatever it was they held back from God in those earlier years."

Magdalena recoiled. "Really?"

"Not all priests," Seripando corrected. "Only priests who pray and grow in virtue. When I was prior general, it was my job to prod these good men to do so, and to awaken the sleeping. If weak prayer grieves the heart, imagine what no prayer must cause."

"Are you sixty?" Magdalena said, turning the page.

"I'm seventy." He smiled. "There is always more to learn, and when I learn it, I love Him more."

She sat forward, sensing an opportunity. "And what you learn—have you ever learned sometimes that you were wrong? That something you held to be very true was in actuality keeping you from God all along?"

"So many people have that experience." Seripando sighed. "Keep reading about Saint Augustine. He'll tell you the same. The most blessed among us have had a moment where God breaks through. In that moment, the heart pops open like a chestnut on the fire." Seripando closed his eyes as though savoring a delicious wine. "Have you had that experience, Sister Magdalena? It's called *metanoia*. It's a Greek word, and it's the moment where you're standing on a road, a road you've intended all your life to travel, and suddenly you change your direction. You were heading for a town in the valley, and instead you turn your feet toward a city you've only heard about, a city on a hill with its lights streaming through the sky. You don't know if you have enough provisions for the journey or what you'll find when you arrive, but you set your feet on the new road because suddenly no other road will ever be enough."

Gooseflesh puckered Magdalena's arms. "That's...that sounds amazing."

"I joined the Augustinians when I was fourteen." Seripando chuckled. "What did I know at fourteen? I was a boy. I had an idea and a lot of energy, and when my parents died, that was a profound suffering. But remember how I said suffering can be a gift? With them no longer paving a path into the legal professions, I found the way open to a life they would never have approved. I seized it."

Magdalena stared, open-mouthed. "I didn't know that."

"I've done so many things." He shook his head. "Always after the next chapter begins, I find I've learned so much that I could have done the previous work better."

Magdalena said, "And the Council? What do you think you'd have done differently at the Council?"

He focused on her. "How curious. Do you think my work here is at an end?"

She tensed. "That's not what I meant."

"I hope still to do things at this Council. Given the chance to repeat it, though, I would have hurried us along." Seripando frowned. "I'd not give us quite as much time to bog down in debate." He reached for her hand. "I know the joke they say about me, that I *dare not* to do anything. They're correct. I'd rather caution than incaution. But perhaps I've been too cautious. Maybe I should have been more direct about challenging the *zelanti* who want to keep everything the same forever and ever and ever."

Magdalena started. "But sir...that would mean challenging the pope."

"The pope is the pope is the pope." Seripando shook his head. "These people who are so afraid we're going to take away the power of the pope: what are they afraid of? That the gates of Hell will prevail? No, Christ said that will never happen. That the foundations of the Church will be moved? No, because Christ said He'd build His Church upon Peter."

He lifted his hand off Magdalena's and lay back on his pillow without energy, but with something of light in his eyes. "They're worried about losing the *extraneous trappings* of the papacy. How could that be? The pope would still be the vicar of Christ even if he were bobbing alone in a boat on the sea, without vestments and without a court. He would be the pope without cardinals around him and without a palace and guards. All the reforms in the world wouldn't take that dignity from him."

Magdalena said, "Then what would *reform of the head* take away?"

Seripando looked momentarily glorious. "It would take away all the things that are unnecessary. It would strip away the things that keep the pope from being fully the pope. Have you ever wondered, if we were able to reform the papacy and streamline the Curia—if we were to remove all these impediments to the pope functioning as the vicar of Christ— then what would happen?"

Magdalena gasped.

Seripando chuckled. "He'd be more the pope than ever before. And what an amazing, wonderful thing that would be. A pope who truly is pope to the world rather than pope to himself."

It was the last conversation Magdalena had with him. Sixteen hours later, in the small hours of March 17th, Seripando died.

# TWENTY-SIX

On March 19th, Magdalena climbed the interior of the Church of San Marco, laden with forbidden books.

Seripando's death had put all of Trent into mourning, but Magdalena kept her face stern and her eyes dry because Simonetta glared whenever he saw her. Her grief wouldn't change a thing. The man was dead, and today he'd be buried in Trent's Augustinian church.

The pope's orders had been fulfilled. What more did Simonetta want?

More, that was all. More control, more orders from the pope, more subversive reformers about whom to tell his nasty tales. For all Magdalena knew, letters had flooded into Rome to report to the pope that she'd dared to cry after Gonzaga's death, and a few days later another letter about how she'd raised her voice.

Because her tears had been noted in the Index of Forbidden Emotions, Magdalena hadn't cried for Seripando. Whenever she'd started to quiver, she'd reminded herself that he was a heretic, and heretics could disguise themselves as nice old men in order to lull the innocent into theological pitfalls that would give way beneath their feet and drop them into Hell.

All the same, in the spirit of Chiara, she'd plundered Seripando's room and helped herself to a few forbidden books.

It was hours before the funeral. No one knew where she was, and no one cared. The nuns at St. Martin's convent would assume she was working at Madruzzo's palace. The nuns in the palace would assume she'd stayed in the convent. Instead she lashed the stash of books to her body in a fabric sack. She tied her leather shoes to a cord and hung them around her neck. Then in the dark hours, she climbed into the church architecture to stash them, forbidden and untouchable.

Chiara would have done as much. No, actually, Chiara would have climbed into the rafters with a candle to read them, sounding them out in Latin one syllable at a time if necessary.

First Magdalena hid *The Confessions of Saint Augustine*. Seripando had lived and died as an Augustinian friar, and why he'd asked her to stumble through this well-nigh memorized book in her faltering Latin was a mystery she couldn't now ask him to explain.

As Magdalena tucked the book into its hiding point, she flipped a few pages of text she couldn't easily read. She'd find someone else's copy of Saint Augustine's *Confessions* and go back over them, but not his. Not the copy touched by his fingers and held near his heart, tinted with the scent of his worn skin and careful eyes. Seripando's copy should be no one else's. Maybe his heresy had soaked into the pages. Maybe someone who read the words he loved to excess would also begin to love them too much, and maybe that person would face a similar end.

In one of the window ledges she stashed a copy of *Novae constitutiones ordinis Santi Augustini*, which Seripando had written himself. She made her way back and then over to another fixture, and there went *Cicero relegatus* and *Cicero revocatus,* also his writings. She had no idea what either book was, but they probably weren't on the Index right now, otherwise Seripando wouldn't have been named a legate in the first place.

But even unforbidden, she didn't want these books remaining in Seripando's suite to be plundered by Simonetta. If Seripando's executioners wanted to further destroy his good name, they should at least do so without his books.

Again she returned to the edge of the church, crept along the masonry and above the pipe organ. Here she stashed yet another work written by Seripando: *Oratio in funere Caroli Vimperatoris.* Again, the contents were a mystery behind the curtain of her basic Latin. Again, Simonetta shouldn't have it.

Another ten minutes passed, and balanced on a window ledge narrower than her foot, Magdalena hid Chiara's unfinished lacework.

Chiara hadn't been a heretic, but Magdalena knew two things with a sharp fury. First, that she had no idea how to finish what Chiara had started. And second, that Nezetta was reputed to be the best lace-maker in the convent, and that if Magdalena could help it, Nezetta's hands would never in a hundred years touch Chiara's piece.

With one final purloined item to hide, she crept back to the edge of the church, but then two black-cloaked individuals entered on the ground level fifty feet beneath her. Magdalena retreated into the stonework.

Lena had been right that you could climb like monkeys through these churches. If Agnella hadn't shown Magdalena how, she'd never have tried, but the richest of the churches had numerous side altars donated by opulent families with luxurious sums to bestow on the Church. Each altar was more ornate than the last, as though trying to make all the other patron saints jealous in Heaven while keeping earthly artisans and artists in full employment. Balconies jutted out over each of the side altars. It was on one of these that

Magdalena flattened herself, close to the cavernous ceiling, and from now on people moved in the church. She couldn't get down without being spotted. Light danced through the stained-glass over the dust-covered top of the balcony as morning passed.

She would have to remain her for the duration of the funeral.

Several priests carried Seripando's casket into the church, probably Augustinians themselves, although Magdalena couldn't tell from this height or this vantage point. She waited while people trickled in. It would be several hours, but she was used to fasting and used to discomfort, so she'd offer it up for the relief of Seripando's soul in Purgatory.

The musicians played. The choir sang. The church filled, and below her filed a procession. From her vantage point, she was able to see everything taking place in the sanctuary area and around the altar. The vaulted roof brought up the sounds below, and she imagined they'd carry down her sounds as well, so she quieted even her breathing.

Speeches. So many speeches, delivered by so many bishops and officials and envoys she knew only by name. The Cardinal of Lorraine, Charles de Guise, spoke. He mentioned that Seripando hadn't wanted episcopal power. He had accepted it only when the pope had insisted on sending him to Trent as a legate. De Guise didn't know it was a mistake for which the pope later made Seripando pay, rather than paying for it himself.

Father Diego Laynez spoke too. Magdalena hadn't asked Seripando about his past, but now she learned that the decades he'd demurred to talk about had been filled with work. He'd been the prior general of the entire Augustinian order for twelve years, and he hadn't disclosed that as part of his work he'd visited every one of their monasteries and convents in order to reform the order.

*Reform.* It kept coming up over and over as more people came forward to speak. According to the Augustinians who had worked with him, he'd wanted to enhance their spiritual lives and make them truer to the works of Saint Paul. He hadn't created new rules for the Order, but rather that they should observe the rules they already had.

Therefore, *reform,* but not in any way *changing.* Making them better monks and friars and preachers by removing the extraneous things and letting them fully be monks and friars and preachers. It was the same thing he'd said about the pope.

That didn't sound like heresy, but Magdalena wasn't a theologian. Martin Luther, confirmed heretic that he was, had been an Augustinian. Could you get more of a condemnation than that? The same order that formed Seripando had given birth to a rift that sliced Europe into pieces, with more heretics emboldened every day. In England. In France. Catholics were dying and Catholics were losing their churches, and wasn't that the final fruit of heresy?

Another bishop spoke. Emperor Charles V had, according to this speaker, called Cardinal Seripando the best preacher in all Europe and had taken great pains to hear him whenever possible. Was that heresy? The Emperor wanted reform too, but was it heretical?

Seripando had revoked the authority of all Augustinians in Italy to preach until he'd restored orthodoxy to the order. He'd forbidden Augustinian houses from receiving any Augustinians about whose teachings there was any grave doubt. In his old age he'd turned down a bishopric and had also resigned as prior general, and he'd tried to retire. But then the emperor and later the pope had called him out of retirement for the council. Therefore he'd set aside his desires and served. At Trent, he'd tried to reform his fellow bishops to make them more like he was: a teacher and a preacher.

Magdalena never moved through the whole funeral, silent like a cat so the populace would never look up to find a figure where no figure ought to have climbed. *Fatherly,* the speakers kept saying at the funeral, as they also had last night at the visitation. Over and over again she heard that Seripando had been fatherly to everyone, guiding and encouraging rather than punishing, recognizing individuals' possibilities and leading by example rather than directing from behind a wall.

Was that what fathers did? Magdalena couldn't say. In her experience, fathers were the people you wrote to in desperation when the expenses mounted, and then a few days later the creditors stopped coming so you could concentrate on buying today's bread rather than paying for yesterday's. A father was the person who once loved your mother but also had responsibilities and a name elsewhere that required constant tending, and you were a burden on both of those.

The pope was a father to the Church too. The pope promoted his nephews (and his "nephews") to be cardinals because he wanted to provide for his children. That was another kind of father.

Seripando had said a father should live in his own diocese and preach to his own children from his own pulpit. That he should maintain a relationship with the priests who worked for him and see to their education. This, at a time when a hundred and ten Italian bishops lived in Rome but had never even seen their own diocese because it wasn't convenient to do so. This, at a time when the great-granddaughter of a pope had needed to beg for a man she hadn't seen in twelve years to send a paltry-to-him sum of money so she could enter a convent and cease being a financial drain on her mother, and that was considered an acceptable means of discharging his duties as her sire.

And that same man had denied any connection to of his children because one was physically flawed, rather than understanding her broken body needed a father even more.

After all of that, when they said Seripando had been fatherly, what did she know of fatherhood?

Magdalena peered down the fifty feet to the floor, at the rows of occupied benches that were so much more full than Mass on a Sunday. Chiara had said something about how an angel feels looking down at the inside of a church. How did God feel? Of the choices she'd just seen, which kind of father was God? Because until this moment, she'd always assumed it was the same: when you got into trouble, you sent God a missive asking for enough capital to set matters right, and shortly the problems disappeared. With that, His fatherly duty had been discharged, and you should continue fending for yourself until the next time you required assistance because He preferred it that way. He had a kingdom that needed tending.

You could live your whole life with that kind of relationship to God. But Seripando had said no, you can't. More emphatically, no, God didn't want it that way.

The last thing Magdalena had meant to stash in the architecture was the most important: a manuscript Cardinal Seripando had worked on every day for the past year. It was a structured all-in-one book that defined every single aspect of the Catholic faith, or at least would do so when completed. He'd called it a *catechism*. He followed the prayers of the Mass and used them as a type of tree trunk for branching off and discussing all aspects of the Catholic faith.

If Seripando was a heretic, and the pope said he was, then heresy would be imbued in the very book the Church had planned to stamp out heresy. That's why Magdalena had taken the manuscript from a drawer before any of the reformers could lay hands on it. She'd tied it with a length of Chiara's crochet thread, and it lay flat at her side in the balcony, dazzled red or green or blue as the sun passed through stained-glass. There must not be heresy passed along to others when Seripando was still so respected. His heresy had to end here.

For hours she remained with the hand-written papers beneath her palm, remembering Seripando's last conversation. *Late have I loved you.* For some, far too late, and far too little.

# TWENTY-SEVEN

Magdalena had to hide a triumphant smile for most of early April.

Simonetta and Hosius (and indeed, all of Trent) had been certain the pope would send word naming Simonetta the new principal legate. The principal legate had at first been Gonzaga, and after his death, briefly, the principal legate had been Seripando. It only made sense to promote Simonetta, already a legate and a veteran of all three Council periods.

So when a letter arrived from Rome with the information that two new legates were en route, and one was to be the new principal, Simonetta stormed around with a deep scowl for days.

The new principal was Cardinal Giovanni Morone. Yes, the same Morone imprisoned by Pope Paul IV for heresy. That Morone.

A Morone who, Magdalena assumed, would have been executed just like Reginald Pole had he not responded to the pope's summons for a heresy trial.

Uncertain why the pope hadn't made the logical promotion, Magdalena kept her head down. There was no one left to speculate with. Not with Lena, who would have muttered something about how popes and winds change direction without warning. Not with Agnella, who would have rolled her eyes and said a man neck-deep in heresy would surely see the benefits of abandoning his heresy after several years in prison. She couldn't with Chiara, who would have asked so many questions that eventually Magdalena would have taken the fallback position: the pope was the pope, and surely he knew what he was doing.

Instead she chose to talk in her head with Seripando, who had died on the orders of the man who had just appointed as his successor an accused heretic. She heard no answers (and would have died of terror if she had), but a year in the cardinal's shadow had injected his voice into her head. Only now that he'd died did she realize how much she'd come to expect his soft-toned observations as the backdrop of life in Trent. As she went about her day (much freer now that she didn't have one individual to follow), she caught herself making the observations she expected to hear from him.

He wasn't mad at her. In her head, Seripando wasn't angry that she'd served the Church by executing him. In her head, he understood and submitted to the necessity of protecting the laity from the clergy who ought to be pastoring them.

But Morone—what would Seripando have said about Morone at one time being in prison and now being sent out to head the very Council intended to root out heresy?

If Morone had made such a comeback, then couldn't also have Reginald Pole?

Couldn't Seripando himself?

Meanwhile, the veryfrustrated legate, Simonetta, the Eye of the Pope who had not seen this coming, snapped orders and gave exasperated answers. The only time Magdalena heard him address the issue directly (while she prepared tea for Hosius) he muttered, "At least it's not de Guise."

De Guise had become more popular by the day. Chiara would have been entranced by his rise—in fact, up until

March 10th, she had been—and now he was a lightning rod for the reformers. Would the Catherinites have to execute him too?

Instead of voicing any of this, Magdalena poured the tea.

Until April 9th, she baked bread, did laundry, and attended the general congregations where she listened to arguments that split hairs and raised hackles. And sometimes, when no one was watching, she glanced at a very irritated Simonetta and indulged in happy spite.

On April 10th, Cardinal Morone arrived in Trent, bringing with him the other replacement legate, Bernardo Navagero.

Navagero was a Venetian politician, had at one time been married, and was now a cardinal. When he arrived, Agnella whispered under her breath, "I should blunt the axe for him too."

Magdalena started. "Did he know what was going on at *Le Convertite?*"

"I have no idea." She huffed. "Probably. Probably couldn't believe Giovanni Pietro Leon would do such a thing, and certainly not on the testimony of a few whores."

Navagero was in his fifties and nowhere near the artistic masterpiece of de Guise. If Simonetta ever got an order to execute him, Agnella would beg Lena to take it on by herself. It was a wonder she had left Venice rather than poisoning the whole city.

By now the Catherinites of St. Martin knew how to inculcate themselves perfectly into any ceremony where newcomers were introduced. The bishops and cardinals and theologians had seen them so often that they no longer saw them at all. The nuns could walk through the seats and up behind the podiums and place items or remove them, whisper messages or deliver notes, and all with complete freedom.

Magdalena was noticed only when she found herself flagged down by a bishop or a theologian and then dispatched on an errand so they didn't have to miss one of the discussions. That was how Morone first noticed them too. "Whatever you need," Madruzzo had said, almost as an afterthought while showing Morone to his suite, "the nuns of Saint Martin are empowered to acquire it for you or otherwise carry out your orders."

Morone was housed in Gonzaga's former rooms. Although it had been aired out after his death, Magdalena imagined she could detect the scent of death in the draperies and the cushions.

Morone looked at Magdalena and Lena as though this were the first time his eyes had registered their presence. Whenever he'd smiled today, the smile had gone all the way to those warm eyes. Now, however, there was no smile. Perhaps in the pope's palace, nuns were commonplace, and there had been nuns aplenty at the day's ceremonies introducing the new legates.

"Are these the Catherinites I've been told about?" He sounded bland. "His Holiness told me that I should expect to be assigned one as a shadow."

Lena bowed. "I'm their abbess, sir."

"I've no need of a shadow. God gave me one, and it always appears opposite the sunshine." He looked at Magdalena. "I presume you've been assigned to me?"

Magdalena lowered her head. "No decision has been made in that regard, sir."

"Then I'll make it," said Morone. "You are my second shadow, and I want you to be as quiet as possible while I get the work sorted. This Council is a disaster, and I need no one else underfoot complicating matters."

Lena said, "I'll take that into consideration, sir."

Morone shook his head. "You took a vow of obedience to the pope, and in Trent, I'm operating as the pope's voice. She'll be my shadow. You, my dear abbess, may go."

Madruzzo looked horrified. Magdalena bit her cheek and struggled against the temptation to look at Lena, who would either be infuriated or horrified, but would not on any account be amused.

"As you wish, sir." Lena's voice was very tight. "Sister Magdalena is relatively new to our order. In the event you require a more experienced assistant, one will be provided. Sister Magdalena," she said in a warning tone, "do well."

That wasn't an instruction as much as a threat. Magdalena bowed.

As soon as Lena had left the room, Morone said to her, "You can sit in the outer parlor. If I require your services, I'll send for you."

Magdalena took the time to say a rosary, then did some of her warmup exercises. Morone had no use for her: that much was clear. If she had to continue in service to him, she might as well practice combat moves and reading Latin because she'd have plenty of time.

There had been plenty of time waiting on Seripando too, but it had been time overhearing fascinating discussions about very fine points of law, issues the average person could live a lifetime without even realizing were at the center of a question, let alone knowing how to resolve. Seeing Morone's attitude, Seripando would doubtless have said, "My dear, dull minds won't at first recognize your useful qualities."

"No, sir," she would have replied. "That wasn't inability as much as willfullness."

When Madruzzo and Morone exited the suite's inner parlor, Magdalena stood. Madruzzo noticed her, then said to Morone, "You really should make use of the Catherinites."

Morone said, reaching for his red hat, "Maybe she can make my tea."

Magdalena reacted without thinking. There wasn't a second between the rage in her head and the motion of her hands, the quick release of the dagger strapped against her inner arm and the whiplike motion as she hurled it at the wall, toward the center of the hat, through the crown, and with a bang, into the wall.

The hat hung there, pinned through its heart.

Morone stared. Madruzzo looked apoplectic. Magdalena trembled, half terrified but far past the time where she cared what these officials did to her. Any indignity was better than the notion that she was no more than the pope's lap dog.

Keeping her voice steady, she said, "I'll need some instruction in how you prefer your tea."

Madruzzo said, "I...I'm very... I'm so sorry, Sir! I—"

"If you don't mind," Morone said, his voice low, "I'd like a moment to speak with my second shadow about the preparation of my consumables."

Madruzzo stared again at the impaled hat.

"Go." Morone sounded confident, his voice smooth. "I can see she takes tea service very seriously."

Madruzzo left with reluctance, his gaze jumping back over his shoulder for one last check on Magdalena in the center of the parlor.

Morone went to the wall where his hat hung like a framed painting. "You may take a seat. Kindly don't hurl the furniture at my head."

She marched to his desk and dropped onto one of the overstuffed cushions. This may have been the same chair she occupied while watching Gonzaga die. She saw no reason not to sit here while her vocation died as well.

All the same, it gave her a sardonic pleasure that Morone couldn't easily remove the dagger. When he finally got it loose, he carried it and the impaled red hat back to his desk, where he set down both with great deliberation. "You've gotten my attention." Sitting, he crossed his legs and leaned back in his chair. "But I admit I'm unclear what message you intended to convey, other than an irrational hatred of my clothing."

"I apologize for any distress I may have caused your hat." Magdalena kept her voice steady, which was hard because she wanted both to apologize and to laugh out loud. "I'm reasonably good at mending, sir, if you care to send it home with me. It's a clean tear."

"No doubt." Morone studied her. "Since you seem to have no trouble speaking your mind, I invite you to continue doing so, and I will grant you the same honor. I am not ignorant of the machinations going on at the council. The council itself is split into factions that make the hole in my hat seem invisible by comparison, and such division is not sustainable."

Magdalena nodded. "Agreed, sir."

"You are operating under a vow to serve the pope, are you not?"

When he didn't go on, Magdalena said, "Yes, as are you."

"Actually, I am not. I never took a vow of obedience to the pope, and that's for the best in this circumstance because I may have to do things the pope would not approve of. You, however, don't have such freedom. I'm aware of your order's obedience to the pope, and I'm aware that his orders are sent to you through Cardinal Ludovico Simonetta."

Magdalena nodded again. Morone continued, "You are under Simonetta's orders to listen to me for any heterodox thoughts and report them back to Simonetta. Simonetta then writes vindictive letters to His Holiness, who makes decisions and recommendations based on, in effect, your reports after they've been thoroughly distorted by Simonetta's pen."

As this seemed entirely too true, Magdalena only frowned.

"For myself," Morone continued, "I've been sent with special instructions to flatter Cardinal Charles de Guise and then embarrass him in public. So I'm quite aware that misinformation and distortion are the rules of law right now. I intend to have nothing whatsoever to do with this nonsense. The Church is about truth. Eternal truth. We cannot get it by playing about with untruths."

Magdalena said, "I understand, but—"

"But," Morone said, "you're under a vow of obedience to report to Simonetta. I'm protecting your soul by isolating you from me. Things you don't hear are things you cannot report to him. You are under no obligation to tell him something you have no idea has happened."

Magdalena opened her hands. "I need to protect you. That's also my vow."

"You didn't protect my hat." Morone's mouth quickened into a smile. "I'm far older than you, and I've played these political games for longer than you've been alive. These machinations are reprehensible to me, and someday they will be reprehensible to you too if you're lucky. For now, I will promise not to put my life in jeopardy while I'm in my quarters, and you can protect my life when I'm outside them. But not," he added, "when I'm conferencing with another bishop or cardinal or theologian. Then you will be on the outside, and you can consider me as protecting you."

Magdalena said, "I disagree."

"Then frame it differently," Morone said. "If you hear nothing to report to Simonetta, then Simonetta can't detract from my good name with the pope. By your ignorance, you will have protected me anyhow."

# TWENTY-EIGHT

Simonetta stormed around, writing with deep scratches into his papers, snapping answers when asked questions, and fixing dark eyes on anyone with whom he interacted. Magdalena could take pleasure in that. She took pleasure in standing behind Morone with her hands clasped in the sleeves of her habit, her eyes downcast, relegated along with Lena to an outside chamber while Simonetta and Morone spoke within. She nurtured a bitter joy in letting Simonetta know in daily reports that nothing of significance had happened. She noted every time Simonetta bristled that Morone had gotten the position Simonetta had thought certainly his own.

This wasn't the proper attitude of a bride of Christ. Therefore Magdalena kept it to herself.

She liked Morone well enough, now that they'd come to an understanding. She'd mended his hat. She learned how he liked his tea and how he liked his office tidied, and she let him know how Simonetta liked his reports written and what sort of information he liked to send back to the pope. Morone adjusted his interactions accordingly, and Magdalena could feel even more vindictive pleasure when Simonetta received a report full of nothing.

Only a week later, however, Morone decided to travel to Innsbruck to speak to Emperor Ferdinand. In this instance, for once, he yielded to Simonetta's insistence that he take his Catherinite shadow.

"You can't make me tea on the road," Morone said as he wandered his office deciding what to bring. "Moreover, there will be no private conferences at Innsbruck for you to report on. Everything the emperor does, he does with his court in attendance. But regardless, the situation is dire enough that Simonetta cannot change a thing. The pope wants me to go."

Magdalena sat mending one of Morone's dressing gowns. "I won't take up much space in the carriage."

"What, no trunks of ball gowns?" Morone looked up with a smile. "Bring your needlework or prayer book or anything you want for spending your own time. The pope is in a terrible situation because our friend de Guise has put him in one. Therefore the pope has authorized me to do anything I must to calm the emperor, and I have quite a free hand. Simonetta knows this."

Simonetta definitely knew it, and it galled him. Magdalena said, "What did de Guise do?"

"Because of de Guise's visit to Innsbruck, the emperor sent two letters to Rome. They arrived almost the same day that word arrived of Gonzaga's death. First, realize that the emperor is far cannier than any games we're playing here. We are the equivalent of schoolchildren compared to his political savvy. The first was a public letter, telling the pope that Emperor Ferdinand wanted to ensure the council went well and that he felt Rome might be working against it. This was mild enough, until the pope received his private letter."

Magdalena took note of Morone's wicked grin. "You said the emperor does everything with his court in attendance."

"That may be the case, but the second letter was markedly different in tone. It left the pope badly shaken. Shortly thereafter came a letter from King Philip."

Magdalena's spine straightened. "Spain is on Pope Pius's side! Spain wants the council to continue."

"Spain also issued something very close to an ultimatum," Morone said. "Neither Simonetta nor de Guise got named chief legate because neither of them would be able to do what I'm about to do." He sighed. "Not that it's going to be easy, but I could use a nun at my side whose purpose is to keep me in line, and at the very least, to pray for my victory. If I don't succeed, I'm concerned about the future of the Church."

There was a knock at the door, and a servant escorted in de Guise with Tadea. "Charles!" Morone strode across the room. "I'm so glad you could consult with me before I head off to Innsbruck. I have some questions because you were just there."

De Guise nodded, but he looked pale. "I'm sorry I haven't been able to meet with you until now."

"I understand," Morone said, clasping de Guise's hand. "I'm so terribly sorry about your brother. I heard the news when I was in Rome. Has the French king taken action yet?"

De Guise said, "I heard today that the authorities tore apart the assassin. Hanged, drawn, quartered, but they failed to do it properly and finally took the man apart with a sword." He crossed himself. "May God have mercy."

Magdalena thought of Agnella's tormentor, whose execution had failed in somewhat the same way. But in the next moment, all the hair stood up on her arm. Assassination? His brother?

Was his brother a heretic?

"I didn't support having the assassin executed," de Guise said, "and especially not like that. But the killer named his employer, and it's Gaspard de Coligny. The king is hardly going to be swift to take action against such a man as that. Therefore my family has declared a blood feud."

Morone gasped. "Are you going to return home?"

"No." De Guise's eyes grew fierce against the pallor of his cheeks. "His killers acted as they did because they were Huguenots. I can strike best against Huguenots from here, at the council."

There were tears in his eyes. His brother. Of course he'd cry. How would she feel if the Marcoli family killed her brother? Or her sister?

Morone said, "Then come with me. I won't take much of your time. Your Catherinite can remain out here with mine."

De Guise said, "Is that wise? We know there are assassination-minded heretics."

"Then they'll have to come through my parlor to reach us, and the Catherinites can deter them out here," said Morone, and he shut the door between them.

Magdalena sat at the window.

Tadea sounded resentful. "You have to do something about Morone to make him give you better access."

"The man's got a head harder than a granite statue." Magdalena shrugged. "He's going to take me with him to Innsbruck, so perhaps I can gain better access there. Especially if he believes there are Lutheran assassins, he'll want me close at hand."

Assassins. Just saying the word made her uncomfortable, and Magdalena got back up, restless. She moved around the study to tidy it up.

Are we assassins?

No, they were special operatives of the pope. They were brides of Christ and defenders of their Mother the Church. They acted by special order only and under the authority of the pope. Executioners, maybe. Assassination was different.

The Church only opted to execute a heretic when there were no other means to rectify the problem. When it was proven. Usually it was the worldly authorities who ordered those executions, but it didn't have to be. It wasn't the pope's fault that he was the worldly authority of the Papal States. He needed freedom to protect his country and his Church. That meant having his own special forces. There were the Swiss Guard who protected Church officials in public. In private, there were the Catherinites. Bodyguards. Protectors. Ascoltrices. And sometimes the executors of special sentences.

She paced the room again, but with nothing left to tidy up, she stood at the window. "I'll have to pack and return tonight. He wants to leave early in the morning, so I should stay nearby."

Tadea nodded. "Simonetta would lose his mind if Morone left you in Trent. We need to know what he tells the emperor."

We're ascoltrices. We're servants of the pope. Magdalena blinked harder as she looked at Trent's rooftops. We're the handmaidens of the Lord, and we're doing God's work.

# TWENTY-NINE

Although not as far a journey as Rome, Innsbruck took a toll. Starting on the morning of April 16th, Magdalena sat in the carriage beside Morone, struggling to keep herself recollected and always at attention. With her dagger on her arm and her rosary at her waist, she watched the roads for bandits and Lutherans. The Emperor kept this part of the country safe, but given the death of de Guise's brother, Magdalena took no chances.

The *assassination* of de Guise's brother. An assassination that two months later had left him in tears and a family in chaos.

Whenever they stopped, Magdalena stretched and worked as much of her body as possible before the legate's entourage stuffed themselves back in the carriage. In the carriage, sometimes she prayed. Sometimes Morone would talk to other members, and she'd listen.

Simonetta would have given his eyeteeth to be here, but he'd have to wait for his report, and it would contain nothing of interest. The men in the carriage said nothing they wouldn't have said before the entire papal court.

And then Innsbruck: the facades charming and striking, the air crisp and thin, the buildings different from Rome and now also different from Trent. They were white. They were squared off. The streets were roomier and straighter. Everywhere Magdalena looked, rooftops joined to rooftops, leading naturally to the desire of running through the whole city without ever once touching the ground.

Finally they reached the palace, Ambras Castle: a fortress in the heart of Innsbruck, towering and tall but without all the architectural accoutrements she'd come to expect from Italian buildings. Straight white walls led to two levels of black tile roof.

She could climb that too. It would be difficult, but she could climb it.

Servants swarmed around their carriage and ushered everyone out onto the paving stones. Although Magdalena longed to linger in the open air, Morone motioned her to follow him.

They entered a tremendous hallway, then were escorted through another foyer and past another series of guards, and then another. A team of extremely fashionable servants met them on a higher floor, and based on the conversation, these were overseers of some sort, as though the palace were its own miniature country within a country within an empire. The entourage's quarters were being sorted out, and a meal would be brought them, and the cardinal would be summoned to meet the emperor just before dinner.

Magdalena stayed very near Morone, and she made note of their path through the building. He would have a whole suite for himself and his small entourage, but she was also the only woman in the group, and therefore the most likely to be culled out and brought to a nearby convent for safekeeping. She had to make sure she could get back to him if that were to happen.

Servants carried up the group's baggage, and then two Spanish-speaking maids tried to escort Magdalena from the room. "Sir!" she called.

Morone stopped them, then said to her in Italian, "What do your kind do about sleep?"

"We don't sleep." Magdalena kept herself from smiling. "We give it up for the Lord."

Morone hesitated only a moment. "You can't stay in my room."

"Of course not. But surely this suite has rooms for servants."

Morone's brow contracted.

She bowed her head. "I'm not going to tarnish your reputation. If you need me to be on another floor, or quartered with the emperor's servants, I'll go. But I have to stay in the palace, and I need to be able to access you for safety."

He frowned. "What if a man tries to tarnish *your* reputation?"

Magdalena said, "Perhaps you could ask your hat."

Morone laughed. "Thank you for the reminder. I'm sure we can find some means to get you quartered."

After some questions, one of the servants showed Morone to a new part of the suite. All the cardinal's rooms were double-doored and plush, the furniture solid as though it had been set in place by God Himself during the second day of Creation. On the other side, though, were smaller rooms, each with a bell on the wall. From the lavish side of the suite, Morone could pull a rope and it would ring on the practical side. Among these smaller quarters, one of the emperor's staff opened a room for Magdalena.

"If anyone comes in to kill me," Morone joked, "I'll ring the bell for you."

To her delight, her tiny room was equipped with a tiny window. She deposited her bag on a bed softer than any she'd ever slept in, then returned to Morone's suite to unpack.

"We'll meet the emperor in an hour." He glanced at her. "Wear your best. You can stay with me, but do your order proud."

"It's his road we traveled," she said. "He's the emperor of the dust on my clothes."

Morone chuckled. "He's the emperor of a lot of things he doesn't care to see, is my guess."

When the time came, everyone in the party had gotten presentable, and again the higher-status servants appeared at the door. Although they gave Magdalena a suspicious look when she joined the party, no one dared suggest to Morone that his menials didn't need to attend the audience.

One of the servants went ahead and announced them to the emperor, and thereafter they were further announced. Guards appeared and guided them into a room larger than some of Trent's cathedrals. Paintings lined the walls, and the ceiling itself seemed made of gold.

A gold ceiling. Did God Himself live in a palace like this?

Feeling small, Magdalena bumped into Morone. He glanced at her, then smiled. It was probably meant as reassurance.

After they walked at least thirty minutes across the hall (it felt longer than the walk from St. Martin's to Madruzzo's palace) a man exclaimed, "Giovanni! Welcome to Innsbruck!"

It was the Holy Roman Emperor Ferdinand. Magdalena recognized him from his portraits.

Morone switched to Spanish as he spoke with the emperor, and the emperor guided him to some cushioned chairs arranged before a fireplace.

Morone introduced his entire entourage, including Magdalena.

"I'm told you're our new chief legate," said the emperor, "and I apologize for taking you away from your very important work at Trent."

"I have even more important work to do here," said Morone. "I greatly desire the council to succeed, of course, but I suspect I want it less than you do."

"Better men than myself have given everything to bring this to fruition," said the emperor, "starting with my father. You were at the very first period, yes?"

If Magdalena recalled correctly, it was Morone's musings on justification at the first period that led to his later imprisonment and trial for heresy. She folded her hands in her lap and looked away as Morone said, "I was. Moreover, we just lost two truly great souls."

"Hence your promotion to chief legate. I'd always wondered why you weren't named a legate from the start. How long have I known you? Since 1536? You've had quite a career." Ferdinand sighed, and his face became very grave. "I was so saddened to hear about the death of Cardinal Seripando. He was a great man. A truly saintly man."

Morone nodded. "It's quite a blow to the Church."

"My father used to invite him to the court all the time. Whenever he could listen to one of Seripando's sermons, he would. We invited him here particularly to remain with us, but he wouldn't." The Emperor shook his head. "Such solid teachings from the man. He wanted to bring us all back in line with what Christ Himself had taught, in every way faithful."

Magdalena's skin was all goosebumps. She snuck a look at the emperor. He spoke in full earnest.

"Cardinal Seripando's very life was a model of the reform we need in the Church," Ferdinand continued. "I see some of the hypocrisies coming forth from Trent, or going into Trent, and it grinds my teeth the way they preach change but practice stubbornness." The Emperor got to his feet and paced. "They take a week to make a decision, then write to Rome to report what they've decided, and then the pope gathers his Curia around himself and they take another week to decide whether to honor the decision. This cannot be." Ferdinand pivoted and fixed his gaze on Morone. "A council was called because the Church requires reform. To then shape the council into an instrument that can never in a thousand years institute any meaningful reform is to dishonor God Himself. I cannot at the end of my life stand before the Lord and make a recounting of what I've done with the great power He's given me if I have to admit that I watched His Church rot from the inside without taking action."

"You aren't refusing to take action," Morone said. "You have exerted every influence you can."

"And I will do more." Ferdinand's voice grew sharper. "I am very glad you're here because I have many things to say to the pope's first man at this Council. With Seripando at the tiller, I had little to fear because I knew the Church had been placed, intentionally or by accident, into the hands of a living saint."

Magdalena's heart skipped, and this vast, cavernous room all at once had no air in it.

A living saint.

Morone gave the emperor a knowing look. "But about me, you're not so sure."

He was smiling, but it wasn't enough to diffuse the emperor.

"About you, no, I'm not so sure. What I want, and what I told de Guise I wanted, and what I told the pope himself I wanted, is for the pope to leave the walls of Rome and get in a carriage and travel up to Trent. I have come to Innsbruck. The least the pope could do is move to Bologna, so as to make the messengers' horses that much more rested."

Morone inclined his head. "His health won't allow it."

Ferdinand said, "His health, or his desire not to have to look his questioners in the face?"

Morone said, "His health, sir."

"If his health is that fragile, then all the more reason to conclude the council before he succumbs to the inevitable." Ferdinand looked completely unconvinced that the Angel of Death was standing watch beside the papal carriage, awaiting the moment they hitched up the first horse. "Do you not see the irony, Giovanni? Trent has spent months arguing about whether a bishop should stay within his diocese while we beg the bishop of Rome to come to Trent, and instead he stays in Rome."

Morone shook his head.

"The health of Seripando, did that prevent him from doing his duty before God?" Ferdinand's voice sharpened. "Did the health of Gonzaga? Or did they instead do what the Church needed and what God demanded, even though it meant surrendering their lives?"

The room had grown around her, like a canyon. Magdalena felt like a mouse at the base of a mountain, the rocks sheer on either side, the deer and the wolves tremendous while she huddled, exposed, beneath the bare branches of a winter-stripped bush. The air felt thin and the room, hot. Dizzy, she sat with her muscles locked so she wouldn't topple off the overstuffed chair and onto the lacquered floor.

"Girolamo Seripando was also given power, and how did he use it?" Ferdinand paced away again. "His election to head the Augustinians could have unlocked luxuries. I know we offered him luxuries if only he stayed with us, and he accepted none of them because any man who could preach the way he could would never accept such accommodations. He was, in effect, a bishop who moved through his entire 'diocese' and cultivated exactly what we needed in our priests. Community. Education. Prayer. That man understood reform, and I thought—in my naïveté I thought—that by elevating him to legate the pope agreed with me." Ferdinand spun back. His dark Spanish eyes bored into

Morone. "But instead we have months of deadlock over the most trivial questions, and that deadlock will end this period of the council with the inevitable death of Pope Pius IV."

Morone started to speak, but Ferdinand cut him off. "Seripando should have been made pope. If he had, the council would have concluded, and the Church would be reformed. If he were at the Church's helm, Seripando would still be alive."

---

In her black garb, black-gloved and black-shod and with her head wrapped in a black scarf, Magdalena slipped out the window that night. Although the walls had seemed sheer from the outside, when actually faced with them, she found them easy enough to scale. She descended to the lower roof, and there she sat, looking at the sky.

Stars. Innsbruck had the same stars as Trent, and Magdalena lay back on the roof tiles to watch them without any dulling effect from the moon. The moon itself was the slightest of curves, like the shred of a fingernail, and tomorrow it would be gone.

She shouldn't fall asleep. Though the night wasn't chilly, she didn't want to awaken numb and stiff and then have to search for toeholds in the wall. Instead she let the night air enliven her. She'd been stuffed into a carriage far too long.

Under the stars she prayed, and she recited psalms long since committed to memory while she listened to the sounds of a world outside the boundaries of the Papal States. Here she wasn't just over the border. Here she was, truly, in German lands.

Even in the nearly full dark, she could keep climbing. She could scale the further walls and slip into the higher floors where the emperor slept. With no major difficulty, she could climb into his window and find him in his bed. If she were really an assassin, she could kill him where he slept.

He was a reformer. He wanted to change the Church. He'd criticized the pope in every way he could and was encouraging Morone to do the same. But she wasn't an assassin. She would never do such a thing.

Lena had said the Roman nuns climbed like monkeys, and now Magdalena spent a little time doing exactly that, making careful note of where she had to return in order to get back into her own bed rather than surprising some unsuspecting maid.

At midnight the church bells would toll for *matins* (which her order normally prayed together with *lauds* at three o'clock) and that would be time for her to get back to her room. She could pray *matins* and *lauds* together at the earlier hour, then let her exhausted body collapse in that tiny room with its tiny window.

Assassins killed for money, whereas she'd taken a vow of poverty. Assassins had no authority, but she worked under the authority of God's representative.

Still, wasn't the Holy Roman Emperor also God's representative on earth? And he'd called Seripando a living saint. Although not living anymore. She had killed him.

There was no way around her being a killer. She'd killed in self-defense back at Santi Cosma e Damiano. Unintentionally, and in order to preserve her virtue, and without thinking about the consequences, she'd killed. In that she felt justified, and if the lives of the saints were filled with stories of women who went to extreme measures to protect their virtue, then she fit right into that framework.

There had been Cavanei who'd paid a man to assassinate Seripando, and again, that she could justify. A man had wanted to kill, and she'd stopped him.

But again: that man had wanted to kill. Was he operating under orders from his Lutheran Church? Was that man only her schismatic counterpart?

There was also de Guise's brother, killed by some monster working under religious and political pressure. That was assassination by definition, but was it different from hers? She was operating under a legitimate authority, the authority of God who was the owner of life and death.

She wasn't an assassin, so there was no reason for her now to be perching on the edge of this roof, tears overspilling her eyes while every muscle in her neck and back tightened up, and with her hands clenched around the stones as she remembered a soft voice and wrinkled skin and eyes that held both welcome and challenge.

Or maybe she should be crying, because assassins don't cry. Assassins collect their money and put away their weapons and feel satisfied with a job well done. They don't cry over a death any more than a lace-maker cries over the sale of a shawl.

The bells rang, and Magdalena finally cried for Seripando. She cried because the emperor had loved him, and it was obvious Morone had respected him. Maybe she'd loved him too. He'd cared about Chiara, and Chiara had also ended up dead. Maybe they were together in Heaven now. Maybe they were together in Purgatory, praying for Magdalena's soul because she was an assassin and the outrage of an emperor had held up a mirror to her heart.

Her own mother probably lay awake right now, crying over the outrages suffered by Fiora and Domenico because the Marcoli family had declared a blood feud of their own.

Gonzaga had begotten five children. Were they mourning in their own beds, clutching an official letter from the pope? Were they outraged about their father's death, thinking he'd gone to Trent against his will to serve the pope and had then given his life in the pursuit of a Council that never would end?

The moon was nothing tonight. Maybe it was grieving too, closing its eyes against a world filled with murder.

Magdalena took to the streets, silent in her steps and not taking care to run through the shadows because in this near-moonlessness were no patches of brightness to give her away. She ran until she reached the Hofkirche, a church at the center of the oldest part of Innsbruck and built by Ferdinand to honor his father, Emperor Maximilian. It was Emperor Maximilian who first had called the council.

Its white facade was lifeless in the dark where it should have shone in the moonlight. Magdalena searched the Gothic structure for a place she could get a grasp, and then she started to climb.

By Rome's standards this wasn't a tall structure. Houses on either side pressed close, and its roof sloped gently on all sides, like a squat pyramid. No, you wouldn't find something this plain in Rome, but it got the job done. She found handholds on one of the layered buttresses, then scrambled up that to a lower roof. From the lower roof she found a series of tiny set-in windows, and from there reached the highest roof. This was broken only by a tower, and up this she climbed next, again using the windows for hand and footholds.

The very top of the tower was hardest because she had to climb outward in order to get over the lip, but once there she wiggled up on her stomach until she had her entire self at the very top.

What could Tadea do with her arrows from this height? Whom could she not take down from this vantage point if the pope only issued the order? How far could Magdalena throw her dagger with the same orders?

How far was it to the ground? And if she jumped, would the entrails of a dead killer look different spread across the walkway of a church?

She couldn't. She couldn't do it because dying in this state meant damnation. Murder was mortal sin. This was eternal death, carried within herself in a locked box, awaiting the moment when her soul met the Almighty and she had to hand over the treasures locked inside. When the time came to render an accounting, what an account she would have to reconcile.

There was no way to make up for the deaths of Gonzaga and Seripando, nor the deaths of any other heretics the pope dispatched her to remove from the sight of the world. A lifetime of penance wouldn't bring them back. In two lifetimes, she couldn't ever make up for the good that Seripando and Gonzaga might have done had they each been given one more year of life to devote to the council.

What could they have accomplished? Reform, maybe? Reconciliation with Emperor Ferdinand? Peace between the Church and King Philip II? Might they even have ensured the return of the Lutherans and Huguenots?

She could confess, but who to confess to? Simonetta would brand her a hysterical woman and refuse to absolve her for her emotions. Morone would hate her if he knew. She didn't trust anyone else.

Standing, she hurled her dagger off the roof. She counted the seconds as it fell, counted the seconds to the clang on the cobbles. But she didn't follow it.

Again came the tears, and this time Magdalena pulled off her head wrap to wipe her eyes. No one would see her up here, and her jerking sobs wouldn't carry, so she let it happen.

She couldn't die this way. She didn't want to go to Hell. But she couldn't live this way either, and the more she sat with the knowledge of what she was, the more she realized that she didn't need to die to go to Hell. In its own way, this entrapment in her own heart was Hell itself.

# PART FOUR
## ROSEWATER

# THIRTY

The next morning, Morone sent every member of his entourage out of the room except Magdalena. When the last one closed the door, he faced her. "What happened to you? Who has hurt you?"

"No one hurt me."

Magdalena's voice was raspy, and she turned from him to clear his breakfast tray from the desk with his notes and his books. He was writing plans in anticipation of meeting with Emperor Ferdinand.

He stepped closer. "Don't lie. Someone hurt you."

Magdalena jumped when his hand came down on her shoulder. The tray fell from her hands, and crockery shattered on the floor. "I'm sorry!" she yelped, dropping to her knees and gathering the pieces as quickly as she could, fishing them out of the puddle of tea on the wooden floor.

One of the servants rushed in, saw her on the floor with the broken tray, saw Morone standing over her, and said, "Sister, allow me to clean it."

Magdalena grabbed the tail of her overtunic. "I'm sorry."

"She's ill," Morone said to the servant. "Please summon the emperor's doctor to examine her."

Magdalena looked up, but her vision blurry with tears. "Sir, I'm not ill. You startled me."

"It's just crockery," he said. "Teacups can be replaced. You look very ill, and I demand to know: who hurt you?"

Magdalena shook her head, unable even to speak. Teacups can be replaced. Cardinals can be replaced too. But Seripando couldn't. Chiara couldn't.

What could be replaced? Her dagger. She'd found it last night in the street, dented in the hilt but otherwise unharmed. It was back on her arm, where it should be.

Morone had gone grim. "I've heard about things that happen to women while traveling. You were left alone last night, and—"

"No one touched me, sir."

Morone looked over her head to another servant. "Please escort Sister Magdalena back to her room."

"I have to stay with you!"

"The palace is secure enough. You need to stay in your cell and rest. The travel has been too much." He stepped forward. "Or are you going to tell me who has hurt you? Because it doesn't matter to me who it is. You say the word, and I will see to it that he's punished. The emperor will listen to me. He'll be punished first by the civil authorities and second by the Church."

Magdalena's throat tightened.

"Very well." He turned away. "Stay here. I'll make sure your room is guarded, little bodyguard, and when I return, perhaps we can talk."

This was how Morone began three weeks of negotiations. For three entire weeks, he would meet once a day with Emperor Ferdinand, sometimes over a meal and sometimes in Ferdinand's study, and sometimes with Ferdinand's churchmen. When Magdalena finally convinced Morone that she'd only been sick from so much travel, she joined them as well.

Morone called her his little bodyguard, to everyone else's amusement. He asked her to take notes for him, which she did. In the evenings, then, she would recopy the notes and he would burn the originals. He would then lock the paper in his desk.

"If you don't mind, I would like to write to my family," she said one day. "It's been two weeks since last I wrote home. My mother will be worried."

Morone said, "I will look at the letter before it's sent," and when she exclaimed in anger, he said, "because there are more in Rome than just your family. I don't need poisoned reports about me flying back to the pope on vulture wings. Write to your mother, but I want to make sure you write only to her."

So Magdalena wrote to her mother, and she kept the language as plain as she could. Morone read the letter before allowing her to seal it, and he gave it to a messenger to carry to Rome along with letters of his own.

Next, Morone showed her his own letter to the pope, and he produced another blank sheet of paper. "You are going to write another letter, this one to Simonetta. Tell him I entrusted this letter to you before I sent it to the pope, and then you are to copy exactly what I've written and send it to him."

Magdalena hesitated. "What does this accomplish?"

"Despite what Simonetta may think," Morone said, "I'm not a wild-eyed reformer. Nor, as de Guise thinks, am I a stone-hearted traditionalist bent on keeping the Curia in the hands of the same rich families who've held the reins for hundreds of years. I need the council to function. That means the pope needs accurate information, and I need Simonetta on my side."

Magdalena said, "And then, once I write this—you send a completely different letter to the pope?"

"No, after I write this, you seal both letters, and together we walk them downstairs to the messenger who is taking it to Rome." Morone's eyes were narrow, and his humor was gone.

"I'm going to have enough on my hands with keeping the emperor happy. I don't need to be looking for the knife in my back from my allies."

That came a little too close to home. Magdalena seated herself at his desk and copied Morone's entire letter. Cardinal Simonetta, I've gotten this letter away from the principal legate in order to send you information on what he is negotiating with Emperor Ferdinand. These are the exact words he's sending the pope. Following that was the painstaking process of copying out five pages of information from Morone. In it were the details of conversations already had, of conversations yet to be wrought, and the names of everyone involved. There was a reminder of everything the pope had asked Morone to achieve and an assessment of each goal's likelihood of success.

Simonetta would love this. He would hate it. He would pore over the letter to hunt for ways to convince the pope that his confidence in Morone was in every way misplaced. He'd try to convince the pope that by doing everything the pope had asked him to do, Morone was failing in his position. Simonetta would also love it because he'd think he had information Morone thought he didn't, and he'd hate it because in the end, there would be nothing to accomplish with it.

Magdalena wrote until her hands hurt, but she finished all the pages. Then she sealed up the letter, and Morone sealed the original. Everything was addressed, and Magdalena found herself accompanying the servant to the main hall where the overseer accepted all the letters (and payment for their delivery) and assured her the Rome letters would go tonight, but the Trent letters might have to wait a day or two.

Back to the suite she went, her head foggy but her sense of direction functioning enough that she never feared getting lost. She was an assassin, after all. Moving through unknown corridors was supposed to be her strength.

When she returned to the suite, Morone summoned her into his office. "Who is Fiora?" he asked. "A great-aunt?"

He'd read her letter, but now he required the context. "My younger sister. She's fourteen, and she has a twisted foot and a short leg, along with some other problems."

Morone studied her. "But you asked your mother if Fiora was still able to get around town."

"I left just after one of the sisters at Saint Sebastian's set her up with a clever set of shoes. Sister Agnella. She made a mold of Fiora's foot and fitted a shoe to that." Magdalena could see Fiora's twisted foot in her head as she spoke. Why was it that after a year and a half she wondered what her sister's face looked like, and she'd forgotten her brother's smile? But all along that one foot was emblazoned in her mind. "But Agnella said Fiora's foot might grow as she got stronger, and once that happened, the shoe wouldn't fit as well. At that point, she'd need a new one."

Morone's eyes had widened. "That's very clever of Sister Agnella."

"Saint Sebastian's runs a hospital for incurables. We had to cobble together workarounds for patients all the time." There were so many one-of-a-kind custom creations for all the various individual ways people had to die. They needed specific kinds of help as one at a time their body parts failed. "Sister Agnella studied the way Fiora limped and then measured her and sat up all night, carving a wedge to fit against her."

"She sounds very resourceful." Morone shook his head as he returned to his desk. "You all do. But I guess that's to be expected."

Magdalena said, an edge in her voice, "To be expected that Christ calls the cleverest women to be His brides?"

Morone looked up. "Is that your experience? That Christ only calls the cleverest? And then, because the cleverest are all behind enclosures, does that leave the dullest women for the raising of children and the management of households?"

"I think He calls the very cleverest to the order of Saint Catherine of Alexandria." Magdalena cocked her head. "But we're a small order, and that leaves plenty of clever women to run the households of Rome. Is there anything else you require, sir?"

"While you're at your reading," Morone said, returning to his work, "see if you can find out where He calls the humblest."

She bowed. "For that, sir, you might want to check the Carmelites. I haven't had the honor of meeting any myself."

---

Because Emperor Ferdinand had other business to attend to than Morone and a recalcitrant Council, Magdalena spent long days wandering the palace and walking through Innsbruck. The compact city felt alien to her, the food strange in the market stalls, the language rough and yet fun to work around. She walked the palace grounds and enjoyed the lengthening daylight. Morone's driver introduced her to their horses, and when he realized she'd never learned to ride, he taught her.

The Emperor's stables contained several sidesaddles. "This was designed by Catherine de' Medici," said the driver. "She thought it ridiculous that a woman couldn't control her own horse, so she added another pommel, and you can sit with your right leg hooked around this part," he showed her, "and your left foot in this stirrup."

One of the stable boys was leading another horse from the stable when their horse let out a loud whinny. "Easy, boy," said the driver. "I know you're friends, but he's got work to do. And so do you."

"Could I use pants and ride astride?" Magdalena said.

The driver flushed. "I suppose you could. But—"

"The horse isn't going to compromise my virtue," Magdalena said, so in an agony of blushes and nerves, the driver let her straddle the horse in the traditional way, with her habit girded and her exercise pants beneath.

As the three weeks wore on, Morone let Magdalena stay in his presence more often, sometimes in the same room while he wrote letters. When she ran out of prayers to pray or liturgical hours to say, she exercised. Morone at first watched with raised eyebrows, but Magdalena would begin with her stretches and then work on the slow-motion movements Agnella had taught in Rome. From there she'd practice the choreographed half-fights in which Lena drilled the nuns whenever she had a chance. They were graceful and smooth, but Magdalena concentrated on the ways in which they would be deadly. She made up her own on some days. She re-enacted her fight with the imposter bishop as well as her fight with his mercenary. She acted out the throat-jab that had killed her confessor at Santi Cosma e Damiano, but there wasn't much to that, only the motion of discovery, the kick behind her to get free, the pivot, the jab, and then the horror when he didn't get up.

Morone exclaimed, "What are you doing?"

"Defending. Striking back." She performed a slow-motion block followed by a strike. Do this a hundred times, Lena had said. Do it slowly and have your muscles learn every sense of the motion. Let your arms feel where they need to go, and then when they need to do it, they'll act with perfection. Chiara had asked, *Is that from the Holy Spirit?* and Lena had replied, *No, it's from your will to survive. It's from the heart of your womanhood and your desire to protect your virtue.*

Now Magdalena knew why: because the Holy Spirit would hardly come into the abode of an assassin. To claim He would do so added blasphemy to murder, so Lena was being careful with their souls.

Morone kept watching from his desk. "That's hardly a defensive move."

Magdalena spun toward him and jumped onto the back of the sofa, then leaped from the sofa to the floor, landing in a shoulder-roll, then back onto her feet. From there she jumped up onto the desk. She roundhouse kicked, high enough to clear Morone's head, and then performed the same block and strike with enough speed to snatch an arrow from the air.

She jumped backward off the desk, landing on the carpet with no sound.

"I beg to differ." She straightened. "I believe it has sufficient defensive capability."

His eyes were wider than she'd ever seen. "You—"

She bowed her head. "We consecrated our bodies to God, and therefore we make sure they're in good condition. To serve." She smiled. "I'm your little bodyguard. Now, if you don't mind, I'll let you go back to your writing."

Then, at the end of the third week, Magdalena took notes during a negotiation where all the disagreements melted like frost in daylight. Emperor Ferdinand and Cardinal Morone reached an understanding, and she wrote the words with astonishment. Emperor Ferdinand would send instructions to his envoys to support the legates rather than supporting the French and the Spanish. Ferdinand also grudgingly allowed that the bishops would continue to vote as individuals rather than as national blocs.

And lastly, the emperor finally conceded that it would be chaos to have everyone proposing their own agendas, but as a concession of his own, Morone agreed the legates would take into account the bishops' and the envoys' desires. This had been the biggest fight all along. The legates could *win* any argument they wanted simply by not having it. "Reform of the head," for example, would never be discussed in the council sessions because the legates wouldn't put it on the docket. *But why?* all the Spanish and French bishops had asked. *Why is it that only the legates decide what's of importance to all of Christendom when the French and the Spanish had come with long lists of questions? Why couldn't the faithful receive from the Eucharistic cup? What should they do about the rites of the Mass celebrated in languages other than Latin?*

The Emperor did continue to insist that the pope reform the Curia, that cardinals should be promoted only on the basis of their merit rather than on the basis of the bed in which they were sired. And he grudgingly added to Morone that having the pope review everything from the council before allowing it to move forward remained an impediment to progress of any sort. "To achieve anything," he said, "you will have to operate independently and let Rome deal with the consequences. To leave things be is the same as not to have a Council in the first place."

With the negotiations concluded, a snowstorm of letters emerged from Innsbruck that afternoon. Morone wrote to the pope and to Carlo Borromeo. Morone wrote to Simonetta while at the next desk Magdalena also wrote to Simonetta, copying the letter to the pope. The Emperor wrote to the pope. The Emperor wrote to all his envoys and to the Spanish envoys. And finally, just before the messengers were dispatched to make as much distance toward Rome as they could in the failing daylight, Magdalena wrote to her mother.

Morone looked over her letter, then allowed her to seal it and add it to the stack.

"We'll leave tomorrow," Morone said. "Our letters will precede us to Trent by perhaps a day, but it's better this way. Give them warning of what's to come."

"The *zelanti* will be pleased," Magdalena said. "De Guise will be horrified."

"No, he won't." Morone shook his head. "He's a politician. He knows that in order to achieve your ends, you oftentimes need to make your opponents think they're achieving theirs. The Emperor's shadow over the council for the past six months has stopped us from achieving anything. As soon as we return to Trent, we'll have the road open."

Magdalena said, "Until the next crisis."

"I want to wrap this up in six months." Morone sighed. "We won't have another crisis."

There was always time for another crisis. Nothing moved quickly. Debates that could have been settled during dinner ended up taking months, and she'd already been away from home for sixteen of those.

Sixteen months during which the Marcoli family sometimes remembered her family after a night of drinking and lay in wait for her brother in the mornings. Months during which Fiora had to go outside only with an escort because the Marcolis had threatened to do to her what their dead priest-relative had tried to do to her sister. (Which then they backtracked: of course Magdalena must have made that up, being ugly and unwanted, and their priest-relative being a paragon of virtue. Except that they would laugh then and say good on him, because the Lutherans could take wives. And what was the big deal?)

She could be home in eight days if she got in a carriage. Five if she rode with the messenger carrying those letters. But at home, what could she do? Climb in through the Marcoli family window and assassinate every one of them in their sleep?

So instead she prepared to return with Morone to Trent.

# THIRTY-ONE

It would take three full days of travel to reach Trent. At sundown on the second night, they found the palace of a certain bishop who was himself at Trent, but whose people were pleased to lodge them for the night. It was an honor. Everything would be made up for their guests. Servants readied a suite and lit fires.

It wasn't until dinners were served on little carts that Magdalena realized she didn't have a room and bed of her own. It was just assumed her body was Morone's personal entertainment, and she had been roomed accordingly. The overseer had glared at Morone, and now she understood why. No wonder, if they thought he was just another Church "reformer" who said the right things and then did whatsoever he pleased.

Teeth clenched, Magdalena slipped into the hallway to find a room of her own. No one paid her any attention. In her habit, once she got away from Morone's suite, she became another invisible member of the staff. Perhaps she was a relative of the nameless bishop or of one of the priests who came in and out of this bishop's palace. The servants didn't pay attention, and Magdalena strode with confidence. If no one noticed a nun, they noticed her even less when she gave them no reason to question her presence.

After a day in the carriage, the sheer relief of flexing her muscles felt like paradise. Maybe she could slip out the window and scale the palace's multiple turrets. Or maybe...and at this thought she smiled. Maybe she could (as suspected) spend the night in a bishop's bed. She'd locate the absent bishop's master suite and spend a night in luxuries no nun would ever replicate.

She already deserved Hell. Surely the concupiscence of a bishop's bed (without a bishop in it) wouldn't damn her further. For one thing, the bishop himself slept there.

At a corner, Magdalena grabbed a laundry basket and then descended the nearest staircase to the servant areas. They bustled with activity, and here she found a place to abandon the basket. At the kitchen she loaded a serving tray. Soon she'd plated a slice of roast with a creamy sauce, plus rosewater buns glazed with sugar, and a small bowl of fruit, all of which she covered with a lid. She also took a small decanter of white wine and a crystal glass, then lay silverware and napkins on the tray. When a chef asked what she was doing, she said, "The master has need of this." The chef huffed but didn't stop her.

Carrying the tray, she strode upstairs with purpose. Master suites were always up high, but not up so high that the master would get out of breath reaching his bed. She followed the carpet where it was more worn and found herself in a ballroom, so she retraced her steps and went the other way. In this part of the corridor she found greater luxuries, more artwork, and statuary. At a sufficiently gorgeous set of double doors, she went inside with her tray and found herself in paradise.

Laughing, Magdalena set down the tray and flung herself on the bed, sinking into its thick blankets and deep mattress. The sunlight slanted at enough of an angle to render the room nearly dark, and she rolled over to gaze out the windows. Orange. Pink. She hadn't thought the sunset would be as gorgeous this high in the mountains, and yet it was even sweeter.

Sitting cross-legged in the bed, she uncovered the tray and devoured the roast. She drank the wine and enjoyed the heady dizziness, then consumed the fruit and lingered over the rosewater buns. They weren't as good as her mother's. For that matter, they weren't as good as her own, but they would suffice.

Yes, she decided, flopping back in the bed, this would definitely suffice. She'd taken a vow of poverty, but so in theory had the bishop. And although she'd taken a vow of obedience, no one had told her not to sleep here or enjoy a meal the servants would probably have given her anyhow if she'd asked. They'd doubtless brought a tray to Morone's suite with double portions, figuring he'd want his lady-friend well-fed and moderately inebriated before bedding her.

She left the bishop's bishopless bed (her preferred way of being bedded) and explored the room, wondering if some servant would come through in the morning just because he was assigned to clean it, and clean it he would even if the bishop never came by. Sadly, she shouldn't take the chance.

She was here now, though. The ceilings were twice to three times her height, with columns lining the walls and unlit sconces. The furniture matched the room: heavy and dark, ornate and artistic. There were two fireplaces, each with a deep mantle and statues on either side.

No wonder priests fought one another to be bishops and cardinals. But priests didn't climb. They would never enjoy this room the way a Catherinite could.

Unsure if it were the wine that made her want this, but quite sure she didn't care, Magdalena slipped off her shoes and girded her habit. In the corner, she scaled the wall, then sat on top of an armoire.

It was dusty, of course. She jumped to the floor, running her hands over her now-greyed habit, then tested the curtains. She used them as a rope and made her way up over the window, perching there to scan the whole room.

A chandelier hung in the middle. Could she jump there from here? Would it hold her weight? That was definitely the wine asking. Magdalena decided yes to the first but no to the second, and she turned her attention instead to the bed canopy. She couldn't land on top of that (she'd plunge through) but she could (and did) jump with her hands outstretched, catching the canopy bar and swinging her body so she landed on the mattress.

The bed lurched and groaned, but it held, and she laughed. She climbed the curtains to make that jump again.

With the room as her playground, she scaled the walls over and over, eventually observing the room from a statue niche. The headiness of wine had diminished, so she sat alongside the Blessed Virgin, who stood with her hands outstretched. Magdalena outstretched her own hands, and she grinned. *Our Lady of Peace,* she thought. *Peace be on this house. I don't have any of my own to offer you, but you could have it if I did.*

The door opened, and Magdalena tensed. Heart pounding, she tucked herself behind the statue

It was dark enough that they wouldn't easily see her, but they'd look closely if they heard a sound. She breathed through her mouth.

"We don't know what he's going to do," said the man who entered. "The council depends on him, but he's the pope's man."

"But the chance," said the second man. "God gave us this opportunity. You can't deny it."

The pair opened the bishop's desk and sorted through some papers. "Morone," one of them was saying. "Morone. Don't you remember his name? He was imprisoned as a heretic."

"They should have gotten rid of him then."

"Who knows why they do things in Rome." The first man shook his head. "Okay, I have what we need."

Magdalena let them close the door, then jumped to the floor. Holding her empty dinner tray, she slipped back into the hallway and followed them, walking as though she were making a delivery. She noted which room they entered, and that there were already several gathered inside, but she walked straight past without turning her head.

When she heard them close their door, she entered the next room, unused and with all its furniture covered by sheets. In a corner she stripped off her black overtunic and her white sheath so she stood in just her black exercise garb. It was late. She didn't have her gloves, but she opened the window and slipped outside, then made her way to the next window.

"It's just him and his concubine, plus four servants," said a voice. "We could take out all six if we have to. If anyone asks, we can deny they ever arrived."

Magdalena's eyes narrowed.

"How many people saw them enter?" said another voice. "Dozens? Six people don't just disappear. Our best bet is to have them leave as planned and then attack on the road, that way whatever happens doesn't point back to us."

Her heart raced. The danger wasn't immediate, but danger it clearly was. She needed to move Morone, and she needed to move him in secret. And yes, she was his concubine. No one had asked, but she was his concubine.

Which was, she had to admit, rather more to advantage than having them think her his bodyguard. If they'd realized, they would have roomed her on the other side of the palace with a generous dose of arsenic in her decanter.

"Do we have to kill the nun too?" said one of the voices.

"His whore?" A sigh. "I don't want to kill a woman. She may not even want to be with him."

"We could give her a chance," said one. "Leave her in another city. She'd have to fend for herself, but it looks like she's pretty good at that."

Raucous laughter. Magdalena's cheeks flamed.

Take her away. Leave her in another city to fend for herself.

She had a chance. An unparalleled chance. She could hand over Morone if they made a deal. They could take her somewhere else, a place no one would recognize her as a Catherinite. She would never have to kill again, never hold a letter with a papal seal instructing her to end the life of a powerful man who held the wrong ideas.

She could even bargain with them for money and then send for her mother. Mother could take Fiora and Domenico out of Rome. They could disappear from those streets, and she could live with them again. It wouldn't be home, but *home* for her was long gone, swept away in the tidal wave of vows and vendettas.

One more death and she'd be free. Whether she did it or they did it, it was only one more death, and she'd be released from these lies she'd twisted herself into.

Although the conspirators felt secure, they kept their conversation hushed, as if maybe they didn't want even God overhearing their plans. It went like this: they knew who Morone was and knew he'd met with the emperor. They considered Morone a plaything of the pope and therefore an enemy of true Christendom. Killing him would throw the council into further disarray, and therefore they, the handful of men they were, had a chance to change Christianity. This was a singular God-given chance to effect real change for the glory of the Kingdom.

Magdalena flinched because she might as well have been listening to herself explaining to Chiara. *I'm sorry. I'm so sorry.*

For Morone to survive tomorrow, he couldn't remain here tonight. If she wanted to save him, the only question was when to leave. Did she need to climb to the second floor right now and break in his window, or could she wait until everyone settled down and then make their move?

But first she needed to decide whether she wanted to do any of that. Whether she shouldn't just go back to the absent bishop's bedroom and let events play out.

How many conspirators were in that room? Six? Could she fight six men all at once? No. Lena had taught her how to fight two simultaneously, but Agnella had said even that wasn't possible. "If you're fighting multiple men," she'd said, "you'll die. You have to line them up. Just move yourself around until they're lined up, and take them down one at a time."

She'd never be able to do that in a room. Besides, were they armed? She had only her dagger. Even assuming she could throw the dagger and kill one before jumping inside, that left far too many. Someone would run for help.

Worse, once she acted, they'd know she was aware of their plot. In danger of getting caught, they'd kill Morone now. Best to wait, whether she wanted to save Morone or save herself.

And of course, it was her first thought as an assassin whether she *could* kill six men at once, not whether she *should*. Filthy soul. Filthy, filthy soul.

Also clear was that everyone had to leave, not just Morone. These conspirators planned to kill the entire party. If she took just Morone, the other four would die. So as the last of the wine left her head, and as the church bells tolled *compline* (and what should have been bedtime) she listened to every scenario the conspirators ran through. They were just as aware of the time as she was. They had until morning, so they didn't rush their decision: if they wanted to kill him in his bed, they could do so just as easily while the local convents were saying *lauds* as at *matins*. If they opted for the highwayman approach, they had several hours. They also had the means to delay Morone's departure until they had helpers on the road.

Magdalena clung to the wall for half an hour while they argued to a resolution: they'd do it in the morning. Morone and his crew would call for their carriage, and some of them would lie in wait on the route while others would follow behind. The ones who followed would flag down the carriage on the pretext of something forgotten, and once the entourage stopped, those on the road would do the deed. They'd remove the woman and kill all the men.

Magdalena returned to the previous room, then with cold-numbed fingers pulled her habit back onto her frozen body.

Confronted with other assassins, what was an assassin to do? She had no belief in honor among thieves. In Rome, there was honor among family members (usually), but another thief was your competition. If someone's family had to get an extra loaf of bread, it should be your own. It was without question in her best interests to hand over Morone and take advantage of the new life they offered.

She could play up her sex and appear helpless. She could work on their belief that Morone was a monster and cry that he'd coerced her. They'd purchase her silence, especially if she traded them access to that suite. Even more especially if she volunteered to do the deed herself.

Shivering, she rubbed her goosebumped arms and wondered what was colder: her body or that series of thoughts.

In a mirror she studied her sleepless eyes and short-shorn hair, her thin mouth and hungry cheeks. No, she couldn't. Her soul was rotten right to the core, but she couldn't make that choice. No more deaths. Not even one. Especially not Morone's. When she went to Hell, at least she'd go to Hell doing her duty by the Church, protecting the man she was assigned to protect.

Back in Morone's parlor she found one of the bishop's maidservants. To the surprise of Morone's valet, she dismissed the woman. Morone's cook, driver, and secretary were already asleep, and she said to the valet, "Don't go to bed. We need to leave."

Before he could object, she slid open the heavy door to the cardinal's bedroom, and she carried in a candle. "Sir, you need to wake up. We have to escape tonight."

# Thirty-Two

Morone looked exhausted, but to his credit he sat up and listened while he became ever more awake. The valet stood in the doorway, and Magdalena waved him in as she pulled a chair closer to the bed to relate everything she'd overheard.

"We have to leave," she concluded. "Now, before they realize you're escaping."

Morone took a deep breath. "Perhaps we can talk to them."

"Talk to them and you'll find a knife in your throat. They don't want to kill you on the premises," Magdalena added, "but they're willing to do so."

The valet said, "How did you hear this conversation? Why would we trust you?"

"Didn't you notice their eyes?" Magdalena asked. "Those weren't servants who didn't want to work. They were angry and restrained. I followed them."

Morone said to the valet, "You can trust her as regards protecting me. That's her duty, and she's quite skilled in guarding officials of the Church. The question is what to do now."

Magdalena said, "We need to get the carriage ready, but without alerting anyone. If they know you're on the move, they're likely to act at once."

The valet said, "The horses are in the stable and will need to be hitched to the carriage."

"Wake the rest of our party," Magdalena said to the valet. "We have until morning, but we should plan now."

She and Morone sat in maddening silence while the valet roused the other three members. Their enemies were planning right now; shouldn't they also be planning? If their enemies were to change their minds and rush in, what could she do? In the room Magdalena saw no shortage of things she could use as weapons, but what of the others? Did any of them know how to fight? Once again, one nun couldn't disable six assailants. Or ten. She probably couldn't handle three.

Morone finally said, "How did you know to listen to their plans?"

Magdalena opted for distraction. "It wasn't just their eyes. I was searching for another room where I could spend the night. They expected me to sleep in your bed."

Morone exclaimed, "They expected what?"

He was more outraged at their bland acceptance of unchastity than their plot to kill him? Smiling, Magdalena said, "You think they didn't believe the same at Innsbruck?"

"Absolutely not," Morone said as the chef entered the room. "Why would they?"

Because most of Christendom expected priests not to honor their vows, Magdalena thought as the driver rushed in, shaken. Because too many women entered convents when they couldn't become brides of men, and not because they longed to be brides of Christ.

Which, if she had to be honest, was why she'd entered Santi Cosma e Damiano. But was it still true? On this night when she could face judgment with a murder-blackened soul, she should at least answer herself honestly.

The valet returned with the secretary, and they all gathered with their candles while Magdalena gave the report again.

Morone said, "They want to derail the council, and they think my death might stop it."

The secretary said, "That would reflect very badly on Emperor Ferdinand."

"I don't care who our deaths would look bad for," Magdalena said. "My job is to make sure Cardinal Morone doesn't die."

Everyone fell silent. How had she come to be in charge here? But all five men were waiting for her direction. "The biggest challenge I see will be getting the carriage ready." She looked to the driver. "How can we do that without anyone noticing?"

"I can go into the stables and ready the horses. They've rested several hours. We can get into the next town at least." The driver frowned. "The carriage will be locked up."

The valet said, "I can get into the carriage house. Lead the horses out one at a time. If we leave directly from the carriage house, we should escape notice."

Magdalena said, "If we leave after midnight, there were be the fewest people around to see us. The main entrance is most likely to be guarded, so we'll need another way out."

The chef said, "When I was in the kitchen, there was a door to the courtyard."

The valet said, "Should we leave right now?"

They all looked at Magdalena. *I'm an assassin, not a general. I don't know the first thing about tactics.* She braced herself. "No, first we let everyone settle down. We have time to pack our belongings, but only the things we can carry out on our own." She shouldn't have to mention that there wouldn't be porters during a midnight escape, but you never knew with officials. "Abandon anything you can't carry, and be prepared to abandon any of that too. Don't pack anything that will make noise. We'll need to take any papers you have," she added to the secretary. "Sometime after midnight, we'll leave. That will give everyone two hours to rest."

They wouldn't be able to sleep. Under the circumstances, who would? This was worse than when she'd had to take out Cavanei.

Morone said, "What if they change their plans and act sooner?"

"I'll stay by the door," Magdalena said, "just in case."

She had nothing to pack, so she helped Morone ready his bag. He'd be abandoning half a trunk's worth of clothes. Then, with her spine pressed to the door she sat, knees tucked up, listening to the hallway and holding her rosary. Even when she couldn't pray, she felt stronger holding it. It was a lifeline and it was a weapon, and it was a cord that tied her to Christ. She didn't deserve His love, but she could still protect a cardinal who did.

At midnight, Magdalena roused the chef and the secretary, both of whom had fallen into a restless doze. The driver slipped downstairs first with the secretary. They would give him a quarter-hour lead time before sending out the chef and the valet. Magdalena had wanted to send out Morone in the second batch, but he refused. "It's only right to ensure their safety," he said. "If I'm killed, so be it, but why should my valet be martyred in my stead?"

From the window Magdalena could make out one figure in the light of the waning moon. He crossed to the stables and slipped inside, and although she listened, she couldn't hear any disturbance from the horses. Those conspirators, knowing they planned to strike in the morning: surely they wouldn't be sleeping well either. They weren't professional soldiers nor were they trained killers. They'd be nervous, reviewing all their plans. What if there were witnesses? What if something went wrong? What if one of them died, and what if the one who died were oneself?

They might even be praying for success. Magdalena had in the past done exactly the same. But praying for harm to come down on a person—was that really prayer? Or was that a curse? And on whose shoulders would God lay that curse?

I'm sorry, she prayed now. If there's a curse, it should come on me. I accept that. But not on Cardinal Morone. Please, Father, not on Cardinal Morone. If one of us has to die tonight, my soul isn't ready to come to you, but it should be mine rather than his. The Church still needs him.

It had never needed her. Christ had many brides. One bride fewer wouldn't create a gap.

Jesus had said that those who lived by the sword would die by the sword. Proverbs said that he who dug a pit would fall into it, and if one rolled a stone, it would roll back on him. Therefore it was fitting that an assassin should be killed by rival assassins. Not desirable, but fitting.

The chef and the valet left the room with one bag each, and Magdalena again waited at the window. This time she actually climbed outside, not turning to note the horror that certainly danced over Morone's face as she exposed herself to the wall of the palace. From higher up she could see better, and the night's chill woke her in a way *lauds* never did. If she had to sacrifice her own life tonight, at least right now she still felt alive and could over that to God with both hands full.

The driver led one of the horses through the courtyard to the carriage house. After the horse was hitched, he'd need to fetch the second. At that point, she'd bring Morone.

Transferring the cardinal was the most dangerous step. There was no way to hide him, and in this house, no way to protect him.

Although there might be one way. She slipped back inside, saying, "Sir, do you have your red hat and cloak?"

He didn't travel wearing red. Those were the ceremonial garments, although as a little girl Magdalena had wondered if cardinals slept in red pajamas.

Morone said, "Still in the trunk," so she pulled them out.

"Sir," she said as he followed her to his bedroom door, "it's you they want dead. If they find us, if there's a fight, I want you to run."

She put his red cloak over her exercise garments and set his red cap on her head. "They're not trained soldiers," she said, to his astonishment. "If there's a fight, they won't think clearly. They're tired and anxious. Let them strike at the red. Let the real red hat escape."

Morone stepped closer. "I can't let you die."

Magdalena clenched her hands. "Sir, you absolutely cannot do anything else. If they fight, the Church requires you to save yourself."

She checked the window to find the smudge of the driver heading back to the stables. "Just a few minutes more."

She stuffed her cast-off habit into her bag, then patted her dagger in its holster. "Aren't cardinals called 'princes of the blood'? Tonight, I'm a princess of the blood."

"God willing, there won't be any blood."

Magdalena signed herself with the cross, then started her stretches. *Matthew. Mark. Luke. John.*

In the stable, a horse neighed, and there came a bang.

Magdalena's heart skipped. "We have to leave. Now."

Another whinny, and she looked out the window. Silence. Everything depended on silence, but you couldn't convince the animals. The horse was balking against the guidance of the driver, head back and hooves planted, and once again he squealed. From the barn came an answering neigh.

Grabbing Morone by the hand, Magdalena ran with him into the hallway, him single-file behind her and her other hand tracing the wall.

Downstairs she could hear doors opening. All those restive sleepers, waiting for the morning when they'd bloody their swords: they weren't going to lie there suffused with curiosity. Guilt was like that: you knew you were wrong, so it made sense that everyone else knew.

Magdalena checked the dark staircase before starting down. The lower level hallway revealed the unsteady glow of a candle, but distant. Morone behind her was in black. In the full dark of the servants' staircase, her red garments might as well have been too.

Down they went. Someone opened a door, ran down the steps, and then slammed another door. They continued descending. Once she pushed Morone into a corner on a landing, but there was no need, and they kept moving. On the ground level they raced for the kitchen, and from the kitchen into the courtyard. The carriage house doors were open, and the driver was hitching the protesting horse into the shafts.

She pressed herself into the doorframe. Voices. And was that metal scraping?

Her heart pounded. "Sir, don't look back. Just run. Go!"

She pushed him into a run and tore off across the courtyard to put herself between the approaching figures and the black-clad Morone. Let the attackers come at her with her visible cloak and distinctive red hat.

They'd kill her. Morone would escape. A necessary sacrifice.

Magdalena let the first attacker hit her while she pivoted her hips to use his momentum. She rolled him up the side of her body, and crashed him onto his head.

She didn't make sure he was down. He'd never get up again.

You can't find three men at once, Agnella had said. Keep them in line.

She flung up the cloak and punched right through it. Distracted, the man didn't see the blow that crashed into his face. She followed with another, then ducked as he kicked her in the ribs.

That cloak was a weapon. As his kick landed, she wrapped the fabric around his leg, trapping it. Threw her weight to the side. Pivoted, twisted, and the second man man went down with maybe a broken leg. Her side stabbed her with every breath. She kicked his temple to keep him on the ground.

The next man was on her too fast, too fast. He punched her in the abdomen, then another blow to her ribs, another, another. A flash of pain as something broke, then another. It was like lightning through her body. She had no distance, no room, no time to come up with a counterattack. She couldn't breathe. Lighting kept striking and she couldn't get past the barrage of punches to counterstrike.

She dropped to the cobbles, then rolled sideways with her side screaming. She leaped to her feet, smashing her shin up into his temple. He went down, blood pouring from his ears and nose.

Morone's carriage rattled into action.

A fourth assailant flattened her from behind, face down into the ground with the red cloak swirling around her. He slammed her face into the ground, and she shoved upward to unseat him while he battered her head and kept her flat with the stones driving into her ribs. Again, the cloak, such a weapon, princes of blood....use it. She struggled within it to face upward while he kept battering her face, but now she had her hands in motion under the cloak. She grabbed the rosary, then drove an elbow up into his eye.

His head snapped backward, and she was up, the rosary around his neck. She twisted him until he went face down, then shoved him to the ground with her knee in his neck. She tightened the cord. The man flailed.

This was it. The next attacker would kill her. Her chest burned as she held the man beneath her, but she hadn't the strength to finish him off. She couldn't even wipe the blood from her eyes. Still, Morone was free. Morone. Morone.

*I'm sorry, God.* Every breath burned and her leg and both arms blazed with pain. Her vision was blacking out. *I'm coming to You.*

"Stop!" A man was running toward her from the carriage. She looked at him, but she couldn't do anything more.

"Stop!" he called again. "Magdalena, come now!"

Morone? But he had to leave. He had to get out of here.

She tried to get off the fourth assailant and fell to the cobbles. Morone yanked her up by the arms. "Leave him!"

Magdalena turned back to the man on the ground and rasped, "We are the princes of blood."

She had no idea where the force in her voice came from. She felt like a corpse that just didn't realize it was dead.

Morone yanked her into a run at the carriage. The driver was shouting at her to get inside, and she flung herself onto its floor while Morone jumped on the sideboard. He slammed the door behind her even as the driver urged the horses to speed.

The floor rattled against her ribs. Every breath was a knife against her lungs. The one who hit her chest, he must have broken something. Broken everything. But all around, everyone was alive. The chef and the valet had their faces pressed against the back window to watch for pursuers, but they were alive. Afraid. Shaking with pain and unspent energy, but alive.

Morone took her hand to lift her to a seat, but Magdalena took it back, curled around herself and her aching ribs and her numb shin. Her head vibrated with the horses' motion, but she was alive. She and her filthy soul had escaped divine judgment for one more day.

# THIRTY-THREE

When they were out on the main road, the driver slowed the horses but didn't stop. "We're going all the way through to Trent," he called down. "If you need me to stop the carriage, then flag me. By sunset, I want us in front of Santa Maria Maggiore."

After a while, Magdalena dragged herself onto the seat and curled up her side. She could only open one eye, and even that was just a slit. Morone gave her a handkerchief to press against her bleeding face, then slid all the way over to make room. The other three stayed on the opposite bench. Every jolt from the carriage knifed through her ribs, so she breathed lightly with her fingers knotted in her rosary. *Holy Mary, mother of God.* She wanted to pray, but she kept finding herself back to just those five words, as if she were pleading without daring to ask a question.

Hell would be an eternity of pain, so she clenched her teeth and listened to the wheels. Sometimes a stone popped up against the carriage to startle her with its bang. Another attack? But no, their attackers didn't morph into pursuers. Their bravery had dissolved like mist when faced with one woman who could take down four men.

Dawn came. She raised her head, but Morone rested a hand on her hair. "Stay down. You're hurt."

A moment after, he started praying in Latin, and the other men gave their responses. *Et cum spiritu tuo.* Reflexively she thought them, but the words didn't come out. He touched her forehead, felt him making a slippery sign of the cross. Then another touch, this one on one of her eyes.

Anointing. He was anointing her for death. When they'd done this for Gonzaga and Seripando, it had been on both left and right, but her right side was down and he didn't try to move her. She'd just have to remain half-blessed.

Ear. Nose. Mouth. Hands.

In low tones, he prayed in Latin. So hard to focus on the words right now. She caught "tender mercy" and "saved by your healing." That was good. Morone would feel he'd helped her just as much as she'd helped him.

After the final amen came silence. Then the valet said, "We should find a doctor."

No, of course they shouldn't. How ridiculous. They should continue to Trent. In Trent, Morone would be safe. In Trent, no one would try to kill him thinking he was the pope's plaything. Or the emperor's plaything. The ignorance in Trent would be of a different sort, and the assassins there were highly trained but also highly restrained.

Morone said, "Leave her be."

*Thank you.* The words never got out of her head. She formed up the answer, but then it stayed, hovering somewhere behind her eyes, and eventually her thoughts returned to that semiprayer. *Holy Mary, mother of God.*

Mary, who was foretold in Eden to be the new Eve, the better Eve. Mary, shown in Revelation wearing a crown of twelve stars and with the moon under her feet. Mary, the Ark of the New Covenant who was Christ. Mary, mother of God whose Son had saved them. And now, with every jolt against Magdalena's ribs, Mary wouldn't leave her head.

The driver stopped briefly at an inn so the valet could get food. They kept the curtains drawn, and then the carriage started up again with freshly baked bread stinking up the interior. Magdalena refused so much as a bite of food. That man who'd gone down with blood from his ears and nose was most likely dead. *Holy Mary, mother of God.*

Protect her own mother. Protect her sister. Magdalena didn't matter, but people were dying because of her, so please, Mary, don't let her mother and sister be among them. It wasn't their fault. It wasn't their fault.

At sundown they arrived in Trent with exhausted horses and exhausted passengers. At the city gates, Morone helped Magdalena get back into her habit before she collapsed again onto the carriage seat. At Madruzzo's palace, he called immediately for doctors and for someone to carry her to a bed. He should have taken her to the convent, she thought blearily while someone lifted her and her grinding ribs to carry her inside. Morone could have left her there and then proceeded to the palace to relish the triumph of successful negotiations.

She ended up in a bed as soft as the bishop's the night before. Morone stood by the door, not letting anyone inside until Madruzzo could produce a doctor.

Rather than the doctor, it was Agnella who rushed in. "Magdalena, what did those monsters do to you?" She stripped back the bed clothes and pulled off Magdalena's wimple, feeling her face, her neck, her shoulders. She positioned her cheek beside Magdalena's lips while groping for her wrist. "You're breathing okay. Your pulse is really light."

Morone said, "Check her ribs. She took a hard blow to her side. I'm afraid the ride in the carriage was too much, but I didn't want to stop until we got her here."

Agnella pointedly ignored Morone. "Can you sit up? Did you fight off the emperor's entire army?"

Four of them. Magdalena tried to count the attackers again in her head. Yes, only four. Not an army.

"I hope he's replacing a dozen corpses right now." Agnella turned to Morone. "You need to leave the room. I'm going to remove her habit."

Walking to the door, Morone said, "You do realize I put her into that habit."

Agnella whirled toward him.

Magdalena gasped and tried to sit up. "Sir, don't joke!" She lifted her sleeve so Agnella could see the exercise clothes underneath. "He didn't touch me. He didn't touch me."

Agnella turned back to the bedside. "The men who did touch you, I hope they're babbling their explanations right now to Christ Himself while Satan shovels an extra load of coal into the ovens." She looked back at Morone. "I told you to leave."

He looked about to protest, but then he stepped out the door and let it shut.

Agnella built a fire and set water to boiling. After she rang for a servant, she requested towels and several long strips of cloth. "I don't need the doctor, but I need the doctor's materials," she told the servant. "If you send a runner for Sister Lena, that would be best."

The soft bed enfolded Magdalena while Agnella parted her from her habit, then gently worked back the exercise clothes. "God have mercy," she whispered. "Have you tried walking?"

Magdalena shook her head.

"Your entire shin is bruised, ankle to knee. You've got massive bruising on your ribs, too. It's like you tried to turn yourself purple. But you failed. Your face is white like the dead." Agnella shook her head. "Lie back. I'll make it good."

Agnella layered her with hot compresses and then spoon-fed Magdalena a very sweet tea. When Lena arrived, she assisted in silence. It was Agnella who decided how to bind up Magdalena's ribs, and Agnella who told the doctor to go back to reading his books since he couldn't be bothered to come during the first hour after he was summoned.

At some point during these ministrations, the warmth of the compresses and the tea and the gentle words of her fellow assassin-nuns soothed her mind. Between one touch and the next, she'd plunged into darkness.

———————◦————————

A candle flickered in the room when Magdalena awoke, and because she never slept on her back, she stayed still. What if she'd been put there because of her ribs? But when it didn't hurt as much to breathe, she tried deeper breaths, then propped herself up on her elbows.

"Take it easy," said a deep voice. Morone's. "If you want to get up, Sister Agnella is asleep in the next room."

Magdalena turned toward the sole source of light. It danced shadows over Morone's tired face. On his lap was a book, either a Bible or a breviary. He'd changed out of last night's clothes, and when Magdalena looked beyond him, she realized no light came through the curtains.

"It's evening?"

"It's well past midnight. Agnella hasn't left you. She wouldn't leave even when she was falling asleep, so this was our compromise. I'm allowed to stay with you, but she's asleep in the parlor."

"You need to sleep too." Magdalena tried to shift onto her side, but her leg hurt when she moved it. She forced her knee to bend and then pivoted so she could look directly at Morone. "You could have left me at the convent. You have important work."

Morone chuckled. "I have the work of God to do, and I can't guess God would be pleased if I left you on the roadside like an empty trunk I'd finished unpacking." He shook his head. "You value yourself as nothing, so I made sure to tell your abbess you saved my life. I also commended you to Simonetta." He looked marginally annoyed when he said Simonetta's name; he should have known there'd have been no responding admiration from the other legate.

Morone continued, "Since your work saved the lives of five people, including my own, I thought it best to ensure you had care enough to survive as well. Interestingly," (and here he chuckled) "your fellow nun won't let the doctor near you, so I might as well have left you on the curb of your boarding house."

Magdalena smiled. "You should feel honored that Agnella let you stay at all."

"I've come to realize I should. She's rather angry."

"Do you know about *Le Convertite* in Venice?"

Morone gasped. "Is she from there? The abuse in that convent was a blight on the face of the Church, and if the Church is doing penance now for her collective sins, surely that ranks right in the top echelon."

Magdalena frowned. "You think that? But—"

"Yes. A priest who violates his sacred vocation and the trust of his flock is far worse than a rabid animal. Satan targets priests because they have great power, and a corrupted priest is worth the efforts of fifty demons. It's why priests rely on entire convents to pray for our spiritual protection and guidance. You can see from the council that even fair-minded men can make fair-minded decisions that result in evil. A priest who gives his will over to the devil is far worse." Morone crossed himself. "I will pray for her to find greater peace and healing."

Morone reached for the sideboard. "Your abbess brought you two letters, both from your mother in Rome. If you care to sit up and read them, I'll light you another candle."

"Oh!" Magdalena hadn't heard from her mother since leaving for Innsbruck. "I'm not sure I can sit up. Can you just read them to me?"

"And reveal your family secrets?" Again Morone had that amused smile, his eyebrows contracted as though he were frowning but his mouth curved up with the joke. "I'm not sure which is the most recent."

"Pick either one." Magdalena sunk back into her pillow. "The everyday is the everyday, and she wants me to feel like I'm still back at home."

"The everyday is a good thing." Morone broke the seal on the first letter.

Mother's words were stilted because she'd never grown comfortable writing, but every week she took the trouble and had Domenico take down her words. Yet despite her clumsy sentences, awkward and untutored, Morone read her words with a care that made them sound gentle. Natural. With eyes closed, Magdalena immersed herself in the world of Rome, in descriptions of the Easter celebrations and the Easter breads in the market, how Mother had baked dozens of loaves and therefore had money for several more letters north. The second letter brought news from the convent at St. Sebastian's, where Gilia was teaching Fiora to read and write. Fiora was outgrowing her shoe. No one there knew quite how Agnella had matched the wooden sole to the curve of Fiora's foot, but they had tried twice to make her a new one. Fiora was leaning more and more on her crutch. Domenico was still working at the docks with Erico and had picked up another job making deliveries. Mother sent her love and her prayers.

Mother couldn't hug her across these hundreds of miles, but for just a moment Magdalena felt wrapped in care and warmth. Mother had no idea what her daughter was really doing. She imagined long days in the chapel, praying wisdom and direction into the men deciding the Church's future. It would break her heart to know otherwise. So she would never know, and she could keep loving her daughter from far away.

Morone said, "Are you in pain?"

Magdalena pulled up the sheet to dry her tears. "I'm fine. Thank you for reading her letters."

"Are you homesick? So am I. You've been through so much at such a young age. Perhaps you can go back, although I daresay we need your services here."

Magdalena's mouth twisted into a frown even though she was fighting it, and more tears seeped into the pillow that billowed up around her cheeks.

Morone said, "You are in a great deal of pain. Please don't lie to me. What can I give you?"

Magdalena blurted out, "Absolution."

She hadn't thought before speaking, but as soon as the word emerged, the tears rushed out twice as fast. She shivered as though she were still clinging to the wind-swept ledge outside the conspirators' meeting.

Morone said, "Do you want me to get Cardinal Simonetta? He's your confessor, is he not?"

Agnella's so-called confessor had refused to let any other priest come into *Le Convertite* to confess the nuns, afraid of his crimes being discovered. All along, the Catherinites had confessed only to Simonetta, not by rule so much as force of habit. Only him. But why?

She without any order preventing her from confessing to anyone else, she said, "I want it to be you. I saved your life. I'm asking for the sacrament in repayment."

"Paying you in sacraments would be simony. I say yes, but only to do my duty as a priest." Morone checked that Agnella was asleep, then pulled his chair closer. "What do you want to confess?"

It was dark other than the candle, and the darkness was the perfect place to spill out all these dark liquids that had corroded her heart. She'd killed a man in self-defense, then killed a man to defend the legates. And then she'd killed a legate. And then she'd killed another. Her voice broke as she fought for the words, the words that would make all of this sound sensible and somehow less than multiple murder.

Mother had steeped roses in water to create slippery, scented rosewater, and Magdalena had steeped death in the water of her spirit in order to create poison, whatever poison this was that came out of her mouth here in the dark. In the jumping shadow of the candle, she couldn't make out the hatred that had to be worked into Morone's face. The laughing eyes: gone. The smiling mouth: frozen. Henceforth she'd be sent out to his front parlor the way she'd been at the start. Maybe he'd banish her further, using his authority to expel the Catherinites from the council, if only to keep himself alive.

She'd grown to admire him, and he to admire her. But seeing her soul, now he'd hate her.

She finished the litany of deaths. Then silence. Morone wasn't moving. Next would come his condemnation.

Morone whispered, "How long have you carried this in your heart? The night you realized all this, was the next morning the day you looked so sad?"

She swallowed hard. "I don't want to go to Hell. My mother—it will break her heart. It will break Fiora's heart."

"It would break God's heart too. You were right to talk to me." Morone shook his head in the dark. "You're so young. Eighteen?"

Eighteen was too young to be already in Hell. "But after I knew what I was, even then, those attackers—one of them is probably dead. Maybe two. When it came time, I acted again."

"There's a difference between self-defense and murder. Think back. The first man, it was an accident, no? You were defending your virtue. There is no crime." Morone had slowed his words. "The second...this is harder, but I can see there might be cause. But Gonzaga was no heretic. And Seripando, a heretic? No. If heresy fills men with such an ardent desire to live a Christ-like life, if it fills bishops with the yearning to pour out the grace of the Holy Spirit on a world thirsty for God's love, then may the Church be filled with such heretics!" He lowered his voice. "Girolamo Seripando was no heretic. Those orders can't have been legitimate."

Magdalena whispered, "Then I'm going to Hell?"

"Not you, little one. Christ had something to say about men who deceived little ones, that it would be better for them to have a millstone tied around their neck and be tossed into the sea. Lie back. Close your eyes."

Morone laid his hand on her forehead. In a low voice, he intoned the familiar words. "Dominus noster Jesus Christus te absolvat: et ego auctoritate ipsius te absolvo ab omni vinculo excommunicationis, et interdicti, in quantum possum, et tu indiges."

Absolution.

He made the sign of the cross over her forehead. Magdalena deflated into the bed, trying not to sob because crying hurt her ribs, but it was a worthy pain.

"Deinde, ego te absolvo a peccatis tuis, in nomine Patris, et Filii, et Spiritus Sancti. Amen."

"Amen," she whispered.

He handed her his handkerchief. "Daughter, what I said about Sister Agnella, I say to you too. You've been used by men of the Church. They've used the best part of you to do it. The guilt of what's been done to you will be laid at the feet of us all, and I beg your forgiveness."

Magdalena struggled to focus on him. Were there tears in his eyes?

Before she could answer, Sister Agnella appeared in the doorway. "She's awake? How is she?" She rushed toward the bed. "You're crying. He didn't hurt you, did he?"

The edge to Agnella's voice was sharper than the executioner's blade she'd blunted. "He read me my mother's letters," Magdalena whispered. "And now...I feel like I'm home."

# THIRTY-FOUR

Daylight. Magdalena studied the room around her until she realized this was actually Morone's bed, the same room in which she'd murdered Gonzaga.

But no, that was gone. Her soul was clean, and Christ's mercy had come into her heart. She was fit to be His bride again.

Letting the pillows take her weight, Magdalena prayed the morning prayer. She had missed *lauds*. She'd probably missed *prime* too.

Restless, she tried to sit up, braced for the pain in her ribs even though Agnella had bound them last night. Her fingers worked over her chest, and she breathed as deeply as she dared. It wasn't as bad as last night, so she pulled back the blankets to look at her leg, which had transformed to a stunning mixture of purple, gold, and black, with extra swelling at the knee.

She'd no idea she could bring to bear that kind of force, and she'd delivered it against the weak point of a man's head. There'd be nothing left of him now.

Next her fingers explored her face. She found a definite swelling over her cheekbone, but at least she couldn't see the damage. She could open both eyes again, so that swelling had eased.

And her soul, although she couldn't see it, probe it, bind it up—her soul too must have healed while she slept because she felt alive and wanting to move. She even felt hunger, and she hadn't been hungry in so long. Her last meal had been the stolen roast beef in the bishop's bed.

Gently she swung her legs over the side. Agnella had left her habit folded on the chair, so she got herself presentable and then edged her way to the inner parlor.

On a couch, Lena flung aside her embroidery and rushed over to her. "Oh, you're awake! We've been praying for you to recover. Cardinal Morone told us what you did, and it's taken a lot of convincing to keep him from writing to the pope for a special commendation."

Magdalena laughed, then winced. "They were going to kill him."

"You've done more than Simonetta ever thought, although he has plenty of trouble seeing past the end of his nose." Lena rang a bell for the servants to bring breakfast, then started a kettle for tea. "I saw the letters you sent Simonetta. Good work taking Morone's letters to copy them out. You even won that battle-axe's trust."

At the mirror on the far wall, Magdalena studied her face. Her nose was swollen, and a bruise stretched from her left eye all the way to her jaw, a more colorful twin of the one gracing her right leg.

The outer door opened, revealing a servant with a tray. Two buns, eggs with a cream sauce, sausages, and a bowl of fruit, plus a servant who looked numb with horror on seeing a beaten nun. Lena strode across the room. "I'll take that. You can go."

Magdalena signed herself and said grace. Lena continued, "Morone summoned your erstwhile host, the bishop of murderers. I forget his name, but he at least had the common sense to affect horror. Whether he was involved in hiring those brutes, whether he would recognize them on the street, or whether he's even been home to his palace in the last ten years isn't our privilege to know, but he had the decorum to apologize."

Magdalena swallowed a bite of sausage. "Should I expect a visit and graciously accept his apology?"

"I assure you, I already accepted an apology on your behalf because his apology took the form of a sizable donation to the convent." Lena smirked. "You did your duty, so he owes you nothing, and all of us know it. But he'll make a show, so we'll take the gift."

Magdalena devoured her breakfast. Last night she'd needed spiritual food, and today she craved the physical thing. The meal before her smelled right, tasted right, and filled her up right. Her soul was right with God, and her body felt rested. Broken, but rested.

Lena picked up her embroidery again. Had she ever faced the same realization, that they were assassins? Or did she grasp with that practical mind of hers the impossibility of answering that question to her own satisfaction? Did she therefore do the mental equivalent of setting it atop the high columns of a cathedral, never to be taken down and never to be examined?

Or worse, had Lena faced the realization with the same tactless revelation of a mirror, accepted it, and moved ahead?

Still, under Lena's fingers, thread and fabric were becoming a work of beauty. She used white fabric and white thread, but the thread formed the letters IHS. She must be making a purificator, or maybe a corpral. No one would see the starched white-on-white beauty unless they got close because the design was not meant to be seen except under very specific, very holy circumstances.

Could a person create sin and beauty at the same time? Or was it rather that the more hardened you became to your own sinful identity, if you actually married yourself to it, then creating beauty became more difficult? As your soul settled deeper into the river mud, did the sweetness you would have created eventually stop oozing out into the current?

In came Agnella with a tray. "The uptight kitchen servants informed me you sent for breakfast, but surely they didn't bring you these!" She set the tray on a table, showing Magdalena a half-dozen tiny plates trimmed with tiny roses, a delicately browned pastry confection at the center of each. "I'm glad to see those monsters didn't keep you down." Agnella folded her arms. "You still look wretched."

"I feel great."

Lena shook her head. "I want you taking it easy for a while. You're going to really feel terrible tomorrow, and healing from that kind of injury isn't trivial."

Agnella pulled up a chair. "Did our abbess tell you what's happening here at the council while you've been getting yourself beaten?"

Lena sighed. "Why would she want to hear that when she can imagine it perfectly fine on her own? It's all bickering and plenty of tug-of-war with the paperwork."

Agnella leaned closer. "Our abbess is omitting the best part. You missed a special general congregation where the Cardinal of Lorraine, the eminent Charles de Guise, talked for three hours."

Magdalena's eyes flared. "About what?"

Lena sighed. "Priesthood. The scrutiny of episcopal candidates. The nomination rights of kings. It will come as no surprise," Lena added dryly, "that Simonetta takes exception to every single thing de Guise says, up to and including 'good morning,' so quite a special letter went off to Rome the next day."

The hair stood up on Magdalena's arms. "We're not going to get an assignment for him are we?"

Agnella laughed out loud. "Simonetta probably prays for that every night!"

Lena shook her head. "De Guise is an annoyance, not a heretic. Even Simonetta can see that."

Agnella said, "But when you start walking around again, you're going to hear a lot of bishops muttering to one another, '*Primus canon non placet,*' because it's canon one of the document that's made everyone's hair turn white. It's the old *jus divinum* problem back again."

Magdalena said, "Still, three hours...to say what?"

Agnella waved a hand. "Oh, but there's more. Every diocese is going to start a school for priests."

Magdalena stopped. "Don't they already go to school?"

Lena laughed. "Not all of them. Isn't that much obvious? The richer ones, of course. But the poorer ones might not even know how to read. They learn just enough Latin to stumble through the prayer book, taught by a parish priest who might not know anything himself. It's why you find superstitions with a life of their own."

Magdalena said, "But how will a school help?"

"Because the schools will be open to everyone." Lena smiled. "This is such a good idea that it has to have come from the Holy Spirit, because I can't believe these men came up with it on their own. All priests will have to be educated. Either they get an education on their own, or they get it through the diocese, but either way, they'll learn all the doctrines of the Church."

Agnella huffed. "Some of them know what's wrong and just enjoy doing it."

Lena said, "Don't disparage the idea. The more priests are educated, the more they'll be able to figure out when someone is a priest for the wrong reasons or shouldn't be a priest at all. They'll catch the evil ones."

Agnella didn't look convinced, so she turned to Magdalena. "Did Morone give you the letters from your family?"

"He did, thank you, and it helped." Magdalena smiled. "Everyone at home is fine and boring."

"Aren't you glad you're here? It's so much more exciting to be beaten by men with murder in their hearts." Lena folded her arms. "You have good senses, but being aware of other people's intentions—that's Bellosa's training."

Agnella snorted.

Lena ignored her. "The fact that you survived their evil intentions is mine."

"I think I had something to do with it too," Agnella added. "I taught you to climb."

"It's like Lena said," Magdalena interjected, "put us near a wall and we climb it like monkeys."

Lena waved Agnella away. "Go do some work for once. You've fooled around long enough. We have a Council to protect and a *primus canon* to *non placet.*"

Agnella snatched one of the pastries off the rose-dotted china. "I'll be back later to check your injuries. For now, do lots of breathing exercises. It's better if from time to time you force out your air."

Magdalena sobered after Agnella left. Turning to Lena, she said, "She's so angry. I'd forgotten after my time in Innsbruck. It's...striking."

"She has a lot to be angry about."

"True, but...forgiveness."

Lena shook her head. "I won't tell her to forgive. I pray that she will. I pray that she works down her un-Christlike anger, especially the anger at men who've done nothing directly to hurt her. But the work is for the grace of the Holy Spirit to do, not for us."

Still, that bristling anger. The defensive posture. The fear. Under it all, whenever Magdalena got hurt, it was the reflexive fear: *Did he touch you?*

When she noticed Lena studying her, Magdalena said, "I probably should keep working for Morone."

"Simonetta will have me crucified in the public square if I dare suggest anything else." Lena laughed out loud. "You copied the man's letters to the pope, for goodness sake. That kind of access isn't something he's going to blink at, especially after Morone started by giving you none at all." Lena set aside her embroidery. "I have to ask this, so speak to me as your abbess. Morone ordered you put in his bed because he wanted to personally assure your safety, and in the condition in which you arrived no one would accuse you of unchastity. But is this the first time you've slept in his bed?"

"What?" Magdalena's eyes flared. "Of course! He never touched me! He very assiduously guarded my chastity!"

Lena rolled her eyes. "Simonetta assumes you won him over with the most feminine of persuasions."

"Simonetta can go put his head up the chimney!" Magdalena exclaimed. "I'm a bride of Christ! Or has the esteemed cardinal forgotten how I ended up with the Catherinites in the first place?"

"Perhaps you'll recall what you just told me about forgiveness." Lena folded her arms. "I'll set Simonetta straight, for all the good it does. Remember what I said about him not seeing past the tip of his own nose."

Magdalena bristled. "Should I refuse to attend Morone at all, since Simonetta believes I'm servicing him in illicit ways?"

Lena shrugged. "Men crave duality. They want their opponents to be evil. They say they hate the sin and then relish the scandal caused by sin. You tell them their enemy isn't as evil as they thought, and rather than being relieved that a soul hasn't abandoned God, they feel disappointed that their enemy isn't evil all the way down. What can I tell you?" Her eyes were piercing. "If, amidst all the scandals of the Church, this is the one Simonetta chooses to hold dear to his heart, what's the harm? Forget your reputation and do the work in front of you. That's what God asks of all His brides."

# THIRTY-FIVE

Agnella predicted the ribs would take six weeks to heal, and said during that time Magdalena shouldn't do too much exercise.

In practical terms, Agnella's prohibition meant nothing. Magdalena still had to carry laundry for the boarding house and spend hours on her feet shadowing Morone, then awaken in the middle of the night for *lauds*. Scrubbing floors hurt too much, but for anything else, whenever she flinched, a nearby sister was certain to assure her that a little stretching would assist her healing. The binding around her ribs was tight, so she did plenty of deep breathing exercises. "Exchange your air," Agnella encouraged her. "Air is good for you. Get out all the old stuff."

The lack of climbing was a true penance. The summer nights stayed warm and the skies clear, and Magdalena looked up at the stars longing to be just that much closer to them. She still hadn't climbed the outside of Santa Maria Maggiore, and the ornate walls begged for her hands and toes.

In early June, Morone moved out of his quarters in Madruzzo's palace into Palazzo Thun, along with Navagero. The council, likewise, had been taken over by Morone. "Cardinal Gonzaga, may God rest his soul," he'd said to de

Guise, "promised we'd take up the issue of episcopal residence when we discussed the sacrament of holy orders. He probably counts himself fortunate not to have to deal with it, but we have to."

"*Jus divinum,*" de Guise had replied in a tone that raised the hairs on Magdalena's neck. "Nothing else will suffice."

That morning, Simonetta had handed Morone a document on episcopal residence, which Morone had thanked him for and then set untouched on the corner of his desk while he pulled out a fresh sheet of paper and began to write. All day he sent Magdalena back and forth to de Guise's library to fetch books or send others back, and once she had to return pushing them on a cart because he requested so many. That horrified Morone. "Your ribs!" he exclaimed, to which Magdalena only replied with a shrug, "Your reform of the Church."

It helped, perhaps more than a little, that Morone was shadowed by a silent nun with a faded purple-yellow bruise around her eyes and a scar on her cheek. During meetings with key bishops and theologians, they'd glance at her and get serious. She was a reminder that men and women had died, and were still dying, because of these questions debated at length in posh parlors.

She continued feeding Simonetta information, with Morone's consent, in the form of the discarded rough drafts of Morone's letters. "I have to undo his influence with Pius," Morone said. "Borromeo is on our side, but as long as Simonetta has the pope's ear, we're fighting wars on too many fronts. We need to keep Simonetta's venom focused on de Guise so we can get as much work through the council as possible."

Magdalena said, "De Guise will hate losing his reputation."

Morone grimaced. "De Guise is like you. He would sacrifice his reputation in a heartbeat if it meant preserving the Church."

She mentioned this to Agnella, who laughed loud enough that the guests on the top floor must have heard. "De Guise's reputation is everything to de Guise! You didn't hear about his fight with Count Luna!"

Ever since the French had arrived, there had been arguments about precedence between the Spaniards and the French. In a way it was helpful: the more the representatives of the two countries battled one another, the less they turned their attention toward the pope's power. United, they could derail the council.

Count Luna himself was a sharp-eyed man with an equally sharp voice and intellect, a man capable of anything. With both Luna and de Guise demanding prime seating and objecting to the other having equally prime seating, the council was having a hard time keeping the peace.

During the June 29th meeting, the legates had arranged for Count Luna to be seated *extra ordinem*, which shouldn't have offended the French because they got to keep their place, and should have pleased the Spaniards because they got a prime spot. The actual result, of course, was fighting that had nearly come to violence. De Guise had lost his temper and come close to withdrawing the entire French contingent. He swore that France would no longer obey the pope for the duration of his reign, and then went ahead with a bunch of invective including (Agnella snickered while relating this to Magdalena as they sat over a basket of mending) that the pope was a simonious tyrant. "The French and the Spanish ambassadors won't attend the same services until this is settled." Agnella snipped off a loose thread. "No one gets blessed because someone has to be blessed first. These are the men deciding the fate of Christendom."

Magdalena had said mildly, "Maybe we need to pray for a change of heart."

To which Agnella had only snorted.

Perhaps Morone agreed. He'd unearthed the memoranda from all the national envoys, the forty-two different points of contentions the different kings and princes had wanted resolved, and he sent a letter containing all of them to Rome, noting that before the bishops could work on any of the particular items, they needed to resolve *jus divinum* and holy orders.

Therefore Morone rewrote the document about holy orders in an attempt not necessarily to please everyone, but at least to prevent too many parties from objecting.

"Try to please everyone and everyone will get angry at you," Morone said dryly. "That's why Christ said *Blessed are the peacemakers*. All parties find them infuriating."

According to Morone's draft, "The conscientious performance of one's episcopal duties is *jus divinum*," so the term was there even though it wasn't applied to a bishop's actual residence. But he'd also shifted the burden from law to conscience, requiring bishops to become pastors to the people under their care, especially to the poor.

De Guise remarked, "Exactly as it should have been from the start."

Count Luna protested, "Residence isn't explicitly enforced."

Morone said, "Read on. We're also going to stipulate that anyone who isn't performing his job loses the benefice."

A momentary silence filled the room.

De Guise said, "So the bishops who would care for the souls under them the right way are going to do so for the glory of God...and the ones who care only for themselves will do their job to keep the income."

Morone's mischievous smile returned.

De Guise said, "It's sad that conscience can be purchased...but I like it."

Morone spend the rest of the night writing a reformulation while Magdalena brought him endless pots of tea and fresh paper and ink. She didn't fetch any further books because, it seemed, most of de Guise's library was already in Morone's parlor.

On June 11th, at yet another meeting, de Guise and the *zelanti* got into a loud argument about the relationship between the council and the papacy, and whether the council could claim authority over the pope or whether the pope could claim authority over the council. "There was a fist fight at the first period of the council," Morone told Magdalena later. "I was afraid today that we would see one at the third."

And then one morning: agreement. For Magdalena it felt like the moment when a disparate band of musicians finished tuning their instruments at random before Mass and suddenly were harmonized to one another. There, on Morone's table, was a document affirming the hierarchical structure of the Church. It didn't go as far as the reformers wanted, and some of the *zelanti* were furious it had gone as far as it had, but it had enough votes to pass. Morone handed it to Laynez to copy out then addressed a letter to the pope asking him to respond as quickly as possible, and to be clear: yes or no.

After everyone had left his quarters, Morone collapsed onto a chair beside the window, letting the breeze blow over him. Magdalena poured a glass of wine and brought over with a tray of cold meats and rolls. He sighed. "This is exhausting, but we have a tactic to go forward. We choose a few key players and convince them to negotiate. They'll bring their tribes into line."

Then they got a response from Rome. The pope had issues with the document.

"It doesn't matter," Morone told de Guise. "We're voting."

De Guise looked shocked, but since he was getting what he wanted, he agreed. After he left, Morone ordered Magdalena to lock the door, and he burned the pope's letter.

She clutched her hands as the paper curled and blackened in the flames.

Morone shrugged. "We're not technically in violation. We've changed the document since the version he rejected, so as principal legate, I say we proceed." He signed himself with the cross. "It's not just me. The pope also wants this Council wrapped up by the end of the year."

# THIRTY-SIX

A fter a tumultuous session on November 11th, Morone proposed that the next session take place on December 9th, and then he proposed that it be the last.

The last session.

No one believed it possible. They hadn't touched half the issues that had driven away the Lutherans. Indulgences? Veneration of images? Purgatory? None of these had seen discussion, and yet somehow Morone wanted it all resolved in less than a month's time.

Forty-two items, to be wrapped up by the end of the year, at a Council that had already sprawled across three decades, three periods, two cities, and five papacies.

Luna objected. Of course Luna objected. But even the Spaniards were ready to have done with this endless council, and the few votes in favor of continuing even one further month were not enough to override the whole.

Magdalena had healed, and that night, she and Agnella scaled the outside of Santa Maria Maggiore. On the roof of the world they watched the stars and laughed about the old men and their endless documents.

"Over by the ninth of December." Magdalena's voice was a hush.

Agnella chuckled. "December 9th of the year that never comes. Miles of paper and gallons of ink, but what have they said yet about Purgatory or the veneration of saints or indulgences?" She waved a hand. "There will have been more Catherinites in Trent than stars in the sky by the time they get all the work done."

Magdalena shrugged. "That's what Morone wants."

"And Count Luna? He'll do anything to blunt the blades of the council to make sure it rolls on forever."

The hair stood on Magdalena's arms.

Agnella said, "He's dangerous. I have no idea what he would dare, and that makes him twice as dangerous."

The next morning, while getting the suite ready for Morone's next series of meetings, Magdalena said, "Sir? I've heard that Count Luna is very opposed to ending the council in December."

Morone didn't even look up. "I assume you heard about Count Luna's opposition from Count Luna himself because he's already told everyone in Trent and has moved on to addressing letters to everyone in Rome."

Magdalena choked on a laugh. Morone added, "He says the whole world is in opposition to ending the council. It turns out that the whole world is *Spain*. All these years, the geography books have been markedly incorrect." He sounded exasperated. "Half the French have already gone home because of the fighting. The rest are hungering to leave as well." He looked up. "And you? Aren't you also eager to return to Rome?"

Rome, where she could get her feet off the ground on a regular basis. Magdalena said, "I will stay wherever the Church needs me."

"Brave words from a brave nun. I don't want the Church to need you here much longer. We're men and not angels, but we'll have to work harder than devils. It's amazing how willing some are to compromise when the reward is being back in their own homes."

When Morone didn't look ready to continue, Magdalena said, "Is Count Luna dangerous?"

"What have you heard?"

Morone looked unnerved enough that Magdalena hesitated, puzzled. "Oh! No, I haven't heard about him in *that* way." Wanting the council to continue forever might be stubborn, but it wasn't heretical.

Morone still studied her. "And if you did hear such things?"

Magdalena shook her head. "There aren't orders, and we don't act on our own."

Morone lowered his voice. "Be plain. If you do receive orders, what will you do?"

Magdalena froze in place.

Mindful of the seal of confession, she had re-told him everything outside the sacrament. Because of that, he could ask her these questions, and she could answer. Now, though, she had no idea what to say.

"Pretend we're in the midst of a heresy trial. What will you do if we convict?"

When in doubt, dodge. "Nothing, sir. It isn't my place."

Morone said, "Was it your place before?"

Heart hammering, Magdalena recoiled. "No. We talked about this. If we're given orders to complete another sentencing, I'm to refuse."

Refusal meant breaking the vow of obedience. Moreover, her refusal would accomplish nothing because any of the Catherinites would complete the sentence in her stead. But if the orders never came, Magdalena never needed to figure out her response.

They needed a change of subject, and changing it back to the original would suffice. "I was only concerned what he might he do to prolong the council."

"Talk. Endless talk." Morone sighed. "He has his faction around him, the way de Guise has his faction, and the Spaniards will slow everything down. If the Spaniards are looking for something to drag on the council forever," he added in a dry tone, "they can read the sheaf of letters I've just received from Rome."

Magdalena walked over to the small pile on his desk.

"They'll go nicely with the others I've received." Morone looked up with mischief dancing in his eyes. "I've made the Curia so very angry."

She lifted the nearest open letter, skimmed to the signature (an Italian name, a cardinal) and then started parsing out angry sentences.

"Why so furious? Threatening, even?"

"The article on the table limits each bishop and cardinal to one benefice." Morone laced his fingers behind his neck and leaned back in his chair. "We're going to lower their standards of living. Rome will become a city of ghosts as every important individual leaves, taking with them artisans and clothiers and other fine individuals. The pope will, you will be devastated to learn, have to rely on men other than cardinals and bishops to consult in the Apostolic Palace. And the worst tragedy of all," Morone said as he sat up again, "is that every one of those letter-writers will have to go live in the diocese he's being paid to shepherd."

Magdalena studied Morone. After a momentary silence, he said to her, "You don't appear as fully distraught as the situation warrants."

He was completely expressionless, so Magdalena said, "Distraught, sir?"

"One might expect sackcloth and ashes for such a grief as this." He laughed. "Even Cardinal Alessandro Farnese has made his voice known. Here."

He came up with one envelope among all the others. Handing it to her, he said, "He's your grandfather, yes?"

"Great-uncle." She took the letter. "I've never met him."

Morone paused, concerned. "Perhaps that isn't your ideal introduction, then. He's a fine man, but threaten his lifestyle and he's not at his best."

She noted the even writing, the lengthy sentences. He wrote in Italian, not Latin, to exhort Morone in the strongest terms. Nevertheless, Magdalena went cold at the accusations. The raw anger. Farnese wanted the council suspended before it took this kind of step. He accused Morone of being a reformer of the worst kind, practically a Lutheran, and threatened that continuing in this line would ensure he was never elected pope.

Morone had gone back to writing. "Heresy?" she whispered.

Morone met her eyes. "He's not accusing me of heresy. He considers me as committing a crime worse than heresy. It's not about losing souls. It's about losing material luxuries."

Magdalena folded the letter in her hands, and she sat quietly.

Finally she said, "I'd never kill you."

Morone didn't look up. "Good to know."

"But they might. If luxury is that important." Magdalena flexed the paper, tracing the rough edges with her fingertips. "Not with a heresy trial. Just...on their own."

"That's why you're here."

"I can't be everywhere."

Morone shrugged. "God can be everywhere. You've protected me already. And rest assured, if at any point they kill me, the council will still ratify this. They will ratify it faster. They'll carry on, and their anger will sway the moderates. Pope Pius has already agreed to sign off on this reform. In order to stop this reform, Farnese and Luna will have to stop the council itself."

# THIRTY-SEVEN

With ten days before the council's scheduled ending, Count Luna banged open the door to Morone's office, a frightened servant at his back. "Morone, this cannot stand!"

Magdalena got one look at Luna's rage-whitened face and took stock of everything in the room that could become a weapon. The fireplace tools, cast-iron and as long as her arm, would serve for defense, but they were unwieldy. The heavy furniture might protect Morone, but she considered the silver tray for the tea service. All she'd need would be to delay Luna long enough that the servants could rush Morone to safety.

Luna reached into his coat, and Magdalena undid the clasp on the sheath. Instead of a weapon, though, Luna pulled a mass of papers from his inner pocket. *"What is this?"*

Morone stepped forward. "Count Luna, I assure you, I have no idea—"

Luna shook the papers. "This whole council is an insult to His Most Catholic Majesty Philip II! You're going to close the council without his say-so. You are threatening to issue recommendations about reforming the princes of the world without ever once considering reform of the head of the

Church itself. And now—" Luna dropped his volume and tone. "Now you are going to bankrupt all of Spain."

Morone kept his voice calm. "I assure you, we intend no such thing."

Luna glared at Magdalena. "What are you looking at, girl?"

If anything could have moved Magdalena away from Morone before, it certainly wouldn't have now. She kept her hands together under her habit sleeves, her right hand clutching the handle of the dagger.

"I assume she's looking at you, trying to figure out what I've done to cause offense." Morone moved toward Luna, something Magdalena thought ill-advised. "Please show me the document so I understand."

Luna thrust the papers at Morone. The cardinal must have recognized it at a glance, but he read for several moments, quite probably collecting his thoughts.

Luna didn't give him the opportunity. "The *cruzada*. The indulgence decree will eliminate the *cruzada* even though Spain has always supported the Apostolic See in every way possible!"

For just a moment, Morone appeared as a man who had been awake for months settling squabbles and stomping out little sparks that had lit on the carpet. Worse, he looked suddenly old. In the lines around his eyes, Magdalena saw the ghost of Seripando.

Luna ranted, but he wasn't getting more violent. Morone listened, and listening to the count would make him more pliable until violence grew further and further from possibility. She refastened the catch on her dagger.

Luna said, "The pope himself granted Spain the right of the *cruzada* in 1497 so we could tax our clergymen. And now *this*," he gestured at the papers in Morone's hand. "*This* is designed to revoke that right. Something we were granted as a *favor* because Spain did so much to spread the word of God and to protect the Church!"

Morone rubbed his chin, but Luna kept going. "The *cruzada* generates as a minimum a hundred fifty thousand ducats a year. Where else will that money come from?"

Morone shook his head. "It's not for me to tell a king how to run his country."

"Neither is it for the Church to tell a king his subjects are not his."

Morone walked to a chair near the fire and gestured that Count Luna should sit. The count didn't move at first, but finally he yanked back the chair. He made the very act of sitting down look resentful.

Morone steepled his fingers. "Spiritual gifts and blessings can't be sold. The Church offers indulgences to encourage good works. She offered an indulgence for almsgiving, and as you can see, that was a tremendous mistake because unscrupulous priests started selling them. We're not very good," Morone added dryly, "at figuring out how opportunistic minds will take advantage of well-intentioned incentives."

Luna said, "That's a beautiful sermon, but now you are insulting Spain by calling us opportunists. This is a strike against Spain, make no mistake, and Spain will not stand for it."

Morone studied him. "And what will you do? Spain alone doesn't have enough votes for *non placet*."

Luna's shoulders straightened.

Morone raised a hand. "I will see about modifying the decree. Since a pope granted the *cruzada* tax, one could argue that we should not modify the pope's wishes."

Luna said, "Do you still intend to end this Council in less than a month? Without His Most Catholic Majesty's approval?"

"Yes."

Luna stood. "Then whatever happens next, it is on your conscience."

Magdalena didn't relax even after Luna stormed from the room. "He's dangerous." The look in Luna's eyes when he charged in: it still haunted her.

Morone said, "I kept him from violence."

Magdalena said, "Political violence is entirely another thing. Didn't you say he wants to keep the council going endlessly because as long as it's in session, King Philip has some leverage against the pope?"

Morone sighed. "But to keep it going now, what could he do?"

What could he do? What had prolonged the council so many times this far? Fears of plague, threats of war, papal deaths, endless deadlocks, a decree from the emperor... With imagination, surely Luna could come up with a new method of prolongation.

Morone looked up, startled. "What hour is it? I have so many visitors today, but the next one is important."

Magdalena's nose wrinkled. "Someone else I need to defend you from?"

"Not at all." Morone offered a smile. "Wait, and I think you'll appreciate this."

Half an hour later, Lena and Agnella came to Morone's office, and Morone summoned Navagero. He asked the three nuns to be seated, and Navagero approached Agnella.

Standing before her, Navagero bowed. "I wanted to offer you my personal apologies for the failures of the Venetian authorities to protect you and all the nuns of *Le Convertite.*"

Agnella straightened. "Sir?"

"We failed you. We trusted Leon, and we didn't believe the women who most needed our help. This is my shame, the shame of all Venice, and the shame of the Church. I offer you my apology. You suffered because of me, and I wish to make it right."

Agnella looked to Lena, who seemed just as surprised as herself, then looked at Magdalena. "How do you think you can do that?"

Morone said, "By making sure it can't happen again."

Morone spread out a document on his desk. "This is the decree for the reform of women's religious orders."

Agnella said, "It wasn't my order that required reform."

"No, it was your confessor who required reform, and may it please God in His mercy to be reforming his soul in Purgatory rather than dropping him straight into Hell." Morone's eyes narrowed. "But here, I want you to know two things. First, we've declared it anathema to force a woman into a convent against her will."

Agnella's eyes widened. "Really?"

"Brides must enter freely into a marriage. A woman who's kidnapped cannot marry her kidnapper. And similarly, a woman forced into a convent cannot become the bride of Christ. Forced vocations will now, and forever, be forbidden."

Magdalena's heart thrummed. "And what else?"

Navagero said, "The papal nephew, Carlo Borromeo, has come up with a beautiful design." He handed her a letter with a drawing, something that looked like a pair of closets. "It is a divided room designed just for confessions. The penitent stays here, on this side of a wall with a screen. She does not see and cannot touch her confessor, but he can hear her. The priest stays on the other side."

Agnella gasped. "People can see where both are from outside! There are curtains, but you can see inside. He can't—" She blinked quickly. "He can't touch her. She's safe."

"Borromeo has already made plans to install one in his cathedral after his return. Soon after, all other churches will be requested do the same." Navagero's gaze lowered. "I was heartbroken for the women of *Le Convertite*. There are predators in the world, but we will make it harder for them to operate. Predators like the darkness and seclusion. We will force them into the light. We will make everyone safer, and part of the reason to do so is because of brave women like you."

Magdalena's ears rang through the rest of the conference. Agnella didn't gush thanks. Neither did Lena. Rather, with reserve she thanked them for their attention, and then in a curious silence, she left.

Instead of leaving with them, Magdalena remained before Morone's desk without moving.

He studied her with curiosity. "You aren't satisfied?"

"No."

Morone sighed. "You were misused as well, but the path to helping you is more complex."

He set his elbows on the desk. His schedule was full to the breaking point. From now until December 9th wasn't nearly enough time to settle all the disputes and define all the beliefs of the entire Church. But he stayed at his desk, giving precious minutes to Magdalena.

"Your order was founded only because ignorance allowed it." Morone steepled his fingers. "I will not defend anything Pope Paul IV did. Nothing. He harmed me, but the harm he did you and your order far exceeds my imprisonment and my damaged reputation." The lines deepened on Morone's face. "He was able to accomplish this only because of ignorance. The answer to ignorance is education, and knowledge is the gift this Council needs to give to all of Christendom."

Magdalena studied him. "How?"

"First, by clarifying what we believe."

"Which gives the Lutherans a chance to clarify what they don't believe," Magdalena put in.

He waved a hand. "By now, we're not going to reconcile with them as a group. They will have to return to us individually, through God's grace. The point is that Catholics will know who we are. Anyone who wants to know about justification or the sacrament of marriage, or if they're curious about indulgences, can look at the documents and read what we have said. Secondly, we will have no more ignorant priests who were trained up at the knee of a similarly ignorant priest. Every single diocese is to open a school for men who will enter the priesthood. Every priest will be able to read."

Magdalena's eyes narrowed. "No more Markus Sittich von Hohenems?"

"Especially no more of that." Morone rubbed his temples. "Christ deserves knowledgeable men, just as He deserves willing brides." He sighed. "I only wish we knew what had happened to Seripando's documents."

Hesitant, Magdalena said, "Which?"

"His catechism. He was at work on a book to define every dogma of the faith in great detail, and canon 7 of the reform decree authorizes publishing it. Emperor Ferdinand especially wants it. But we've never found his manuscript."

"I know where it is."

Morone's head snapped up.

"I hid it. He was a heretic, so he could have included heresies and perverted the whole Church." Her eyes widened. "Don't you know how much Satan would love to infiltrate that kind of document?"

"Almost as much as I would love you to get it back for me!" Morone exclaimed.

Magdalena said, "Then let's go."

Morone instructed his servants to turn away everyone for the rest of the afternoon. Then Magdalena led him toward the Augustinian church.

The silent church's prior approached, bowed to Morone, and asked how he could help. Morone said, "We believe something was left in here."

The prior nodded. "Can I help you find it?"

Magdalena said, "Actually, I'd prefer to look alone. Can we lock up the church?"

The prior insisted on staying inside, but he did bolt the doors. Morone said, "This church has been in use for nine months since you hid it. Surely someone would have found it by now."

Magdalena girded up her habit. "Not where I put it."

The prior stared at her. "What did you hide?"

"A manuscript," said Morone, but he cut off the word as Magdalena slipped off her shoes and started scaling the wall.

Up twenty feet she climbed, the architecture yielding handholds out of polished stone, and ever upward she moved. Knowing their eyes would be on her the whole time, she fought nerves and continued toward the vaulted ceiling. Oh, this beautiful church! She'd last seen it when she'd bid goodbye to Seripando. What a gentle man. May he forgive her for her sins. Christ had forgiven her and cleansed her soul, but maybe in Heaven Seripando still hadn't overcome her betrayal.

At the top of the pillar, she slipped over the ledge and found the manuscript just where she'd left it, though now covered in dust. She looked over the side. "I'm going to drop it down for you."

Morone sounded terrified. "How are you going to get down?"

"I need to get a few more things." She let go the manuscript, which slapped into the floor with a bang and probably created a small cloud. Next she scanned the architecture and tried to remember exactly how many books she'd stashed.

One at a time the architecture yielded Seripando's works, and finally *The Confessions of Saint Augustine*. The last she tucked into her habit.

Only one thing remained: Chiara's little bundle of crochet thread and unfinished lace. Magdalena touched it, then whispered, "Goodbye," but she left it there. That wasn't hers. Forevermore it should be no one's.

Once on ground level, she retrieved her shoes and ungirded her habit. Morone's face was whiter than the marble altarpiece, his voice thinner than parchment. "You shouldn't do that. You could fall."

The crack of Gilia's arm on a pew resounded in Magdalena's mind as she settled the fabric of her wimple. "Sometimes we do."

The prior signed himself with the cross. "Please don't hide anything else up there."

On the street, Magdalena dissolved in giggles. "For the rest of his life, whenever he says Mass, he's going to look into the ceiling corners."

"Not just him." Morone hugged the books to his chest. "That was the most frightening thing I've ever seen."

He hadn't seen her on the church roof in Innsbruck. Magdalena stared at the cobblestones. "Promise me this manuscript contains no heresy."

"None. Moreover, it's going to go to the Curia, where it will be pored over and clarified and revised by an entire team of cardinals who will argue more about the finest points of the text than any subgroup of bishops and theologians have here at Trent. We've also specified that a missal and a breviary need to be drawn up and purged of superstition, and for the same reasons. Rest assured, the results will all be orthodox."

Magdalena sighed. "Thank you. Thank you for everything you're doing. They told me it was up to our order to save the Church. But the one doing it is you."

"No," said Morone as they turned the corner to Palazzo Thun. "It's the Holy Spirit."

The front door of Palazzo Thun slammed open, and a servant ran out. "Sir!" he exclaimed, holding a letter aloft.

"Sir, we were just coming to find you. It's a letter from Rome. The pope is dying!"

# THIRTY-EIGHT

All four legates had gathered in Simonetta's quarters at Madruzzo's palace.

"We've had two letters at the same time," Morone said in hushed tones. Outside was already growing dark, and inside they had all the lamps lit. The Catherinites moved about taking care of necessities while the legates kept their chairs close to the fire. "One is from the cardinal-nephew. Both were written on the twenty-seventh, and both say the pope is dangerously ill."

Navagero murmured, "He may already be dead."

Morone said, "As long as we haven't been told he's dead, God willing, he is alive. But what remains is to close the council."

Simonetta said, "If the pope dies while the council is in session, it suspends automatically."

"We cannot risk it suspending," Morone said.

Simonetta nodded. "I agree."

Navagero said, "So what do we do? The documents aren't ready for voting. The ninth is ten days away."

"We move up the calendar," Morone said. "What's the soonest we can get the work completed and begin the final session?"

Simonetta said, "The final session will require reading all the documents from the previous two periods of the council, that way we get a *placet* from the French for the documents drawn up while they weren't here."

Hosius rubbed his temples. "That's going to take at least a day on its own. Maybe longer."

"We can do with only the first paragraph of each," Morone said. "But the remaining documents? Can we draw them all up by the second?"

"Absolutely not!" Simonetta exclaimed. "Even with all the committees working overnight—"

"Change them from doctrinal issues to reform issues," Morone said. "That ends the necessity for debate. A committee can draft a reform article, then condemn excesses, superstition, and fraud."

Simonetta gasped.

"Even so, it would take until at least the third," Navagero said. "His Holiness will have to stay alive for four more days."

Morone shook his head. "We'll all pray for him to outlive the council, but both these letters are grim." He lifted one. "It's pneumonia, I believe. Borromeo writes that the odor of death clings to the room, and his uncle's arms are covered with spots."

Magdalena exclaimed, "What?"

The four legates looked at her, as if for the first time registering the nuns' presence. Magdalena rushed over to Morone. "What kind of spots?" She whipped around to Lena. "How could—Who would even order that?"

Morone was uncertain. "What are you saying?"

She turned to Simonetta. "Did you order that? Did Luna make you do it?"

Simonetta's eyes had widened. "Absolutely not!"

"You said Luna couldn't stop the council from ending," Magdalena exclaimed to Morone. She dropped to her knees before his chair. "Sir, listen to me. *Luna can stop the council*

341

*from ending.* He can kill the pope, and then the council automatically suspends. At Luna's meeting with the Spanish bishops, they talked about what would happen if the pope were to die. I don't know how he got that poison, but this letter says it's poison."

Navagero reached for her hand. "Child, child, it's an illness."

"It's poison that's supposed to look like an illness," Magdalena said.

Lena snapped, "You're hysterical. Leave the room, now."

Morone raised a hand. "I know what she's talking about, and I don't think she's hysterical."

Simonetta stared at Morone. "What do you think she's talking about?"

"I am the pope's principal legate. I've been told everything I need to know, so I know about *carrying out sentences.*"

Magdalena looked up at Morone, eyes filled with tears. "Sir—"

Morone turned to Lena and read out loud from Borromeo's letter about the pope's condition. The sudden onset, the coughing, the weakness, the odor of death, and finally the flat grey spots marking his skin. "Does that sound like the poison?"

Lena glanced at Simonetta, who nodded at her.

She said, "Yes, sir. That's the way ours works."

"Would your order in Rome under any circumstances attempt to use it on the pope himself?"

"I cannot speak for Sister Bellosa," said Lena, "but I would never do it. We've taken an oath of loyalty to the pope. The only one who could give such an order would be the pope himself."

Magdalena said to Lena, "Could Count Luna have gotten hold of it?"

Nezetta, who accompanied Hosius, said, "I've never told the recipe to anyone, but it's possible he obtained it from the same sources I did. It's a Spanish book, but I reworked the formula. His may not be as effective," she added, "but then again, it may even be more so. The pope has been in fragile health for a while, or so he claimed when he refused to travel to Trent."

Magdalena wrapped her hands around Morone's. "We need to stop this. You need to send a message to Cardinal Borromeo. Tell him what's happening and get him to check every single person who visits the pope, to prepare the pope's food himself, to—"

Simonetta shook his head. "Would that even be enough?"

Nezetta said, "It can be reversed. With lots of water, a healthy man can recover. But the pope is not healthy."

Navagero raised a hand. "Pardon me, brothers, but what are you talking about?"

Simonetta folded his arms and scowled. Morone said, "The Catherinites are charged with keeping us safe, but they're also empowered by His Holiness the pope to carry out sentences of execution for heresy. One of the means they utilize is a poison that works in the manner described by Borromeo."

Hosius exclaimed, "Are you mad?"

Sister Lena looked annoyed. "Of course he's not mad. And while I agree it sounds like the same substance, what are we to do? We're hundreds of miles from Rome."

Morone said, "I'll write Borromeo tonight and instruct him on what to do."

Lena said, "We need to let the Roman nuns know as well, so they can protect him. They can move quickly. They run a hospital for incurables, so it would seem natural that they get involved if the pope is dying."

Morone started to speak, but Magdalena blurted out, "Send me."

Lena exclaimed, "Absolutely not!"

"Send me! You have to send a courier, so send me!" She looked right in his eyes. "Sir, let me go. I'll recognize the poison if it's the same. I'll be able to protect him if they try direct means. I'll insist they read and believe your letters."

Morone shook his head, frowning. "We will send a courier with the letters. I'll write to the convent in Rome, but sending you seems—"

"Extreme? This is an extreme situation."

"You can't make the trip," Simonetta said flatly. "You are young, you're a nun, and you can't go at speed. A courier will arrive in three days. It will take you five, and you've said yourself that speed is essential."

Morone said, "In the morning, I'll get a number of leading bishops to push the final session forward. We'll have a general congregation on the third and the final session immediately afterward."

Magdalena rushed from the room, and in the outer parlor she stood with her face in her hands.

Behind her, Lena said, "You told him."

Magdalena shook her head. "We have to get to Rome. We have to save the pope."

"I am not an idiot, despite what those men may think." Lena strode forward and clapped her hand on Magdalena's shoulder. "The pope never said a word about us to him."

"He watched me kill four assassins!" Magdalena exclaimed. "He's not an idiot either! Right now, what matters is saving the pope and closing the council. I want to get to Rome. We have to stop the Spaniards from preventing the final session. We're here to save the Church!"

"Hush!" Lena stepped closer. "None of us are idiots. Remember your chief weapon as a Catherinite. No one sees us. No one notices us because we belong everywhere. Of course you should be down there, and of course those men don't think you should. Let them write the letter. Let them arrange a courier. And when the courier goes to Rome, that courier should be you. You, and I think Agnella and Tadea."

Magdalena nodded.

"No one notices us. This is the key. I will tell them you were too hysterical to remain, and they'll believe me. You get to the convent. Pack whatever you want and get your sisters. Return here. I will meet you at the door. I will have their letters."

Magdalena whispered, "You're going to take the blame?"

"I am going to fulfill my vows. So are you. If there's blame for that, then I accept it in whole. These men can gnash their teeth in celebration of our success while the Church survives for another fifteen hundred years." Lena's eyes narrowed. "Go."

Magdalena took off, but her heart hurt. She could die doing this, and Morone would know the last action she'd taken had been direct defiance. Simonetta already thought of her as an emotional child, but Morone would never see her again.

At the convent, she tore inside and found the nuns in chapel. It didn't matter that she was interrupting their prayer. "Tadea, Agnella! You're needed!"

In the hall, she said, "Pack for Rome. Now. This is an emergency." In as few words as possible, she explained the situation.

Agnella said, "I know what to bring. Wear your exercise clothes and pack both your habits. It's going to be a cold trip."

Magdalena rushed to the kitchen to load a bag with bread, cheese, dried fruit, and fish. Agnella filled two waterskins, then rifled through the dispensary.

Tadea met her in the hallway, dressed in men's clothing, and thrust a bundle of clothes at Magdalena. "Pull this on. Most couriers are young boys. Guess what you are now?"

Fifteen minutes later, they had returned to Madruzzo's palace, three boys carrying black sacks. Out of breath, Magdalena said, "Lena said she'd give us instructions."

A carriage pulled up to the door, and Lena jumped out. "In, all three of you. Here." She handed two sealed envelopes to Magdalena. "One is for the Rome convent. Don't stop though—go straight through to the pope's residence." She turned to Tadea. "Use the letters for—"

"I know what I need to do," Tadea said. "Thank you."

Agnella said, "Once in Rome, I'll run for Bellosa."

"Keep them safe." Lena looked over her shoulder. "The driver knows you're to ride all night and change horses as necessary." Lastly she handed them a bag of coins. "God be with you."

She slammed the door, and the carriage rattled off. To Rome. To Rome, and a pope who might already be dead.

# THIRTY-NINE

G od had made it a big world, and they couldn't travel it quickly enough. Even riding through the night, stopping only to change horses and drivers with the bill charged to the pope, they wouldn't be able to reach Rome until after dark on December 2nd. They prayed on the way, and they tried to rest when they could, but the constant motion kept them awake and nervous.

December 1st. They had stopped to change horses, and Magdalena sat wringing her hands. "The process took ten days with Seripando." She kept doing the math in her head, and then she'd do it again out loud while Agnella and Tadea stared out the coach window. At night it had been worse because they couldn't see the countryside, and distance felt like no progress at all. But now it was daytime, and it still felt as if they would never reach Rome. "Borromeo sent his letter on the 27th. For the pope to get sick enough to write, he might already have been dosed for three days."

Agnella kept her voice flat. "We're doing the best we can."

"What if he dies?" Magdalena was still dressed like a boy, but she reached into her pack for her rosary. The beads fit around her fingers. "What if they hold the final session thinking he's alive and then find out afterward he'd already died? Is the session invalidated?"

Agnella huffed. "Who knows how these men think? They may come up with a reason it's invalid. Or on the other hand, they may make the next pope's election contingent on him recognizing the validity of a session held before word reached Trent."

Tadea stretched "For all we know, on the morning of December first, they received another letter saying he was already dead."

"True. But so help me, even if I have to cut open the pope's chest and keep his heart beating with my hands, I'm going to keep him alive until the fifth." Agnella laughed out loud as Magdalena gasped. "We'll find a way. Worrying won't make the horses move faster."

"Well, as long as the horses are stopped, I have work to do." Tadea pulled a leather case from her bag and spread the contents on one of the seats. "You never asked me why I ended up at Saint Sebastian's. It's such an interesting story." She smirked as she got out the letter from Morone. "As it turns out, sometimes when you're from a very rich family, your tutors teach you skills just to keep your attention from wandering. For example, with just a little work, you can imitate anyone's handwriting. Or," she added, working with a very fine blade around the seal on Morone's letter to the pope, "you might learn how to replace a seal so no one knows the letter was breached."

Magdalena leaned forward. "What are you doing?"

"We'll need authorization to stay with the pope. We can infiltrate the Apostolic Palace just fine, but once discovered, we'll need Morone's permission to keep us there as the pope's protectors."

Agnella said, "It would be better if we had Simonetta's."

"Oh dear," Tadea said, pulling out another letter. "I guess I'll need to make one of those too."

She worked in silence, her hand steady as she created a letter that, had Magdalena found it on Morone's desk, would have thought was entirely his work. An ill pope and a concerned Borromeo wouldn't notice the subtle differences.

Agnella said, "Why hasn't Lena been using you for this all along?"

"Of course she has. Who do you think wrote the letter to Cavanei?" Tadea fought a wicked smile. "But to answer your question, sometimes if you do this often enough, your former convent doesn't want you." The frown lines deepened on her forehead. "And after enough offenses, maybe your own family no longer wants you either."

Magdalena shuddered. "That's awful."

"We all got here in awful ways." Agnella sounded subdued. "It's why we're so good at our work."

Magdalena said, "I wish it hadn't happened that way."

Agnella nodded. "I wish it hadn't happened too."

The driver called to them, and Tadea put away her writing just as the coach rocked again into motion. Agnella said, "I wonder who the new pope will be."

Magdalena sighed. "Not Morone. I told you about all the letters from the Curia. Cardinal Farnese himself said Morone would never become pope."

Agnella said, "If you cut the strings of the purse then yes, men will remember that long after they've forgotten every other bruise you dealt out."

There wasn't the same anger as before. Had Navagero's apology softened her that much? Had it been the measures he'd taken to ensure no one else would be raped by her own confessor?

<hr />

The evening of December 2nd. Their coach slowed, and Agnella called upward, "Is everything all right?"

Tadea lifted her head off the bench where she'd been sleeping. "Stopping to change horses," the driver called. "You'll get a new driver, too."

The nuns got out of the coach while the horses were changed. Magdalena stretched, and Agnella did her regular warmup exercises on the further side, where the men wouldn't see her. "It sounds like everything is crazy in Trent right now," one of the men said as he hitched the first horse to the coach. "We just had another man come through and change horses en route to Rome."

Agnella said, "Did he say why?"

"Didn't say much at all. His Italian was lousy," laughed the stable hand.

Tadea said, "German?"

"Spanish."

Magdalena's eyes widened. Agnella said, "What else did he say? Anything about the pope?"

"Nothing. Really impatient. He'd nearly run his horse to death. We've got a boy walking the poor thing so it doesn't come down with chills after being so overheated."

Magdalena said, "We need to get moving. Now. We need to catch up to that rider."

The new driver said, "We'll never catch a man on a horse."

"Get as close as you can, then." Agnella's voice had authority. "Are we ready to go? Let's start now."

The coach lurched to a start. Tadea was the first to speak. "We don't know it's Luna sending word to his assassin."

"I know enough about men to say it is." Agnella huffed. "Thank goodness the moon is nearly full, because we're going to have to ride all night."

The moon had been full on the 29th. Even knowing Morone's plans to end the council, Magdalena hadn't gone out onto the rooftops for one final run. It had been cold. It had been unfathomable that the council would actually end.

And because travel in the winter would be more difficult than travel in the spring or summer, Magdalena had told herself that she would see more full moons in Trent, that there would be more climbs to the roof of Santa Maria Maggiore.

Now they traveled, stopping for minutes rather than half an hour and letting the horses walk rather than allowing them to stop. The driver (first one, then another) gave the names of the towns or cities they passed. Magdalena could close her eyes and imagine their respective bishops, but not their locations on a map.

They prayed the liturgical hours, estimating time by whatever means they could. They prayed the rosary, and Magdalena sounded out passages from Saint Augustine's *Confessions*, the only personal item she'd brought from Saint Martin's. Well, the book and by accident the letter from Alessandro Farnese, which she'd tucked into the book for safekeeping.

"This should be our last stop," Agnella said, returning from speaking with the driver as they changed horses again. They'd just finished *vespers,* and Magdalena was parceling out one of the loaves of bread and one of their cheeses. "We're close enough to Rome that we should arrive after dark, but before midnight."

Magdalena said, "We can't wait for morning."

"We can get inside," Tadea said. "I have the letters. Right now, I could get us into the Apostolic Palace treasury room with ten burly men carrying shovels and an ox cart. We just need to convince the Swiss Guard to answer the gate."

Agnella said, "If they don't answer the gate, then I'll get us in, and we'll need your letters to keep us inside after they find us."

Time to resume travel, but as soon as the coach moved, it gave a sickening lurch. All three nuns were flung to the side. "Whoa!" called the driver, and then a moment later, the side door opened. "We have a problem."

They climbed out to find the coach was sunken into the mud on one side. "Get it out!" Magdalena exclaimed. "We have to get to Rome!"

Tadea put a hand on Magdalena's arm. "This will take hours. It's stuck."

"But—"

Agnella said, "We can dig. We can push. Let's unload everything we can and get the horses to pull."

Magdalena said, "Wait! The new horses, can we just get them saddled? There are horses here. We can borrow the horses and ride for Rome."

Agnella exclaimed, "I can't ride a horse!"

"I can ride." Tadea looked at the driver. "Get two more horses saddled. She and I are going. You take Agnella and follow us." She pulled out the bag with the coins. "Here. Do it!"

The man ran for the stables. Tadea turned to Agnella. "We'll head right in to the Apostolic Palace. You go for the convent. You'll be a couple of hours behind, but we'll need you as soon as you can get there."

Agnella said, "Can you make it all the way?"

"It's been a while since I rode a horse, but sure. Like I said, when you can forge a signature, you can get anything you want." She snickered as the driver returned leading two horses. "Follow as soon as you can."

The driver helped Magdalena to mount, which turned out to be much easier in boy clothing than in a hitched-up habit. But once she got used to it again, it was no different than being on horseback in Innsbruck, other than the bag she carried and the cold that grew more intense the longer they rode. Both nuns had gloves, but the gloves weren't proof against the December evening. Magdalena struggled to keep her hands from going numb.

They made distance faster than they had in the coach, to the point where Magdalena wondered why they had used the coach in the first place. But that was insanity: she could do this for an hour or two, but not for thirty-six. Even the paid couriers, who did this every day, wouldn't dare ride from Trent to Rome in thirty-six hours. The Spaniard sent from Trent had nearly killed at least one horse in the process. Maybe he'd push hard and kill another one. Maybe when it died, it would take him too so that they'd find his body in a ditch, that man's message to speed up the assassination ultimately defeated by two nuns who knew how to call it off.

Her legs ached and her head ached, and that took her mind of the pain in her hands. They pressed on, sometimes trotting and occasionally letting the horses walk. Tadea said at one point, "I wish I'd kept up my riding, though. You don't forget, but the muscles forget what they used to do."

Magdalena said, "Agnella is curled up in fur rugs in a coach, nibbling on bread and cheese and jealous about how lucky we are to be at the source of the action."

Tadea laughed out loud, then urged her horse again into a trot.

# FORTY

At the gates of the Apostolic Palace, Tadea and Magdalena dismounted in silence. They brought the horses to the papal stables and gave money to the stable hands, who gladly took the horses with their papal livery but looked askance at the pair of "boys."

Tadea said. "We come from Trent with an urgent message for the pope from Cardinal Morone."

"The doors are locked for the night," said one of the stable hands. "You can ask the guard at the gates."

The guard at the gatehouse was unimpressed by their credentials and didn't at all care to see Cardinal Morone's letter. "You cannot see His Holiness tonight. We have orders to keep the gates locked."

Magdalena's eyes widened. That meant the pope was still alive.

She glanced at the palace: yes, he had to be alive. If he'd died, lights would be in all the windows as everyone bustled about with the work you needed to do after a death. There would be church bells and mourning sounds. A living pope meant hope for the council.

Tadea lowered her voice. "Are you questioning the wisdom of the pope's chosen representatives? We've also been sent by the Ludovico Simonetta, cardinal of the Datary, *Oculus Papae.* We are not without credentials."

Tadea's highborn breeding had given her the ability to turn arrogance on and off. In their day-to-day living, Magdalena had never seen anything like it.

"You will lose your job in the morning if we aren't admitted," Tadea added.

The guard remained unimpressed. "I'll lose it now if you are. His Holiness is quite ill, and you won't see him anyhow tonight. This is something you would know if you were actually sent by Cardinal Simonetta or Cardinal Morone."

Two other guards remained inside the gatehouse, watching, but not at all alert. Based on the direction of her eyes, Magdalena predicted the calculations Tadea was making in her mind. Magdalena had her dagger on her arm, but Tadea's crossbow was stashed in her pack. The guard had a sword, plus a dagger, plus he wore armor. All of them did. Without the armor, the pair of them could have taken out all three men without doing long-term damage, but the armor meant incapacitating them might be deadly. The guards didn't deserve that.

Magdalena said, "Perhaps one of you could carry our letter inside to the chief butler. Let him be the one to make the determination."

"You won't lose your job if you disturb the butler." Tadea sharpened her voice. "But when it turns out that we're correct and the pope needs to see this information right away, then you won't lose your job in the morning either."

After consideration, the guard called one of his men. Tadea removed one of the letters from the leather folder, but then she kept her hands in her bag. The junior guard who took the letter was maybe a year younger than Magdalena, the sword ungainly at his side. *He could be Domenico.*

At the other end of the street, glass shattered.

Tadea cried out, "Are we under attack?"

She yanked Magdalena against the gate as the chief guard rushed into the street, the other guard at his back.

"In!" Tadea hissed. "Now!"

They rushed through the unlocked gate, following the path of the junior guard. The junior guard came rushing back, and Tadea shouted, "There's fighting in the street! Turkish pirates! Help them!"

The junior guard ran to the gate. They darted into the bushes.

"Crossbow," Tadea whispered. "Fired it right out of the bag."

"Scale the walls," Magdalena breathed. "The pope's suite is bound to be lighted. Doctors and such."

"True." Tadea looked upward. "But not toward the front."

The chief guard stormed up to the main door shouting an alarm about intruders, so they sidled along the side of the palace, then around the corner.

At five days past full, the moon was bright enough to see by, not bright enough to cast shadows. Every window was dark on this side, but they moved around to the back.

Behind a bush, Magdalena pulled off her boy clothes. "They're not looking for nuns. And black is best right now."

"Good call. We should get in quickly," Tadea whispered, "or onto the roof. They're bound to search the grounds."

"Turkish pirates?" Magdalena asked.

Tadea's voice was low as a breath. "If you live in the south, Turkish pirates are a considerable problem. He had a southern accent. Over here, go up. There's a balcony halfway. Most likely that—" and she pointed to a different, more enormous balcony halfway down the building, "is where the gentleman himself sleeps."

Magdalena girded her habit and tucked her shoes into the top of it, then scaled the wall. More and more guards were calling to each other through the still air, so she hurried as best she could. At the little balcony, she lifted herself over the railing and settled onto the marble.

She looked back over the edge and waved to Tadea. But instead of coming closer, Tadea said, "Here!"

Tadea's sack flew aloft, and Magdalena caught it. "Go!" Tadea shouted, and then bolted across the middle of the garden.

Magdalena stared as Tadea flew across the grounds, and the guards pivoted to follow her.

The bag contained Tadea's folder and the letters, but not her crossbow. Hoping Tadea knew what she was doing, Magdalena edged a door open to a dark room. And with that, after three days and losing all her companions, she was inside the Apostolic Palace.

# FORTY-ONE

During her book test, Magdalena needed to move through a room without disturbing a sleeping man. This was the same. With her entire body sheathed in black and her feet bare, Magdalena stayed low to the carpet and moved without making a sound through a bedroom with all its curtains drawn.

Deep breathing told her someone else was in the room. She breathed with the same depth and pace as the sleeper. Easy. Stay in synchronization with those breaths. Don't give the person anything to hear that might alert his dreaming mind to the reality of her presence. Be nothing more than a dream.

On the far side of the room, Magdalena made out three doors, any of which might creak when opened, and two of which probably led dead ends. She pressed her hands flat to the carpet and concentrated on the texture. It was springy here, in the corner. It was less springy in the center, where feet trod. Here it was more worn. There it was rough, and therefore this was the path most traveled, so this way Magdalena traveled as well.

Her saddlesore muscles protested with every move. She was exhausted, but energy coursed through her, energy that came either from disbelief that she was doing this or from

God Himself. She'd vowed to protect the Church and the papacy. Here she was doing both. May God in His mercy help her.

She reached for the knob, and with a slowness born of fright, she let the knob warm beneath her hand. Then, when she felt confident in the rhythm of the deep breathing, hers and the sleeper's, she began to turn. The catch opened, and Magdalena rose all the way to her feet. She swung the door just enough to slip through, and she held it in place while taking in her new surroundings.

This room was wider, more silent, quite probably the outer room of the unknown sleeper's suite. Good. She propped the door in its nearly open state so it wouldn't close with a click, then moved further in, careful not to step into the furniture or into a wall. In this room there wasn't even moonlight for a guide. She straightened her habit and replaced her shoes, then located another door. This she opened with less care for silence, and it rewarded her by yielding a hallway, illuminated at one end by moonlight streaming in a window.

The large balcony and the lit windows had been in this direction, so Magdalena followed the hallway. This part of the palace was opulent. Was all of it? Was this hallway more so than the rest? Was it less opulent because fewer people saw the pope's private quarters?

Her legs trembled as she moved to where the suite must be, and here she found grand doors. When she pressed her ears to those doors, she could hear nothing.

His private suite wouldn't open directly into his bedroom. She'd seen enough lavish quarters and private palaces by now that she expected no fewer than three rooms before she'd find the bed chamber. There would be a public parlor and a private parlor and a sitting room and a room for his reading. So through the suite she worked her way, bracing herself at every turn for the moment she reached the one that was occupied.

And finally she found it, a room where on the other side she could detect noise, and beneath the door a little light.

She hadn't found a tray or a basket to make herself look natural, so she merely opened the door and strode in.

The chamber reeked of death. Magdalena walked across its expanse with purpose, directing her steps toward the poster bed at the center and the attendant seated at its side. She'd remember this stench until the last days of her life. It would always trigger the memory of Seripando and his lanky hands.

But it ended here. She would associate Seripando's death with this smell, but not the death of Pope Pius IV. He had to survive.

The attendant stood. "Sister, forgive me. I didn't expect anyone else. Galiano isn't supposed to come until midnight."

Aware that she might be facing an assassin, Magdalena bowed her head. "Galiano asked me to come up in his place. I didn't realize I was early. My apologies." She bowed her head, then clasped her hands at her chest. "I'm Sister Magdalena DeCasalvis, of the convent of Saint Sebastian and the hospital for incurables."

On his bed, Pius raised his head. "Catherinites," he murmured. "It is over, then."

"Sir, I will stay with you and pray over you." She softened her voice. "I've tended many a deathbed, and you aren't lying in yours. I believe Galiano sent for me in error. Nevertheless, I will remain until dawn."

Magdalena examined the tray by the fire, dotted with a dozen glass jars, any of which might contain Nezetta's concoction. "Are there any medications I should dispense during the night?"

The attendant said, "I'm not in charge of that. The doctor comes in every hour."

She rested a hand on the attendant's arm. "Go get some sleep. I'll remain with him in prayer."

Prayer and investigating, and quite possibly a little mayhem.

The attendant looked to the pope. "Are you sure, Your Holiness? I can stay as well."

"No, you may go. I'm only one man," he murmured. "I don't need two people with me all night."

After the attendant left, Magdalena went straight for the little jars. One at a time she pinched out the tiny stoppers, sniffed the contents, and set them back. One brought tears to her eyes: theriac, and its heady balm of musk and cedar and lavender. Forever and always, theriac would smell like Chiara's death. *Saint Chiara, pray for me. I'm trying to make it right. Pray for me and for the pope. I don't care what happens to me, but the pope has to live two more days.*

The fifth jar was death. Jarred death, jarred by the hands of a person just like Nezetta. She upended it over the fire.

The liquid hissed as it made contact. Magdalena turned to find Pius looking direct at her.

"My daughter, what are you doing?"

"Sir, I'm saving your life."

Magdalena opened the sack, then pulled out Tadea's folder with its sealed envelopes. "Sir, I am indeed a Catherinite, and I've come from Trent, from the legates, carrying letters for you. This is from Cardinal Morone. He explains what's happening, and I'll beg you to trust him. This one is from Cardinal Simonetta. I assume his letter says the same."

The pope took the letters. "It is his seal. But why are you here?"

"I'm your protector. Catherinites take vows to serve the pope. We need to protect you." Magdalena returned to the little bottles near the hearth. "Someone in the Apostolic Palace has been sent by the Spanish to poison you. They want to prevent the council from ending, and with Cardinal Morone driven to end it at the next session, they've only one way to do that. They plan to kill you in order to invalidate the final session."

Pius looked up from Morone's letter to stare at her.

"I've come from Trent," Magdalena said. "I've vowed my loyalty to the papacy, so I'm here to protect you."

"But who would poison me?" he asked.

"I believe it may be the man who's been administering these medicines. Galiano?"

"Bartolome Luis de Galiano?" The pope's eyes widened. "He's the steward of the palace!"

Also the man whose orders had prevented her and Tadea from entering through the front door.

A clock struck in the streets, and soon another. Eleven thirty. The next shift was supposed to arrive at midnight, so she hurried through the rest of the bottles. Nothing else smelled of death. Even the ones she couldn't recognize put her in mind of green earth and summer nights.

And then the last, the scent of summer itself, a breath of rosebuds tight in the first moments of the morning.

"Rosewater," she whispered. She set that to the side with the theriac.

A kettle sat on the hearth, so she filled a cup and added a splash of rosewater. "You have to drink lots of water, sir." She turned to him. "You've been poisoned to make it look like pneumonia. Our order knows poisons, and we know how to diminish this one. You can rid yourself of it, but you have to drink and drink and drink."

Plain water with the memory of roses. She carried it to him, warm in her hands. "Sir, please. I vowed to obey you. Please now obey me."

She

the cup to his lips, and although weak, he drank. After a few sips he said, "No more," and she set it aside.

At the fire again she filled the poison bottle with boiling water, then dumped it and filled it a second time. Nezetta had retired the kettle in which she'd brewed their poison, never to be used again. Was it so effective that it could soak into glass too? Magdalena took a brand from the fire and inserted it into the mouth of the jar to fill it with smoke. Then she let it cool and rinsed it again with boiling water.

Time passed too quickly. She had Pius sip more water, then returned to the poison jar. She pushed a fingerful of theriac salve into the neck of the bottle, then washed it down with lukewarm water. Then, after sealing the jar, she shook it vigorously to melt the salve.

The killer might well have more, but he wouldn't know to carry it in. He might just use the substitute and count on the smell of the room rather than the smell of the jar.

Without much time, Magdalena scanned the room. With its opulent furniture and statuary, more opulent than even the German bishop's bedroom, the chamber offered a dozen places to climb and even more places to hide. She needed to choose well, though. She had to be able to see. She had to be able to respond.

She could remain at the pope's bedside, fully visible, and count on being ignored as her sisters always were. But a killer—no, a killer suspected everyone, and a killer would mistrust her presence because she wasn't the one he expected to find. He'd demand she leave.

"Sir," she said, "take one more drink." With this swallow, he finished the cup. "I'm going to have to hide when Galiano comes in. I don't know if he's the assassin, but I need to be able to watch. If he tries to harm you, I need to be free to intervene."

Pius looked concerned. "What will you do, a little girl?"

She gathered herself. "With all due respect, sir, I'm going to do exactly what my order is trained to do. Exactly what you've ordered us to do many a time. This will only be the first time you've witnessed it yourself."

She refilled his cup and reminded him to keep drinking.

"Daughter, please," the pope said, "give me my Bible too. If this is my last night on earth, I want God's word close to my heart."

The Bible was on the night stand near his cup, and she gave it to him. Then as bells tolled midnight, she scaled the wall and disappeared into the enclosure around a statue of Saint Joseph.

Saint Joseph, protect me. You protected the Christ child. Please protect the pope. The Church needs your prayers.

She withdrew into the darkness and kept her attention trained on Pius where he sat up in bed. Nezetta hadn't told her how long it would take for the poison to leave his body, or how much water he'd need to drink. Cups of water? Rivers? She had no idea, and now there was no way to ask.

# FORTY-TWO

The bedchamber door opened, and in came the dark-eyed steward. He exclaimed, "Sir, where is Foscari?"

"Ah, Galiano. I sent him away early," the pope said. "He was so tired, staying up all night with an old man. I knew you would come, so there was no need to inconvenience him."

Galiano straightened the pope's blankets. "You should sleep. Carlo told you to sleep."

Carlo Borromeo, the papal nephew. Of course he'd be intimately involved, and a man so holy would suspect no one of such an evil.

"This may be my last night on earth," Pius said. "I want to spend it in prayer and contemplation."

Galiano shook his head. "If Carlo thought it your last night on earth, he'd be here with you."

The steward's movements were practiced. As he moved about the room, Magdalena judged him second by second. Was he too tense? Was he too relaxed? Motions betrayed motives. Was this man the keystone in the assassination plot? Or was he just the chief steward in the Apostolic Palace, waiting on his master and praying for his recovery in between plumping pillows and boiling water for tea?

From high up the wall, Magdalena took note of the pope too. Now that she wasn't busy, she realized how small he was, how similar to a dying Seripando. Aged, fragile, but with a core of iron. She'd informed him he was being poisoned and that the next man into the room was quite likely the murderer, but he'd maintained calm. He sat in bed now and spoke to the putative killer as though nothing more pressing were happening than choosing the correct blend of tea.

He wasn't afraid of death. Come to think of it, neither had Seripando nor Gonzaga been afraid of death. Cavanei in the alleyway had pleaded for his life, but the legates had not. The pope had not. He wanted to survive, but at the same time she sensed a certain surrender that hadn't been present at the hospital for incurables.

Life wasn't something you lost. It was something you enjoyed and used and at the end rendered back to God. These men had spent so much time pondering eternity that on its doorstep, they felt trepidation but no fear. Awe. Respect. But without any horror.

Regardless, he needed to survive, and Magdalena would ensure he did.

The pope asked for his water, and she smiled. Yes, he wanted to ensure he survived as well. Willingness to surrender your life wasn't the same as eagerness to do so.

Galiano said, "One moment, Your Holiness," and took the cup to the little tray, where he reached directly for the blue bottle.

Eyes narrow, Magdalena tensed. Killer.

The man added a few drops of would-be poison to the cup, then returned it to the pope. "This cup is still warm. When did Foscari leave?"

Oh, no. That was a bad judgment call on her part.

Pius shrugged. "Not terribly long ago."

The man didn't hand the cup over but kept his hands around the stem. He was too far for Magdalena to leap at him. Her dagger, thrown from here, might kill the man before he had the chance to do any damage, but likely not. She worked the clasp free and slipped her fingers around the handle.

The man scanned the room. He knew there was a letter downstairs from Trent. He may even have read it. In the pope's bed right now was another letter from Morone outlining the entire plot.

Galiano set the cup on the side table, then paced around the room. He looked into corners whole holding his candle. He peered beneath the bed, and Magdalena remained still like a cat, her black clothing covering her entire body, her head covered with the black scarf, the pale skin of her hands submerged in her sleeves, and her face down. If he saw her, she'd spring.

How many were involved? If she subdued this man, how many could take his place? She couldn't defend the pope's chamber for two days against a room suffused with armed guards. Even the pope's own protests wouldn't keep her alive if the guards deemed her a danger.

When he didn't find her, Galiano looked even more nervous. He pulled the bell for the servants.

The pope said, "Please sit. You seem unsettled."

"There was a disturbance on the grounds earlier tonight." Galiano turned back. "A pair of boys tried to get through the front gate."

She and Tadea should just have scaled the fence. Tadea had been so sure her letters would get them all the way inside. They hadn't realized the danger would be so close to the point of entry.

The man continued, "I'm concerned one of them could have broken in here."

Pius said, "Why such concern? How would they have done so?"

"I don't know how. But it seems as if someone's been here, and you might have been asleep."

Pius waved a hand. "Someone who found me asleep and did no harm is not a danger."

"We don't know that." The door opened, and the steward called, "Bring me guards. Post them at all the doors to the suite. Position one on the balcony too."

The steward returned to the table of medicine bottles and again picked up the blue one. He slipped out the stopper and sniffed.

His eyes widened, and he stared at Pius.

Guards arrived. Galiano told the one for the balcony, "Stand with the curtains drawn, so no one will see you." He sent the rest out of the room to guard the doors. "Do not come inside. Your job is to keep anyone from coming in," he snapped, "and you can't do that if you come in first."

"No intruders have gotten into the house," the chief guard said. "There were only two boys, and we chased both of them away."

"Your incompetence let them onto the grounds in the first place. I don't trust that they haven't come back."

This was probably a good judgment call, considering that if they'd chased off *two* boys, it meant Tadea had snuck back behind the fence to let them chase her off a second time.

As the guards took their places, Magdalena wondered who this setup would benefit. Clearly Galiano thought it benefitted himself, but why didn't he want at least one guard in the room? Why didn't he ask them to search?

Maybe he was going to wait for the pope to sleep and then kill him directly. It would mean a death sentence once the pope's body was discovered, but the assassin would have served his purpose. Or rather, the purposes of the Spanish Crown as interpreted by Count Claudio Fernandez de Quinones Luna.

Six months ago, wouldn't she have done the same? Hadn't she stood in a bedchamber resolving to die in service of the Church?

Here was a better question, though: in a palace surrounded by people who wanted Morone dead, what would she have done if she'd suspected one was sealed up in the same room?

That was easy. She'd have armed herself, and she'd have flushed out the attacker.

The steward's actions made sense in that light: why he'd want guards at the doors but not inside. If guards were inside, they'd arrest or kill the intruder while leaving the real assassin no closer to finishing his job. Instead, he wanted to cause a commotion with no witnesses. During the fight, he could strike the pope, and when the guards entered, he could blame the pope's death on the intruder.

That must mean Galiano had no more poison. Good.

God, help me get through this. She kept her head tucked as the man resumed searching. I think I know what he intends, but I don't know how to prevent it.

Galiano wouldn't leave the circle of lamplight near the pope's bed. As much searching as he did, he did it in the light because the darkness was her weapon, and this room was full of it. In fact, the whole world was Magdalena's weapon, and Magdalena's body was her weapon. She just needed an opportunity to use what she had.

Light snoring came from the bed. The pope had fallen back to sleep.

Galiano heard it too. Pitching his voice low, he said, "I know you're here. You might as well show yourself."

He drew the heavy bar across the door, nestling it into the holder without a sound. Next he secured the balcony doors as well. That done, he took up a candle and stepped into the center of the room.

"I can immolate us all." His voice flowed low and smooth, a river of poison. "The judgment of God will come on all of us, but God will know I've saved the Church. You, on the other hand, will burn for eternity. Burn now and die. Burn forever afterward."

If he did try to light the room, she'd spring for him, get the doors open, and carry the pope to safety. But this was only a threat, and she recognized threats.

Galiano said, "No?"

*No, of course not.* This man might be willing to set himself on fire, but he seemed far too sane to make that his first option.

The man's whisper filled the cavernous spaces of the room. "If they find him dead, they'll believe it was you."

It was the book test all over again. The man was a heretical book with a venomous snake locked inside. You had to secure the book without freeing the snake. Only this time, there was no one waiting on a ledge to receive the book.

He took a step toward the sleeping pope, then set the candle down again on the side table. Good, no fire.

But then Galiano pulled a knife from his belt and turned to the Pope.

Magdalena pulled off her shoe and flung it across the room, and when it slammed into the wall, Galiano turned. Magdalena leaped from her niche to the carpet. As Galiano swung back toward her, she sprang onto a desk and leaped halfway up the wall, kicking off sideways to change direction.

He raised his blade as she crashed into him, grazing her side and then rolling under her so she slammed into the side table. Glass shattered all over the floor.

Galiano turned to the bed and drove his blade down into the pope's heart.

The pope cried out.

Magdalena screamed, lunging toward the pope. No, there still had to be time to save him, time to keep him alive just for a couple of days. Even if he died, he shouldn't die now, die with everything mere hours from completion—

Guards banged on the main door, calling to Galiano to let them in. Galiano shouted, "An assassin! An assassin has killed the pope!"

He was between her and the pope, but she needed to get to the bedside. Kill Galiano and stop the pope from bleeding out. If she could.

Magdalena charged Galiano, feinting with one hand, then checking him to the side of the head with the other. Whenever she twisted, the glass in her shoulder and the slash up her side lit up like fire, but she had no choice, only to do the same again and do it faster. She tried to throw him to the floor, but he evaded and punched her in the gut.

She jerked her head forward and hammered her skull into his nose. Blood spurted out as he staggered backward, and she leaped, driving her knee at his head. Again he dodged, then rolled beneath her to sweep her legs from beneath her when she landed.

He slammed her head into the ground, then got on top of her, knee to her chest. Atop her, he wrapped his hands in her habit with his arms crossed. "An assassin nun." He wrenched her sideways so he was sprawled her with one leg locked between hers, tightening his choke hold. "How cute."

Her side screamed with pain and the glass ground into her skin, and now she couldn't breathe. She thrashed, but his fists in her habit and his leg around hers left her with nothing to use but her arms and the ground. The whole world was her weapon, but where was her weapon now? Her blood couldn't get to her head and the air couldn't get into her lungs. The world darkened.

She had to get to the pope. She had to slow the bleeding. He had to live until tomorrow. She had to...

Darkness. Ringing in her ears. Fire in her lungs.

Then the pressure was off her throat and she gasped so hard it hurt. She drove her elbows back into Galiano's chest as nausea swamped her. Galiano went down on his back, fresh blood coursing along his temple.

At the edge of the bed, blood on his night shirt, was the pope. In his hand was a large metal cross with a crimson tint. "Leave her alone!"

He stood only a second, then collapsed onto the bed.

Magdalena leaped onto Galiano and locked her body over his, kneeling in the glass. The pope was alive! Alive for now. Alive! She grabbed Galiano's forearm and shoved it to the floor, then with her other hand got under his upper arm and gripped her own wrist. As hard as she could, she pivoted his elbow toward his hips and then pried his shoulder upward.

Alive. The pope was alive.

Galiano screamed, thrashed. It took all her upper body strength to keep his shoulder pried up and his head jacked to the side, her body on his. He rolled, kicked at her. Her own blood ran over her eyes, and every time he thrashed, her slashed side stung in protest. She registered the banging at the door again. It must have been going on the whole time, but she hadn't noticed. Glass crunched under Galiano as he struggled, and every movement drove the glass shards further into her knees.

Her arms shook with the strain. Dizzy, nauseated, Magdalena pressed as low to him as possible so she could keep him under control. He had an endless reserve of strength, whereas she was disoriented, exhausted, bleeding. She couldn't do this for as long as it would take for the guards to splinter the door. She might not be able to do it for another minute.

More glass shattered: the balcony door. The lone guard burst in with his sword drawn, rushing for her and the pope and the man on the floor, running on the slivers and creating even more with his boots.

The guard dropped his sword and yanked her off Galiano.

"No!" the pope cried, "Not her! Galiano tried to kill me!"

The guard let go. "What?"

But in that second Galiano had leaped up, staggered, and grabbed the guard's sword.

"No!" Magdalena rushed between him and the pope as Galiano raised the sword for a killing blow. Her hands shot out to his wrist and his opposite elbow. She caught him with the blade over her head, the pope at her back and the guard at Galiano's.

With a twist she wrapped his arm around so the sword arced through the air. She locked his elbow and his wrist until with a pained cry he let go of the sword and she took it by the handle. Then as he collapsed to the ground, she swung the sword down to his neck.

She didn't stab. With the point at his throat, she stood, staring, blood coursing down her face and down her side, her heart pounding, her breath hard.

"I am the bride of Christ." She glared into his eyes. "Keep your hands off my family."

Galiano stared, afraid even to inch backward. Blood trickled down her arm while she kept the point at his throat. Her journey started with an Adam's apple. It would end with one too.

The guard ventured a timid, "I'll...I'll take the sword, sister."

She didn't hand it over. "Open the door." It came out a whisper. The rasp of her voice was the very thin line between the life of the pope and his death, the life of the council, the life of the Church itself.

Uncertain, the guard glanced at the pope. He must have nodded, because the guard removed the bar from the door. That was the scene greeting the guards when they finally entered: a bleeding nun standing over their bleeding steward, pressing a Swiss Guardsman's sword to his throat, and a pope sitting up in bed with blood on his shirt.

"Arrest Galiano," the guard said.

As soon as they'd secured him, Magdalena dropped the sword and rushed to the pope. "Sir—you're bleeding. Let me help you. Please. You have to stay alive."

"I'm alive, daughter." The pope extended a frail hand to her blood-covered one. "See. God's word has saved me after all."

He opened his night shirt to reveal nothing more than a scratch, then handed her the dagger with which Galiano had struck his death blow. The blade and penetrated right through the cover of the pope's Bible, through all the pages, and out the other side. But it hadn't gone further, only enough to penetrate the dressing gown and the top layers of skin.

Magdalena dropped to her knees at the side of the bed, head on her arms. She shook out of control, again overwhelmed with cold and nausea. *Oh, my God, thank you. Thank you. I couldn't save him, but You did.*

The pope stroked her short hair. "Daughter, you're bleeding."

She didn't answer, unable to say anything more to him, unable to say anything even to the guards when they arrested her. They gave her a towel to press to her side and led her downstairs to a cell. She did it without protest. It didn't matter what happened next. The council would conclude, and Christendom would be saved.

# FORTY-THREE

The papal prison wasn't a bad place to spend a night, although the guards weren't entirely sure what to do with her. The pope had said she was innocent, but given the circumstances, they didn't trust him to be of sound mind at the moment.

Borromeo had been awakened, and groggy as he was at first, followed by how distraught he was next, he wasn't sure what to do with her either. She was left in a holding cell, therefore as was former steward Bartolome Luis de Galiano, and calmer minds would have to sort it out in the morning.

Magdalena huddled on her thin pallet beneath a thin blanket, listening to guards deliberating down the hall. She'd have to break out and sneak back into the papal chambers at some point to retrieve the letters that would free her from this prison. She'd have to send word to Morone. She'd have to do a lot of things, but while cataloging them all, she unintentionally did the thing she needed to do most and fell asleep.

Church bells broke into her dreams before dawn, and when she stretched, the brilliant pain in her side roused her fully. She ought to have seen a doctor or a surgeon. Everything else in the holding cells was silent beyond a curious scratching that didn't sound like mice or rats, and when she looked up, she found Bellosa at the barred window.

Even turning her head to the window sent ripples of stiffness and pain down her back and a throbbing dullness to her skull.

Her former abbess said, "You're quite a troublemaker. I'm sure to receive a charming letter from Cardinal Simonetta in the next several days, but it won't be as interesting as the report I had last night from Sister Tadea."

Gingerly, Magdalena sat up. Her ribs didn't grind, so they probably weren't broken. She didn't try moving her legs. "She found you?"

"She fetched us all. We were all over the grounds, but not in time. She had gone ahead of us and heard the fighting in the pope's bedroom, but in her words, the balcony guard was a useless hand-wringer, so she shot out the glass on the doorway. That made up the man's mind to go inside and do his job. Tadea climbed onto the balcony just in time to witness the end of the fight. Which, I'm told, you lost."

Magdalena deflated. "Forgive me. God saved us all."

Bellosa shook her head. "He had to. No one else was about to do it." She pulled, and the entire set of window bars came free. "I have no idea why they think imprisoning you in such a flimsy cell is a good idea, but here we are." She slipped inside, then settled on the pallet beside Magdalena. "When Agnella arrives, I'll have her look over your injuries. You're frightful. I assume that's not all your own blood."

Magdalena hadn't been given a wash basin nor had she the strength to use one if she had. The would-be killer's blood was probably all over her face. It certainly was on her hands. No wonder the guards hadn't known what to do.

Bellosa pulled out her handkerchief and started rubbing at Magdalena's cheek. "It would be impolitic to break you out, so I'm going to stay. I've placed myself under arrest."

At the window, Gilia said, "Do you need another in there?"

"Can you get word to my mother?" Magdalena said.

"And worry her to death? Since we're talking about decisions that would be impolitic—"

"No, if you could send word to deliver rosewater to the pope. Please. He's got to drink lots of water to counteract the poison, and hers is…well, it's not magic. But it's close."

Gilia huffed. "Fine. I'll go, since you're making me extremely jealous that I didn't get to travel to Trent."

Tadea appeared after Gilia vanished. "I'm staying too. I need to get my arrows back."

Magdalena laughed as Tadea climbed through the window, then winced at the sting in her side.

Tadea continued, "It was quite the havoc at the convent last night. Apparently the ruckus we made at the Apostolic Palace was enough that the Swiss Guards dispatched everybody they could, so sneaking in was quite the challenge."

Bellosa started massaging Magdalena's neck and shoulders. It hurt like crazy, but Magdalena closed her eyes and tried to relax those muscles. Bellosa said, "I had sisters on the roof, but no one else had gotten into the building by the time the assassin made his move."

Agnella appeared and handed a loaf of bread and a cheese through the window.

Rome. Magdalena was back in Rome, surrounded by friends and with her duty at an end. By the end of the day, the council would have closed. They'd succeeded.

While Bellosa worked the stiffness out of Magdalena's body, the sisters prayed *prime* in the cell. To the crowd of guards at the entrance, Tadea explained, "We're nuns. We're used to cells." Unnerved by the crowd of nuns and the unbarred windows, they sent upstairs for help.

Gilia returned with a jug courtesy of Magdalena's mother, as well as a medical kit from Saint Sebastian's. The nuns were crowded shoulder-to-shoulder, but they managed to give Agnella room to treat the injury on Magdalena's side.

Theriac. The smell filled her, and Magdalena blinked back tears. Agnella thought it stung, but it only felt as if she'd brought Chiara into the cell with her.

Gilia scouted out a basin of water and towels. It was in the middle of washing off the encrusted blood that the guards announced the presence of the cardinal-nephew, Carlo Borromeo.

The nuns stood, Magdalena leaning on Agnella to maintain her footing. They passed her forward toward the bars. At least she was cleaner than she'd been an hour earlier.

Looking over all the nuns packed in, Borromeo tried to sound in control. "You've created a lot of confusion in the Apostolic Palace, but I believe I shall have to ask you to create just a little more. I've been ordered to invite last night's honored guest to accompany me upstairs, but if the rest of you would like to join her, I see no reason to exclude you."

Agnella said, "Or rather, you see no way to exclude us."

Borromeo gave a sage nod. "That does seem to be the case. Either we all take the stairs, or else you'll climb in the windows."

Magdalena took her first step and then couldn't go further, so Agnella got under one arm and Tadea under the other, and they managed the long staircases one painful step at a time. Even now Magdalena found herself analyzing the corners for hiding spots and potential weapons.

After a long, slow journey punctuated with three resting places (thank goodness for the plush chairs in the alcoves) they finally reached a smaller suite, not the grand suite from the night before.

"There's some need to clean the master suite," Borromeo explained, "and we felt he would be more comfortable in smaller quarters without access to outside. Also, the Swiss Guards feel that rooming him in an unexpected place will provide an additional measure of safety."

Bellosa found Magdalena a chair and let her collapse into it. "The rest of us will stand from respect," she said, "but Sister Magdalena is injured."

Borromeo had gone pale studying Magdalena's condition. "I didn't realize the guards hadn't summoned a doctor last night. They should have. I most humbly apologize for not seeing to it myself." He looked at her. "Your name is Magdalena? My uncle was unclear last night."

"Sister Magdalena DeCasalvis." A standard opening tactic for questioning, she'd been told. Ask a question the detainee won't mind answering.

Borromeo nodded. "Please, tell me in detail what happened. I've already spoken to the guards and to my uncle, but they're as bewildered as I am."

Bellosa spoke before she could answer. "With all due discretion, Cardinal Borromeo, I'm not certain how much we are allowed to disclose. Our nuns in Trent uncovered a plot to kill your uncle, the pope. They came under the authorization of Principal Legate Morone to prevent the assassination, and last night Magdalena was able to gain entrance to the room in order to protect him. As you can see, she succeeded. If you doubt the facts of the case, then I invite you to imprison my entire order. As her abbess, I take responsibility for her actions and the actions of all my nuns in this matter."

Borromeo turned back to Magdalena. "Yes, your authorization. I saw the letter you gave my uncle. Quite a skilled copy of Morone's handwriting, but not exact."

Magdalena closed her eyes.

"Most of it is his wording, though, so I assume you were working from an actual letter."

The nuns remained perfectly silent.

Having made his point, Borromeo said, "Tell me about Trent."

"The council will close today." Magdalena kept her eyes lowered. "Your uncle had to survive until the council closes in order for the council itself to be recognized as authentic. The Spanish under Count Luna wanted to prevent that."

Borromeo said, "I'm aware of that much. I wrote to Morone instructing him to ignore Luna's machinations and close the council as quickly as possible. But the council will hold its final session on the ninth, not today."

Magdalena swallowed hard. "The only way for the Spanish to prevent the council from closing was to ensure the death of the pope. When Cardinal Morone heard about your uncle's illness, he pushed forward the final session by five days. He sent word back to you about the plot to poison the pope, but we didn't think that sufficient, so we intercepted his message and came ourselves."

Borromeo said, "All of you?"

"Three of us." Magdalena didn't look up or otherwise specify the other two. "We are charged with loyalty to the pope. Our vows required us to come."

Borromeo shook his head. "There was no time for you to have come from Trent."

Agnella said, "How many people have you told about the planned confessionals?"

Borromeo sat up. "You know about that?"

"I've seen the drawings you sent to Cardinal Navagero," Agnella said. "For the protection of penitents who can't be shut up alone with a confessor. To be installed in your home cathedral and later in every church in the world."

Bellosa said, "We know about the letters written by many in the Curia to prevent the limitation of benefices."

Tadea said, "We know about the commissioning of seminaries."

Agnella said, "Primus canon non placet."

Tadea said, "*Jus divinum*. Reform of the head."

Magdalena said, "I've seen with my own eyes the draft of Seripando's catechism. Sir, we were at Trent. Until the evening of November 30th, I was in Trent."

Borromeo rubbed his chin. "What happened to Morone's original orders?"

"They're in a leather folder in the papal bedchamber, tucked behind a statue of Saint Joseph."

Borromeo dispatched one of the servants to find it. "While I verify your story, tell me, what do you want?"

That much was simple. "I want the pope to live. I want the council to succeed."

"Anything else?"

Magdalena added, "I want you to bring him this jug of rosewater. He has to drink it to flush the poison out of his body."

Borromeo looked puzzled. "Rosewater?"

"He can drink plain water if he likes," Bellosa said, "but for now he may drink nothing stronger than rosewater."

"Lots of it," Magdalena added. "He needs to drink as much as he can."

Borromeo called over another servant. "Please see if His Holiness is willing to receive visitors."

While waiting for a response, Borromeo asked more questions about Trent, but his tone had changed from tentative to curious. What had they decided about the veneration of images? How did Morone plan to forward the timetable by five days? Didn't they agree it was a stroke of genius to change issues from the doctrine category into the reform category? It became harder and harder to keep speaking past the exhaustion and the pain, but shortly a servant returned with leather folder—and Magdalena's travel bag. While Bellosa helped her get the habit back over her exercise clothes, Borromeo withdrew the original letter. He couldn't have reached the second line before he said, "Yes, this is Morone's hand," and then pored over the remaining text, his eyes betraying first unrest and then anger.

The second servant returned. "He would like to see just the one."

Magdalena strengthened herself against the pain and took her mother's rosewater jug, then followed the servant up the hallway. "Only stay for a few minutes. He's very weak."

The smaller chamber was still larger than the convent's refectory, with four guards standing at the corners. It smelled of death, but not as strongly as last night.

The servant showed Magdalena to the pope's bedside, then withdrew.

She bowed. "Sir, thank you again for your help last night."

"It is I who should thank you." The pope glanced at the jug. "What are you carrying?"

"Rosewater, from my mother. You have to drink it all."

"Not all at once, I hope!" He laughed. "Come closer, daughter."

She stepped nearer. Her side was throbbing, and she hoped she'd be able to continue standing through the whole interview.

"You look more like a nun today." The pope sighed. "So much trouble. Christ said we would suffer if we followed Him, but who would have anticipated so much of the trouble would come from other Christians? Come here where I can touch you. Then kneel."

When Magdalena had gotten to her knees, he could put his hand on her head. He whispered a prayer. First of thanks, then of a blessing. His hands were shaking.

Her head tingling, she took painful steps toward his side table, where she filled a cup with rosewater. "Rest, sir, and heal. And know that no matter what, by tonight the council will conclude."

# FORTY-FOUR

After the pope's dismissal, Magdalena found herself quite bewilderingly with no immediate mission. So she went back home, home to Saint Sebastian's, certain the pope would summon her back and force her to give a more thorough report.

But the summons didn't come. Every day, it didn't come. And every night, with no message and no coach and no visitors from the Curia, Magdalena had gone to bed thanking God for another day spent caring for those in the hospital. All of December, she had filled her time with washing bed linens and spoon-feeding withered men who couldn't raise their heads. She comforted the parents of children contorted by muscle spasms and prayed at the bedside of paper-thin women who waited to see the Blessed Virgin coming in their final hours.

Honest work, done for God's most honest people. At the day's end, she'd do her final exercises and worship at *compline* with her sisters. Then she'd sleep like the dead until *lauds*.

Mother had been delighted to have Magdalena back from Trent, although she fussed that surely Magdalena was thinner now, her eyes deeper and darker, her words more cautious. By the end of a week, Agnella had fitted Fiora with another shoe and a new crutch. "We'll teach you how to defend yourself too. One of the bishops from the East showed me an interesting trick with a staff, and I think we can adapt it for you."

They had spent all Advent this way, fasting and praying, working and praying, exercising and praying. Rome was still Rome. All was well.

Then, on December 28th, came the summons. Magdalena must again appear before the pope. "I'm only surprised it didn't come sooner," Bellosa said as they hurried through the street, shawls tight around themselves. "When Cardinal Morone returned from Trent, I expected it the same day."

At the Apostolic Palace, a pair of guards (neither of which Magdalena recognized, thank goodness) ushered them to the door, and from there another guard took them to a parlor to wait. Two of the Swiss Guard stood at the door to the papal offices—the proper ones this time. Magdalena sat with her hands folded in her lap.

The next time the door opened, however, it was not to the papal offices, but from the hallway. In came her mother, her brother, and her sister.

Magdalena stood. "Why are you here?"

Her mother lifted a letter. Fiora, in her least threadbare dress, exclaimed, "A Swiss Guard came this morning! They brought us in a coach!"

Magdalena wrapped her hands around each other, then grabbed Fiora in a tight hug. What had Morone said to the pope? Could it be that Morone wasn't behind this summons at all, but rather Cardinal Farnese? What would he do to his bastard relations? Moreover, what would he do to his bastard relation who had worked so hard to make sure the council concluded—and therefore reduced his standard of living?

The five of them were shown into the papal suite, and then from an outer room into an inner room. Fiora gasped and gaped and pointed until Mother hushed her. Domenico kept himself under better control, but Magdalena could see he was unnerved. It hadn't occurred to her how she'd gotten used to pomp and decoration, the fantastic ornamentation of rich men's homes, and how she'd taken to eyeing architectural features as nothing more than potential handholds.

The owners of the statues and paintings were only men, and flawed men at that. Some deeply so.

In the third room, the guards gave them over to the pope himself, seated at his desk and flanked by two cardinals.

Magdalena stepped forward and bowed. "Thank you for receiving us, Your Holiness." Then one at a time she bowed to the cardinals. "Cardinal Morone. Cardinal Simonetta. It's a pleasure seeing you again."

The pleasure appeared to be entirely hers. Simonetta for one wore a deep scowl, and she didn't dare glance at Morone.

The pope said, "I am so glad you all could come to me. Sister Magdalena, please forgive me the impertinence of inviting your family, but I did so want to meet the woman whose hands made the rosewater you delivered after my illness."

Magdalena's mother flushed. "It's an honor to have helped, sir."

The pope smiled. "Your daughter did me a great service, and then I repaid her by taking your rosewater. I'm afraid that was not much of a repayment, and as such I stand in your debt." He leaned forward, elbows on the desk. "Cardinal Morone has spoken to me of your family's situation, and I would like to assist."

Mother glanced at Magdalena, horrified.

Magdalena braced herself. "Sir, I didn't tell my mother what happened the night I returned from Trent, only that my early return was in the service of the Church."

385

The pope smiled. "Quite a service it was. Ma'am, you ought to know that your daughter saved my life, and that while in the north at the council, she saved the life of Cardinal Morone as well. The Church itself owes her a debt, and while God Himself repays all our debts in eternity, I would like to make a start on repaying this one now. Name a gift, and I'll give it to you."

Mother's eyes had gone huge. It wasn't fair. Her mother wasn't at all prepared for such an offer. Surprised like this, she could ask for money, and most likely the pope was expecting exactly that. Given time, Magdalena could have thought of an appropriate response, but without giving it any time, her mother said, "Sir, if a reward is forthcoming as you say, I would appreciate if you could establish my son in a position with the Apostolic Palace."

Magdalena's eyes widened, but not as much as the pope's did.

Her mother bowed her head. "I'm sorry if I'm asking too much, sir, but his job now is dangerous and the pay minimal. I worry when he's gone before dawn and back after dark."

The pope raised a hand. "Of course we can bring him onto our staff. Young man, what kind of work would you like?"

Domenico was either mortified or terrified into silence. Magdalena said, "Sir, I would suggest you employ him as one of your guards."

Pius grinned at her. "Sister Magdalena, that is a splendid idea." He turned to one of the servants. "Bring the chief of the Swiss Guard." He returned his gaze to her mother. "That seems too small a gift. You, ma'am? Would you like a job in our kitchens too?"

Mother wrapped her hands in her skirt. "Yes, sir. I would very much appreciate that."

"I will make sure that is done by the end of the day. In fact, if you're both working here, we can also arrange for an apartment."

There were thank-yous and tears, and then the servant escorted out Mother, Domenico, and Fiora.

Magdalena remained. Through the entire interview so far, Simonetta had not ceased glaring at her with venom, and in her peripheral vision Morone just seemed stern. She avoided his eyes.

With only Bellosa at her side, Magdalena returned her attention to Pius. "Thank you, sir, for your generosity to my family."

The pope's voice had lost its garrulous tone. "Unfortunately, now I need to deal with you. I'm told you are a more complicated situation."

Bellosa said, "As her abbess, I am prepared to discipline her within our order."

The pope rubbed his chin. "I agree that's entirely within your purview. The Catherinites served me well during the council, and yes," he cut off Bellosa's next words, "I'm aware you did no more than your order vowed to. But still, I recognize the work you've done."

Magdalena said, "And the evil we've done as well."

Simonetta folded his arms. "As I warned you, Your Holiness, this one speaks her mind."

"I've heard her speaking her mind several times, and it hasn't harmed me." The pope sighed. "Daughter, I agree that I have made terrible mistakes while in the process of heading a council intended to correct the Church's mistakes. My decisions cannot be undone."

Magdalena tried not to see Morone's eyes or Simonetta's. Simonetta would be furious. Morone, she didn't know and didn't want to find out. Until the moment she looked, he could be furious, or he could be piteous. Either would be terrible.

She steeled herself. "Cardinal Seripando told me that as pope, you can dispense a lot of conditions, but even the pope cannot dispense sin. Your Holiness, I'm ignorant. I have no formal training. I don't understand half the theology the bishops discussed at the council, but I was assured by men far more knowledgeable than myself that your orders were for the Church's benefit."

Simonetta began to speak, but the pope raised a hand. "Please, I want to hear what she has to say."

"Sir, when I learned what the Church actually teaches, I realized I'd been exposed to genuine holiness. I just hadn't been able to recognize the light because of what I had been taught in the dark. Cardinal Morone told me of the council's plans to educate upcoming priests, and to put all the Church's teachings into books. Sir, ending ignorance is not just about banning the wrong kinds of books. It's about creating the best kind of books and distributing them into the hands of everyone who needs them."

The pope said, "Cardinal Morone has shown me the documents. I will carry them out to the last letter. If I find anything to be lacking in their reforms, I myself will add to them. No one will be exempt, and no excuses accepted. At Trent, the Church did a great work, and now it is up to me to see its fulfillment."

Magdalena blinked hard. "Please, sir, I had blood on my hands before I entered our order, but now I bear even more. I've confessed and been forgiven, but as you said, my evils cannot be undone."

Pius looked grave. "In a way, though, it can be undone. Your skills, have they been used only for wrongdoing? Of course not. You have saved Giovanni Morone's life. You have saved mine. You even saved Cardinal Seripando's." The pope raised a hand to cut off her protest. "Not now. Now is my turn. Your brother, you had no difficulty with offering him to the Swiss Guard, so I know you appreciate the work of a soldier and an officer. You too acted as a soldier and an officer. But your order will have to be reorganized."

Bellosa exclaimed, "Sir?"

Pius turned to her. "You will not be charged with carrying out any further sentences. Protection, yes. Executions, no. The time for secrecy is ended, if indeed such a time ever existed. Now is the time for daylight."

Daylight. The daylight she'd longed for on top of the Innsbruck cathedral. Daylight.

Pius continued, "The council has shown the need for daylight and education, the need for secrets to be proclaimed from the housetops. It has shown the need for discussion and understanding rather than the need for silence and force."

Bellosa bowed.

"You must no longer be the clandestine arm of the Roman Inquisition. You will, however, be required for other purposes. For listening. For protection."

Magdalena's legs trembled. "Thank you, sir."

The pope smiled. "Now, you may go."

Cardinal Morone said, "Before you do, I require your attendance in my office."

The world went grey.

Morone led Magdalena from the papal offices away from Bellosa and a still-scowling Simonetta. Simonetta could scowl for years if he wanted to. It didn't matter. Magdalena kept repeating to herself what had happened.

They were freed. She wouldn't have to leave her order.

Daylight. Everything kept in secret could be proclaimed from the housetops.

In a smaller parlor, a servant built up the fire. Morone had her sit on one of the overstuffed chairs. He took another.

She clutched her hands together. "I'm sorry, sir. I disobeyed you, and that was a betrayal of your trust."

"It was quite a lot of things." In his voice was the guarded tone he'd used with the emperor at Innsbruck. "I expected never to see you again. I didn't predict that you could forge my handwriting well enough to deceive everyone but Borromeo, but I should have foreseen your commitment to headstrong disobedience."

Her entire body tensed as though a murderer were back in the room. "The forgery at least wasn't my work."

"You did deprive yourself of the tumult at the last moments of the council, when we declared it ended, and Charles de Guise, the much-loved Cardinal of Lorraine, burst into a deep-throated rendition of *lauds*."

Bursting into laughter, Magdalena looked up. "Did he really?"

"I didn't want to be outdone." Morone smirked. "I followed it up with *Te Deum*. Most of the bishops were crying."

Magdalena smiled. "And you, sir? Were you crying?"

"Like a baby." He slapped his leg. "The relief of that thing being done, after eighteen years? Anyone would have cried."

Magdalena relaxed into her chair.

Morone steepled his fingers. "Borromeo is already making plans to return to his diocese to live there full-time, and I have been put in charge of the consistory." He only sounded aggrieved. "If I was looking forward to a dearth of meetings, then God in His wisdom has judged against me. I shall have them in abundance."

Magdalena nodded. "Here in Rome?"

"I believe so, although keep in mind that many members of the Curia are about to scatter to their own dioceses, many of them to a place they've never before seen. The pope will no longer employ bishops for administrative tasks. There will be a number of empty chairs and irritated faces until we straighten out all the difficulties, but His Holiness seems to think I'm the one to straighten them."

"And Cardinal Simonetta?"

"Back in charge of the Datary, although one hopes he will have less to do now that dispensations aren't to be handed out like wine glasses at a party."

Finally Cardinal Morone met her gaze, and for a long moment he studied her. "Thank you for your swift action. His Holiness did survive, and I'm told he survived in no small measure because you did a number of things you ought not to have done."

She lowered her head.

Morone added, "If you'd listened to anything we said at the council, you'd have known that you cannot commit evil in order that good may result. But that's something for you to take up with your confessor, whoever that unlucky priest may be."

Magdalena chuckled. "I told Saint Sebastian's confessor about the little confession booths. He was amused. He says they will be hot."

"Purgatory will also be hot. Tell him to offer up his sufferings for the holy souls, while he sweats and listens to nuns enumerate their subtle sins and their near-perfect forgeries." Morone got to his feet. "I'm glad that Pius provided for your family. He asked what might be done for you, and whether you might benefit from having Cardinal Farnese acknowledge your branch. Knowing what I do of the man, I suggested he find other means."

Morone took Magdalena's hand as she stood. She gave him a demure smile. "Without saying too much, sir, I believe shortly Cardinal Farnese will have helped us more than he ever intended."

Morone met her eyes with questioning, and then his questioning look turned into a smile tinged with mischief.

# FORTY-FIVE

Darkness. Darkness, stillness, and only the sounds of breathing. It was another bedroom, just like the book test and entirely different, because this time, the snake lay in the bed, and Magdalena crouched with it between her knees.

She leaned over the breathing figure, and when she'd found his ear, she whispered, "Wake up, Marcoli."

The man startled, and just as quickly she had her hand over his mouth. "Not a word. That metal against your throat is a knife. Stay still or die."

He could breathe through his nose. When he didn't move, she settled back to sit on his chest. "Listen, Marcoli. You have angered the Farnese clan for too long. You have harmed too many. Our patience grows thin."

Beneath her, he was completely tense. Softly enough not to awaken his wife beside him, she breathed into his ear. "Call off your vendetta. Any harm to Fiora or Domenico or Magdalena, and every male in your family will die in the same night."

The man tried to nod beneath her hand.

"End it or I will come back, and you won't wake up. My proof is on your carpet."

She'd already positioned the envelope where he would find it, sealed with Alessandro Farnese's seal (one of them; surely he wouldn't miss one) and written in his handwriting. The threats were remarkably similar to the ones he'd sent Morone, only this time they didn't threaten merely a career.

Magdalena said, "Remember, no words," and sprang from the bed.

Marcoli shouted, "Stop!"

Magdalena flattened herself against the floor as an arrow shot through the open window, tore through the bed curtains and thunked into the wall behind Marcoli.

He gasped. She jumped onto the window sill, then leaped for the rope hanging alongside the building, scaling it in seconds. By the time he reached the window, she was already on the roof. He was looking down at the street for a retreating intruder.

A second arrow thudded into the house just alongside his window. With a gasp, he pulled his head inside.

Stifling a laugh, Magdalena ran along the rooftop until she reached the corner, where she scaled down the wall. On the other side of the street, she met Tadea climbing down the edge of the building with her crossbow strapped to her back.

"Two more to go," Magdalena said.

"Only two? This is fun." Tadea grinned. "Let's hope Agnella has the next house scoped out for us before we get there." And the nuns took off running through the Roman night.

# THANK YOU!

Thank you so much for reading about Sister Magdalena and the parkour nuns!

The research behind this book was daunting at first, and later kind of insane. The three books I relied upon most were *Virgins of Venice* by Mary Laven, *Trent: What Happened at the Council* by John W. O'Malley, and *The Papacy and the Levant* by Kenneth Meyer Setton.

It's a truism that you shouldn't have two fictional characters with similar names, but here history defeated me. Cardinals Seripando and Simonetta had very similar names, and it wasn't my fault. Neither one had a nickname that I could swap in, and both were vitally important. I tried to keep their names as clear as possible in the text, and I apologize for any confusion. Cardinal Seripando seems to be as wonderful as I wrote him (or even more wonderful!)

Seripando and Gonzaga did, indeed, die during a two-week interval during the third period of the council. With this occurrence as with all other major events, including the order in which certain issues were discussed, I stuck as closely as possible to events as they took place. Cardinal Reginald Pole, for example, did die after refusing to return to Rome for a heresy trial. The lecherous priest at *Le Convertite* did exist, and he died just as described. Pius IV did suffer a life threatening illness that hastened the closing of the council, from which he recovered with astonishing rapidity.

No documents exist to prove or disprove the existence of a clandestine order of assassin nuns. But Psalm 18:29 says that with God you can charge an army, and with God you can scale a wall. Magdalena has done both. You may draw from that any conclusion you wish.

Thanks so much to everyone who helped. Karina Fabian, Eric Mentzer, Laura Maisano, Heather Turner (who did a fabulous job editing and fact-checking!) and Lisa Johnson. I'm grateful for all your patience, encouragement, and insights.

If you enjoyed reading about Magdalena, may I suggest...

Ever since God created humanity, the seven Archangels of the Presence have been there to assist, to guide, to help.

They never expected the help to go both ways.

From long days spent as travelers to fiery moments destroying cities...from tricky underground operations (and accidentally setting off one of Satan's secret weapons) to the everyday grind of guardianship, the angels struggle to show God's presence to the people in their charge. But sometimes, in ways they never expected, even they can learn and grow.

**Check out the full series at
http://janelebak.com/seven-archangels-saga/**